SIOBHAN CURHAM

Frankie Says
Relapse

Hodder & Stoughton

First published in Great Britain in 2003 by Hodder and Stoughton
A division of Hodder Headline

1 3 5 7 9 10 8 6 4 2

A CIP catalogue record for this title
is available from the British Library

ISBN 0 340 82370 4

Typeset in Plantin by Hewer Text Ltd, Edinburgh
Printed and bound in Great Britain by
Mackays of Chatham plc, Chatham, Kent

Hodder and Stoughton
A division of Hodder Headline
338 Euston Road
London NW1 3BH

For Tina, Ginny and Jeanette

ACKNOWLEDGEMENTS

I would like to thank the following people for their phenomenal love and support over the past year.

Judy Chilcote, for being so much more than an agent; your friendship, shopping tips and Dr Phil quotes have proved invaluable.

Sara Hulse, for being the best editor I could have wished for; your loyalty and advice have made this past year a joy (not to mention your fashion tips!)

Lucy Dixon for hours of endless fun touring the bookstores and radio staions of London; a gold embossed ordanance survey map is in the post!

Everyone else at Hodder especially the Sales and Marketing teams and Wayne 'wellard' Brookes.

Jeanette and Steve Smith; my own personal sales force!

My family; especially Mikey for threatening to have 'my guts for garters' if I ever went into teaching and giving me the confidence to pursue my dream and Anne, for being nothing like Helen (honest!).

Tina, for providing me with so many fabulously naff memories from the Eighties and gallons of lemon squash!

And last but never least, a huge thank-you to Colin for making me the happiest football widow in the land.

Chapter One

Friday afternoon, 4 p.m.

It was Friday afternoon, late May, and bank-holiday boredom was beckoning. As I drove home from the school run feeling suitably dejected I had prepared for three interminable days of Barbie versus Scooby-Doo. I had prepared for my credit card to take a battering as I became ever more desperate to buy my kids' silence. I had prepared for endless treks around garden centres in the search of the latest in Scandinavian decking – yes, I was even prepared Stepford-style for the 'quality' time I was about to be sharing with my husband – but I was completely unprepared for a Betterware salesman to be lying prostrate across my driveway.

'What are you doing?' I cried, in mock indignation, leaping gleefully from the car. For the sight of this corduroy-clad representative, recumbent in a sea of abandoned catalogues was quite possibly the most exciting thing to have happened to me in a decade.

My prone purveyor of plastic products raised his head slowly to meet my gaze. With his pockmarked skin and mossy teeth he had the kind of face only a mother could love – and a bifocally challenged mother at that. Running a fleshy hand through his coarse ginger hair, he let out a strangled moan.

I briefly contemplated bustling my children into the relative safety of the house, but on seeing the rapt expressions on their faces I thought better of it. Why ruin their fun? After all, this was probably going to be the highlight of their break. God, even the latest Westlife video didn't cause Megan's jaw to drop quite so low, and as for my son Frankie, well, judging by his frozen stance this was beating the most nerve-tingling episode of *Scooby-Doo*.

'What are you doing?' I repeated, warming to my role of morally outraged middle-class mother. To add depth to my character I beeped the alarm on my Range Rover and prodded my caller with the toe of my Jimmy Choo slingback.

Wincing, he heaved himself into a seated position. 'What is it with you Pinner people?' he spluttered, gazing forlornly into the middle distance, 'Are you telling me you never need plastic containers? Or do they have to come gilt-edged from John bleeding Lewis?'

Rendered speechless for the first time in recent memory, I shrugged my shoulders and allowed him to continue.

'Where else can you get sixteen assorted containers for four ninety-nine?' he demanded, apparently to no one in particular – unless, of course, he was chronically cross-eyed on top of everything else. 'Not at John bleeding Lewis, that's for sure. I've been walking these streets for six months now and all I've had is an order for a static-free duster and a poxy left-handed potato-peeler.'

At this point I tried to interject with a gasp of admiration at the sheer enterprising brilliance of a static-free duster, but with the burden of six months' bitterness to unleash he was un-stoppable.

'And to cap it all,' he yelled, his face turning a disturbing shade of puce and clashing horribly with his marmalade beard, 'to cap it all, you can't even be bothered to leave the catalogues outside, as instructed. No, you just discard them in your stainless-steel, John bleeding Lewis pedal bins, with not a thought for Muggins here who has to foot the bill.' The Betterware Breakdown clutched his head in his hands and sobbed, at which point my compassionate eight-year-old daughter Megan began to howl with laughter behind her veil of curls.

'Mum, who's John bleeding Lewis? Is he a baddy?' Frankie enquired, his bright blue eyes as wide as saucers.

'Oh, yes,' I couldn't resist affirming. 'One of the most evil baddies on Planet Earth!'

'More evil than the Tar Monster?'

'Oh, yes, much more evil.'

'Did John bleeding Lewis zap that man with his laser-gun?'

'No, I think he stabbed him with his poxy left-handed potato-peeler!'

At this point both of my children roared with laughter – I accept sole responsibility for their warped sense of humour.

'I'm going to pee my pants!' Frankie shrieked, clutching on to Megan.

'As long as you don't *poo* them,' Megan cackled, uttering the one word guaranteed to send her younger brother into further paroxysms.

The Betterware Breakdown stared uneasily at the three of us sniggering and snorting, then stumbled to his feet. 'I'm sorry, I don't know what came over me – it's just—'

'Look, for Christ's sake, give me a catalogue,' I interrupted. After all, he was the first person to have made me laugh in God knows how long – it was the least I could do.

In the end I plumped for the demonstration model of a delightfully tacky pink plastic travel clock. Tenderly described as the 'essential bedside companion' it made for a highly practical purchase as I urgently required both an alarm clock and some companionship during my increasingly frequent sojourns in the spare bedroom.

Greatly rejuvenated by his change in fortunes my Betterware salesman bounded off down the street, and as I unlocked the front door and kicked off my shoes I couldn't help wondering if I had been the unwitting victim of an elaborate new sales technique. Known as the Plaintive Pitch, it was probably being practised in role plays throughout the land.

Bizarre encounter over, it was back to reality with a sickening lurch as soon as I entered the kitchen. There on the counter, where I had flung it earlier in disgust, was the snotty letter from my editor at *Gal Pal* magazine rejecting my latest offering of coffee-break fiction for being far too dark. 'Warped' was the adjective she used, before informing me haughtily that although her sappy readers enjoyed a good 'twist in the tale' they certainly would not appreciate anything quite so tasteless as the implication of incest. I had been quite stung by her cutting criticism, having found the notion of a bored housewife inadvertently ending up on a lonely-hearts date with her spotty teenage son rather entertaining.

Oh, well, I thought, reaching into the freezer for the chicken nuggets and oven chips, better rewrite her surprise date as her dullard husband. But I couldn't help wondering what the hell was the point in a twist so predictable that even the Prozac-popping readers of *Gal Pal* would have worked it out by the second paragraph.

I was wrestling with a tin of Scooby-Doo pasta shapes – and wondering absentmindedly if Betterware did a left-handed tin-opener to go with their potato-peeler – when my son decided to drop his latest bombshell.

'Mum, I want to change my name,' he declared, helpfully littering the floor with the half-chewed contents of his lunch-box, a mud-splattered PE kit and reams of school correspondence.

'But why?' I asked, incredulous. Did the child not appreciate the honour of being named after the finest eighties band this country produced? Just wait until he was a few years older and I played him my limited-edition Mersey mix of 'Welcome To The Pleasure Dome' – then he'd understand.

'I hate Frankie – it's stupid!'

I gritted my teeth and glowered at my four-year-old Philistine.

'So what exactly do you wish to be called, then?' I enquired, yanking at the tin-opener.

'Daphne.'

Momentarily stunned, I lost my grip on the tin-opener and showered Megan's Britney Spears rucksack with tomato sauce.

'Daphne!' I spluttered. 'But that's a girl's name!'

'So.' I want to be a girl.' Frankie pouted, a little too effeminately.

'Muuum!' Megan wailed, with all the harmony of a hydraulic drill. 'What have you done to Britney?'

Glancing helplessly at the rucksack I couldn't help empathising with my daughter's distress, for with the scarlet rivulets trickling down Britney's face and the splatters across her body it did indeed appear as if she had been the victim of a particularly brutal slaying.

'I want to be a girl,' Frankie wailed, tugging a little too insistently on my raw silk sundress.

'You're a little weirdo, that's what you are,' Megan hissed, rescuing Britney from my evil clutches and storming upstairs to her bedroom.

I was about to run after my pouting princess (the elder one, that is) when the phone began to ring. Racing into the living room I tripped on an abandoned steam engine and hurtled arse over tit into a Lego minefield. Explosions of pain shot through my foot, up into my thigh. This better be good, I seethed, grabbing the telephone from the coffee table.

'Hello! Caitlin Kennedy!' I barked – or, rather, yelped in agony.

'Oh, good afternoon, is that Mrs Delaney?' came a twittery voice down the line.

'No, this is Ms Kennedy.' My heart sank with the awful realisation that I was about to become the victim of a cold call. Anyone who knows me knows that I refused point-blank to take Sam's name the day we tied the knot (or should that be noose?). The only people brave enough to call me Mrs Delaney are double-glazing salespeople or teachers at parents' evenings.

'Oh, good afternoon, Mrs Delaney. I'm calling from We Sue Big and I was just wondering if you'd had an accident that wasn't your fault in the last three years?'

As I sat on the floor nursing my throbbing foot I pondered the ludicrousness of this tweety-voiced woman calling me seemingly at random because she'd 'just wondered' if I'd had an accident that wasn't my fault.

'Well, as a matter of fact I have.'

'Really?' Tweety-pie could barely contain her delight, 'Well, did you know, Mrs Delaney, that you may well be entitled to some compensation?' In the background I could hear her shuffling excitedly with her script. 'Here at We Sue Big we operate a no-win no-fee policy, so you just can't lose.'

'Oh that's excellent,' I taunted, knowing full well that my sarcasm would completely bypass Budgie Brain.

'Okay, Mrs Delaney,' she tweeted. 'If I could just take a few details about your accident. First of all, how long ago did it happen?'

'Oh, about a minute,' I replied. 'You see, I tripped and sprained my ankle while racing to answer this completely pointless call. So I tell you what,' I hobbled into a standing position to administer my lethal parting shot, 'do me a favour and go and sue *yourself* big and when you've finished perhaps you would be good enough to forward me my compensation cheque. I take it you have my address?' I paused just long enough to hear her flap about in panic before slamming down the phone. What a God-awful day. And just when it seemed it couldn't get any worse, I heard those four little words guaranteed to fill me with dread and fear.

'Hi, honey, I'm home!'

Chapter Two

No, it wasn't Jack Nicholson grinning insanely and brandishing an axe. It was far, far worse than that. It was my husband
Sam, grinning inanely and brandishing a kilo sack of organic
porridge oats.

'Jesus!' he gasped, dropping the sack on to the coffee
table. 'This thing weighs a bloody ton!' He removed his
glasses, took a neatly folded tissue from the breast pocket of
his shirt and dabbed at his perspiring brow. 'How's your day
been, then?'

I couldn't fail to notice the look of apprehension upon his
face as he awaited my reply.

'Oh, great,' I declared, watching the corners of his mouth
curl their way into a relieved smile. 'If you enjoy receiving
snotty rejection letters, bringing a Betterware salesman back
from the brink of breakdown, discovering your son has
transsexual tendencies, alienating your daughter by desecrat-
ing her Britney Spears bag and then twisting your ankle in a
bid to answer a call from a bunch of ambulance-chasers. My
day was just great, thank you. How was yours?'

Sam's face crumpled and, for a split second, the sight of
those huge blue eyes clouding over and that bottom lip starting
to quiver gave me the strangest urge to rush over and stroke his
unruly mop of curls. Needless to say, I refrained.

'Yeah, it was good,' he uttered, half-heartedly. 'I finally
finished the bloody Wilkinson audit.'

This was good news indeed. Sam had been working flat

out on the 'bloody Wilkinson audit' for the past six weeks now and it must have been a tremendous relief to see the back of it.

'That's great, Sam. So does this mean you've got Saturday off for once?'

'Yeah, 'fraid so.'

'Well, let's celebrate. How about we get an Indian tonight and crack open a bottle of plonk. Low-alcohol Lambrini, of course,' I added reassuringly – my husband must be the only Irishman in North West London to prefer a sparkling perry to a frothing pint.

Sam glanced anxiously at the sack of oats on the coffee table. 'Oh, er, I'd love to, Caitlin, it's just that I'm on the final day of my detox and I really don't want to blow it now. Could we not make it tomorrow instead?'

'Detox, schmetox. Stopping it one day early won't hurt. God, the way you eat, if there's a toxin left in your body it won't be long before it dies of solitude!' I had the vision of a golden onion bhaji in my sights now and, like a missile with the munchies, I was homing in on my target.

Sam shook his head solemnly. 'I'm really sorry, Caitlin, but day four is the most crucial of all. If I blow it now my universal body-wrap will have been for nothing. I tell you what, you go ahead and order an Indian and I'll make myself a bowl of porridge.'

I stared at him with his sickeningly glowing skin and gleaming hair and fought the urge to ram his organically grown porridge oats right up his colonically irrigated arse. Why did he have to be such a – well – such a woman? Sometimes I felt as if the roles had been well and truly reversed in our relationship. I can't remember a time when I really gave a toss about my appearance. Well, I can, but that was before, and what did I know back then? I was just a stupid kid. Don't get me wrong, I'm not one of those women you see lolloping about in the school playground in a pair of saggy-kneed leggings and a tea-stained Gary Barlow T-shirt. I like to look presentable and have a wad of store-cards to rival the best of them, but that doesn't mean I waste endless weekends trawling the high street like my best friend Karen in the relentless pursuit of the perfect bargain. Or endless hours analysing myself in front of the mirror, searching for yet more flaws to add to the list. Getting my hair cut off was the best thing I ever did. Who needs a flowing mane when you can have a gamine crop? Not me, especially when it shortens your morning routine by about forty-five minutes. And, let's face it, living with Sam and Megan I'm lucky if I get five minutes in the bathroom in the morning.

I looked at Sam gazing wistfully at his sack of oats and sighed as my vision of bhaji heaven began to fade from view. 'Don't worry about it,' I conceded, too fed up even to bother sulking. 'I'd promised Karen I'd go over to hers tonight anyway – she wants to have some kind of séance or something. I tell you what, I'll ask her if she can try to make contact with your appetite, shall I?'

Before Sam had time to respond, Frankie came flying into the room, his school tie wrapped around his forehead like some miniature soldier of fortune. 'Mum, Mum, the John bleeding Lewis Monster has set fire to the cooker!'

On cue the smoke detector in the hall began emitting its daily shriek and I realised that, yet again, the chicken nuggets had been cremated. I hopped through to the kitch-en, pulled the flaming pan from the oven and waited for Frankie to hand me a soaking tea-towel to smother the flames. As you can see our health-and-safety routine has been well practised.

'Okay, kids!' I yelled, grabbing my car keys. 'Looks like it's fish and chips again. Can I get you anything, dear?' I asked, poking my head round the living room door, where Sam now sat with his head in his hands. 'A free-range pickled egg perhaps? Or some GM-free mushy peas?'

Sam glanced at me nervously. 'No, it's okay, I'll just make myself some porridge – with chopped apricots,' he added, somewhat desperately.

Chapter Three

Before I go any further I ought to state for the record that my husband hasn't always been so anal. True, he was the only man I met at university who had an endowment policy – but, then, he was studying accountancy. And, as I said before, he's the only Irishman I know who hates getting drunk, but that definitely has its plus points. At least I've never had to put up with him declaring his undying love for his best mate or woken up to find him about to take a piss in the wardrobe. Nevertheless, things have undoubtedly deteriorated during the fifteen years we've been together.

Fifteen years! God, now I know why they call it 'life'. It never was the most passionate of relationships even in the beginning, but I don't believe there's anything wrong with that. The flames of passion can be hugely overrated, if you ask me. The trouble with fire is that it may start off by warming the cockles of your heart, but left unchecked it won't be long before it sends you the way of my kids' chicken nuggets: burnt to a frazzle and singed beyond all recognition. No, what I had with Sam was more your night-storage heater than your roaring log fire. Something safe and reliable to snuggle up to, something that made sense at a time when little else did.

I remember the first time I saw him, hovering nervously around the film-society stall at the freshers' fair and something deep inside me – in that place where I could still just about experience feeling – clicked. Looking into those crystal blue eyes and seeing my own fear reflected back was all it took. We fell into our comfortable little world of snatched coffees between lectures, surreptitious cinema dates and shared economy pizzas – Sam ate like a normal person back then. We held hands in the park, kissed nervously in the back row and finally we had sex – I was his first, he was my second. And within a year or so we were just like all the others: confident, ambitious, optimistic – on the surface, at least. We graduated. I got my dream (?) job as a features writer for a women's magazine and he began the seemingly endless slog of accountancy exams. We got engaged, took out a joint mortgage, dragged ourselves to mass every Sunday for six whole months in order to appease our parents and pledge our troth in the local Catholic church, and then, following the rulebook to the last letter we produced two children, one of each. (I drew the line at the golden-retriever clause, but Frankie did own a hamster until I neglected to feed it one busy Whitsun week.)

And here we are, a life sentence later, and somewhere along the line something has gone horribly wrong. Something inside me that I thought I'd buried for good, or smothered into submission, has started to claw its way back to the surface, and everything I'd have turned a blind eye to before – the organic porridge oats, the colonic irrigation, even the universal body-wrap – has started to gnaw away at me. All I seem to hear over and over again in my head are the words, 'What am I doing here?'

What am I doing here? It's Friday night and, as the rest of the female population hauls on her high heels and totters off to the local fleshpot, I'm at my best friend Karen's house about to embark upon a séance. A séance, for Christ's sake! I'm afraid I lost all faith in the notion of 'the other side' the day I forked out fifteen quid to Gypsy Rose Lee, the imaginatively monikered fortune-teller to the stars and 'various members of Royalty'. I remember perching myself in her poky little caravan in the middle of Pinner fair, almost overcome by her dog breath, only to be informed that I was a happily married mother. Call me a cynic, but the platinum wedding band on my finger and the two kids I had in tow might have provided more of an influence in this incisive insight than any spirit guide. And as she rambled on about my moving to a house with a number seven on the door, and I listened to the excited shrieks and thumping bass line from outside, I couldn't help feeling like a bit of a twat. That fifteen pounds could have got me three goes on the Cage *and* a jumbo hotdog. Speaking of food . . .

'What's happening on the lemon squash and biscuit front, Karen?' I called anxiously. 'My stomach's beginning to feel as if my mouth's been sealed.'

'Chance would be a fine thing,' Karen muttered, from the kitchen, followed by the unnecessarily loud clatter of crockery. 'Coming right up,' she trilled, from behind the door.

The lemon squash and biscuit tradition dated way back to the beginning of our friendship some twenty-five years ago when Karen and I spent every available minute in each other's homes. Well, mainly me in hers if I could help it – Karen always had far nicer biscuits and far saner parents. Even during our teenage-rebellion years we would always partake of a glass of lemon squash and a plate of biscuits before embarking upon the obligatory bottle of Strongbow and the packet of ten B&H. And now that we were women of the world, or of North West London, we might have graduated to Marks & Spencer's homestyle lemonade and their finest Belgian selection, but the sentiment still remained.

While I waited for my hostess to appear I cast my eyes enviously about her living room. Oh, to have my own place – my own place in Chiswick, light years away from Pinner. A place with no toys, no mess – a veritable Lego-free zone. A place where I, too, could burn clusters of scented candles without fear of a certain little person using them as a funeral pyre for his sister's Barbie. A place where I, too, could display sparkling crystal ornaments below head height. A place where I could curl up on the blissfully stain-free sofa, as I was now, with the remote control in my sole possession, safe in the knowledge that I could watch *Friends* uninterrupted by requests for bedtime stories or, even worse, a programme on BBC2 about growing your own vegetable patch. God, how I envied Karen sometimes for her globe-trotting job and her girl-about-town apartment. Okay, so maybe the mountain of self-help books and the ouija board on the coffee table were a bit off-putting, but apart from that her home felt like a welcome haven from my own madhouse. Some things just never change, I guess.

Or perhaps they do, I thought, dumbstruck, as Karen emerged from the kitchen and plonked a tray in front of me. There was nothing amiss with the customary jug of lemonade, standing proudly in all its thirst-quenching glory, ice cubes and lemon slices bobbing merrily on the surface. No, it was what lay on the plate next to it that was the problem. The insipid beige circles of blandness. Where were the Belgian delights, all golden, crispy and delicately encased in silky chocolate? Even a good old Bourbon or custard cream would have been preferable to this travesty of tradition. For there, peering up at me in all their blanched embarrassment sat a plate of Rich Tea biscuits. Rich Tea!

'What the hell?' I spluttered, gesturing feebly at the plate.

'What?' said Karen, tossing her blonde curls surprisingly defiantly for one who has committed such a social *faux pas*.

'Rich Tea?' I could barely spit out the words. 'In all our years of friendship we have never resorted to Rich Tea. Not even that time when I'd had the flu for two weeks and couldn't get to the supermarket. I still managed to rustle up some Garibaldis!'

'Oh, yeah, they were great,' Karen practically sneered, hands on hips, in a shameless display of effrontery.

'At least they had currants in,' I retaliated. 'At least they held some kind of appeal for the tastebuds. I mean, what exactly is the point of a Rich Tea biscuit? You just put them into your mouth and they dissolve into oblivion. You don't even know you've eaten one!' I collapsed back into the sofa in despair.

Karen gathered her embroidered satin caftan around her and pointed to her stomach.

'Look!' she cried.

I looked at her pot belly and sighed. I hated it when Karen was due on – like one of those pathetically doting fathers-to-be who end up experiencing their partner's morning sickness, I seemed to share every second of Karen's premenstrual tension.

'You look fine,' I said, in what I hoped was a suitably soothing voice.

'No, I don't. I look like somebody's stuck a bicycle pump up my arse and inflated my spare tyre,' Karen barked. The one good thing about her PMT was that it made her language far more colourful and she wasn't so sickeningly nice. 'It's just not fair,' she continued, waving her hands about wildly, like Mystic Meg on acid. 'You eat like a horse and look like a pixie, whereas I pick like a pigeon and end up looking like a bloody great heifer!'

'You look fantastic,' I said, and I wasn't bullshitting. You know when you're about twelve years old and your body plays that cruel prank commonly known as puberty? Your scalp begins to seep oil into your previously lustrous locks, your skin erupts in pustules, your teeth jostle for space in your increasingly overcrowded jaws, and you feel about as awkward as a Brown Owl in a brothel. And then some well-meaning Minnie (usually your mother) reassures you that true beauty comes from within – at which point you take to your bed for three months. Well, in Karen's case, this much-misused statement was true. Her beauty really did seem to evolve from somewhere within. Like rays of sunlight, her infectious giggle, her theatrical body language, her genuine kindness all radiated a warmth that drew people to her like a magnet. We were like chalk and cheese, really. Her blonde and buxom, me brunette and bustless. Her with her wide open face and oval chestnut eyes, me with my feline features and even cattier tongue.

Tonight, though, as Karen towered over me she seemed to be glowering with defiance rather than radiating warmth.

'Yeah, well, as of today I'm on a diet, so I'm afraid it's Rich Tea biscuits and low-calorie lemonade all round,' she huffed.

'God, what is wrong with you people?' I wailed. 'I've just left Sam at home chewing on a dried apricot in the hope that I'd discover a chocolate-filled oasis waiting for me here, and instead what do I find? Yet another neurotic with an eating disorder!'

Karen plonked herself down on the floor and filled two glasses with lemonade. 'You leave poor Sam alone – at least he takes a pride in his appearance. Most men succumb to the dreaded middle-age spread the minute they've got you up the aisle.'

'Taking pride in your appearance is one thing, but resorting to organic porridge oats and Rich Tea biscuits is quite another,' I retorted. 'I mean, it's positively sado-masochistic.'

Karen took a sip from her glass and sighed. 'I've got to do something, Cait, I'm thirty-three years old and what have I got to show for it?' She cast her eyes mournfully about her beautiful flat before taking a nibble of her Rich Tea. I couldn't help noticing the faintest trace of a grimace flicker across her face before she crammed the rest of the biscuit into her mouth.

'What have you got to show for it?' I echoed, in what would have been an incredulous tone if I hadn't already heard this a million times before. 'Only a wonderful flat in Chiswick and a high-flying career as a marketing exec for a wine company. Not only do you get to travel the world getting pissed on free plonk but you managed to escape from Pinner too, you lucky cow! If you want to feel sorry for anyone you should feel sorry for *me*.'

Karen snorted. Either that or she was having difficulty digesting her Rich Tea.

'You!' she cried indignantly – it had obviously been a snort. 'Feel sorry for you with your adoring husband and your lovely kids and your flexible job from home – from your cosy family home, full of children's laughter and beautifully handcrafted toys?'

I stared at Karen in astonishment – she was obviously suffering from some kind of starvation-induced delusion.

'You have the perfect life, Cait. Do you realise that if we had been living in the middle ages I'd have been burnt at the stake by now? Still on the shelf at thirty-three!'

I stuffed a Rich Tea into my mouth and waited patiently for it to dissolve. Like when you discover you've boarded the wrong train and you're winging your way to Worthing instead of being whisked home, the evening had taken an unexpected turn for the worse.

'But you've got the delectable Marcus,' I offered, 'a globe-trotting executive complete with his own apartment. I can't imagine a more perfect relationship. You get sex on tap and you retain full control of your TV remote. You get free access to the contents of his pants without having to pick them up off the floor and wash them afterwards. How cool is that?'

'Marcus schmarcus!' Karen hissed. 'You don't understand, Cait, it's all very well having a high-powered career and your own place but it can get pretty lonely, too. Sometimes I find myself gripped by the most terrible sense of melancholy when I'm here on my own. It's all I can do to stop myself picking up the phone and begging Marcus to move in with me. A remote control is no substitute for a life's companion, you know – not even when they're having a *Sex in the City* night on E4.'

I raised my eyebrows, but refrained from reminding Karen that her moments of 'melancholy' always seemed to coincide with the onset of her period and within a week she was always back to her treat- 'em-mean, keep- 'em-keen self.

'Marriage isn't all it's cracked up to be, you know. Things aren't always as perfect as they might seem,' I murmured sagely, before rinsing my mouth with lemonade. 'And what's the point of having everything perfect on the surface if there's absolutely nothing underneath? My life is a bit like one of those display cakes at the baker's, really. Beneath all the fancy icing there lies a hollow, cardboard shell.' Sometimes I amazed myself at my profundity.

Karen evidently didn't share this sense of awe. 'Oh, for God's sake, Caitlin, are you ever going to wake up and appreciate what you have got?' She slammed her glass on the table, causing the Rich Teas to quiver. 'Or are you going to stay trapped in the past for ever?'

God, her hormones really were raging tonight. Yet for some inexplicable reason I felt unable to respond. In fact, I felt frighteningly close to tears. My phantom PMT was taking hold. It was time to change the subject. 'So, are we going to have this séance or what?' I asked, trying desperately to keep the embarrassing tremor from my voice.

Karen looked at me and suddenly her face unfurled into its familiar warm smile. 'Sure, sure. I'm sorry, Cait, I'm just a bit tired and emotional – it must be the build-up to tomorrow's new moon or something. I didn't mean to bite your head off, it's just that I worry about you sometimes.' Karen glanced at the pile of self-help books on the coffee table. 'Today is a gift, you know,' she uttered wisely. 'That's why it's called the present.'

I let out a snort of laughter. That's what I love about Karen's

Oprah-style psychobabble: it always makes me feel better, although perhaps not quite in the way it's intended.

'Okay, let's get cracking.' Karen began clearing the coffee-table of its clutter of books, remote control, magazines, lemon squash and biscuits until only the ouija board remained. 'I'm a bit nervous, actually,' she confessed, moving the board to the centre of the table. 'I've never done one of these before, it's a different ball game from the tarot, you know.'

Although the ouija board was a first for me too, I have to say that I wasn't the least bit nervous. I mean, it was all a load of bollocks, really, wasn't it? There was no way a glass could move unaided: somebody had to be pushing it. I watched as Karen placed an upturned glass in the middle of the board, between the words 'Yes' and 'No'. All around the circumference the letters of the alphabet formed a frame of gold. Karen looked so excited, so hopeful, it would be a crying shame if nothing were to happen, if we ended up sitting there like a pair of prize prats waiting in vain for a message from beyond the grave. It was the least a friend could do.

So we sat there for a minute or two, eyes closed with fingertips resting on the rim of the glass, while Karen asked over and over again if there was anybody there and if they would only give us a sign. Then, fighting the overwhelming urge to collapse into fits of laughter, I slowly, gently, began to push the glass across the board.

Karen's eyes flew open. 'Are you pushing it?' she hissed.

'No,' I lied, trying to look as shaken as she did.

'Oh my God, it's somebody from the other side. Who's there?' she asked nervously. 'Tell us your name.'

Slowly the glass shuddered its way across the board, picking out letters, which Karen duly recited in a nervous little voice. 'C...A...D...B...U...R...Y...F...I...N ...G...E...R...'

Karen gazed blankly for a second before pushing the glass

away in disgust. 'Cadbury finger. Ha, ha, very funny. Honestly, Cait, you shouldn't mess about with the spirit world, you know. I was shitting myself.'

'Oh, come on, Karen, you know nothing's going to happen. We're not starring in some Hammer horror movie. Look, why don't we open one of your work freebies and watch *Sex in the City* instead?'

Karen sighed dejectedly. 'All right, but let's have one more try – and this time no mucking about.'

'Okay, okay.'

I put my finger back on the glass, closed my eyes and began fantasising about the Australian chardonnay that would soon be blazing a trail down my throat. Suddenly the glass jerked forward.

'Shit!' I opened my eyes and looked at Karen.

She was staring at the glass. 'Is that you again?' she whispered.

'No,' I whispered back, 'I promise. Did your hand slip or something?'

'No, I haven't moved a muscle.'

'Me neither.'

'Oh, shit!'

We both sat in stunned silence as the glass began slowly to edge its way across the board.

'Who's there?' Karen asked, her voice trembling. 'Tell us your name.'

Once again the glass began to move, but it was different this time, faster and smoother and, more worryingly, I wasn't pushing it.

'W . . . I . . . L . . . L . . .' Karen read out, and suddenly my heart began to pound, 'S . . . C . . . A . . . R . . .'

My stomach seemed to leap into my throat, burning at the back of it, every hair on my body bristled, and although my finger was resting on the glass as lightly as could be, I knew exactly where it was going before it even got there.

'L . . . E . . . T . . . T.'

Will Scarlett. I heard someone screaming – I think it was me – and then the smash of glass.

'Oh, my God,' Karen was saying, over and over again, 'I've read about this kind of thing happening in the *News of the World*. I'm so sorry, Cait. Are you okay?'

I was on my feet, tears coursing down my face.

'I've got to go home!' I cried. 'I've got to go home!'

Chapter Four

Like reading last thing at night and waking to discover that an entire chapter has been lost, I arrived home from Karen's unable to recall a single mirror, signal or manoeuvre of the thirty-minute journey. As I screeched into the drive the house was already shrouded in darkness, a full eight hours' sleep being a vital part of Sam's detoxification process. For once I didn't slam the door behind me or clatter up the stairs singing 'Bat Out Of Hell' – waking Sam was the last thing on my mind.

Something strange had happened to me at Karen's and I felt like a woman possessed. Not, I hasten to add, by some fiendish spirit who was about to make my head rotate three hundred and sixty degrees while I cackled, '*They're here!*' No, I'd been possessed by a desire rather than a demon: the sudden and overwhelming urge to unlock a certain door in my mind. A door that had been slammed shut a lifetime ago. And I knew exactly where I could locate the key. It may have been buried under a mountain of junk for years but, like a tracking device bleeping away incessantly in the background, I'd never been allowed to forget its existence.

I tiptoed across the landing to the spare room and eased the door shut behind me. Over the past few months our fourth bedroom had become less spare and more spoken for as I'd gradually claimed it for my own. Row upon row of my books and notepads had slowly filed their way on to the pine shelves. One by one the naff watercolours on the walls had been replaced by my favourite Dali prints and framed photos of the kids, and the economy polyester duvet set deemed suitable for guests had been traded in for a far more comfortable duck-down version.

I grabbed the duvet, bundled it on to my trusty wicker chair and clambered on top. God, how I hated being such a short-arse. I lunged for the hatch in the ceiling, managed to yank open the door and hook a clothes-hanger to the bottom of the loft ladder. As I pulled gingerly on the hanger the ladder shot down with a clatter loud enough to wake the dead, let alone the detoxifying. I held my breath and waited for the flurry of footsteps, but all remained quiet. Reassured that the coast was clear, I crept to the top of the ladder, wincing with every creaking, groaning step. On reaching the top I fumbled about in the darkness for what seemed like an eternity until I finally located the light cord. With a deafening click the loft was flooded with a fluorescent glare. I found myself surrounded by boxes and bin-liners, – wave upon wave of clutter emanating from the loft hatch like the rings inside a tree trunk, chronicling the history of our time in the house.

The central, most recent ring consisted of piles of books and magazines from my long-overdue office clearout. *Plotting the Short Story, Writing for Cash, So you Want to be a Freelance Writer*, all lay discarded among copies of old magazines from the days when it still meant something to see my name in print. The days when I actually felt proud to be the author of such dubiously titled tales as 'One for Sorrow Two for Roy' and 'Curl Up and Diet'.

Cringing, I trampled over my collected works straight into a mound of baby clothes, once again hoarded for nostalgic rather than practical purposes. I shuddered as I caught a glimpse of Frankie's old changing-mat, yellow foam erupting from a split in the plastic cover. What on earth had possessed me to keep a memento of the nappy-changing nadir of my life? Skirting around it I trod on a plastic bag and something squeaked – Megan's Sweep puppet, I thought, automatically, recalling the hours spent trying to prevent yet another crying fit by sticking my hand up a toy dog's arse and jabbering like a moron.

Shuddering, I made my way to the darkened recesses of the loft and the assembled crates that had remained unpacked from when we moved in. The baggage from our previous lives that we hadn't quite managed to offload. I immediately spotted my extensive record collection and Sam's flea-ridden teddy bear, Digby. Studiously avoiding all contact with Digby, I caught my toe in a bin-liner and a swathe of ivory satin spilt on to the floor – my wedding dress, lying half crushed under my very first record player. I gazed fondly at the red leather-effect lid, and eased it open to examine the long, grooved spindle in the centre of the turntable. Built to hold up to six singles at any one time, it had seemed like state-of-the-art technology to a music-loving thirteen-year-old, listening in awe as Shakin' Stevens faded out before Kim Wilde plopped down on top of him.

Then I saw it. Lurking at the back of the loft, a shabby cardboard box advertising the wares of WavyLine food stores. I felt a sickening lurch in my stomach, but whatever it was that had taken over my body that night made my arm reach out for it and, before I knew it, I was delving inside.

First out was a slightly off-white T-shirt. FRANKIE SAYS RELAX! the faded black lettering demanded. I held it to me and inhaled deeply. Recoiling from the smell of damp I reached into the box again and pulled out a bundle of yellow newspaper cuttings and a tattered piece of paper: a return coach ticket to Nottingham dated 14 February 1985. Although the loft was still baking in the trapped heat of the day I suddenly felt frozen to the core. My hands trembled as they reached into the box again, this time pulling out a miniature brass Davy lamp, a battered copy of *On the Road*, a piece of stone and a seven-inch single. Holly Johnson grinned from the worn sleeve looking suitably dapper in a long black smoking jacket and white gloves. 'The Power Of Love'. The chorus echoed through my mind as I glanced nervously about the loft. Suddenly the hatch seemed an awfully long way away. What if the lightbulb were to blow and I was plunged into darkness? I reached hastily into the box and finally found what I was looking for. A battered A4 notebook bulging at the seams and covered in childish scrawl.

As I studied the pale blue cover I caught sight of something so bloodcurdling, so spine-chilling, that I almost flung the thing to the floor in horror. I squinted in the semi-darkness, but my eyes weren't deceiving me. The girly, curly script really did say, 'I luv Kajagoogoo'! Jesus. What was I doing? Did I *really* want to open this can of worms? Was I *really* ready to face up to the demons that lay dormant within those ragged covers? Why not let them sleep for another seventeen years? I turned the book over and my heart skipped a beat. There in the centre was a faded yellow sticker with COAL NOT DOLE printed in black. In a blinding flash I saw a picture of myself in my school uniform, the same sticker, shiny and bright, proudly displayed on my blazer lapel. And I heard a ghostly chanting in my ears – 'Dig deep for the miners,' it echoed. Clutching the notebook to me, I tripped and stumbled my way back to the loft hatch and down the ladder.

I didn't resume breathing again until I was curled up safely in bed, still shivering under fifteen togs of duck-down. I turned the cover with trembling hands, forcing the lid off my Pandora's box, and began reluctantly to read.

Chapter Five

Monday 3, March 1984

Dear Anne Frank,

I have decided to dedicate this diary to you as, apart from Madonna, you are my sole source of inspiration in this dreary, mundane existence. Only you can truly comprehend the feelings of imprisonment and isolation I have to endure, day after day, week after week, surrounded by people who don't understand me, in this Godforsaken place called Pinner.

Five Things I Hate Most About Pinner

1. Pinner People.
   With their cheesecloth clothes and gold sandals bought from hideously tasteless boutiques like My Fair Lady and their dreadful coiffures rinsed and set rigid in salons such as Cheveux by Peter and Geoffrey, Pinner people have to be the most dull, straitlaced people imaginable. This is no place for anyone with the slightest spark of vitality or originality to grow up. With every day that passes in this God-awful place I feel another drop of my creative juices trickling down the drain.

2. Bugger all to do.
   Unless you are over sixty and have a penchant for

Darby and Joan clubs and bring and buy sales, there
is absolutely nothing to do. Young people in Pinner
are forced to hang around in parks listening to Dean
French's ghetto-blaster while gagging on flat cider and
carving graffiti about Duran Duran in the hut. This is
okay when you are thirteen or fourteen, but by the
time you reach fifteen it becomes incredibly tiresome.
There are only so many times you can declare your
undying love for John Taylor on park furniture before
wanting to fling yourself into the duckpond in
despair.

3. Appalling Snobbery.
   Pinner must be the only place in Britain that refuses
   to have a chip shop for fear of lowering the tone.
   Instead we are left with an over-abundance of
   tearooms and a Greek restaurant called Paphos –
   surely Pathos would be more apt?

4. The Queen Elizabeth Estate.
   It is hard to believe that a place that forbids a chip
   shop should house a council estate, and I'm sure if
   the Pinner Round Table had anything to do with it
   the Queen Elizabeth and all who live in her would be
   bombed tomorrow. However, such a place does exist,
   tucked away discreetly behind a barrier of conifers
   and barbed-wire fences so as not to offend the
   sensibilities
   of the local bourgeoisie. After all, the sight of those
   discarded mattresses and burnt-out cars could really
   ruin one's journey to the golf club. (As a reticent
   resident of the Queen Elizabeth I think it's hilarious
   that a town planner somewhere thought it fitting to
   bestow such a regal-sounding address upon us.

Surely Albert Steptoe Towers would have been
more fitting. I mean, I can hardly imagine the
Queen ever tripping her way through the discarded
glue-bags and hypodermics in order to pay her
namesake a visit!)
5. Calibre of Local Celebrities.
I believe you can tell an awful lot about a place by the
calibre of its local celebrities. Hence Liverpool has the
Beatles and Frankie Goes to Hollywood while Pinner
gets Bob Holness and Ronnie Barker.

I rest my case.

I apologise for beginning my correspondence in such a
negative way, Anne, but I really have had the most awful
day, so bad it has driven me to write a diary. It was either
that or a suicide note. The day began with an argument
with my mother, Helen – nothing unusual there but this
time was particularly frustrating. I was running late for
school – the hem on my skirt had come down again –
Karen was waiting patiently on the doorstep and just as I'd
tacked it back up, Helen yelled at me to come into the
kitchen. Actually she didn't yell – my mother never yells,
she leaves that to my dad and me – but she definitely
raised her murmur by a fraction of a decibel. As I entered
the kitchen, where she was busy grating an apple into a
bowl of what looked worryingly like hamster bedding, she
said, without even looking up, 'You're wearing makeup.'

And I said, 'No, I'm not,' I mean, it was only one coat
of Twilight Teaser, for Christ's sake, Karen is allowed to
walk around looking like Siouxsie Sioux all the time.

'Wipe it off,' she said, in her infuriatingly calm voice,
passing me a piece of kitchen paper.

'No, I won't,' I responded, turning to leave.

'You're fifteen years old,' she said, in the tone you'd use

to address a fifteen-month-old baby. I mean, I'll be able to have sex legally in less than a year – although the chance would be a fine thing!

'Exactly,' I replied, 'I'm fifteen years old – I'll be able to have sex and elope to Gretna Green soon, so what harm is a bit of lipstick going to do?'

'That's exactly what I'm worried about,' Helen said, with a shudder. 'Now, wipe it off. Can't you see that makeup is just another way for society to oppress women? By wearing makeup all you're doing is degrading yourself for the benefit of men. You're a beautiful girl, Caitlin, you don't need to paint yourself like a clown to get attention. And, besides, true beauty comes from within.'

At this point I heard a snigger from the doorstep where Karen was waiting, in full war paint as usual. God, it was so embarrassing. It's bad enough when my mum goes off on one of her Germaine Drear rants in private, but in front of my best mate was just too much. If I'd stayed there any longer she'd probably have got me to burn my training bra in the toaster! So, ignoring her murmured protestations, I marched out, and on our way down to the bus stop I applied a coat of Karen's strawberry lip-gloss on top of my Twilight Teaser, which tasted foul, but at least I had the last laugh.

Or so I thought until Wank-face Wainwright kept me behind after maths to give me my second lecture of the day on the evils of cosmetics. I would have stayed and argued the point but I had English next period, and this is one of my best chances of the week to spot Alex Moon. He is quite possibly one of the most beautiful boys I have ever laid eyes on, and right now is the only thing I look forward to about going to school. Of course, he's in the sixth form and far too cool to acknowledge me, but I am happy to make do with snatched glimpses in the corridor and surreptitious glances across the playground – all from my direction, I regret to add. But not today on this bluest of blue Mondays. No, by the time I had raced over to the English block, reapplying my Twilight Teaser on the way, the corridor was deserted, the classes having all been called in. I was devastated. Oh, how I live for a glimpse of that shiny wedge haircut and those moody brown eyes and the way he walks like a man. A man among boys. Oh, if only he would notice me too. All the other boys are so immature, with their squeaky little voices and their disgusting fluff-sprouting, acne-covered faces.

Things got even grimmer at lunch-time. I binned my wholemeal Marmite sandwiches and went to the ice-cream van with Karen to get a hot dog and hopefully a sighting of Alex. But he was nowhere to be seen and, even worse, we ran into Donna 'the Mattress' Maddox and her mates. After running the usual gauntlet of abuse – I always find it bizarre being called a 'fucking weirdo' by a girl who thinks white stiletto ankle boots and purple legs make for a cool combination – we returned to school completely demoralised. I don't know what I'd do if I didn't have Karen. She is the only person I have anything in common with – the only other teenage girl on the Queen Elizabeth who doesn't want to have a baby so she can get a flat of her own. If it weren't for my nights spent at Karen's drinking lemon squash and eating biscuits while plotting our escape from this hellhole I think I'd go insane.

Which brings me to the final part of this dreadful day of disaster. I arrived home from school comforted slightly that I was one day nearer to the weekend and the prospect of an evening at Karen's listening to the Orgasmatron remix of 'Relax' only to receive a double-whammy of doom. First, the rancid assault on my nostrils informed me that we were having bacon and cabbage for tea – again. My dad has been living in England for seventeen years now, has he not heard of the saying, 'When in Rome . . .'? It's hardly fair of him to keep inflicting his bland, boiled offerings on me and Helen night after night. And, worse still, making Helen cook it for him. Where are her feminist principles when it comes to my dad? That's what I'd like to know. As I took a deep breath and entered the kitchen I was greeted by the pair of them staring at me grim-faced.

'I hear you've been wearing makeup to school again,' my father said, by way of address.

'It was one coat of lipstick.' I sighed.

'Don't you know makeup's not allowed in school?' my father asked, stroking his beard in the way he always does when he's trying to appear serious.

'Yes, it is.'

'Well, it isn't where I teach.'

Thankfully, my dad teaches at a school on the other side of the borough – it would be the final straw if he taught at Pinner Hill. The Mattress would have a field day if she could add 'teacher's pet' to her list of insults. Not that I could ever be accused of being Joe's pet: he always sides with Helen and tonight was no exception.

'And I hear you completely ignored your mother when she asked you to take the muck off your face.'

I looked at my mother, who was disappearing in a fog of foul-smelling steam by the sink, and I wanted to throw the colander of cabbage all over her smug, makeup-free face. God, she is so weak, always running to tell tales to Joe while waiting on him hand and foot. And she accuses *me* of being subservient to men.

'I was running late. I wiped it off on the way to the bus stop,' I offered lamely.

My father sighed and took a sip from his mug of Bovril. 'If your mother asks you to do something you do it,' he said wearily, in that voice of his that says, 'I've been dealing with unruly teenagers all day long and I really don't expect to have to come home to one.' 'So I'm afraid you're to stay in tonight.'

'What? Can't I even go round to Karen's?'

'No, and before you start, if I hear any more from you you'll be staying in for the rest of the week.' And with that Joe vanished behind his copy of the *Guardian*.

So here I am, Anne, lying on my bed, still feeling sick from the after-effects of the cabbage with only my diary for company, and I've never felt so desperate. I know that what I'm going through is nothing compared to what you had to endure, locked up with that awful Mrs van Daan and the dreadful Dr Dussel, but at least you had Peter. At least you knew what it was like to fall in love and have somebody fall in love with you. I just can't begin to imagine how wonderful that must feel.

Tuesday 4, March 1984

Dear Anne,

Well, what a difference a day makes! You will never believe what happened to me today. Not only did I see Alex Moon but he actually spoke to me! I still can't believe it as I lie here on my bed drunk on love (and lemon squash and vodka).

Karen and I were bunking off PE – Karen's got her period and it was cross-country running – so we escaped to the third-year toilets. Luckily the Mattress and her mates weren't around so we had a really good laugh about her fluorescent green leg-warmers. Anyway, then I remembered I still had half a B&H in my coat pocket so I decided to sneak to the cloakroom to get it. And that's when it happened. That's when all of my prayers were answered and I finally got to speak to the object of my desire. I was in the cloakroom fumbling about for the cigarette when suddenly I heard footsteps. Thinking it was a teacher or, even worse, the Mattress, I dived behind the coat pegs, but it was all right, it was him. Alex Sex on Legs Moon. He looked at me and I looked at him and as our eyes met I felt the strangest sensation (I don't think it was an orgasm or anything, but things certainly got pretty tingly). And then he smiled. He actually smiled. At me. And then he opened that beautiful, pouting mouth of his and said, 'Wotcha.'

To me. Alex Moon said, 'Wotcha,' to me. And I said, 'Wotcha,' to him. He finally knows I exist. God, he is even sexier up close. He has a scar next to his eye and a tiny gold hoop earring in his right ear. I could barely speak with excitement when I got back to the toilet. Karen was well jealous.

Have spent the evening at Karen's. Her family are so much cooler than mine and what happened tonight is a perfect example. When I left here earlier my mum was writing to one of her political prisoners in South Africa while my dad was playing his banjo along with his Clancy Brothers LP. I left the house with 'Up the long ladder and down the short rope, to hell with King Billy and God bless the Pope' ringing in my ears, only to get round the corner to Karen's house to find her dad checking the oil on his motorbike while her mum, Debbie, reclined on the settee in a red satin wrap, polishing her nails. Karen's parents are wicked. I would give anything for a dad with tattoos and leather trousers instead of a beard and a banjo. And I can't imagine how much fun it must be having a glamorous mum to share makeup and beauty tips with.

Anyway, we managed to sneak about a quarter of a bottle of vodka into our jug of lemon squash before retiring to Karen's room to listen to our four different mixes of 'Relax' while I performed action replays of my cloakroom encounter with Alex. By about the tenth time (and half-way through our jug of vodka squash) we concluded that the way he said, 'Wotcha,' definitely implied he was interested. Oh, please, God, let it be true. I would give my signed Thompson Twins album for a date with Alex.

Failing that, we have come up with an action plan to find some real men, which is as follows:

1. Check out the local youth clubs.
2. Go to the roller disco at Harrow Leisure Centre.
3. Try to gain entry to the Victory pub – notorious for its under-age drinking.
4. Go on a CND march (serious last resort!).

Sunday, 9 March 1984

Dear Anne,

Complete disaster on the hunt-for-real-men front. I will now report the tragic results of the first stage of our action plan.

Our investigation of local youth clubs got off to a flying start. Not only did we discover that one existed in the Pinner Methodist church hall but, even better, they were having a disco this Saturday. Karen and I spent the whole morning in Watford shopping for new clothes. She got a gorgeous snood from Chelsea Girl, just like the one Nik Kershaw was wearing on *Top of the Pops* and I got some black lacy fingerless gloves and a new pair of pink footless tights. We also got a packet of silver bangles to share and two sachets of Shaders and Toners from Woolies. Then we spent the afternoon at Karen's getting ready.

We were supposed to be getting ready at my house, but you'll never guess what my pain-in-the-arse parents have done to me this time. I swear their sole purpose in life must be to humiliate me in the most cruel and bizarre ways imaginable. Karen and I arrived back from Watford full of excitement about the evening ahead. I should have known it was a mistake coming back to mine when I spotted the heap of manure steaming away in our front garden.

'Oh, my God,' Karen sniggered, 'it smells like *Emmerdale Farm.*'

Then, without warning, the front door burst open and out came Paddy O'Brien, possibly my dad's most embarrassing mate, with his alcohol-pickled face and his white bouffant hair, bellowing something like, 'Ah, sure, b' Jaysus, yer coddin' me, y'are.'

To which my dad replied, at the top of his voice, 'Sure, thanks for the shite, Paddy, I'll see ye down O'Flaherty's later.' And then, to make matters even worse, my dad walked over to the pile of manure, bent down and inhaled deeply. 'Aaaah – the smell of the land,' he sighed to Karen and me – we were trying desperately not to gag, her with laughter, me with mortification. 'How do you girls fancy an afternoon at the allotment?' he enquired. And I don't even think he was joking!

Hastily we made our way upstairs to what I thought would be the refuge of my bedroom, only to discover Helen hovering around by the door. 'Ah, Caitlin,' she said, somewhat sheepishly, I noted, 'I've, er, put something up in your bedroom. I hope you don't mind. It's just that with all those posters of millionaire pop and film stars you insist on plastering all over your walls I thought the room needed a bit of balance.' And with that she scuttled downstairs.

Oh, Anne, I can't begin to tell you how angry I was when I walked in to find one of Helen's political collages running practically the whole length of the room. Sandwiched between the Human League and Holly Johnson was a sea of brown bodies and swollen bellies.

While we had been shopping in Watford my mother had spent the entire morning making a collage of pictures of starving Cambodians.

'Flippin' 'eck!' Karen exclaimed. 'It's even worse than the "Meat Is Murder" one.'

I shuddered as I remembered tossing and turning beneath the photos of cleavers and carcasses that Helen had hung over my bed last year when she was trying to persuade me to become vegetarian. 'Why can't she just leave her collage-making to her primary-school pupils?' I wailed, dangerously close to tears from the sheer humiliation of it all.

'Come on,' Karen soothed. 'Get your things together and we'll go round to mine.'

I bundled my clothes and collection of crucifixes, bangles and beads into a bag and headed off to Karen's once more, but not before scrawling 'Frankie Says Relax!' on every single one of those swollen brown bellies.

The afternoon improved rapidly after we arrived at Karen's. The glamorous Debbie helped us with our hair while she played the Torvill and Dean music over and over again on the record-player. (I didn't have the heart to tell her it was called Ravel's 'Bolero' not Ravin's 'Bollaro'.) Karen looked great as usual. Debbie put about half a pot of gel on her hair and backcombed the ends until she looked just like Madonna on the 'Holiday' video. I wish my hair wasn't so long and dark. It's so difficult to do anything with. In the end I put a sachet of mahogany toner on it and tied it back with a piece of black lace. Then we got dressed. I wore my slashed teabag T-shirt over a bright pink vest, my shortest black skirt, new pink footless tights and my black ankle boots with the gold buckles on the sides. I felt so glamorous and grown-up that part of me wished I was going on a date with Alex. If he saw me like this he'd realise I'm not just some dumb schoolgirl but that beneath the school tie and blazer there is a sophisticated woman dying to burst out. Karen looked fantastic in her snood. Of course she had to wear it round her neck so as not to ruin her hair.

We spent about an hour in her bedroom practising our Madonna routines – I love that punching dance she does, it's great for releasing tension. I kept imagining Helen standing right in front of me every time I lashed out. Karen's dad offered to give us a lift. I wouldn't have minded, but Karen said it would be too embarrassing. He drives a metallic blue Capri with 'Gaz and Debs' across the top of the windscreen, which admittedly is a bit naff, but at least they have a car and a sporty one at that. My parents must be the only teachers in the land who don't own a house or a car. The private ownership of property is for parasites, or so says the gospel according to Joseph Kennedy. It's bad enough living in a council house, but if we had a Capri life would be a little more bearable.

Anyway, having declined the offer of a lift Karen and I set off on foot. While Debbie had been busy Immac-ing her legs, Karen had managed to pinch four of her cigarettes. I wish Helen smoked. The only thing she leaves lying around the house are assorted health foods. I can just picture Karen's face if one day in the park I turned to her and said, 'Look, Karen, I've managed to nick four sun-dried prunes!'

As we walked along smoking, enough drivers beeped at us. Dirty old perverts. I felt well grown-up, though. With hindsight, that was probably the highlight of our night for things went rapidly downhill the minute we reached the Pinner Methodist church. We should have known, really. I mean, a church hall is hardly going to be a hotbed of disco debauchery – it's hardly the Wag Club.

Oh, Anne, we walked in – and I'm still shuddering at the recollection – to find the place full of kids. When I say full I don't mean full to capacity, there was only about ten of them, but every single one must have been twelve or under. And as they stood in awkward little groups pressed against the walls, giggling and fidgeting, what looked like a traffic-light turned on its side flashed away in time to 'It's Raining Men'. Oh, if only! The only thing it was raining last night in the Pinner Methodist church was shame and embarrassment. Karen and I looked at each other in horror – but before we could do a runner the DJ caught sight of us and was shouting at us over his microphone to come and join the party. And when I say DJ, please don't picture Steve Strange at the wheels of steel – or even Ed Stewpot. No, the DJ in question was actually the Reverend Jeremy Wilkinson, known throughout Pinner for his legendary evensong sessions. We were trapped in some awful Sunday-school soirée, and the worst thing was, those little brats in their Velcro fasteners and velour party frocks had the nerve to laugh at what we were wearing!

I will never be able to walk past the Pinner Methodist church again without suffering a traumatic flashback of Karen and me sprawled on the floor doing 'Oops Upside Your Head' at the front of a line of giggling imbeciles.

Wednesday, 12 March 1984

Dear Anne,

I don't think I'll ever understand my parents. While I'm upstairs dying of a broken heart all they can do is talk about the bloody miners going on strike. I mean they're two teachers living in London, for Christ's sake, they've never set foot in a pit in their lives.

I haven't seen Alex all week, I think he may be off sick.

Oh, please let him be back tomorrow, I can't bear another day in that prison without a glimpse of him to help me make it through the day.

I have played 'Hello' by Lionel Ritchie twenty-seven times since I got home from school. Joe just yelled up the stairs, 'Mary, Mother of Jaysus, will ye tell yer man it's not him we're looking for!'

God, he is so unfunny!

Chapter Six

Friday night, 11 p.m.

Oh, my God. I flung the diary to the floor and groaned. How could I ever have been so gut-churningly shallow? How could I almost have been brought to climax by somebody saying, 'Wotcha'? Could I really have been that desperate? Had I ever been that horny? These days, I had more chance of having an organic tofu omelette than an orgasm. Even my trusty vibrator had been put out to pasture, with the recesses of my under-wear drawer now doubling as a twilight rest home for tired dildos.

I peered over the top of the duvet at the seemingly innoc-uous notebook lying discarded on the floor and felt as if I were marooned on a desert island being circled by a taunting shark. Excruciating extracts rang through my head. 'Oh, how I live for a glimpse of that shiny wedge haircut' . . . 'Oh, if only he would notice me too' . . . 'The way he walks like a man. A man among boys.' God, it was like Barbara Cartland does St Trinian's.

When I had retrieved the diary from the loft, I'd been so scared of what else it contained that I'd been totally unpre-pared for this exercise in degradation. But before I had time to shrivel up and die from the sheer embarrassment of it all I heard the pitter-patter of footsteps across the landing followed by a somewhat cautious tap on the door. I glanced at my essential bedside companion, whose bright fuchsia hands informed me it had just turned eleven o'clock. Frankie must have been having another nightmare.

'Come in,' I called softly, and on cue the door burst open and Frankie flung himself on to my bed.

'I was dreaming about the John bleeding Lewis Monster. He turned me into a chicken nugget!' Frankie mumbled, his hair tousled and eyes squinting in the glow of the bedside lamp.

'Okay, snuggle up and I'll tell you a story,' I offered, pulling back the duvet, relieved to have a diversion from my excruciated state.

Frankie clambered in next to me and nestled his head in the crook of my arm.

'Tell me the one about Daphne and the gigantic dog poo, Mum,' he murmured, stifling a yawn.

'Okay. Once upon a time there was a beautiful girl called Daphne . . .'

Frankie's eyes sprang open. 'Was she wearing her pink tights?'

'Yes, she was wearing her pink tights.'

'And her pretty purple dress?'

'Yes, she was wearing her favourite purple dress and matching purple shoes.'

'And was her hair curly or straight?'

Jesus Christ! Surely it was only a matter of time before I found Frankie at his sister's dressing table, attired in her finest Barbie underwear, face shimmering with glitter and giving himself a French manicure.

'Her hair had been lovingly teased into a mass of Titian curls,' I obliged.

Frankie smiled contentedly and closed his eyes.

'One day Daphne was on her way to the shops when she accidentally trod in a gigantic dog poo . . .'

As my purple-clad heroine battled her way through the excrement, Frankie's sniggers turned slowly to snuffles and he slipped once more into sleep. Careful not to wake him, I edged my way into a lying position until our faces were level. Gently brushing the curls from his heart-shaped face, I gazed at the crescents of his closed eyes, fringed with the sort of eyelashes any woman would die for. As the air whistled through his red satin bow of a mouth I was suddenly overcome by a rush of pain and fear. Some people make it so easy for you to keep your guard up, with their endless tantrums or irritating habits, but there was a vulnerability about Frankie, a spontaneous warmth, that made it impossible not to reciprocate. As I watched him lying there, all crumpled pyjamas and downy skin, half of me wanted to gather him up as close as I could, to try to recapture the days when he was still a part of me, and the other half wanted to leap from the bed in terror. For I had experienced this feeling once before and the thought of losing it again was too much to bear. A tear worked its way down my face and plopped into Frankie's hair. How could I go through life too terrified to love my own children? What kind of a mother was I going to become and, more importantly, what kind of damage was I going to wreak? Surely I had a responsibility to Frankie and Megan to face up to my demons while I still had the chance. So, with a reluctant heart and a trembling hand, I reached out of bed for my diary.

Chapter Seven

Monday, 17 March 1984

Dear Anne,

Complete disaster on the hunt-for-real-men front – part
two! For some reason I thought the roller disco might
prove more successful than our night of Methodist misery,
but it was not to be. We arrived at Harrow Leisure Centre
clad in footless tights and leg-warmers, inspired by an
afternoon of leaping around Karen's bedroom to her *Kids
From Fame* LP. As I took to the floor with the wind racing
through my hair and the music pounding through my body
I really felt as if I might live for ever. The hall was about
ten times bigger than the one at the church; there were
proper disco lights, a huge glitter ball suspended from the
ceiling and – I couldn't help noticing – some gorgeous boys
hanging around by the side. But therein lay the problem:
that's all they did, hang around the side sniggering and
nudging each other as us girls flew past. As I skated round
and round like a stuck record I soon realised that no Leroy
Johnson was going to be sweeping me up over his head to
the sounds of 'High Fidelity'.

In fact, quite the opposite was true. For, about two hours
into the disco, when the boys had drunk enough Coke to
venture on to the dance floor all they wanted to do was
ram into us and send us flying. Landing flat on your back
with some mullet-haired monstrosity leering down on you
is hardly the most romantic way to spend a Saturday night.

Karen and I returned to her house for late-night lemon squash and biscuits and listened to Tears For Fears' *The Hurting* for two hours solid while nursing our aching feet and tender limbs. I'm going to be black and blue all over in the morning. All I want is some love and affection. Will I never meet a real man?

Thursday, 20 March 1984

Dear Anne,

Caitlin Moon, Caitlin Moon. Caitlin Moon. Mrs Caitlin Moon, pleased to meet you. On the bus home from school this afternoon Simon Bradshaw shouted to Alex, 'Are you going to the Vic tomorrow?' From behind my copy of *Just Seventeen* I held my breath and waited for the words I yearned to hear. 'Yeah, laters,' he grunted, masterfully swinging his sports bag over his shoulder and leaping from the bus. Alex Moon will be in the Victory pub tomorrow night and so, hopefully, will me and Karen. This has to be fate. I have to look gorgeous – I think I might borrow Karen's stone-washed drainpipes with all the gold zips.

Friday, 21 March 1984

Dear Anne,

As that miserable Mancunian Morrissey would say, 'Heaven knows, I'm miserable now.' Oh, God, everything is going so horribly wrong – at this rate it won't be long before I'll be traipsing through Pinner with a bunch of daffodils sprouting from my backside on my way to a Dungeons and Dragons convention! Why can't I be cool and pretty and fit in? Why do I always feel out of place wherever I go and whatever I do? I'll tell you why – because I have THE PARENTS FROM HELL, that's why. The

way I feel right now I could quite happily murder them as
they sleep, under that hideous 'ethnic' blanket, hand-woven
in Botswana exclusively for Oxfam. God, I hate them, I
hate them, I hate them!

As you know, tonight was supposed to be the night
Karen and I enjoyed our first drink in a public house. Our
first visit to a pub that didn't involve perching on a stool
drinking copious amounts of Coke and eating endless
packets of crisps while my dad traded abuse with fellow
Irishmen about how they were all a bunch of yellow bellies
and bogtrotters. It was to be our first drink as adults,
sophisticatedly sipping Cinzano and lemonade while
exchanging small-talk and making eyes at Alex Moon.
There would be no drunken old Irishmen giving us fifty
pence for the fruit machine or, even worse, 'some sweets'.
It was going to be the beginning of a new chapter in my
life – the night when I came of age – or so I thought.

It all started remarkably well, considering we got ready at
my place. We had had fish and chips for tea so for once
the house didn't stink of boiled vegetables. And by the time
Karen arrived neither of my parents were engaged in
embarrassing pursuits. Joe was busy marking books at
breakneck speed so that he could spend the rest of the
weekend alternating between the allotment and
O'Flaherty's, and Helen was engrossed in her current tome
about the oppressed women of Mozambique.

Karen flung her bounty of half a bottle of Tia Maria and
three slightly misshapen cigarettes on to my bed and
sighed. 'You're so lucky,' she said, 'living here, with your
parents.'

I couldn't quite believe my ears either.

'I can't stand it at home.' She sighed, backcombing her
hair frantically in front of the mirror. 'I've got nobody to
talk to. All I get is my mum wittering on about perm

solutions, while my dad polishes his leather trousers and tinkers about on his bike. And then, to cap it all, I've got those bloody little brats and their bloody Transformers tearing all over the place screaming, 'Robots in disguise.' At least you can have a decent conversation with your parents; at least they read books. The only book my mum possesses is the *Reader's Digest Guide to Holidays on the Channel Islands.*'

'But your parents are so cool,' I replied, grabbing her industrial-sized can of hairspray. 'They're so trendy. They actually like Duran Duran – and they let you have a Sodastream.' Helen only allows me to drink milk or watered-down orange juice at home. I think she'ld rather I drank cyanide than any kind of fizzy pop.

Karen snorted. 'They're so working class. They have no ambition or drive. Do you know what my mum said to me tonight? She said that Geoffrey has promised me a place as a junior stylist when I leave school next year. And she thought I'd be happy at the prospect. As if I want to spend my days sweeping up hair and rinsing out rollers. I mean, your parents want you to make a success of your life, don't they? They take it for granted you'll be applying to universities in two years' time. Mine take it for granted I'll be applying blue rinses.' Karen took a large swig from the bottle of Tia Maria. 'Have you got any Depeche Mode?'

Thankfully, the combination of Tia Maria and 'People are People' jolted Karen from her melancholic madness and we set off for the pub. Not before a grilling from my father, though.

'Sweet Jesus!' he declared, staring pointedly at our hair. 'You don't fancy earning yourselves a bit of extra pocket money down the allotment, do ye? I could do with a couple of scarecrows.' He leant back in his chair and guffawed. 'So, where are you off to, then? Brookfield Farm?'

Listening to *The Archers* is yet another of my parents'
humiliating habits.

'Are you wearing makeup?' Helen piped up. God, the
hypocrisy of the woman, so concerned about the oppressed
state of her 'sisters' in Africa while all the time waging her
own campaign of oppression against her very own
daughter!

'It's only a bit of eye-shadow,' I lied, looking down at the
floor and shuffling towards the door. 'Anyway, we're only
going round to Karen's.'

'Hmmm,' said Joe. 'Well, don't stay out too late, Worzel,
I've a load of runner beans to plant tomorrow, I could do
with your help keeping the sparrows at bay.'

It wasn't until we'd got to the park and I'd changed into
Karen's stiletto-heeled boots, applied a quick squirt of
Poison and pretended to smoke a cigarette, that I regained
my confidence. After all, I wasn't trying to attract a middle
aged, banjo-playing Irishman, was I? I knew Alex would
appreciate my teasingly combed coiffure.

As we wobbled our way down the high street we got
more attention than ever from the horn-beeping perverts of
Pinner. Without wanting to sound like Helen, I really don't
know how women can bear to wear stilettos for any longer
than five minutes at a time. My toes felt as if they were
being crushed in a vice and my whole body felt thrown off
its axis. How on earth does Debbie manage to wear them
all day long in the salon? Even her slippers have two-inch
kitten heels! As we neared the pub my heart began
pounding faster than the bass line in 'Blue Monday'. With
a last-minute scrunch of the hair and slick of the lips we
nudged open the heavy oak door and marched – a little
unsteadily – to the bar.

The Vic is so much nicer than O'Flaherty's, with its oak
beams, low ceiling and Dubliners-free jukebox. Of course, I

didn't notice any of this at first. I was too busy examining the carpet while a squeaky-voiced Karen ordered the drinks. I thought I was going to be sick with nerves as I waited, cheeks aflame, for the barman to shout, 'Call the police, we've got a couple of kids here,' but he didn't. He simply poured the drinks and then he even asked if we wanted ice and a slice! As we made our way to a table that lurked invitingly in a darkened corner I wanted to leap for joy. I was an adult at last! No more swigging Strongbow on park benches for me. From now on my life was going to be a hectic social whirl of nightclubs and cocktail bars. As Rufus and Chaka Khan pounded from the speakers and I sipped slowly on my Cinzano and lemonade (we had deduced that our combined pocket money would only stretch to two drinks each) I experienced a feeling of such intense happiness that I cannot begin to put into words. And then, as if things couldn't get any better, I caught a glimpse of a gleaming chestnut wedge above a pair of achingly moody eyes making their way through the crowd – most of Pinner Hill sixth form by the looks of it – towards us. 'Alex!' went up a cheer of recognition from the table next to us, echoing my own inner cry of joy. Alex, holding a pint of beer and a packet of twenty B&H, raised the corners of his scowl into the faintest of smiles, and then as he sat down he glanced over in our direction and – get this – he actually raised his eyebrows in acknowledgement!

Oh, Anne, for one brief moment in time I must have been the happiest girl alive. I should have realised then that it wouldn't last, that it was far too good to be true. It makes me feel physically ill to recall what happened next, but I know that I must record it. I must put it down in writing for future reference in case I ever find myself wavering and feeling anything other than pure contempt for my parents. God, my pen is actually shuddering as I

write this, huddled in bed at eleven o'clock on a Friday
night when the rest of the world and Alex Moon are still
out drinking and enjoying themselves.

Karen and I were pretending to be engrossed in a debate
over who has the nicest hair – Nik Kershaw or Howard
Jones – while glancing feverishly at the adjacent table when
it happened. 'The Re-fle-fle-fle-fle-flex' was fading out on
the jukebox when what sounded like a mortally pissed
version of the Furey brothers and Davey Arthur began
bellowing through the pub. Gradually the excited chatter
tapered out as everyone began searching for the source of
such an affront to the eardrums. However, there was
something sickeningly familiar about the wailing voices –
invoking images of torturous Saturday nights at
O'Flaherty's – that meant I didn't need to see the white
bouffant hair and purple nose or the Aran sweater and
brown cords to realise that it was Paddy O'Brien and my
father. As the voices grew ever closer and Karen began
chanting, 'OH MY GOD!' over and over again in time, my
eyes burnt with tears of humiliation. How could he do this
to me? And in front of Alex and half of the sixth form as
well. My life was effectively over. All I had ever wanted
was for Alex to notice me. Well, he noticed me tonight, all
right. The entire pub noticed me, blushing the shade of a
tormented tomato while two geriatric Paddies serenaded me
with 'Sweet Sixteen'.

'Well, well,' Joe said, when they had hummed and
howled their way to the end, 'what have we here?'

'Looks like the Wurzels!' Paddy O'Brien bellowed, before
launching into a chorus of 'Combine Harvester'.

'So, what do you think your mother would have to say if
she knew you were out drinking in a pub?' Joe asked,
before downing half a pint in one go.

Part of me wanted to stand up and shout, '*I'm out*

enjoying my emancipation – she should be glad I'm not being circumcised or dying of malnutrition in some mud hut in Africa!' But, of course, I'd already been humiliated enough for one lifetime. All I wanted to do was crawl out of that place on my hands and knees, away from the finger-pointing and sniggers of my fellow Pinner Hill pupils.

'Come on,' Karen hissed. 'Let's get out of here before they start doing "The Irish Rover"!'

As we pushed and stumbled our way to the door with Joe and Paddy's chuckles ringing in our ears, the final nail in my street-credibility coffin was administered with the immortal words, 'Fucking weirdo.'

I turned to see the Mattress sneering at me from beneath her two-inch-thick Maybelline mask. Frozen with horror, all I could do was stand there while her pouting, Saucy Sable mouth belched smoke rings into my face. In the end Karen had to grab me by the arm and drag me from the pub. I was inconsolable all the way home, not helped by the fact that my entire body seemed to be staging an uprising against the stiletto-heeled boots. As I wobbled and staggered my way back up the high street I felt cheap and ridiculous.

Karen, however, seemed remarkably chipper. 'Do you realise what this means?' she said excitedly, pulling up her snood.

'We are now social outcasts, banished to the library at break-time with Pisspants Parry and Arthur Cocker,' I replied, sorrowfully.

'No – I'm not talking about school, I'm talking about our lives,' Karen said, her lace-clad hands gesticulating grandly.

'Our lives are effectively over. Didn't you see the Mattress? She'll never let us live this one down.' It had started to rain now and I could feel my hair begin to collapse like an undercooked soufflé.

'Sod the Mattress – we got served! We went into a pub on our own and got served with alcoholic drinks. Who cares about school and the Vic and Pinner? The whole world is our oyster now. Just think of all the different pubs out there. We could even go to Watford!'

I hobbled up the path behind her, inhaling the scent of dissolving Elnett and thinking mournfully, but Alex Moon doesn't drink in Watford.

I was so depressed I declined Karen's invitation of lemon squash and biscuits, and went straight home to be greeted by yet another appalling sight. There was Helen, standing at the kitchen counter kneading a lump of roughage-riddled dough, her wooden elephant earrings bobbing in time with her pounding fists as she warbled, 'Kumbaya'! Oh, Lord – just how many personal tragedies can a girl take in one night?

Chapter Eight

Dear Anne,

BAN THE BOMB!

I can't believe it has been an entire month since I last wrote to you, but as you can probably tell I have been busy undergoing a period of personal growth during the past few weeks. My eyes have been opened to the terrible outrages going on on this planet and the mushroom-shaped cloud hovering ominously over mankind. I feel, even more than before, a connection with you and your experiences in the annexe. As you listened to the horrific events of the war on your radio and watched the Nazis rounding up your fellow Jews outside, you must have undergone a similar kind of personal journey. I am sure that if I die tragically young and my parents uncover my diary they will highlight this entry as the one where I became a woman. 'It was the CND march on the nineteenth of April that changed her,' they will say, before performing one of their dire folk songs in my memory.

This has nothing to do with the fact that Alex Moon and the Mattress are now an item. I had begun to question my obsession with the opposite sex long before that shock discovery. When you stop to think about it, what does it matter if the most gorgeous boy on the planet finds the unwashed Sinner of Pinner attractive? The way Maggie-

Thatcher-Milk-Snatcher and President Reagan are going, we won't have a planet left for much longer. What kind of people spend millions of pounds on weapons of mass destruction when half the world is starving? What kind of boy finds a girl with nicotine-stained fingers and teeth attractive?

God, I just cannot believe it! I could have accepted it if he had gone out with Rebecca Hamilton or one of the other golden-haired goddesses of the sixth form, but the Mattress? The other week, Karen and I were in the queue behind her for dinners and we noticed that her skirt had burst its seams right over her bulging backside, leaving her knickers on display for all the world to see. Not only were they going grey but they had a big old bloodstain on them as well! GROSS! When she heard us giggling she turned round and said, 'Shut your mouth, Paddy weirdo' – she never says anything to Karen. I so badly wanted to respond with something like, 'Nice pants, Mattress, where did you buy them? Staines?' But I know I would have got a spotted dick and custard shoved in my face so I refrained. How can he *possibly* find her attractive?

Hold on a second . . .

Sorry about that. Ever since Marvin Gaye was killed Helen has been playing 'What's Going On?' *ad nauseam.* I've just put 'Against All Odds' on again to drown it out. I can't believe Marvin Gaye was shot dead by his own father, but on reflection it's probably a more favourable fate than being slowly tortured to death by a campaign of humiliation and oppression. As I listen to Phil Collins I know that to wait for Alex is all I can do, it's just a chance I've got to take, but it seems so dreadfully unfair. And the question is, would I really want him now he's been with her? God knows what kind of diseases he might have picked up. Karen reckons she might even have crabs! And, from my discovery the other night, there is no way she will be keeping them to herself.

It was about midnight and I was coming home from Karen's, taking the shortcut through the flats, when I heard a strange groaning noise behind the bins. My head awash with images of glue-sniffing maniacs intent on rape, I hurried by – only to have my way blocked by a snarling, fang-baring Alsatian. As soon as I heard a girl's voice shriek, 'Rambo!' I knew it belonged to the Mattress, but I was completely unprepared to see Alex come shuffling out with his trousers around his ankles.

'Oh, it's you,' she sneered, her lipstick smeared all over her chin. 'What do you want, weirdo? Having a good look, woz yer? Yer fucking perv.'

I don't know who was more embarrassed, me or Alex. Probably Alex, due to his state of undress. I would have run home if I hadn't been so terrified of the rabid Rambo ripping me to shreds. Let me tell you, Anne, it's extremely difficult to stroll away casually when your heart has just been shattered into a million pieces by the cackling, crab-infested witch of West London.

But I digress. Yesterday was one of the most amazing days of my life. Karen and I decided to go on a CND march. Although this was previously part four of our hunt-for-real-men strategy, I must stress that neither of us is shallow enough to use something of such global importance as a dating agency. Helen was amazed when I told her we would be coming along. It would be the first protest march I had attended of my own free will. In her role as local CND branch secretary, Helen had arranged to rendezvous with her fellow left-wing lentil-lovers at Harrow-on-the-Hill station at 10 a.m. As Karen and I got ready – given the gravity of the situation we opted for the Madonna-meets-Phil-Oakey look – we plotted to make our escape as soon as we reached Hyde Park. However, we had not counted on encountering Jasper. With his sun-kissed mullet and tanned skin, he stood out like a beard-free beacon among the gaggle of *Guardian* readers on platform four. Clad in various shades of pastel cotton and a pair of white espadrilles he looked like a cross between Don Johnson and Jesus Christ.

'Take a look at that,' Karen whispered in awe, pulling her finest Madonna pout.

Preferring a more subtle approach I bowed my head and shot surreptitious glances every time Jasper had his back turned. As we boarded the train Karen shoved her way shamelessly to the same part of the carriage as our *Miami Vice* with me following meekly in her trail. Sometimes it pays to have a pushy friend. I ended up so close to Jasper that when he stretched one of those lovely tanned arms to the overhead rail I couldn't help but notice a tuft of golden hair creeping out from under the arm of his lilac vest top. As the train rattled and rocked its way towards London and the sun filtered in through the grimy windows I felt my misery over Alex begin to burn away like an early-morning mist. The world felt like a wonderful place again – apart, obviously, from the awful threat of nuclear apocalypse.

By the time we reached Hyde Park Karen, in her irritatingly bubbly way, had managed to find out all there was to know about Jasper. He was eighteen years old and the son of a surgeon living in Moor Park. His mother, Mrs Montague, was the headmistress at Helen's school – could this be Fate? – and he was about to take his A levels before studying politics at Manchester University. Suddenly Alex Moon seemed so shallow and inexperienced. Jasper knows so much about life. Karen and I clung to his side like two sponges, soaking up his views on everything from world politics to the music business. (From now on I will be buying the *NME* every week – Jasper says *Smash Hits* is for impressionable kids with pocket money to burn.)

The scene in Hyde Park was incredible: a perfect re-creation of the swinging sixties, with women in plaits and tie-dyed attire, nestling barefooted babies on their hips – or, in some cases, to their breasts! Men with brightly coloured braided string around their wrists sat cross-legged on the grass, actually rolling joints in broad daylight! I didn't see anybody making free love, though. Jasper said he had given up smoking 'ganja', as he calls it, because it made him feel too paranoid. As the sun beat down and various impromptu performances of 'Give Peace A Chance' started up around the park, part of me wanted just to lie back and inhale the mellow atmosphere, breathing in the spicy aroma of ganja and vegetable samosas. But I couldn't afford to relax: I was far too terrified of letting Karen worm her way in with Jasper. Her incessant chatter was the only thing ruining the tranquillity of the day. I don't know how she finds it so easy to speak to somebody as worldly as Jasper. I was terrified of saying the wrong thing – of appearing immature or inexperienced – but Karen genuinely didn't seem to care! I could have died when she told him about our night at the Methodist disco. Jasper has been to the Wag Club – one night he even trod in Boy George's vomit!

By midday it was time for the march to begin. It was bloody miles to Trafalgar Square. I'm so glad we decided against the stiletto heels in the end: not only would we have ended up crippled, but we would have looked ridiculously out of place. I had hastily removed my lacy fingerless gloves and three of my crucifixes within five minutes of arriving. For once Helen actually looked quite normal in her cheesecloth smock and red clogs. On and on we

marched, and by this time I have to say I was beginning to
tire of John Lennon or at least the two lines of John
Lennon that were being endlessly chanted. 'Give Peace A
Chance' really was all we were saying. I was also beginning
to tire of the constant battle for Jasper's attention. I wish
Karen would realise she is just not his type. A man of his
experience needs somebody a bit more understated and not
quite so naïve.

It was when we drew close to Downing Street that things
began to hot up. A group of people in front of us with wild
staring eyes and BAN THE BOMB! banners belonging to
something called the Social Workers' Party suddenly
decided to sit down in the middle of the road. Before I
knew it we were all sitting down, yelling, 'Give Peace A
Chance!' at the top of our voices. It was great. For the first
time in my life I felt like I was part of something, I loved
those people with their dreadlocks and wispy beards, and
their pale vegetarian faces. We were united in our cause,
we cared about our planet, and we weren't afraid to do
something about it.

'Come on,' Jasper hissed, leaping to his feet. 'We'd better
move it, the pigs are coming.'

I turned to see a line of police slowly shuffling their way
into the crowd and suddenly everything erupted. It was
amazing to see so many peace-loving people acting so
aggressively.

'Fuck off, scum!' they shouted, flinging their placards
into the air and surging forwards. As the police – or should
I say pigs? – began to shove back, I felt really confused.
My only previous experience of a police officer was PC
Tony Hartley who used to come to my infant school with a
road map and some matchbox cars to teach us the Green
Cross Code. He was red-faced and jolly and used to bend
his knees and chortle, 'Evening, all!' He never glared at us

and brandished his truncheon like these policemen were doing. And he certainly never charged at us on horseback. Karen and I grabbed Jasper by the hand and began to run. It was even better than playing Knock Down Ginger. As we stumbled our way into Trafalgar Square I felt such an adrenaline rush that I vowed to attend every protest march I could find from now on. Especially if Jasper is going too.

Wednesday, 23 April 1984

Dear Anne,

Never have I been elevated to such heights of excitement only to be instantly plunged into despair! This evening, when Helen was at her monthly Greenpeace meeting and Joe was gnawing on a plate of pigs' trotters in front of *The Sweeney*, I was startled from an old *Blue Jeans* annual by the phone ringing. Knowing that Joe would sooner stand to the national anthem than answer the telephone I raced downstairs to get it.

'Hello,' came a tantalisingly manly voice at the other end. 'Is that Caitlin?' My heart performed a triple salko. Finally a man who didn't answer to the name of 'Gramps' had phoned for me.

'Yes,' I replied, hopefully not too eagerly. Could it be? Oh, please, let it be.

'Caitlin, it's Jazzy.'

'Who?'

'Jazzy. Jazzy J.'

There was a confused silence.

'Oh, shit, sorry. I don't think I told you girls my handle. It's Jasper, Jasper Montague.'

'Oh.' I breathed a sigh of relief, immediately followed by a gasp of excitement. It was Jasper on *my* telephone, phoning *me*. I scrunched my hair and glanced around the hall nervously. That tatty poster of Nelson Mandela would have to come down before we went on a date. There was no way I would allow Jasper over the threshold of this house of humiliating horrors, but the poster was clearly visible from the front door. Although his mother was a member of the Labour Party I had the feeling that it would be Monet rather than Mandela adorning their Moor Park walls.

'I hope you don't mind me calling like this. My mum gave me your number.'

'Oh, no, not at all,' I replied, attempting a sultry voice, *à la* Mae West.

'Are you okay? You sound like you've got a throat infection.'

I coughed. 'Yes, I'm fine. It's probably all that shouting from Saturday.'

'Oh, right. Yeah, it was a good gig, wasn't it? The pigs certainly got what was coming to them, didn't they?'

I thought of Jasper legging it down Whitehall and felt a little confused. 'Yeah, too right, fascist bastards.'

'Anyway, I was just wondering . . .'

My heart leapt. *If I'd like to go for a drink? If I'd like to go to the Wag with you and Boy George? If I'd like to go on a demo against our totalitarian police state?* Yes! Yes! Yes!

'You don't happen to have Karen's phone number, do you? I got the impression she had a bit of a thing for me and I thought I might take her out one night.'

Oh, Anne, how it pays to be pushy. You play the cool sophisticate and you just end up being used as some kind of dating bureau, whereas Karen acts with the subtlety of a hound dog on heat and she ends up on a hot date with Jazzy J.

Saturday, 26 April 1984

Dear Anne,

As I lie here all alone on a Saturday night I can't help but be consumed by hate. I hate my parents (obviously) for abandoning me to my sorrow to go to some bastard barn dance in Northwood Hills. I hate this house. I hate this estate and its illiterate, illegitimate residents. I hate the Mattress and Alex Moon. I hate Karen and Jazzy J, wherever they may be on their stupid date. I hate the way Debbie permed Karen's hair for her this morning and made her look even more like Madonna when all I look like is a tear-stained version of Dr and the Medics. I hate the way Mr Crosby next door keeps playing bloody 'Chopsticks' on his home organ – can't he think of a more productive way to spend his retirement? I hate the way the needle has gone on my record-player when all I want to do is play 'Against All Odds' at full blast. But most of all – I HATE ME. I must be the most unpopular misfit on the planet. I think of other fifteen-year-old girls out on dates with their boyfriends or on sleepovers with their girlfriends and I realise that I have nothing. No boy has ever shown any sign of interest in me, and now I am losing my one and only friend to a mullet-haired mouth-almighty from Moor Park. I think it's time I re-read *Are you there, God? It's me Margaret.*

Sunday, 27 April 1984

Dear Anne,

Karen and I aren't speaking. All I did was point out that Jasper was a tad hypocritical in claiming to be a member of the proletariat when he chooses to spend Saturday night at his father's golf club, and she stormed off home in a huff – she even took her Kajagoogoo album back and she hates Limahl!

At least he didn't take her to the Wag to meet Boy
George.

                              Monday, 28 April 1984

Dear Anne,

School is the pits. Wank-face Wainwright kept me
behind again today to lecture me about my lack of
enthusiasm and how if I want to take my maths O level a
year early I'll have to stop daydreaming in class. What does
he expect me to do? I mean, given the choice between
fantasising over Paul Rutherford or theorising over long
division I'd take Paul any day. I can't believe the rumours
that he's gay – with his leather vest top and clipped
moustache he seems all man to me.

Karen still isn't talking to me so I ended up in the library
at lunch-time. How much lower can I possibly sink? At
least I haven't discovered the joys of Dungeons and
Dragons – yet.

                              Wednesday, 30 April 1984

Dear Anne,

I AM SO BORED! I tried making conversation with my
parents tonight (see how desperate I have become) but
all they want to talk about is the bloody miners. When I
pointed out that we lived hundreds of miles away from
the nearest coal mine and therefore it was nothing to do
with us – well! You'd have thought I'd said I was
standing as a Conservative in the school council
elections.

'Nothing to do with us?' Joe bellowed. 'It's got
everything to do with us. Thatcher is out to destroy the
working class. It's the miners today, it'll be the teachers

tomorrow. We have to stand united against the shrivelled-up bitch.'

'Language, Joe,' Helen cautioned, before putting on their God-awful Pete Seger LP. 'I think we ought to have a public meeting about the strike,' she said. 'Maybe we could get a couple of miners to come and speak.'

Never had a night of lemon squash and biscuits seemed more appealing. Is politics all they can think about? God, how I miss Karen and our chats about men.

Saturday, 3 May 1984

Dear Anne,

Hurrah! Karen – or should I say Carron? – and I are talking again. It's only been a week but she seems so different. She has decided to change her name to Carron ('less council estate') and all she wants to talk about is the 'wonderful' Jasper, but at least I have my friend back. At least I have somebody to go to the cinema with. We went to see a brilliant film called *Footloose*. It was about a small town in America, a lot like Pinner, actually, where the grown-ups decide to ban music. Can you imagine how awful that would be? I don't think I could live without hearing Frankie Goes To Hollywood at least twice a day. Mind you, if it meant I didn't have to listen to that bunch of sideburned saddos Helen has become obsessed with it might not be so bad. They are called the Flying Pickets, which is quite apt, really, given Helen's current fixation with the miners. They wouldn't be so bad if they could play any instruments but all they do is stand around going 'bah, dah' and grinning in that irritatingly *Guardian*-reader way.

Friday, 9 May 1984

Dear Anne,

Have had a really good week. Jasper's mum and dad won't let him out during the week now as he has to have private tuition for his A levels so I have managed to see Karen every night. She is thinking about running away from home in September and getting a job in Manchester as she can't bear the thought of them being apart – am trying not to think about the dire consequences this would have upon my own life. (He still hasn't taken her to the Wag.)

Monday, 12 May 1984

Dear Anne,

Was watching the news tonight about a demo in a place called Mansfield. Arthur Scargill was calling on everyone to bring down Thatcher. I thought Joe was going to wet himself. Seeing all those miners shouting at the police reminded me of my own brush with insurrection at the CND march. It almost made me wish we lived in a pit village. It must be well exciting.

I can't believe we've got two miners coming to visit next week. Knowing my luck the Mattress will be walking past just as they arrive, all blackened faces and northern-speaking. Within twenty-four hours it'll be all round the school that I'm an Arthur Scargill lover. What is going on with that man's hair?

Tuesday, 20 May 1984

Dear Anne,

Have spent the evening having my eardrums assaulted in Karen's house. Debbie is in the grips of Torvill and Dean mania so 'Bolero' was blasting incessantly from the living room. The boys were having some kind of break-dancing contest in the hall and Gaz kept revving up his bike right under Karen's bedroom window. All of this hardly helped calm her tortured mind. At the moment all she wants to do is listen to China Crisis and eat chocolate digestives. Seeing the way things are going with her and Jasper has made me seriously reconsider the disadvantages of being alone. As far as I can tell, Karen comes pretty low on the 'delectable' Jazzy J's list of priorities. When he's not with his private tutor he's at rugby practice or, even worse, playing Dungeons and Dragons! Can you believe it? It just goes to show you never can tell a person from first appearances. I don't believe he's ever set foot in the Wag, let alone Boy George's vomit.

Got home to find Helen cleaning feverishly.

'What's wrong?' I asked, feigning amazement. 'Is there a new moon or something?'

'Don't be so silly,' she retorted. 'I'm getting things ready for our guests.'

That shows how warped my parents are – the amount of polishing that was being done you'd have thought we had Charles and Di coming to visit, not two striking miners.

'Will you be coming to the meeting?' she asked, giving her Native American headdress a quick flick of the duster.

'No, it's all right.' Although Carron's going to Popmobility with Debbie tomorrow night I would rather stay home and watch Helen's sunflower seeds dry than sit in a Scout hut with a bunch of old fossils listening to two moustachioed northerners talk about life 'down pit'!

Chapter Nine

Thursday, 22 May 1984

Dear Anne,

OH, MY GOD! I can't believe what has happened. It's three o'clock in the morning and I should be feeling exhausted, but if love be electricity then currently (excuse the pun) I have been clad in polyester, struck by lightning and plugged into the mains. My entire body is coursing with ecstasy. I suppose I really ought to start at the beginning.

Yesterday afternoon, having trudged home from school with the weight of half the library and the general pressures of teenage angst heavy upon my shoulders, all I could think about was collapsing on to my bed with the latest copy of *Just Seventeen*. However, as soon as I opened the front door and heard unfamiliar chortling coming from the kitchen I realised that Helen's coal-miners had arrived. I attempted to creep upstairs undetected but, of course, old Elephant Ears heard me.

'Caitlin, come and meet our guests,' Helen called, in an unusually effervescent voice.

I slung my bags to the floor and trudged into the kitchen to be greeted by the most splendidly unexpected sight. I know it sounds silly as they haven't worked for almost two months now, but I had half expected to see two soot covered men wearing helmets and carrying lamps. I had not expected to see one cheery-faced, middle-aged man

clad in a biker's jacket and jeans sipping a cup of tea. And
I most certainly had not expected to see the back of what
looked like a drop-dead gorgeous hunk sitting tapping his
tanned fingers on the kitchen table. For some reason I just
couldn't tear my eyes from those fingers. They were so
scuffed and brown. Then, before I had time to rush up to
my bedroom, rip off my school uniform and make myself
look remotely cool and sophisticated, he turned round. I
saw immediately that he was the older man's son. The
heart-shaped face and imp-like grin were a dead giveaway.
However, where the older man had a silvery, shorn crop to
disguise a receding hairline, he had a full head of honey-
coloured hair, spiky at the front in a Tiny Tim quiff. As
soon as our eyes met, my entire body seemed to combust
with embarrassment. I looked down at my hopelessly
unfashionable school uniform and sighed. Why couldn't I
have worn my mini-skirt today? What an earth had
possessed me to choose the kilt?

'Caitlin, this is Bob and his son Jed. They've come down
from Blidworth to speak at tonight's Labour Party meeting.
Do you want a glass of milk?'

Oh, the sheer unadulterated shame of it!

'No, thanks,' I mumbled. 'I'll just go and get changed.'
And with that I beat a hasty retreat to my bedroom. Once I
had brought the temperature of my face back below boiling
point I rummaged through my wardrobe for something
suitable to wear. With his leather jacket and jeans, Jed was
obviously not a New Romantic. Jed. Just his name seems to
holler masculinity. I can picture him now racing around the
Nottinghamshire countryside on his motorbike, his T-shirt
flapping against that brown, muscle-bound body. Anyway,
school uniform consigned to the bottom of my wardrobe, I
writhed my way into my tightest pair of drainpipes and my
FRANKIE SAYS RELAX! T-shirt, and hastily applied a quick

coat of electric blue mascara. Replacing Kenny Loggins with 'Free Nelson Mandela' I yanked the needle on to the vinyl and cranked up the volume on my record-player. Then I opened the door just enough to let Jed hear that I was the kind of politically aware person who cares passionately about prisoners of apartheid and striking workers. My heart skipped a beat when I saw him coming out of the bathroom.

'Good song,' he said approvingly, in a husky northern accent. 'Have you got any UB40?'

Thank God for Helen's '*Labour of Love*' LP.

'Yeah,' I said, cheeks back on the boil.

'So, do you do requests?' he asked, with a grin, the skin at the sides of his grey eyes crinkling like brown-paper fans.

'Yes, if you want.' I suddenly remembered the packet of Bodyform sitting on top of my dressing-table. 'Hold on a second,' I said, and dived back into my bedroom. I hastily hid the sanitary towels, my school bag and my James Galway album (a spoof Christmas gift from Joe) and gave my bedroom a quick once-over. I like to think of it as a welcome oasis from the chaos downstairs. I pride myself on the fact that there isn't a single hand-woven rug, blanket or garment in sight. Now that Helen's Cambodian collage has been destroyed, every inch of wall space is adorned with posters from *Smash Hits* – a veritable mascara, eyeliner and hairspray fest. I retrieved my CND badge from the bottom of my wastepaper basket and set it proudly on top the record-player.

'Okay, you can come in now,' I said, flinging the door open.

Jed walked in and cast his eyes around. 'Bloody ell, you've got more posters than our Maxine,' he remarked.

'Sit down,' I said, pondering the identity of 'our Maxine' and gesturing to the beanbag in the corner. I don't think my internal thermostat could have coped with Jed sitting next to me on the bed. '*Labour of Love* okay?' I asked nonchalantly, as if I owned the entire UB40 back catalogue, while praying he didn't ask for some obscure earlier release.

'Aye, sound,' Jed replied in a voice that made me want to melt.

<u>Six things I fancy about Jed:</u>
1. His husky northern voice.
2. His flinty grey eyes.
3. His cheeky grin.
4. His syrup-coloured skin – definitely good enough to eat!
5. His golden brown spiky hair.
6. His body – he is only a couple of inches taller than me, but he looks so strong.

Oh, what I wouldn't give to lay my head against those broad shoulders and to be held in those muscular arms!

But I digress. After putting UB40 on the record-player I perched on the edge of the bed and tried to look as if having a gorgeous man in my room was just a run-of-the-mill everyday occurrence. My hormones, meanwhile, did a conga in celebration.

'So, you're still at school, then?' he asked, nodding towards the pile of folders and books cluttering up my desk.

'Yeah.' I casually attempted to stretch my legs and nearly slid off the bed.

'Doing your O levels are you?'

'No, not till next summer.' There was no way I was going to tell him about the two I was taking a year early. I didn't want him thinking I was some kind of swot.

'You're joking – so how old are you, then?'

'Fifteen – sixteen in September,' I added hastily. 'How old are you?'

'Eighteen – nineteen in March,' he added, with a
chuckle.

I breathed a sigh of relief. Three years was nothing. Joe
is six years older than Helen.

'So, are you really a miner?' I asked, my face
immediately turning the colour of red, red wine at the
stupidity of my question.

'Yeah – why, am I different from what you expected?'

'Yes. No. I don't know.' (God, I can hardly bear to write
this down.)

'So, what did you expect, then?' he asked, resting his
chin on his hands and staring at me intently.

I thought of helmets, lamps and canaries, and blushed
even redder.

'Don't tell me, covered in coke dust, wearing a helmet,
with a pick slung over me shoulder?' He took one look at
my sheepish expression and burst out laughing. 'Oh, well,
sorry to disappoint you.'

'Oh, no – you haven't disappointed me!' The words
wriggled out like eels before I had time to restrain them for
being so excruciatingly uncool.

Jed gave me a knowing grin, then flicked through the
stack of records on the floor next to him.

'I can't wait till strike's over and I can buy some records
again.' He sighed, pulling out my Human League album.
'You haven't disappointed me either,' he added, with a
wink.

'What do you mean?' I asked, my heart on freeze-frame.

'Well, you're all right – for a southern lass.'

'Oh.' While I tried to work out if he had just paid me a
compliment, Jed got to his feet and looked out of the
window. He seemed fidgety, restless. Once more the image
of a caged canary popped into my head.

'So, what's this place called again?' he asked.

'Pinner,' I replied, unable to disguise my lack of enthusiasm. 'Home to pastel linen two-pieces and Bob Holness.'

'I thought this were London.'

'Well, it is, sort of. It takes about half an hour on the tube.'

'The tube,' he repeated, dreamily. 'I went on that once, when Forest were playing in Cup Final. Me and me dad had to get the tube to Wembley. So, what's the night life like round here? I bet it's ace.'

I thought of the Methodist youth-club disco and sighed. 'Well, Pinner's pretty dead. I usually go up to the West End with my mate Karen, to the Wag or the Mud Club.' *Oh, if only!*

Jed stared at me blankly.

'It's where people like Boy George go.'

'Oh. Right.' Jed looked distinctly unimpressed. 'Are you going to this meeting tonight?'

Oh, Anne, I hope you're not too appalled at my fickle nature, but seeing some real live miners in the flesh suddenly gave the strike a whole new perspective – a human angle – and I thought it only right that I show my solidarity.

'Oh, yes, of course,' I replied. 'I went on a CND march the other week,' I added, nodding at my badge as if for proof.

'Really?' This time he seemed genuinely interested. 'I saw that on the telly.' Suddenly Jed grabbed my hairbrush from my dressing table and began rapping into it to 'Red Red Wine' as if it was a microphone. When I started to giggle he pulled me to my feet and before I knew it we were both skanking around my bedroom like a couple of ganja-smoking Rastas. As we chanted and giggled and danced I had a small taste of what it must be like to have a boyfriend and I never wanted it to end.

Then Helen yelled up the stairs, 'Caitlin, come and get your aduki burger. Joe's taking the guys to the chip shop for tea.'

'What's an aduki burger?' Jed asked, mystified, putting his microphone back on the dressing-table.

Once more my face flamed. 'It's a burger made from aduki beans,' I muttered. 'My mum's a vegetarian and she keeps trying to convert me.'

'Hasn't it worked?' he asked.

'No. I could never give up bacon sandwiches.' I explained.

Jed laughed. 'Aye, you can't beat a bacon butty. Mind you, I wouldn't mind trying one of them aduki things.'

So while Joe and Bob went off to the chippy, Jed and I feasted on bean burgers. Helen was overjoyed at Jed's interest in her carcass-free cuisine – he even tried some Marmite gravy. I think he genuinely enjoyed it too. He certainly doesn't seem like the kind of person to be false about such things. He calls a spade a spade, as Joe would say. By the time we'd finished our honey-sweetened, wholemeal apple crumble he had made fun of my accent, my Frankie T-shirt and my collection of Care Bears, but all in such a good-natured way I found it impossible to feel tense. I only wish I could have found it as difficult to blush!

'Don't you take any crap from him, young lady,' said Bob, when he and Joe returned from the chippy an hour and a half later, mysteriously reeking of beer and cigarettes. 'He's a cheeky young bugger that one – got more lip than Mick Jagger.'

At seven o'clock we set off for the meeting – thankfully, Helen and Joe didn't question my change of heart although Joe did give me a knowing wink when I expressed my concern to Bob about the miners' plight. As I walked through Pinner alongside Jed I couldn't help fantasising that this bronzed specimen of masculinity in his plain black T-shirt and faded jeans was all mine. Oh, how fantastic it would have been to feel one of those strong arms around my waist or those manly fingers taking my hand. I literally floated down Bridge Street. If only Karen could have seen me. She's welcome to Jasper Montague now I've finally found a real man.

The meeting was actually quite good and not only because of my new-found personal interest. Bob spoke for about forty minutes about the problems facing the miners and how they need our help and solidarity as the strike drags on. Luckily he is one of those speakers who like to throw in little jokes every couple of minutes so the time flew by. It was hilarious watching Helen pretend to laugh at the one about the frigid lesbian. I could have sat there all night next to Jed, dreaming of those hands running through my hair and trying to imagine what he looked like naked.

But, as always where my parents are involved, things took a drastic turn for the worse at the end of the meeting. Jed had gone to the toilet (thankfully) and everyone else was discussing which pub to go to for a post-meeting pint.

'You'll be all right walking home on your own, won't you, Caitlin?' said Helen – the bitch – before giggling inanely at Bob's Neil Kinnock impersonation.

I could barely conceal my disappointment. Why can't she ever lighten up? What harm would it do to let me come along? But I could see Helen was revelling in all the male attention. She even had her favourite turquoise beads on – the last time she'd worn them was when Ken Livingstone was elected leader of the GLC.

'But can't I just come for one? I'll drink lemonade.'

'Not on a school night, sweetie. Your exams start in a couple of weeks.'

Sweetie? When had she ever called me sweetie? I wanted to rip her stupid beads off and stuff them into her smirking mouth. It was so unfair. As tears began to sting the corners of my eyes I decided to beat a hasty retreat. The last thing I wanted was for Jed to return from the toilet and witness my humiliation. That would have been the final straw.

As I trudged along Bridge Street, unable to quell the veritable sodastream of sobs bubbling up into my mouth I imagined Helen hurtling down a disused mineshaft somewhere in northernmost Nottinghamshire.

Suddenly I heard footsteps running up behind me.

'Hey, wait up!' a voice called, instantly sending shivers up my spine. It was Jed. My initial jubilation was soon replaced with horror. My tears were sure to have caused a mascara massacre. Sure enough, a quick wipe of my face with the back of my hand left it streaked with electric blue. But it was too late. Panting slightly, Jed was at my side. As soon as he saw my face his smile faltered. 'What's up?' he asked.

Seeing his concern only made me want to cry even more. Yet again in my cursed existence everything had gone disastrously wrong. 'Oh, nothing, just hay fever.' I sniffed, frantically wiping more electric blue gunk from my face.

'Hmmm,' he said, sounding unconvinced. 'Well, do you mind if I walk you home? I don't fancy spending the rest of the night with a bunch of old folk – no offence to your parents or owt, it's just that I'd rather come back with you. If you don't mind. Just say if you'd rather be alone or you've got summat else on. Here—'

Before I knew what was happening he had brought one of those rough brown hands to my face and gently wiped away a remaining splotch of mascara. 'Bloody hayfever,' he said softly. 'Can be a right pain, can't it?'

I nodded gratefully.

'Come on, then,' he said grabbing my arm. 'Let's get UB40 back on. Or would you prefer that Frankie Goes To Hollywood shite?'

As I chased after him pretending (extremely badly) to be outraged, I felt propelled by a sudden surge of happiness – perhaps good things could happen to me, after all.

The sun was setting when we got back to the estate, with the last dying rays reflecting gold off the windows of the flats. Everywhere seemed to be basking in a magical glow. It felt like one of those early-morning dreams where you know in the back of your mind that what's happening isn't real – you know you aren't really enjoying a Frenchy with Holly Johnson and I knew I couldn't really be walking alongside somebody as nice as Jed – but I was happy to wrap myself up in the warmth of the moment and luxuriate in it for as long as possible.

I wondered what kind of house Jed lived in. Something told me it wouldn't be like Jasper's mansion in Moor Park.

'What's it like in Blidworth, then?' I asked.

Jed laughed, 'Oh, not too different from this, really.' He glanced at an upturned shopping trolley lying abandoned in the car park. 'When me dad said we were coming down to London I thought we'd be staying with some right posh do-gooders. I didn't really want to come, to be honest – I thought you'd all be looking down your noses at us.'

I skipped over a shredded car tyre and laughed. 'Hardly. At least, not here on the Queen Elizabeth.'

As we rounded the corner of the flats I heard the clip-clop of white stiletto ankle boots and a low-pitched snarl. The Mattress and her canine counterpart. My stomach lurched as I waited for the usual torrent of abuse. But the strangest thing happened. She didn't say a word. When I plucked up the courage to raise my eyes to her face I saw that she was far too busy gaping like a lip-glossed goldfish at Jed. As we drew level she pulled on Rambo's lead, bared her yellow teeth and said, 'All right, Caitlin?'

I couldn't believe it. I didn't even think she knew my name. I nodded curtly before turning into the front garden.

'Friend of yours?' Jed asked, as I unlocked the door.

'No way,' I replied. 'She only spoke to me because of you. Blokes and blowjobs are all she thinks about. We call her the Mattress.'

'Aye, there's lasses like that back at home.'

I thought of Jed with his trousers around his ankles being serviced by some northern version of the Mattress and shuddered.

Surprisingly, I didn't feel awkward when we got back to my bedroom, and Jed certainly seemed at home, the way he headed straight for the record-player and put on 'Relax'.

'Bent as a nine-bob note,' Jed said authoritatively, as Holly began howling.

I tried to stifle a frown. 'No, they are not!'

'Of course they are – all that leather and facial hair, just like the Village People. It's a dead giveaway. So, have you got a boyfriend?'

I was beginning to realise that Jed was a firm believer in the direct approach, which, combined with his revelation about the Village People, caught me completely off-guard. How could I tell him I'd never had a proper boyfriend? How could they be gay and sing about being in the Navy?

'No. Not any more.'

Jed sat down facing me on the end of the bed and raised his eyebrows quizzically.

'I was dealing with somebody called Alex, but it's all over now. He was too immature,' I said, tossing my hair over my shoulder like the advert for Harmony hairspray.

'Dealing with him?' Jed asked, perplexed. 'What do you mean, you used to do drugs or summat?'

I laughed in what I had hoped would be a sophisticated tinkle, but came out sounding more like a childish squeal. 'No. Dealing. It means seeing somebody. I suppose you still say *courting* up in Blidworth.' My cheeks flared at my clumsy attempt at flirtation.

'Cheeky cow,' he said, getting up from the bed and looking through my bookshelves. 'For your information we say dating. And it's Blid'th not Blid*worth*.'

'So. Are you?' My need to know overcame any sense of cool.

'Am I what?'

'Dating? At the moment.' I pretended to straighten the duvet so that he wouldn't notice my by now radioactive face.

'I might be.'

My heart sank.

'Then again I might not. This looks good,' he said, holding up a copy of *The Outsiders*. 'I bet you're dead intelligent, with all these books and all. I can't believe how many your mam and dad have got downstairs. Your living room's like a library.'

I shrugged my shoulders and wished we could have been magically transported to Karen's house and her solitary copy of the *Reader's Digest Guide to Holidays on the Channel Islands*.

'I think it's sound,' he said, studying the blurb on the back of the book. 'I wish I'd paid more attention at school, but it didn't seem worth it at the time, not when I knew I was going to end up down the pit.'

(Oh, Anne, is there anything quite so tragic as the unfulfilled potential of the working class?)

'You can borrow it if you like,' I said, nodding to the book. 'It's excellent.'

'Really? Sound.' Jed beamed with delight.

'What's it like being on strike? It must be awful.'

Jed looked at me carefully, as if he were weighing up whether to let me in on a confidence. He sat back down on the bed and my heart tremored as his knee brushed against mine. 'To be honest, it's bloody brilliant. Just being outside in the sun all the time and not a mile underground covered in shit. And I'm getting to go to places I'd never dreamt of going before and meeting people from other pits all over the country.'

'And Pinner,' I added.

'And Pinner,' he said, with a grin. 'Especially Pinner.'

(Oh, Anne, what do you think he meant by especially Pinner?)

'So, do you not enjoy being a miner, then?' I asked, unable to contain my thirst for more information.

'I hate it,' he said, his face clouding over. 'I love being outside too much.'

'What would you be if you could do anything?'

Jed laughed, 'A forester.' Noting the look of surprise on my face he explained, 'Blid'th is right next to Sherwood Forest – I must have spent most of me childhood clambering up a tree or making a camp below one.' His eyes took on a dreamy glow. 'There's summat magic about woods, the smell, the light. Well, you ought to know, being a book-lover.'

I stared at him blankly.

'Well, think of how many famous fairy tales were set in woods because of the atmosphere – *The Babes in the Wood*, *Hansel and Gretel*, *Goldilocks and the Three Bears*. Let's face it, *Little Red Riding Hood* wouldn't have been nearly as spooky if her grandma had lived in a cul-de-sac in town!'

I laughed, 'Yeah, and *Robin of Sherwood* wouldn't be

nearly as romantic if Michael Praed had chosen to hide away in marshland.'

'Exactly.' Jed fixed me with one of his amazing grins. 'How about you? What do you want to do when you leave school?'

'Well, I might go to university,' I said feigning uncertainty, although with the parents I've got, higher education is about as preordained for me as Jed's life down the pit. 'But eventually I'd like to be a writer.'

'Seriously?' Jed looked impressed. 'What kind of a writer?'

'Oh, a novelist,' I replied breezily. My writing must be the only thing I can talk about with any confidence.

'That's brilliant. Bloody hell, you're really different, you are.'

'Different from what?' Suddenly I could hear the Mattress shouting, '*fucking weirdo*' in my head and my heart sank.

'Different to other lasses.'

'In what way?'

'I dunno. You're interesting. Everything about you's different. Even your name. Caitlin.' Jed stared at me thoughtfully for a moment, 'I'm going to call you Cat, though.'

'Cat?'

'Yeah, you look just like a cat with those green eyes and that shiny black hair. Not to mention those whiskers,' he added, with a chuckle.

I grabbed a pillow from behind me and clouted him round the head and then, before I knew what was happening, a full-scale pillow fight had erupted. It was fantastic – all that physical contact and unbridled passion.

About ten minutes later, as we lay in a breathless heap on the floor, Jed stretched out his hand and stroked my hair. 'It's so soft,' he whispered.

For once I was grateful I hadn't had time to backcomb it into its usual lacquered labyrinth.

'So, tell me about your writing, then, are you doing anything at the moment?'

Oh, Anne, as I lay there on the floor telling him all about the short-story competition I won last year and the outline I had in my head for my first novel – I even told him about this diary although no amount of tickling could get me to show it to him – I felt so blissfully happy. Finally I had met somebody who actually seemed interested in me and wasn't put off by my weirdness.

Of course, my perpetually pain-in-the-arse parents returned home before anything of a more amorous nature could occur and, of course, the hateful Helen had to shout up the stairs about it being past my bedtime, but none of that seems to matter at the moment. As I lie here thinking of Jed asleep downstairs on the sofa I feel so excited and happy and scared. All I have ever wanted was to find that special somebody for me. Helen has Joe, Karen has Jasper, the Mattress has Alex and Rambo. Could Caitlin have Jed? Oh, please, please, let it be so.

Chapter Ten

Saturday morning – unfeasibly early!

I was chasing Jed through a forest, ducking beneath low-hanging branches, and skidding on leaf mulch as he darted this way and that. I kept calling his name, but he wouldn't turn round. He just kept running and running. Slowly I began to gain on him until he was within reach. Panting, I stretched out my arm and, with a lunge, managed to grab hold of the back of his T-shirt. It was faded and crumpled and streaked with brown.

'Jed!' I called. 'It's me, Caitlin.'

And finally he stopped. And he began to turn. Come on, I willed, just show me your face, but then, without a word of warning, I was propelled into the air. It was as if the ground had turned into a giant leaf-covered waterbed. Every time I tried to regain my footing I shot back upwards, losing my grip on Jed's T-shirt, and once again he disappeared into the forest, leaving me bouncing aimlessly on my own.

'I am the John bleeding Lewis Monster and I am going to get you with my poncy potato-peeler!' a voice roared inside my head.

What the hell?

I opened my eyes and was blinded by the torrent of brilliant sunshine flooding the room. Shielding my face with the back of my hand I squinted at the figure bouncing inanely at the foot of the bed. Frankie.

'What are you doing?' I croaked, burying my head under the duvet and hoping it was all some terrible nightmare. Perhaps if I shut my eyes I could slide back to Jed. But it was not to be.

'Die, Dog Poo!' Frankie shrieked, launching himself on top of me.

'For God's sake, Frankie, I'm trying to get some sleep,' I yelped, flinging off the duvet. It was already sweltering and it was only six thirty. Six thirty! Along with spontaneous sex and sightseeing holidays, Saturday morning lie-ins had been sacrificed long ago on the pre-parenthood funeral pyre.

'Daphne!' Frankie yelled, thrusting his cross little face into mine.

'What?'

'My name's Daphne, not Frankie.'

I groaned and hauled myself upright. Although not a drop of alcohol had passed my lips the previous night I felt something remarkably similar to a hangover setting in. My head was pounding and my mouth tasted like a mouldy sandpit. I also felt that fuzzy sense of disorientation as fragments of the previous night's events drifted into place. The séance. The rooting around in the loft. The diary. Jed. My skin began to tingle.

'What's for breakfast, Mum?'

I stared blankly at Frankie – Daphne – as my mind whirred into motion. The diary. Where the hell was the diary? I looked on the floor, but there was no sign of it. Shit. What if Sam had crept in on his way to his dawn *t'ai chi* session and found it while I was asleep?

'I said, what's for breakfast, Pieface?' Frankie began bouncing once more, his saggy pyjama bottoms revealing a miniature version of builder's bum – or perhaps, in his case, a decadent display of *derrière*.

As he bounced his way up the bed towards me I heard a

crumpling sound from beneath the duvet. The diary. I reached under and pulled it out. It looked even more battered than before.

'What's that? Is it a story book?' Frankie asked, collapsing down next to me, his black curls sticking like liquorice boot-laces to his flushed face.

'Sort of,' I replied, shoving it down the side of the bed, 'Come on, then, let's get some breakfast.'

'Read me a story. Please.'

'Not now, it's breakfast time. I'll read you one after.'

'Okay.' Frankie followed me off the bed. 'Mum?'

'Yes.'

'Who's Jed?'

'What?' I felt sick – my phantom hangover was complete.

'Who's Jed? Why were you shouting at him? Is he a monster?'

I sat back down on the bed. 'No, mate, he's not a monster. I was just having a bad dream about – about the Jedi. Yes, the Jedi from Star Wars.'

'Oh.' Frankie took my hand in his sticky little paw. 'Were you Princess Leia?'

'Yes. Yes, I was.'

'And did you have your hair up in those round circle things or down and wavy?'

Crisis averted, I made my way downstairs to find Sam, juicer in hand, staring at the photo of his fatter self on the fridge door. 'I can't believe I ever let myself get that over-weight,' he said, nodding to the fridge.

I looked at the picture of a jolly, healthily well-built version of Sam sipping a lime green cocktail on a beach in Bali – our honeymoon destination – and sighed. It wasn't just the toxins that had been purged from his body in recent years, but his ability to relax and have a good time too. I watched as he began to slice a banana manically.

'Would you like a smoothie?' he asked, depositing about half an orchard's worth of fruit into the juicer.

In the old days I would have come back with some naff joke about being perfectly happy with the man I had thank you very much and given him a hug, but not any more.

'You've got to be kidding. A cup of tea and a fry-up will do me.'

As I removed the bacon and sausages from the fridge I felt more than a little nauseous. It was far too hot for a fry-up and, if I was honest, the thought of an ice-cold smoothie seemed wonderfully inviting. But for some reason I felt so angry and bitter that all I wanted to do was lash out. Clattering a frying-pan on to the hob, I flung in about half a pint of oil. As the juicer roared into motion I sat down at the table and clutched my head in my hands. It was only seven o'clock in the morning but I could already feel myself knotting with tension.

'Are you okay?' Sam asked, spreading Frankie's toast with Marmite. 'Did you have a bit too much to drink last night? You know, you really shouldn't drink and drive, Caitlin. What would you do if you lost your licence?'

I wanted to scream, but I settled for sarcasm. 'No, for your information I didn't touch a single drop last night. Not even low-alcohol Lambrini.' I plonked some sausages into the frying-pan and dragged the laundry basket in from the hall. With every pair of Sam's neatly folded pants that I flung into the washing-machine I felt increasingly angry. What was I doing here, washing *his* pants, listening to *his* lectures? Why had I ended up with *him?* I slammed the door of the washing-machine and yanked the dial round to the correct programme. God, my whole life felt automated, one endless cycle of school runs, burnt teas and boredom. Then, in a quite unexpected twist, the washing-machine exploded.

Well, it didn't exactly explode, but it did emit a strange clanking noise, followed by an almighty bang.

'Wow!' Frankie exclaimed, a piece of half-chewed toast plopping from his gaping mouth on to the floor. 'It must have been a bomb.'

'Jesus!' said Sam, ashen-faced. 'What happened?'

'It was a bomb, dad,' Frankie explained, authoritatively. 'I think the John bleeding Lewis Monster planted it there yesterday.'

I wasn't sure if I had an overwhelming urge to laugh or cry, so I bit my lip and added four rashers of bacon to the frying-pan.

'Well, aren't you going to do something?' Sam asked.

'Like what?' I replied, turning the sausages in their tide of oil.

'I don't know – phone somebody or something?'

'Why don't you phone somebody? I'm busy,' I retorted, like a belligerent child.

'Well, who?' Sam gazed at me helplessly, a beige smoothie moustache fringeing his top lip.

'Try my address book under Washing-machine Repair Man.'

Sam trotted off obediently leaving me free to force down my panful of fried flesh.

Two hours later our 'happy' family unit was trawling around the supermarket in search of a week's supply of sustenance. Once again I was back on autopilot, marching purposefully down each aisle, slinging in sacks of chicken nuggets and oven chips along the way.

'Must we always have junk food for tea?' Megan pouted. 'Can't you make a shepherd's pie or something once in a while? Jessica's mum is always baking.'

'Jessica's mum has the face of a warthog and the personality of a blanched peanut. No wonder she never ventures out of the kitchen.' I added a four-pack of frozen pizzas to the trolley.

'One more complaint from you, young lady, and you can join your brother in the crèche. Now, let's go and find your father.'

Her father was lurking in the hot-beverages aisle, studying the rainbow spectrum of herbal infusions. Barging past him I grabbed a mammoth box of PG Tips from the shelf and flung it into the trolley.

'Teabags for our toxin-riddled friends,' I explained, haughtily.

'Can we get some cappuccinos?' Megan enquired. 'Brit-ney Spears says she never starts the day without a cappuccino.'

Sam's Botox-injected forehead attempted to wrinkle itself into a frown. 'Oh, Megan, I really don't think so, you're a bit young to be drinking caffeine.'

'Of course you can,' I interrupted, thinking of Helen's dictatorial Sodastream ban and hurling two boxes of cappuccino sachets on top of the PG Tips. 'Now, let's go and get some Coke.'

I had just got the shopping unpacked and the children silenced with two huge beakers of cavity-causing, caffeine-crammed cola when the washing-machine repair man arrived.

'Sam,' I trilled, 'the washing-machine man's here.'

For some reason Sam finds it excruciatingly embarrassing to communicate with a male member of the working class. I don't know whether it's guilt at his own success or a sense of masculine inferiority but it makes for extremely entertaining viewing. I sat down at the table and pretended to read *OK!*.

'All right, mate? What seems to be the problem, then?' With his skinhead haircut, Millwall tattoo and sovereign rings, Ted, the washing-machine repair man, was about as working class as they come.

'All right, mate?' Sam echoed, in a Mockney accent to make Guy Ritchie proud. 'It's the old washing-machine – it's gawn and blown-up on us, like. Can I get you a drink? A beer or sumfink.'

I retreated behind my magazine and groaned.

Ted glanced at the clock on the wall and shook his head. 'Nah, you're all right, mate, it's a bit early for me. I'll just have a cup of char if you've got one going.'

Sam looked confused.

'He means tea, dear,' I said, in my best Hyacinth Bucket voice. 'Would you like it with caffeine or without? Herbal or non? Brown or green? My husband's something of a tea connoisseur, you know.'

My husband had turned redder than a sunburnt bristol, as Guy Ritchie might say.

'Oh, smashing.' Ted rubbed his gold-plated hands in glee. 'Have you got any Lapsang Souchong?'

One hour, two pots of Lapsang Souchong and three hundred pounds later, our washing-machine was repaired, Sam and the tea-loving Ted had, rather irritatingly, bonded, and the kids were reaching a boredom crisis point.

'This place is soooooo boring!' Megan wailed. 'Why couldn't I have been born in Kentwood, Louisiana, like Britney? Pinner's the pits!'

Her wailing reminded me of my diary, and I had a sudden urge to be on my own. 'I don't suppose you could take the kids out for a bit?' I asked Sam, with as much sweetness as I could muster. 'I really ought to get on with altering that short story for *Gal Pal.*'

Buoyed up by his bonding session with Ted and an out-rageous quantity of caffeine, Sam readily agreed. 'Come on, kids, let's give your mum a bit of peace and quiet to get her work done. Who fancies a McDonald's?'

The whole room fell silent.

'What, really?' Megan asked, incredulous. 'With *you?*'

'Do we have to have milk or can we have lemonade this time?' Frankie enquired.

'Are you sure?' I asked. 'But what will *you* eat?'

Sam grinned, almost cockily. 'Oh, they do a pretty good beanburger.'

I thought of Helen's aduki burgers and smiled.

'Anyway, my detox finished today. You haven't forgotten we're going out tonight, have you?'

Oh, shit. I had.

'Is Auntie Karen babysitting?' Megan asked, a little too hopefully for my liking.

'Yes, I think so,' Sam replied.

'Oh, great. I can show her my new Britney video and we can talk about boys.'

'She won't have her hair up in a ponytail again, will she?' Frankie asked.

'I don't know,' I snapped. Suddenly I felt like a stranger, unwanted and unwelcome in my own home. Perhaps they'd be better off with a mother like Karen who enjoyed talking about Britney and playing with Barbie and had a long mane of golden curls.

'Come on, kids, let's go.' Sam grabbed the car keys from the table. 'I'll take them to the pictures after – give you a chance to relax and get ready for tonight.'

I tried not to wince as he kissed the top of my head.

'Great. Thanks.'

As soon as they'd gone I was about to make a beeline for the spare room when the phone rang. Remembering the nightmare call from the day before, I picked up the receiver and yelled,

'Good morning, Salesmen Haters Anonymous, how may I help you?'

'Cait, is that you? It's me, Karen.'

Karen sounded strange – stilted and embarrassed.

'Oh, thank God for that, I thought it was going to be yet another sales call.'

'No, it's only me. I was just checking you were okay, you know, after what happened last night.'

'Of course I'm okay. I was just a bit overtired, that's all.'

'Are you sure? Look, there's something I've got to—'

'Honestly, I'm fine,' I interrupted. 'Now, listen, are you sure you want to babysit tonight? We'd totally understand if something better's come up. I mean, it can't be much fun being stuck in with somebody else's kids on a Saturday night. It's bad enough when they're your own.'

'Don't be silly, I love your kids and, besides, I've told Marcus I'm going clubbing with the girls – got to keep him on his toes when I haven't got him on his back,' she added, with a giggle. 'You and Sam go out for once. Enjoy yourselves.'

'Are you sure?' I implored. The thought of Sam and me staring forlornly at each other over a vegetable pasta bake made me shudder. Wherever we ended up dining tonight, enjoyment certainly wasn't going to be on the menu.

'Of course I'm sure. I'll be over about seven. Listen, Caitlin, I've got a confession to make—'

'Right, I'll see you at seven, then – I must go, I've got a man here fixing the washing-machine.'

I threw down the phone and legged it upstairs. I didn't want to hear Karen's confession, all I wanted to do was get back to my diary . . . but there was something else I had to do first.

Getting my old record-player down from the loft was tricky but somehow I managed it. Wiping the dust from my hands I settled back on the bed, wincing slightly as the needle crackled its way over the scratched vinyl. My eyes filled with tears as I listened to 'Against All Odds'. What was I doing here, in this house, in this marriage? Why couldn't I have been with the only person who ever knew me at all? I felt as if I'd spent the last seventeen years in a coma and had woken up in the wrong life. I was supposed to have escaped from Pinner. I was supposed to have been writing novels, not naff short stories. I was supposed to have been with Jed, not Sam. Where had it all gone wrong?

Chapter Eleven

Thursday, 22 May 1984

Dear Anne,

It is eleven o'clock at night and I feel more worn out than Boy George's eyeliner. Yet every time my head hits the pillow my heart starts to sing. All day long I have thought about Jed. I don't know how I made it through maths without getting a detention or a lecture, at least, from old Wank-face. As I stared out into the playground all I could think of was Jed on the back of Bob's motorbike racing back up to Nottingham. Back up to his picket line and his struggle against capitalist oppression. Karen was off sick today (Debbie has taken her to a hairdressers' convention in Clacton-on-Sea) so I didn't have anyone to share my news with. If she's not back tomorrow I think I might burst. It was wonderful to get home tonight, to shut myself in my bedroom and lose myself in thoughts of Jed. Every time I listen to the masturbation megamix of 'Relax' I think of our pillow fight and of his hand stroking my hair. Oh, Anne, do you think he feels the same way about me as I do about him?

Evidence that Jed fancies me:
1. The way he said '*especially* Pinner' and that I hadn't 'disappointed' him.
2. The tender way he wiped the electric blue mascara from my face.

3. The fact that he preferred to come home with me rather than go to the pub with the others.
4. The way he compared me to a cat. Could he have meant sleek, feline and sophisticated? Either way it beats being likened to a dog.
5. His enthusiasm during the pillow fight and the way he stroked my hair.
6. Asking to borrow *The Outsiders*. Could this just have been an excuse to keep in touch?
7. The way he came to my room before he left this morning and asked me to write to him. Why would he want me to write to him if he wasn't interested?

Oh, how wonderful it would be to receive a letter from Jed – to see a Nottinghamshire postmark among all the African ones when the mail arrives. I'm going to play it cool, though. I've decided not to write until tomorrow at least. I think I will try to get some sleep now.

1 a.m.
Still can't sleep. Does Jed like me or not?

Evidence that Jed does not fancy me:
1. He was probably being sarcastic when he said '*especially* Pinner'. And when he said that I hadn't disappointed him he also said, 'for a Southern lass'. In other words I wasn't too hoity-toity.
2. The age difference – he seemed so shocked when I said I was fifteen. Oh, if only I was sixteen. It is so frustrating being a woman trapped inside a girl's body.
3. He probably has a girlfriend back at home. I found out that 'our Maxine' is Jed's older sister, but he seemed to play his cards pretty close to his chest when I asked him if he was dating. Why, if he had nothing to hide?

4. He thought I was weird. Although he didn't actually say 'weird', what else could he have meant by 'different'?

5. He probably only wiped the mascara from my face because he didn't want to be seen in public with an electric-blue-streaked freak.

6. Let's face it – who would want to spend the evening with my parents and a bunch of old fossils from the Labour Party? No wonder he asked if he could come back home with me.

7. When he said I looked like a cat why did he say I had whiskers? Oh, God, please don't say I'm starting to sprout a beard and moustache like Mabel Pearson at number twenty-eight.

8. I was the one who started the pillow fight. Of course he would join in – he's a boy. He stroked my hair because – well, I don't know, because he wanted to see what it felt like or something.

9. He was just showing a polite interest when he borrowed *The Outsiders*. He'll probably use it as a doorstop for a couple of weeks then send it back. Or maybe he won't send it back at all. Yes, I bet I never hear from him again in my life. It's hardly as if we're likely to bump into each other, is it?

10. The distance. Even if he does like me, how could it work when we live so far apart? When would we ever get to see each other?

11. He probably only asked me to write to him because he wants a pen-pal. He said himself he was really enjoying meeting different people from all over the country. He probably asks everyone he meets to write to him. I have just become a tiny cog in some colliery correspondence network.

12. He hates Frankie Goes To Hollywood.

I have to face it. We have absolutely nothing in common.
I think the facts speak for themselves. Not only have I
disproved all of the evidence in favour of him fancying me,
I have found a further four pieces of evidence to prove that
he has no interest whatsoever. Yet again I am left burying
my face in my pillow of despair.

                                        Friday, 23 May 1984

Dear Anne,
Have just had an ace night over at Karen's. It was really
sound. Jed is on my mind so much at the moment I even
find myself starting to speak like him! Karen was really
happy to hear my news and she thinks Jed definitely fancies
me. She says the pillow fight was a dead giveaway.
Apparently that's what all men do when they want to have
a snog but are too shy to ask. They beat you about the
head with a pillow – it's a throwback to their caveman days
or something. Karen says that Jasper practically smothered
her with his mum's bolster before giving her the best
Frenchy of her life. Oh, if only Jed could have given me a
Frenchy instead of just stroking my hair. Trust Helen to
arrive home in time to sabotage our fun.
   Of course, Karen and Jasper have moved on from the
pillow-fighting stage of their relationship by now. Last week
she let him undo her bra while they were watching a video
nasty. Jasper's parents own a video-recorder and it isn't a
Betamax either. As someone who's only allowed to watch a
portable black-and-white television at the weekend I'm not
sure of the significance of this but Karen assures me that
VHS is the height of modern technology. Anyway,
tomorrow night Jasper wants Karen to have sex with him
while his mum and dad attend the Moor Park Rotary Club
bridge evening! He says it's the right thing for a woman of

the eighties to do. It's time she took control of her own body and gave it to him, basically. Karen is crapping herself. I've got to go round there tomorrow to help her prepare. I don't know how much help I can offer in my accursed virginal state, but I'll do my best. You never know, maybe one day I might be preparing to give myself to Jed.

Saturday, 24 May 1984

Dear Anne,

Well, I got to Karen's bright and early and we set off to Pinner to purchase the necessary pre-sex paraphernalia. Everything from hair-lightener to hair-remover – I bet the Mattress doesn't put in so much preparation for her liaisons behind the bins. When we got back to Karen's house it was eerily quiet – Gaz had taken the boys to a Transformers' roadshow and Debbie was working all day in the salon.

'Come with me,' Karen whispered mysteriously, then led me into the satin-frilled oasis of her parents' boudoir.

Oh, Anne, what I wouldn't give for a room like that. With its elegant white furniture and gilt-edged mirrors it's exactly like the Sindy bedroom. The dressing-table is draped in pink lace and houses more bottles of perfume than Boots. All around the edges silver hairbrushes and velvet jewellery boxes jostle for space. It is a world away from Helen's toothless comb and solitary stick of lip-salve on the bathroom windowsill. But the *pièce de résistance* has to be the frame of lightbulbs surrounding the dressing-table mirror. As soon as Karen switched them on I felt transformed into a film star, all gleaming hair and glowing skin. As I squirted myself with Anaïs Anaïs I could have sworn I saw Fallon Colby from *Dynasty* gazing back at me!

There are even more mirrors on the wardrobe doors. Or should I say the *fitted* wardrobe doors? Fitted wardrobes just seem to ooze class, unlike my parents' hulking great monstrosity, stooping over the bed with its heavy oak panelling and pong of mothballs. I bet the handles don't fall off Debbie's wardrobe every time she opens it either. I can't believe how many outfits she owns. And as for shoes, she must have a pair in every colour of the rainbow and in every imaginable design. Some have little holes cut out of the toe, some have slingbacks, some have gold flowers attached to the front, some are in leather and some in shiny patent, but all have at least three-inch stiletto heels. I couldn't help thinking of Helen's collection of clogs, espadrilles and Scholl sandals lurking like lumbering life-rafts under her bed. Why, oh, why can't she have a gold plastic shoe rack crammed with elegant footwear for me to raid? I can hardly imagine helping myself to a pair of her moccasins if Jed ever asked me to have sex with him.

Karen plumped for a pair of navy stilettos with a bow at the front, before opening her dad's side of the wardrobe. Once again I was hit by a pang of envy as I took in the sea of leather, denim and Sta-prest. There was not a scrap of corduroy in sight.

'What are you doing?' I asked, as Karen riffled through the clothes. Much as I admired Gaz's collection of leather trousers I didn't think they'd make for the ideal seduction outfit, particularly with the navy stilettos.

'Looking for an instruction manual,' Karen explained, pulling out a large book from behind Gaz's cowboy boots. Surely it couldn't have been the *Reader's Digest Guide to Holidays in the Channel Islands?*

'What is it?' I asked.

'The *Kama Sutra*,' Karen whispered knowingly.

I tried to stifle an excited giggle. 'Let's have a look.'

I followed Karen eagerly back to her room. The jug of lemon squash and plate of biscuits she had prepared earlier remained sadly neglected on top of her chest of drawers as we began ploughing our way through *The Illustrated Kama Sutra*.

Oh, Anne, if I was nervous about sex before I'm absolutely terrified now. I always imagined that a woman lay motionless on her back while having intercourse. Of course, I know that in some cases people try it standing up – every other week there's a letter in *Jackie* from some poor misguided soul who believed they couldn't get pregnant in that position. But from what I can gather from the *Kama Sutra* a woman is expected to contort herself into the most unfeasible positions imaginable – in some cases this even involves twisting your legs back to front! And the worst thing of all is that in most of the pictures the women still manage to grin enthusiastically, as if rotating your head three hundred and sixty degrees is the most natural thing on earth! In one particularly disturbing picture a woman is being lowered from the ceiling in some kind of pulley contraption right on top of her prostrate husband's erect willy – or 'member', as they say in the *Kama Sutra*.

'I need a drink,' Karen muttered, when we'd got about half-way through the book.

While she ran downstairs to raid her parents' mini-bar I educated myself about the noises a woman is supposed to utter while making love. I had always imagined some kind of puffing or panting being involved – or even the groaning noise I heard behind the bins the night I caught Alex and the Mattress at it, but never had I imagined myself shouting, 'Hun! Hun! Hun! Hin! Hin! Hin!' Or, even worse, at the moment of 'congress', whatever that might be, shrieking, 'T'hap! T'hap!' Not wishing to depress Karen further I shut the book hastily and waited for her to return.

'Oh, Caitlin, what am I going to do?' she wailed, passing me a bottle of Babycham before flinging herself on to her bed.

'You'll be okay,' I said, unconvincingly, before gagging on my sickly beverage. 'Just don't let Jasper attempt the "Stab with a Lance" position.'

'Oh, my God, what's that?'

'It's where he suspends you from the ceiling with four cords attached to your hands and feet and then swings you backwards and forwards on to his *member!*' I collapsed on to the bed in a giggling heap.

Karen began to snigger. 'Why do you think they call it a member? Member of what exactly?'

'Well, what about the name for our thingy? The perfumed garden!' I snorted, causing Babycham bubbles to fizz up my nose. 'It's even worse than pussy!'

We rolled around on the bed for a bit, clutching our sides and nudging each other.

'Oooh, baby,' Karen shrieked, 'stab my perfumed garden with your lance-like member now!'

'Hun! Hun! Hun! Hin! Hin! Hin!' I yelled.

'What?' Karen stopped laughing, and stared at me.

'Oh, nothing.' I pulled myself upright. 'Seriously, though, Karen, he's not going to want to try anything like that, not if he knows it's your first time.'

'But that's just the point. He doesn't. He thinks I've done it before.'

'What? To who?'

'I didn't want him thinking I was totally inexperienced so I told him I'd done it with my last boyfriend.'

'But you were only twelve years old when you went on that date with Tony Bradbury. You only went to the corner shop for a quarter of cola cubes!'

'I know, but I couldn't tell Jazzy that. The fact is,

nothing's ever been up there before, not even a tampon. What if it doesn't fit? What if I'm sealed up? Oh, God, I think I'd die of embarrassment if he couldn't get it in!'

Karen got to her feet and put Tears For Fears on the record-player. We sat there for a while, contemplating her impenetrable perfumed garden and drowning our sorrows in Babycham while Curt and Roland mused about it being a very, very mad world.

'I've got it!' Karen exclaimed, jumping to her feet and running from the room. She returned a few seconds later brandishing a long, tapered candle – the kind you would use at a dinner party.

'What are you going to do? Conduct a candlelit vigil to the Goddess of the Uncharted Hymen?' I asked.

'No, I'm going to lose my virginity,' she announced, a little weakly.

'Yes, I know, but what has that candle got to do with it?'

Karen gazed intently at the candle. 'That candle has everything to do with it,' she said mysteriously. 'I'll be back in a minute.' And with that she took her candle and left.

I sat on the bed and let the significance of her words sink in. Unable to bear the thought of Karen 'stabbing' herself with a waxen table decoration I returned to the *Kama Sutra*. On page seventy I found a description that perfectly fitted the Mattress.

The Hastini is short of stature; she has a stout coarse body and her skin, if fair, is of a dead white; her hair is tawny, her lips are large; her voice is harsh, choked and throaty and her neck is bent. Her gait is slow, and she walks in a slouching manner; often the toes of one foot are crooked. Her kama-salila has the savour of the juice which flows in spring from the elephant's temples. She is tardy in the act of love, and can be satisfied only by prolonged congress.

She is gluttonous, shameless and irascible. Such is the Hastini, or elephant-woman.

Finally Karen returned to the bedroom, clutching the candle proudly, a smile flickering upon her flushed face. 'God, I need a fag.' She sighed, opened her window and retrieved a half-smoked cigarette from her musical ballerina jewellery box.

'So? How did it go?' I asked, staring at the candle curiously.

Karen lit the cigarette butt and inhaled deeply. 'Oh, fine,' she said breezily, puffing perfect little smoke rings out of the window. 'Here, do you want a drag?'

I took the cigarette from her and held some smoke in my mouth for a few seconds. 'Did it go in?' I enquired, through a fog of uninhaled smoke.

'It most certainly did,' Karen announced proudly. 'Take a look at this.' She waved the candle in my face and pointed to a small groove about four inches up. 'I got it in this far!'

Recoiling in disgust, I nearly sprained my ankle on Karen's *Girl's World*. 'Oh. That's great. Congratulations. Did it hurt?'

'No, not at all. It was a bit uncomfortable at first, but you soon get used to it.' Karen placed the candle into her underwear drawer with a knowing smile. 'Right, that's that done. Now for my strawberry peel-off face mask.'

Sunday, 25 May 1984

Dear Anne,

For some reason I have woken up at six o'clock and can't get back to sleep. Could it be something to do with Joe's thunderous snoring next door? As it is far too early to go round and find out if Karen got stabbed by Jasper's lance last night I have decided to write to Jed. The trouble is I don't know what to say. How do you write to somebody you don't really know at all? I know I've had no trouble writing to you, Anne. God, in the past two months you've learnt more about me than even Karen knows. But the thing is, I want Jed to like me. I don't want him to see me as some kind of a misfit, with only one friend and the parents from hell. No, I want him to see me as cool, sophisticated and popular. Perhaps I will write a letter in rough here for practice.

> *Dear Jed,*
> *I hope this letter finds you in good health. Things have been so hectic since you left you would not believe. On Thursday night I caught a movie with some friends and on Friday I went with some of the guys to the Wag. Boy George was there and he was sick all over the cloakroom. Gosh, those popstar types certainly know how to party! Last night was a bit of a quiet one – I just had a few friends over for a girly night in. We watched a few video nasties on our new VHS recorder. How is the strike going? I am watching the news every night to keep abreast of developments. I hope you are enjoying The Outsiders.*
> *Must dash now, I have an appointment at my beautician's.*
> *Best regards,*
> *Caitlin Kennedy*

Oh dear! I think I'll try going back to sleep.

Well, that was a disaster. I was just drifting into a delicious slumber, dreaming of riding pillion on Jed's motorbike, when I was rudely awoken by a hammering on the front door. 'Will yer get up, yer lazy gob-shite?' a voice bellowed through the letter-box.

I leapt out of bed and peered out of the window to see Paddy O'Brien pacing up and down our garden path surrounded by a mountain of toilet rolls. His white hair was more bouffant than ever and he was wearing a tatty burgundy jumper with a diamond design and a pair of ankle-flapping nylon trousers.

Oh, Anne, what is the use of pretending to Jed that I am cool and sophisticated? The fact is, I have no social life, my family doesn't own a colour TV and our toilet rolls are delivered by a leprechaun on acid. The chances of my perfumed garden ever being sown are less than zero!

Chapter Twelve

Dear Anne,

God, how I hate bank holidays! Oh, I bet they're
wonderful when you have somebody to share them with,
somebody to stab you with his lance all day long like
Karen. But for the lonely hearts of this world they are
just three endless days of pain and solitude. Karen
popped round last night on her way to Jasper's to let me
know that she is now officially hymen-free. I know I
ought to be happy for her but I can't help feeling a little
jealous. She seemed so different – so womanly. When I
asked her why she was wearing her snood on one of the
hottest days of the year, she giggled and pulled it down
to reveal a huge love-bite. How cheap and
unsophisticated. If she's not careful she'll end up looking
just like the Mattress.

On the news tonight Arthur Scargill was at a place
called Orgreave. He said he wanted miners to come there
from all over the country. I wonder if Jed will go. I'll
have to watch the news every night from now on to try
to catch a glimpse. I wish Arthur Scargill would do
something with his hair. I'm sure it would help the
miners' cause a great deal if he didn't look quite so
unkempt.

Wednesday, 28 May 1984

Dear Anne,

Oh, joy! I've received a letter from Jed. My hands are still trembling with excitement as I write this. I was forcing down my bowl of brutally unsweetened malt flakes while racing to finish my maths homework when Joe placed an envelope in front of me. Such was my state of post-bank-holiday gloom it didn't occur to me for one moment it could have been from Jed. Until I saw that it was addressed simply to 'Cat'.

'Who on earth calls you Cat?' Helen enquired, putting down her copy of *Political Prisoners' Monthly* to peer over my shoulder.

'None of your business,' I muttered, then raced upstairs to the bathroom.

With the door securely locked I perched on the side of the bath and carefully eased open the envelope. Oh, Anne, I've read it so many times I know it word for word (if only I had the same power of recall when it comes to algebraic equations!).

Dear Cat,

So, how's it going? I hope you haven't forgotten me already – not that that's likely, of course. Are you still playing that Frankie shite? Have you heard their new single, 'Two Tribes'? It reminds me a bit of the strike. Sometimes I feel like we're at war with the police – our village has been taken over by them. Have you been watching the news? Me and my dad are off to Orgreave tomorrow – should be interesting. I've nearly finished The Outsiders. *It's sound. Our Maxine keeps taking the mickey out of us and calling us a bookworm, but I don't care. There's bugger all else to do at night and I get sick of sitting round talking about strike all the bloody time. Do you have any more books I could borrow? Have you got* Catcher in the Rye? *I've always wanted to read that one.*

I suppose you've got exams coming up now and will be studying hard. I think it's sound you want to be a writer. Maybe one day I'll write a book. About the strike or summat and all the people I met. Of course, I would write at least a chapter about the lass I met down in London who looks just like a Cat and keeps me up half the night thinking about her. When the strike's over the first thing I'm going to do is come down to London – maybe you could take me to the clubs you go to. I'm not too keen on meeting Boy George, though – I don't suppose you know where Paul Weller drinks?

Anyway, I've got to go now. I've got to help me mam take some old clothes down the Welfare. Write back soon and if you send me another book I might even write two chapters about you in me memoirs!

Love,

Jed

I keep him up half the night thinking about me. Oh, Anne, that has to be the nicest compliment I've ever been paid. I'll treasure this letter as long as I live. I must take it round to Karen's to show her and ask if I can borrow Gaz's Jam LP.

Of course, when Jed says he's up half the night thinking about me it could always be because he can't get over how weird I am. OH, GOD!

Thursday, 29 May 1984

Dear Anne,

Believe it or not I am actually writing this during a maths lesson. Old Wank-face is at the doctor's – could he finally be seeking treatment for his appalling halitosis? – and we have been left with a pile of photocopied notes and a supply teacher from Planet Tasteless Tank-top. While my fellow classmates amuse themselves with paper fights and pushing the tank-topped one to the brink of mental meltdown I am going to compose a letter to Jed. Here goes.

> *Dear Jed,*
> *Thank you so much for your letter – it made my day.*

No, no, far too grateful and therefore desperate – Karen says I must play it cool.

> *Dear Jed,*
> *Thanks for your letter. I'm glad to hear you're enjoying the book. I've enclosed the* Catcher in the Rye, *it's even better than* The Outsiders. *I think you'll like Caulfield, the narrator. I've been watching the latest about the strike on the news. It must be horrible having the police all over your village – it must be a bit like that CND march I went on. Good luck at Orgreave.*
> *How dare you say Frankie are shite? Honestly you northerners have no taste at all. 'Two Tribes' is brilliant. Have you seen the video where Reagan and the Russian leader sprawl around in a ring? You will be pleased to hear I have a brand new Frankie T-shirt saying,* FRANKIE SAY WAR HIDE YOURSELF! *Do you want me to get you one? No, I didn't think so. According to my mate's dad, Paul Weller drinks in a pub called the Nags Head in Morden. Maybe when you come down after the strike we could check it out.*
> *I'm in a maths lesson at the moment – even more boring than watching a UB40 video, ha ha! I wish I could be with you at Orgreave giving my support instead of sitting here surrounded by immature imbeciles.*

Oh, well, I suppose I'd better go now and pretend to do a bit of work. Write again soon.
Love
Cat

Karen said it was okay to put 'love' as that was how Jed had signed his letter. I wonder why he signed it 'love', when he could so easily have written 'yours sincerely' or 'best wishes' or even just 'from'? Obviously he isn't *in love* with me, but he must like me quite a bit. Then again, he could just be a very warm person. Yes, the way he was always play fighting with his dad, he's obviously just affectionate to everybody.

9.30 p.m.
Oh, Anne, I'm so worried about Jed. I've just watched the news and eighty-two miners were arrested at Orgreave today. Arthur Scargill looked quite hysterical – he said that Britain had become a police state and he urged union members to go there in their thousands. I hope Jed is all right. I want to phone him but I'm too nervous.

10 p.m.
Jed is okay! Bob just phoned to speak to Joe. They got back safely. Although there were about five thousand miners there they were heavily outnumbered by the police. Bob wants the Harrow Miners' Support Group to organise a coach trip up to Orgreave next Saturday. Joe can't make it as he's already arranged to go to a beer festival in Kilburn with Paddy and, of course, Helen was dead set against the idea. Honestly, that woman is all mouth and no combat trousers. If she's not going, there's no way she'll let me. After what I've seen of Orgreave on the news I can't stop daydreaming about running hand in hand with Jed across a field being chased by mounted police. Just as I'm

about to be cracked across the head with a truncheon Jed pulls me beneath a hedge and holds me in his arms where we melt into a French kiss. It would be so romantic. I think I'm going to go to bed!

Friday, 30 May 1984

Dear Anne,

Arthur Scargill has been arrested! As he was dragged away by the police he shouted, 'nineteen eighty-four – Great Britain!' Kept looking out for Jed on the news, but no sign of him. I can't stop thinking about being at Orgreave with him, it makes me feel all tingly inside. I need to come up with a cunning plan.

Saturday, 31 May 1984

Dear Anne,

Karen has agreed to come to Orgreave with me – she reckons Jasper would jump at the chance. At the moment he is modelling himself on one of Helen's heroes, Che Guevara – he has dyed his mullet black and taken to wearing a beret in the middle of summer. Apparently Jasper reckons Orgreave could become the Cuba of the 1980s, whatever that means. I don't really care as long as I've got somebody to go up there with. Karen and I spent the morning at Watford market – I bought the brand new Frankie picture disc and Karen got a tin of magnolia-scented talc. Jasper wants them to do a sixty-niner tonight while they babysit his niece Petunia – how vile! Mind you, the evening I've been having makes even a magnolia-flavoured sixty-niner seem appealing.

As part of my cunning plan to get to Orgreave next weekend I will have to go to the support group meeting on Tuesday to get details of the coach trip. And in order to go to the meeting I will need to worm my way into my parents' good books. Hence I have just spent the most boring two hours of my life debating with Helen whether the miners ought to have had a strike ballot. Anything to make my interest look political rather than personal – or should I say passionate? It certainly paid off, though.

'It's so good to see you showing an interest in something other than boys or makeup,' Helen said, making me a congratulatory Ovaltine.

'Well, I guess I'm finally growing up,' I replied (through gritted teeth I can assure you). 'I'm really starting to understand the importance of fighting for what you believe in.'

Helen attempted to stroke my hair, but it had been so heavily lacquered her hand bounced right back off. 'I'm so proud of you,' she said, and I'm sure I spotted a tear in her eye. God, you'd have thought I'd told her I'd just finished writing my first novel or something!

'So, would it be okay for me to go along to the support group meeting on Tuesday – to find out more about the strike?'

Helen practically orgasmed. 'Yes, of course – you can let us know what happens. Your father and I have both got parents' evenings. But you'll have to come straight home afterwards, what with your exams about to start.'

Bingo! I grabbed my mug of mortally malted milk and leapt to my feet. 'Sure. In fact I think I'll go up and do a bit of revision right now.' And with that I escaped to my bedroom to listen to the Jam and reread my letter from Jed for the fifty-millionth time.

Tuesday, 3 June 1984

Dear Anne,

Well, the first part of my cunning plan is complete. A coach is leaving Harrow bus station for Sheffield at 7 a.m. on Saturday and I intend to be on it. Now I must phone Jed.

I think I'll leave that part for tomorrow.

Wednesday, 4 June 1984

Dear Anne,

Oh, God, every time I go to phone Jed my stomach seems to lurch into my mouth rendering me incapable of speech. If I don't hurry up Helen and Joe will get back from their Amnesty International meeting and I will lose my only chance. Right, here goes . . .

Complete disaster! Oh, I've made such a fool of myself. I finally managed to dial the whole number without slamming the receiver back down and as I listened to the ringing tone I thought I was going to hyperventilate. For some reason I'd assumed Jed would pick up the phone so I kept reciting my first line over and over in my head, *Hi there, it's me, Cat.* When a woman answered I was totally thrown off-guard.

'Hello,' she said, in an accent even stronger than Jed's.

I was momentarily struck dumb.

'Hello,' she repeated, a little aggressively, making me feel even more nervous.

I deliberated whether to hang up, but then I would never be able to call back again – this was my one chance. Besides, it was probably only his mum.

'Who the fuck is this?' the voice hollered. 'If that's you, Derrick, you can take yer scabby cock and shove it up yer arse!'

I coughed and took a deep breath. 'Er, is Jed there, please?' I managed to squeak.

There was silence at the other end this time. When she spoke again the woman's voice seemed considerably posher.

'Jed? No, he's not back yet. Can I ask who's calling?'

'Yes, of course – it's Cat.'

'Who?'

'Cat.' My cheeks began to burn and I thanked God that this was not the year 2000 and we didn't all have video-phones.

'Cat?' She seemed to spit it out.

'Yes. Well, it's Caitlin, really, but Jed likes to call me Cat.'

'Does he, now? Well, I'm not sure how late he's going to be – Cat – but I'll tell him you rang.' And with that I heard a click on the line and she was gone.

I ran upstairs and buried my face in a cold flannel. What a total nightmare. Who the hell was that woman? It can't have been his mum – if it was, then who the hell was Derrick and his 'scabby cock'? Oh, God, I feel so embarrassed. I bet she doesn't pass on the message, but I'll never be able to phone back just in case she did and Jed doesn't want to talk to me. My one chance and I totally blew it.

Thursday, 5 June 1984

Dear Anne,

My heart feels as if it is tied to a pogo stick at the moment – up, down, up, down. I don't think it can take much more of this emotional bouncing. It began to soar when the phone rang at five past seven this evening. I can be certain of the time because *The Archers* had just begun and as this renders my parents glued to the radio I took the call.

'Cat, is that you?' a voice enquired. A beautifully husky northern voice.

'Yes.' As I leant against the hall wall for moral support the Nelson Mandela poster collapsed on to my head and I couldn't help yelping in alarm.

'Are you all right?' Jed asked.

'Oh, it's only Nelson Mandela,' I said trying to compose myself. 'I think his Blu-tack has dried out.'

'Right.' Jed sounded bewildered. 'Listen, thanks a lot for the book and the letter, I got them this morning.'

'Oh, that's okay,' I replied, kicking Nelson Mandela under the stairs. 'Have you finished *The Outsiders?*'

'Yeah, it were great, and I've already read first twenty pages of *Catcher in the Rye.* That lad Caulfield is a right laugh. So – our Maxine said you rang last night. Sorry I didn't call back sooner, but we didn't get back from Orgreave until gone midnight.'

So that woman had been Jed's sister – I breathed a sigh of relief.

'Yeah, that's why I was ringing, actually.' I paused for a moment to check that *The Archers* was still on. After hearing reassuringly rural voices from the kitchen discussing the delights of pig swill, I continued, dropping my voice to a whisper. 'You see the Harrow support group are organising a trip up there on Saturday and I was going to come along with some of my mates.'

'Really?' Jed whispered back. 'Bloody hell, what am I whispering for? What are *you* whispering for?'

I felt a familiar burning sensation rising in my cheeks (Anne, for future reference and to save on ink, you may as well assume that if I'm talking to or about Jed I'm blushing!).

'Well, you see, my parents aren't going and I know they won't let me – not because they think I'm too young or anything, it's just my exams are coming up – so I'm going to have to pretend I'm studying in the library all day.'

Jed chuckled. 'Well, you'll certainly learn a lot at Orgreave. Listen, I'll find out from me dad where your coach is arriving and I'll make sure I'm there to meet you.'

My heart pogoed even higher. 'That would be great.'

'Then I can give you your present.'

'My present?'

'Yeah, to say thanks for the books. It's not a lot, mind – money's a bit tight at the moment.'

'Sure.'

Oh, Anne, I wouldn't care if he'd got me a lump of coal – just the fact he's got me a present at all makes me feel like the luckiest girl alive!

Just then I heard that awful bouncy theme tune from the kitchen followed by the scraping of chairs. 'I'd better go now,' I whispered.

'Yeah, me too. Well, I'll see you on Saturday in Sheffield, then.'

'Yeah.' (I know, I know, for an aspiring writer I don't always have the best way with words.)

'And, Cat . . .'

'Yeah?'

'I've got a new T-shirt. It says, *I Don't Give a Fuck What Frankie Say!* Do you want one?'

So, I should have gone to bed ecstatic, shouldn't I? I should be lying here now dreaming once more of Jed rescuing me from the clutches of the police state and I would be, if it weren't for my so-called friend Karen and her stupid beret-wearing boyfriend sabotaging my fun. About half an hour after Jed rang and I was floating around my bedroom ceiling between the posters of Holly

Johnson and Howard Jones on cloud nine, I received a call from my so-called *best* friend (God, I'd hate to think what a *worst* friend is capable of) informing me that her and her supposedly revolutionary other half will not be able to come to Orgreave, after all. And do you want to know why? Is it because Che Montague is manning the barricades in some other insurrectionary uprising? Is it because he has been incarcerated by our police state under the Prevention of Terrorism Act? No! He can't go because his mum won't let him! And to make matters worse his mum is going to Orgreave herself. Mrs Montague – Helen's boss. Although she has only seen me once before at a school fête, what if she recognises me and reports back to Helen? What am I going to do?

Friday, 5 June 1984

Dear Anne,

As Arthur Scargill might say, 'The workers united will never be defeated!' Or, in my case, substitute 'lovers' for 'workers' (obviously there is a certain amount of wishful thinking going on here). This could be my only chance to see Jed again and I don't care if my parents find out. I'll cross that picket line when I come to it.

Karen came round tonight, all grovelling and apologetic – she's even lent me her brand new Sony Walkman for the coach journey! Anyway, she has promised to be my alibi and tell her parents she's going to the library with me when really she's going shopping with Jasper. Then, in the evening, she's going to call her mum and get her to pop round and tell Helen we've gone to watch a film.

After a jug of diluted orange juice and a plate of carob-chip cookies we spent the rest of the evening coming up with a suitable disguise to stop Mrs Montague recognising me. According to Karen she spends half her time getting pissed on cooking sherry so it shouldn't be too difficult. My disguise is now laid out ready on the end of my bed, a baseball cap, a pair of reflector sunglasses, a pair of white cycling shorts to be worn under Karen's turquoise ra-ra skirt and a matching stripy vest top. In a bid to maintain a sexy yet discreet image I am going to limit myself to one crucifix and my smallest gold hoop earrings. My alarm is set for six o'clock – I told Helen that Karen and I are going to Paphos for breakfast for a pre-revision treat. I felt a bit bad when she gave me five pounds to pay for it, but it will come in handy for provisions for the coach. Not that I'll feel calm enough to eat. The prospect of seeing Jed again is playing havoc with my digestive system. Could all my dreams be about to come true? On the battlefield that is Orgreave, might I finally see some love action?

Chapter Thirteen

Dear Anne,

Well, I've made it on to the coach and as I sit here huddled in my seat at the back I'm trying really hard (a) not to retch and (b) not to look conspicuous. (Obviously if I fail at (a) then I don't have a hope of achieving (b)!) God, I hate Karen for deserting me in my hour of need. Not only am I the only person here on their own, I am also the only person under the age of twenty – the only person under the age of sixteen! I'm trying really hard to play it cool, listening to the Jam on Karen's Walkman and scribbling away in my diary, but I'm terrified that at any moment somebody is going to march up the aisle shouting, '*What the hell is this child doing unaccompanied?*' then throw me out on to the pavement. The mixture of nerves and the fusty smell of stale cigarettes and petrol fumes is making me feel quite ill. If only we could get going. Aha! The engine has roared into life – and about time too. OH, NO! Oh, it can't be.

Oh, Anne, you are not going to believe what has happened. Just as we were about to pull away from the bus station there was a strange shrieking noise from outside followed by a loud banging on the side of the coach. We were all flung forward as the driver slammed on his brakes. Then, as the doors gasped open, a woman's voice squawked, 'Good heavens, wait up, young man!' I peered down the aisle to see the unmistakable sight of Mrs Montague emerging up the steps of the coach, like a gaudy parrot rising from the ashes. Giving her canary blonde top-knot a reassuring pat she turned to peer at the driver over the scarlet rim of her spectacles. 'Now, just you let me get seated before you pull away, I know how you bus-driving types make it your life's work to maim us more mature members of society!'

As I watched her sweep down the aisle, a hideous vision in Hawaiian blouse and nylon shorts, I just knew she was going to end up next to me – it was the same feeling you get when a weirdo boards a crowded tube, breathing heavily and rubbing his crotch and you just know he's going to pick your back to masturbate against. I pulled my cap down over my face and pretended to be asleep.

'Young lady!' she bellowed, prodding my arm. 'Is this seat taken?'

I shook my head and reluctantly removed my bag from the adjacent seat.

'Thank you. It's Caitlin, isn't it? Where's your mother?'

So much for my cunning disguise. I removed my cap and reflector sunglasses and reverted to Plan B. 'Oh, she couldn't make it, she wasn't feeling too well. But it seemed a shame for us both not to come. Besides, I'm meeting up with a friend of hers in Sheffield, Bob Weyman.' Anxiously I wound the wires of Karen's Walkman around my fingers as I awaited her response.

'Ah, one of her little miner friends. I see. Well, it's a good job I came along then, isn't it? I can keep my eye on you for her. Have you seen the state of some of the reprobates on this bus? Good Lord, where have they all crawled out from? And I always thought Harrow was a respectable borough.' Mrs Montague lowered her voice from a bellow to a mere shout, 'One young man down at

the front – don't know if you saw him, dreadfully pale
chappy all in black – has even got a ring through his nose.
Through his nose! Looks like a cross between a bull and a
vampire bat! Murraymint?' And with that she began rifling
through her handbag, offloading a powder compact, a
bottle of Tweed, several starched handkerchiefs
embroidered with her initials and a silver hip flask on to my
lap before finally locating a battered tin of mints.

Half a tin of mints, two and a half hours' droning about
Jasper and several large swigs from her hip flask later and
she is finally asleep. Her snoring is almost as loud as her
foghorn of a voice, with every gasp from her fuchsia-
painted mouth causing a little puff of powder to erupt from
her nose.

We have just passed a sign for Sheffield city centre. Part
of me will be so glad to get off this coach – the 'reprobates'
at the front have been chanting, 'One solution, revolution,'
ever since we left Birmingham and that, combined with
Mrs M's cloying aroma of alcohol and Tweed, are making
the whole journey even more unpleasant than the school
trip to Thorpe Park when I was sick all over Alison Edlin.
It's starting to get unbearably hot, the ventilation funnel in
the ceiling seems to be wedged in Mrs M's direction, and
even though I'm completely stationary I can't stop sweating
– my aquamarine eyeliner is probably smudged all over my
chin by now. However, much as I am dying for this
journey to end, another part of me is praying we get stuck
behind a jack-knifed lorry. What if we get to Sheffield and
Jed isn't there? What if I have to spend the entire day with
this headmistress from hell? What if I get arrested? What if
I get trampled on by a police horse? Oh, my God, what am
I doing here? Why aren't I spending my pocket money on
a new twelve-inch and some cherry-flavoured lip gloss at
Watford market? Or even revising at Pinner library? Yes,

why aren't I studying? I've got two O levels coming up – I should be at home with my books, not on some Communist coach pretending to be a coal miner. Oh, God, here we are, Sheffield city centre. Please, please, let Jed be there. I'll do anything you want – I'll do all my homework on time, I'll become a vegetarian, I'll even make a collage for Helen. Just LET JED BE THERE!

He was there. I saw him as soon as the coach pulled into the car park. A group of them was standing next to a rusty old minibus, laughing and smoking in the sunshine. As we shuddered to a halt I prodded Mrs M in the side, causing her to snort like an overpowdered rhinoceros.

'We're here,' I hissed. 'Excuse me, must dash.' And with that I squeezed my way past her liver-spotted knees and into the aisle.

'Wait up! Wait up!' she shrieked, staggering to her feet and sending the tin of Murraymints clattering to the floor. 'Oh, drat!'

As she crawled around the floor retrieving her mints, I seized my chance and hurtled down the aisle, barging past bull-vampire hybrids and sending banners flying. Leaping from the bus I careered straight into Jed.

'Steady.' He laughed, catching hold of my arm. 'I don't know, throwing yourself at me already.'

'No, you don't understand,' I muttered (and I'm sure I don't need to describe the colour of my face), 'I'm trying to escape from somebody. You've got to help me.'

Jed stared curiously at the coach as an assortment of social workers, anarchists and antichrists staggered down the steps, blinking in the brilliant sunshine. His white T-shirt and faded jeans emphasised the depth of his tan, and his hair sparkled with gold flecks, but such was my state of desperation I didn't have time to appreciate this vision of sun-kissed sensuality.

'Please,' I implored, tugging at his arm, 'can we go or

we'll be stuck with her and her Murraymints for the rest of the day?'

'I quite fancy a Murraymint,' Jed mused, before noting the look of horror on my face. 'All right, don't worry. Where are your mates?'

'They couldn't make it – long story.' I jumped as a hand grasped my shoulder from behind.

'All right, Caitlin, how's your mam and dad?' I turned to see Bob beaming at me. Like Jed, he was extremely brown, his shorn hair almost white in comparison.

'Hello. They're fine. They couldn't make it, erm . . .' I looked at the floor for some kind of divine inspiration, but all I saw was a Chewits wrapper and what looked worryingly like a used condom.

'Don't fret, lass, our Jed's told us to keep us gob shut. I just hope you got plenty of studying done on the bus.'

I breathed a sigh of relief, but it was short-lived.

'Caitlin! Wait up!'

I heard Jed snigger as Mrs Montague appeared at the coach door waving her tin of Murraymints manically.

'One of your mates, is she?' he whispered in my ear.

The combination of Jed's breath on my skin, Mrs M leering down at me and the overwhelming heat suddenly made me come over all faint. 'Do you have anything to drink?' I asked weakly.

Jed's smile faded. 'Sure. Are you okay? Here, Dad, where's that bottle of Coke?'

Bob retrieved it from a carrier-bag on the ground. 'You all right, lass? Must have been like an oven on that bus.'

Jed opened the bottle and handed it to me. 'I'm really glad you made it,' he said, smiling. 'To be honest, I wasn't really expecting to see you.'

'Really?' If he only knew the lengths I'd been to to get there.

Jed dug his hands into his jeans pockets and glanced around the car park. 'It means a lot to us, you know. To think that people are willing to come from all over the country to show their support.'

My heart sank along with the mouthful of syrupy warm Coke. Jed obviously saw me only as a supporter of his cause. He was probably just as glad to see Mrs M as he was me – in fact, from the grin spreading across his face as he watched her careering down the coach steps he was even *more* pleased to see her.

'Chuffin' 'ell. Look, Dad, it's Edna Everage!'

Mrs M marched her way over, blissfully unaware that half of the pearl press studs on her blouse had somehow popped their way undone, leaving her pendulous breasts on full display. 'Goodness me, Caitlin,' she barked indignantly, 'what on earth was that all about? Anyone would have thought there was a fire, the way you disembarked. Was it really necessary to be so hasty? Honestly, young people nowadays, no time for common courtesy.'

'Too right, madam, too right,' said Bob, beaming broadly at Mrs M's cleavage.

Mrs Montague, peered over the top of her glasses and smiled. 'Well, hello there,' she purred, offering him a slightly trembling hand (the hipflask-wielding wino), 'I'm Marjorie Montague, how do you do?'

'Very well, thank you. Bob. Bob Weyman. Nice to meet you.' Bob grabbed her hand and shook it vigorously, causing Mrs M's breasts to quiver in unison.

Following Bob's gaze she looked down at her chest. 'Good grief – now, how did that happen?' Completely unfazed, Mrs M did up her blouse. 'Must have been when I was on all fours. So, I take it you're one of our mining fraternity?'

'Aye. And you? Don't tell me – with a fine figure like yours you'd have to be a model.'

'Jesus, Dad,' Jed muttered, under his breath. Then he looked at me and shrugged sheepishly. 'Oh, well, at least he'll keep her occupied.'

By this time everyone had disembarked from the coach and the car park had become a sea of social workers, Socialist Workers and striking workers.

'Okay, folks, listen up!' A burly man of about fifty clambered on to a crate to address the crowd. 'I'd just like to thank all of our comrades from down south for travelling all this way to show their solidarity.'

Comrades, solidarity – Helen didn't know what she was missing.

'Now, the plan is we're all going to walk to Orgreave through Sheffield city centre to cause as much disruption as possible.'

Mrs M let out a groan. 'Walk? Good Lord, how far is it? What was the point in paying for a coach?'

The miner wiped his brow with the back of a shovel-sized hand. 'We're expecting thousands here today, so this could be the turning point of the whole strike. If we stop the bastards getting coke out of Orgreave we'll win this thing for sure, so good luck, lads.'

'What about the lasses?' Mrs M heckled.

I hung my head in shame.

'Comrades, if I could just have quick word.' An anxious-looking young man wearing a pair of red dungarees and clutching a Socialist Workers' banner began to speak. 'All of those comrades from Harrow will need to meet back here at seven o'clock this evening for the coach. If anyone gets arrested, remember you're entitled to one phone call.'

I looked at Jed and smiled weakly. What if I were to get

arrested? I had my maths O level in two days' time. Should
I use my one phone call to tell Wank-face Wainwright I
was languishing in a prison cell in South Yorkshire? What
the hell would he say to that?

'What's Orgreave like, then?' I asked casually, as we
began making our way out of the car park. 'Is it as bad as
it looks on the telly?'

Jed laughed bitterly. 'Worse, much worse. Don't worry,
I'll look after you.'

I smiled as my fantasy of the past week slowly edged
its way closer to reality. As we got out on to the street
we joined a stream of miners marching behind colourful
banners, embroidered with the names of collieries from all
over the country. South Wales, North Yorkshire and, of
course, Blidworth. I have to admit that at first it was a
bit embarrassing walking down the middle of the road,
blocking all the traffic, but as the shoppers and passers-
by shouted messages of support, I couldn't help feeling a
little proud. As I strode along next to Jed it was easy to
imagine that I was a young miner's wife marching side
by side with her embattled husband, united by love and a
struggle against capitalist oppression. I felt just like
Winnie Mandela – a younger, more glamorous version,
obviously.

'I never really had much time for politics before,' Jed
said, nodding at a Rastafarian brandishing a Labour Party
banner, 'but this strike has been a real eye-opener. I mean,
you have to take an interest, don't you? You can't just sit
back and accept all the shit that goes on. It's like you going
on your CND marches and buying that Nelson Mandela
single and coming here today – you care about what's
happening in the world. All I used to care about was
having an ale with the lads and who Forest had drawn in
the Cup.'

Suddenly I felt about six feet tall. It's a wonderful thing to be blessed with a social conscience. I resolved to join Anti-Apartheid and sponsor a starving child as soon as I got back home.

Chapter Fourteen

Of all the bizarre things that have happened today the ice-cream van has to be the most surreal. As we marched our way to the top of the hill overlooking Orgreave I felt a growing surge of excitement welling up inside me. There were thousands of us – a sea of jeans and T-shirts and yellow 'COAL NOT DOLE' stickers. Then down below, forming a dark blue ring around Orgreave itself, were the police, rigid behind a wall of Perspex shields. They seemed so far away down there, like toy soldiers guarding a model fortress. At the top of the hill the atmosphere was relaxed and jovial, a fusion of different accents exchanging banter – mainly football-related.

'Here, Jed, did you bring the ball?' A young man with a tattooed dragon breathing fire up his forearm appeared before us and stared curiously at me. I turned away, as if I'd just spotted someone I knew, and wished that I, too, were clad in denim and a T-shirt. What on earth had possessed me to believe that a mass picket was a suitable setting for a turquoise ra-ra skirt?

'Aye,' Jed replied, tipping a football from his bag, 'Come on, then, lads, let's show these Sheffield Wednesday boys how football's played. You don't mind, do you?' he said, touching me lightly on the arm.

'No, of course not,' I replied, my pale skin tingling beneath his tanned fingers.

As I watched Jed tearing about all over the field, flicking

the ball this way and that and effortlessly trading wisecracks with complete strangers, I realised he was the kind of person everybody warmed to. The captain of the football team, the classroom jester – the school hunk. While part of me felt proud that someone like him could have shown a fraction of an interest in me another part felt depressed with the certainty that I would not be good enough.

Suddenly a jangly version of 'Greensleeves' filled the air, replacing my sense of foreboding with memories of school lunch breaks and tea-time on the estate. Surely it couldn't be an ice-cream van? But it was. Chugging over the hill, in all its pink and white stripy glory, came a Mr Whippy – to roars of appreciation from the crowd.

'Well I never,' gasped Mrs M, shielding her eyes from the sun as she strained to take a look. 'You don't suppose he's got a mini-bar back there, do you?'

I shook my head and laughed.

'Here, Cat, fancy an ice cream?' Jed came bounding over, flushed and breathless. And then, before I could say, 'Multiple orgasm', he had torn off his T-shirt and tucked it into the back of his jeans. Oh, Anne, even my literary skills would not be able to do justice to his Adonis-like physique. It took every ounce of concentration for me to request a ninety-nine and not make the obvious Freudian slip.

'How about you, Marjorie?' Jed asked, with a wink.

'I'll just have a can of ran – shandy, if I may,' Mrs M stammered.

As Jed sauntered over to the ice-cream van Mrs M let out a sigh.

'Good Lord, if I were five years younger . . . You're a very lucky girl, Caitlin.'

'What do you mean?'

Mrs M dabbed at her brow with one of her starched

handkerchiefs. 'To have such a succulent specimen of manhood interested in you – the boy's a stallion!'

My heart began to race. 'What do you mean, interested in me?'

'Oh, come on, dear, don't be so coy. It's obvious – the way he was fooling around with that football, the way he keeps looking over at you – the boy's besotted. And he's not the only one, by the looks of things,' she added, scrutinising me over the rim of her glasses. As usual my cheeks gave the game away. 'I thought as much,' she shrieked, rubbing her hands with glee. 'And does your mother know about this budding romance?'

I shook my head and frowned.

'Don't look so terrified, your secret's safe with me – you lucky, lucky girl.'

Shortly after Jed had returned with the ice creams a roar went up from the front of the crowd and within seconds all the bodies that had been sprawled on the grass, soaking up the sunshine, had leapt to their feet.

'Here we go,' said Jed, hastily cramming half of his cornet into his mouth.

'What's happening?' I asked, standing on tiptoe to look down the hill. Nothing seemed to have changed – the police line still stood firm around the imposing concrete silhouette of the coke plant.

'Look,' said Jed, placing one arm loosely over my shoulders and pointing towards the plant with the other, 'the second lot of lorries is getting ready to leave.'

Squinting, I could just about make out three or four bottle green lorries lined up on a slip road beside the plant.

'Where?' I asked, feigning confusion – anything to get that arm to rest there for just a few seconds more.

A shout was welling from the front of the crowd, sweeping back towards us like a wave, '*MAGGIE,*

MAGGIE, MAGGIE, OUT, OUT, OUT!' I felt a flood of embarrassment as the wave reached us – it was just like having to sing in assembly – so I opened my mouth and mimed. In marked contrast Mrs M began chanting with great gusto and, again, I was reminded of school assemblies – it must be a prerequisite for a head teacher to be able to sing obscenely loudly and out of key.

Then, without warning, we began to move forward, down the hill. Down the hill and towards the police. Down the hill and towards the police who, all of a sudden, didn't seem quite so small. Now it was me who felt like a miniature figure, dwarfed by a sea of shouting, burly miners – Holly Hobbie in her ra-ra skirt and curls hopelessly lost in an army of Action Men about to be attacked by a battalion of toy soldiers. Or should that have been Zulus? For suddenly, above the chants of '*HERE WE GO, HERE WE GO, HERE WE GO!*' came a repetitive ominous thud in a scene straight out of Joe's favourite film, *Zulu*. Only this time it was the sound of truncheons rather than spears being banged on the shields.

I felt a hand take mine and squeeze it firmly. I looked up to see Jed yelling defiantly, 'THE MINERS UNITED WILL NEVER BE DEFEATED! Don't worry,' he shouted in my ear. 'Stay by me and you'll be sound.'

I smiled weakly. It was strange, really. For days I had been dreaming of this moment, but now it had arrived it had taken on a nightmarish quality. In my fantasies I had felt safe and secure – now I just felt terrified.

A miner standing next to Mrs M reached into his canvas rucksack and brought out a fistful of stones. 'Come on, lads!' he shouted. 'Let's show 'em what we're made of this time.' And with that he flung the stones in the direction of the police line.

'Now, now, there's no need for that kind of behaviour,' Mrs M retorted. 'You'll get us all arrested.'

The thudding of the truncheons on shields grew louder, there was a roar from the front of the crowd and all hell broke loose. The miners, who had been advancing towards the police line, had turned and were running back towards us.

'Come on!' Jed yelled, pulling me by the hand. 'It's the fucking horses!'

I don't know how I managed to keep my espadrilles on in the ensuing panic as we tripped and stumbled our way back up the hill. I glanced over my shoulder and saw mounted police charging up towards me, truncheons raised. People were yelling, screaming, and then suddenly 'Greensleeves' rang out, only barely audible above the din. I turned to my left to see Mr Whippy leaping about behind his counter shouting and punching the air, like a spectator at a boxing match. As we tore past I couldn't make out exactly what he was saying, but between the expletives there seemed to be a predominance of 'pigs', 'filth' and 'Met scum'.

As we crossed the ridge of the hill I lost my grip somehow on Jed's hand and was carried away in a stream of miners fleeing straight towards what looked worryingly like a railway line. We were trapped. I stopped and turned to see groups of police on foot following the horses, picking out miners and dragging them away. I had a desperate urge to pee. Where had everybody gone? Where was Mrs M? Where was Bob? Where was Jed?

Where was Jed? In my dream he was meant to have pulled me to safety by now, not left me floundering in this awful nightmare. Hearing a strangled moan I turned to see a police horse flailing on its side, its rider trapped underneath, writhing in agony. For a split second I saw the policeman's eyes through his visor and I could have sworn they looked just as terrified as mine.

Just as I was about to burst into tears I heard someone call my name. 'Cat!' I spun round to see Jed running towards me, blood trickling down his face. 'Quick,' he shouted, grabbing me by the arm. 'We've got to cross the railway line into the village.'

My PE teacher would have been proud as I raced with Jed over the railway line and into Orgreave – I must have beaten any Pinner Hill cross-country record hands down. It wasn't until we got on to a residential road leading into the village that the panic began to subside and people stopped running.

'It's all right, they've stopped charging.' Jed sighed, stooping over to catch his breath. 'Fucking hell, that was the worst yet. Are you all right?' He raised his head to look at me.

I tried in vain to stop shaking. 'Yeah, fine. I think. What about you? What's happened to your head?' Half of it was now almost covered in blood, ketchup-like streaks matting his hair.

'I got a clout from a truncheon when I was running up the hill. God, I panicked when I thought I'd lost you. Don't you do that to me again, you hear?' Jed grabbed me by the hand and pulled me towards him.

'Jesus, son, what the hell have they done to you?' Bob came jogging up beside us, puffing and panting.

Jed put his hand to his head and winced. 'Got a wallop from a truncheon, didn't I?'

'Here, give us that T-shirt.' Bob pulled Jed's T-shirt from the back of his jeans and twisted it into a makeshift bandage. With his bare, bloodied chest and his headband Jed looked more like a mercenary than a miner and I'm relieved to report that, amid all the madness, I was still able to appreciate such a glorious sight.

'Caitlin – oh, thank the Lord!' Mrs M staggered her way over. A rather different Mrs M from the one I had last seen. Her topknot had slid half-way down the back of her head and strands of hair were now sticking out at right-angles, creating the appearance of a tribal headdress. Added to this, streaks of lipstick now adorned her face, her glasses were dangling from one ear and she was clutching a Revolutionary Communist Party banner.

'I was afraid you might have been trampled underfoot by one of those awful beasts. I didn't know how I was going to face your mother in the staff room if anything had happened to you. Can you believe what we've just witnessed? It's an absolute outrage.' Mrs M turned to face the massing ranks of miners gathering in the lane. Brandishing her banner she raised her voice to its customary bellow: 'Come on – what's the matter with you? Have you all lost the use of your hands or something? Arm yourselves before the second onslaught. Grab anything you can. Let's kill the bastards!'

A cheer went up from the crowd, and before I knew what was happening, people were dismantling fences and even a stone wall to use as missiles. My heart sank. All I wanted was to be out of there, away from the violence. Away from this twilight-zone village where nothing seemed to make sense. Where policemen clomped you on the head instead of chuckling, 'Evening, all.' Where headmistresses incited people to riot rather than yelled at you to behave. Where young men who, minutes ago, had been eating ice cream and playing football were now covered in blood and crouched on the floor.

I looked at Jed and realised for the first time that the miners' strike wasn't just an opportunity for me to find a boyfriend. It was slightly more serious than that.

'Here, Jed, take Caitlin round the back of them houses.

This is no place for a young lass.' Bob pointed to an alleyway in the middle of a row of houses to the left of us.

'But, Dad, what about you?'

'Don't be soft, I can look after meself. It's you two I'm worried about. You need to get that cut seen to. The last thing you need is another clout. Now, go on, follow those others before the police make another charge.'

Jed and I followed a trickle of miners making their way down the alley. As I tripped and stumbled past the old chip papers, flattened cigarette butts and a dented Tizer can, the noise behind me reached a crescendo. The clatter of stones and roar of abuse raining down on the police filled me with dread – how long would it be before they retaliated once again? Not long at all, as it turned out. Just as we made our way on to the green behind the houses we heard a shout go up from the crowd.

'RUN!'

'Oh, shit!'

I turned to follow Jed's gaze. There, about two hundred yards behind us on the green, was a massed rank of police, marching steadily towards us, truncheons drawn, shields raised. Some even had Alsatians, straining on leads. The Mattress and Rambo suddenly seemed about as menacing as a little old lady out walking her Westie.

Jed ushered me in front of him. 'Come on,' he said. 'You'll be okay.' But I couldn't help noticing that his earlier bravado had vanished without trace.

I clenched my fists and broke into a jog. My legs felt weary and my heart was pounding. It felt as if there was nowhere left to run to. The green seemed to stretch on for miles, and they were bound to catch up with us eventually. And if they didn't, the dogs certainly would. I ran faster and faster. Past the endless walls and back gates of the houses to our right. How I wished I were behind one of those walls, inside one of those houses, with the door double-locked and and all the windows firmly shut. Then, like one of those concealed doors in a Nancy Drew mystery, one of the gates magically swung open and a wizened walnut of a face peered out. 'Quick, lass, get inside,' the walnut ordered, beckoning with a gnarled brown hand. I grabbed Jed's arm and pulled him in through the gate behind me.

'Get in the house,' the walnut's voice commanded, with a quaver. I heard a bolt slide shut behind me but, not daring to stop and turn round, I ran straight towards the open back door of the house and into somebody's kitchen. The next thing I knew I was slumped against the wall, trying to catch my breath and swallow my tears while a little old man clanked a tarnished kettle down on to the stove and attempted to light a match with trembling hands.

'Here, let me,' said Jed, taking the matches from him and lighting the hob. 'Thanks, mate, thanks a lot.' He took the old man's hand in both of his and shook it vigorously. 'I thought we were for it then, I really did.' He turned to look at me. 'You all right, Cat?'

I opened my mouth to utter some sunny response like, 'Yes, fine, never better,' but all that came out was a shuddering sob. I was so embarrassed, yet the more embarrassed I became the more I wept. It was awful. Before I knew it, Jed was right in front of me and those strong arms were round me and my face was pressed against his bare chest. It was fantastic. I could hear his heart pounding, loud and strong like a bass drum, and in that moment I felt safer than I've ever felt in my life.

'It's all right,' he was murmuring into my hair. 'It's all right. They can't get us now.'

'Bloody Big Brother – that's what this is!'

Jed and I jumped apart as the old man hollered, shaking a feeble fist at the grimy kitchen window.

'They think I don't know, but I do. I've been watching them, see. They think they're watching us, but I've been watching them – from the shitter window, with me binoculars. Big Brother. Think about it,' he shouted at us. 'You, missy, tell me what year this is.'

I gulped nervously. 'Nineteen eighty-four.'

'Speak up!'

'Nineteen eighty-four,' I repeated, fighting the urge to giggle.

'Exactly. Nineteen eighty-bloody-four. And they thought I wouldn't realise, but you can't pull the wool over my eyes, no siree, Bob! Don't suppose you've read George Orwell – they've probably burnt all the books by now. But they won't get their hands on mine. Buried them in the backyard, see.'

The whistle on the kettle began to shriek, and as the kitchen filled with steam and Jed and I exchanged a surreptitious grin, everything began to feel all right again. It was pretty ironic, really, that taking tea with a paranoid old man in string vest and braces somewhere in deepest South Yorkshire should return me to some sense of normality, but it did. As we helped ourselves to jam tarts and slabs of stale fruit cake, slurping from chipped mugs of sugary tea and discussing the delights of George Orwell (Jed has read *1984* and *Animal Farm!*), the battle outside seemed at last to wane.

'Can I use your bathroom, mate?' Jed asked, pointing to his head. 'Need to sort out the old war wound.'

'Of course, of course. You know what you need, don't you?' The old man shuffled over to a red Formica cabinet that leaned unsteadily against the wall. He delved inside and withdrew his wrinkled hand with a flourish to reveal – a tin of Spam.

'Spam!' Jed and I declared in unison, kicking each other under the table.

'Aye, Spam – best bloody alternative to a hand grenade on the market. Only twenty-nine p a tin down the Co-op,' he added. 'It's the corners, see – lethal, they are.'

We all gazed at the shocking pink square tin resting in the palm of his hand.

'Right – well, thanks, mate, thanks a lot.' Jed pushed back his chair and got to his feet. 'Er, Cat, you couldn't give us a hand, could you?'

I leapt to my feet. 'Yeah, sure.'

As soon as we got upstairs and into the bathroom we collapsed into fits of laughter.

'Big Brother is watching you,' I hissed, pointing a trembling finger at Jed.

'Spam!' Jed uttered.

'What was that all about?' I asked, wiping a tear from my eye.

'No. Spam. Look.' Jed was gazing over my shoulder, his mouth agape.

I turned, to see what I assumed had once been a bath packed full of bright pink square tins. 'Oh, my God.'

'And take a look at this.' I followed Jed's gaze to the toilet cistern, on top of which were a pair of binoculars, a copy of *1984* and a Swiss Army penknife. Directly above the cistern was a small window that had been whitewashed barring one small aperture, just the right size for a pair of binoculars, I noted.

'Spooky,' said Jed.

I nodded. 'But I'd still rather be in here than out there.'

'Aye.' Jed gingerly removed the T-shirt from around his head. The blood had caked itself into clumps of his hair. 'Can you give us a hand washing this lot out?' he asked.

I tried not to nod too eagerly. As Jed bent his head over

the sink I sponged tepid water over it. Watching the blood dissolve away down the plughole my entire body began to tingle. It was just like eating Space Dust, only this time it wasn't just my tongue crackling and fizzing. It was the strangest feeling I've ever experienced, both wonderful and terrifying. When the water ran clear I reached for a frayed towel draped over a mangle contraption. 'There you go,' I said, patting his head softly with the towel. 'Hopefully this dressing should do the trick.' Thankfully the old man kept copious supplies of cotton wool and Elastoplast as well as tinned meat. As I applied the final piece of plaster Jed drew himself upright so that our faces were level.

'Thank you,' he whispered. 'Thank you.'

And then, suddenly, our lips were touching and our arms were wrapping their way around each other, pulling our bodies close. As I closed my eyes it was like looking through a kaleidoscope: an explosion of stars went off inside my head. His lips were so gentle upon mine, easing them open to make way for his tongue. I felt myself slacken in his arms. I can see now why the sappy heroines of bodice-ripping sagas clutch their hands to their breast gasping, '*Take me, take me now*,' for I felt completely at Jed's mercy. Drowning in desire in my first ever French kiss.

'They've gone! They've gone!' Jed and I leapt apart as the old man banged on the bathroom door. 'Now's your chance to make a break for freedom.'

Jed opened the door to reveal the old man standing on the landing, holding out a *Jim'll Fix It* T-shirt. 'Here, put this on, son, you'll look less conspicuous.'

Jed threw me a sideways grin, 'Cheers.'

'And help yourself to Spam from the bath.'

'Aye, will do.'

Reluctantly bidding us farewell and wishing us luck in

our continued battle against Big Brother, our Spam-loving saviour returned to his outpost on top of the toilet cistern and we set out cautiously through Orgreave. The village had an apocalyptic air about it. The ground was littered with all kinds of debris – rocks, stones, wooden fence slats and shredded banners. In the distance the burnt-out carcass of a motor vehicle was still smouldering and on the corner a BBC news crew were loading their equipment into a van.

'Bloody hell.' Jed sighed, as we made our way over the village crossroads. 'I've seen some things during this strike but today has to take the prize. Are you sure you're all right now?'

I nodded and smiled. 'Yeah, fine. It was all a bit – unexpected. I've seen it on the TV, but it's not the same, is it?'

Jed nodded and frowned. 'I hope me dad's okay. I wonder where everyone's gone.'

Instinctively we lowered our heads as we walked past a police van.

'Best bet is to make our way back to Sheffield – he'll have gone back to the car park with the others.'

I nodded and followed Jed along the road to Sheffield city centre. A signpost informed me that I had one and a half miles left with Jed. In about half an hour I would be back on the coach, hurtling towards Harrow. It felt like something inside me was beginning to tear.

As if he had read my mind Jed leapt in front of me, blocking my way. 'So, when am I going to see you again, Cat?' he asked, folding his arms assertively. He still looked gorgeous, despite the picture of Jimmy Saville beaming from his chest, all cigars and sovereign rings.

I lowered my gaze to my previously white espadrilles, which now bore more of a resemblance to army-regulation camouflage, thanks to the assortment of grass and mud stains.

'There's no way I can have you going back to London thinking this is how I treat lasses on a first date. Letting them get battered to a pulp in a field! You're going to have to let me make it up to you.'

First date! Maybe I hadn't dreamt that kiss, after all.

'Well, what do you suggest?' I asked – and I only wish it could have been in a confident purr rather than an embarrassed squeak.

I suggest you come up and stay with us in the summer. Just for a couple of days or summat, see how it goes.' Jed looked at me quizzically. 'What do you think?'

I think I died and went to heaven, right there and then, in that country lane, surrounded by fields and hedgerows and the occasional passing police van. All I could do was smile and nod.

'Right, that's settled, then. Oh, and before I forget,' Jed fumbled in his jeans pocket, 'your present.' He brought out a small paper bag and handed it to me, 'It's not a lot,' he said, scuffing the toe of his trainer in the dust by the roadside. 'I'm pretty skint at the moment, what with being off work and that.'

I reached into the bag with trembling fingers, and felt something hard and cylindrical. On pulling it out I saw that it was a miniature brass lamp, the kind that miners used to use, the kind I had imagined Bob and Jed would be carrying on their visit to Pinner. I examined the intricate engraving around the base: *NUM National Strike 1984.*

'Thank you,' I whispered, my fingers coiling tightly around the metal.

Jed coughed and I could have sworn he was blushing, but maybe it was just the heat. 'Well, like I said, it's not a lot, but at least you've got something to remember me by.

Not that you should need anything, of course,' he added, his trademark cheeky grin returning. He grabbed my hand and set off down the road. 'Come on, then, let's go and find the others.'

When we finally got back to the car park we were both smothered in hugs, Jed by Bob and me by Mrs M. It's hugely ironic – I'd set out that morning to disguise myself from her – but I couldn't help feeling a tremendous sense of relief as I was reunited with her bosom.

Perhaps it's just an overflow from the ocean of *amor* Jed has unleashed in me, but as she snores away on my shoulder on the coach back to Harrow I can't help feeling a strange sort of affection for this hipflask-wielding headmistress. What happened today in Orgreave is the kind of event that bonds people for life. A bit like the Peterloo Massacre or Bloody Sunday.

As I gaze out at the sodium lights forming an amber path through the darkness, my lips still tingling from where Jed kissed me goodbye and my fingers still wrapped around the lamp he gave me, I know that nothing in my life will ever be the same again.

Chapter Fifteen

Early Saturday afternoon

'Ten B&H and a box of matches, please.'

As Mr Patel frowned at me over his copy of the *Racing Post* I felt something most peculiar happening to my face. It was as if I had clambered straight out of a chest freezer into a sauna – my cheeks pulsated with the unexpected heat. Surely I couldn't have been blushing. I clenched my fists and cleared my throat. For Christ's sake, I was thirty-three years old – seventeen years over the legal requirement for purchasing tobacco – so why the hell was I acting like a guilty schoolgirl? Because that bloody diary was making me regress into an emotional, *angst*-riddled teenager, that's why. God, all I needed was a snood and a Frankie Goes To Hollywood T-shirt and my transformation would be complete. FRANKIE SAYS RELAPSE! For a split second I seriously considered hotfooting into Harrow to get one printed.

'That'll be two hundred and twenty-seven pounds, please,' said Mr Patel, handing me my contraband. Actually, he said, 'Two pounds twenty-seven pence,' but it might as well have been two hundred.

'How much?' Jesus, I remember when you could get ten B&H for a quid and still have enough change for a packet of Hubba Bubba and a sherbet dip! How did kids afford to smoke, these days? I rummaged frantically through my purse for some pound coins. In the end I had to tip the contents all over the counter. 'I don't suppose you sell singles, do you?' I asked weakly, stacking up piles of one and two pence pieces.

'No, my dear, only to the children,' Mr Patel replied, tapping his fingers impatiently on the Lottery machine.

I resumed my counting, cheeks aflame. In the end I managed to scrape together two pounds seventy-four – just enough for the obligatory packet of Polos as well.

Back in the sanctuary of my bedroom I put 'Two Tribes' on the record-player and surveyed my shrine. I had retrieved the WavyLine box from the loft and arranged its contents in a small display on the bedside cabinet. The miniature brass Davy lamp, the crumpled T-shirt, the stone, the book and 'The Power Of Love'. I couldn't face seeing the coach ticket so that remained in its hiding place beneath the old newspaper cuttings. Wincing as the needle scratched its way through the opening chords, I moved across to the open sash window and lit a cigarette. Bloody hell! Despite the outrageous hike in price, cigarettes hadn't improved one little bit. But the awful taste of ashtrays only served to reignite my nostalgic obsession and, once again, I felt compelled to return to my diary.

Chapter Sixteen

Dear Anne,

Well, I now know what it feels like to be a napalm victim! For the past two days I have been hobbling around in agony from the worst case of sunburn outside Benidorm. As you can imagine, my blistered appearance rather put paid to my story of revising in the library all day Saturday. Luckily my parents were still out when I got home on Saturday night (O'Flaherty's were having a 'Bacon and Cabbage' night sponsored by Danepak). When Helen crept into my bedroom to make sure I'd got home okay, I buried myself beneath the duvet. Luckily she didn't stay too long – if I'd had to remain under that polyester firetrap for a second more I'm sure my glowing skin would have ignited the whole bed! By the time I surfaced the next morning, as shiny and red as Kojak's lollipop, I had come up with the perfect explanation. As it had been such a lovely day Karen and I had done our revision in the park.

I still can't believe how easily I got away with it. Whoever said honesty was the best policy had obviously been lying. If I had been honest and said, 'Actually, Helen, the reason I resemble a mortally embarrassed lobster is because I spent the entire day demonstrating outside a coke plant in South Yorkshire rather than poring over my books in North Harrow,' I would have got the most almighty bollocking of my life and been grounded until my A levels.

But by being dishonest I received nothing but sympathy and Aftersun all day long. I was also free to go round to Karen's to fill her in on the previous day's drama. Oh, it was wonderful to be the one with all the news for a change. And what news! I'm sorry, but what happened to me on Saturday beats any shopping trip to Carnaby Street with Jasper hands down. Especially as they had been perusing the latest Dungeons and Dragons models!

While she was in London Karen bought herself a pack of tarot cards. Apparently the cards you select are meant to prophesy your future. Karen is growing quite desperate to prophesy her own future with Jasper. Or if, indeed, she has one. (He has been talking about going to work on a kibbutz over the summer, to find himself picking oranges – or was it to pick oranges and find himself?) Anyway, Karen attempted a trial reading on me last night but it didn't quite work. She was having trouble telling her Major Arcana from her Minor and spent most of the evening leafing through the instruction booklet. Even when she did manage to work out the identity of a card there were added complications. For example, the first card I picked out was the Three of Swords, which apparently means I am about to become embroiled in a love triangle. As if! Anyway, Karen got herself all in a fluster because she couldn't decide if the card was 'upright' or 'reversed'. In the end she plumped for upright and read the forecast in a tone more fitting for a funeral service than a fun night with a friend. Apparently at least one, if not all, of my triangle will be hurt through the choices that have to be made. What a load of rubbish! Unless, of course, Jed has a secret wife!

It's a shame Karen couldn't have foreseen what an absolute nightmare my first maths O-level paper was going to be. I brought my lamp along as a lucky charm, but try

as I might I just couldn't concentrate on the exam with it
on the desk in front of me. However hard I tried to focus
on long division all I could think of was Jed and that kiss.
For the rest of my life I will have a fondness for Spam. If
only Helen wasn't vegetarian I would have Spam
sandwiches for my packed lunch every single day.

Wednesday, 10 June 1984

Dear Anne,

God, I hate the Mattress and her zit-infested chin. She
thinks I can't see the mini-range of pustulous peaks
beneath that layer of foundation but I can. The bacterial
bitch! I was leaving the library at lunch-time after doing
some last-minute revision for my final maths paper when
suddenly, without warning, I found myself being propelled
across the corridor. My books were sent flying and I ended
up sprawled against the wall.

'If it isn't the fucking weirdo swot,' the Mattress snarled,
baring her beige teeth and sniggering to her bunch of
inbred mates.

As I turned to pick up my books she grabbed me by the
blazer and pinned me against the wall. 'What's all this,
then?' she sneered, pointing at the sticker on my lapel,
'COAL NOT DOLE'.

'Oh, you can read!' I couldn't help exclaiming, which,
with hindsight, wasn't the wisest thing to do as the next
thing I knew I'd received a sovereign-plated slap across the
face. On top of the sunburn the sting was unbearable and I
couldn't stop my eyes smarting.

'Ooh, look, she's starting to cry,' the crusty crone
cackled, before stabbing a nicotine-stained finger at the
sticker. 'Coal not fucking dole – where does she think she
bleedin' is? A bleedin' coal mine or sumfink?' And with

that she and her pox-riddlled posse turned on
heels and clattered off down the corridor.

Needless to say, this was not the ideal preparation
my second exam and as I sat in that hall consumed by
feelings of hatred for Wank-face Wainwright, the Mattress
and square roots, all I wanted to do was fling my pencil to
the floor, race from the hall and somehow find my way
back to Jed. I feel so confused at the moment. I don't feel I
belong at school, I don't feel I belong on the estate, I don't
feel I belong at home. I don't really feel I belong anywhere
apart from with Jed.

Thursday, 11 June 1984

Dear Anne,

You will be relieved to hear I have had a much better
day today. I received a letter from Jed! It wasn't very
long, but at least he wrote. He said he'd needed three
stitches to his head when he got back to Blidworth, but
he still seemed more concerned about how I was. He
asked me to phone him 'if you get the chance'. If I get
the chance? As if I can possibly think of anything better
to do! Of course, I'm a bit worried about getting through
to his sister again – she sounded pretty scary the last
time. Jed says that after his head injury she stopped him
going back to Orgreave – apparently you don't argue
with 'our Max' (I'm sure Derrick and his 'scabby cock'
would agree with that!).

Have got my English comprehension exam tomorrow. I
have decided that I'm going to write a story about a young
miner and his wife going to Orgreave. I'm sure I can find a
suitable title.

Friday, 12 June 1984

Dear Anne,

Well, I have to say I have never seen such a bunch of uninspiring titles in my life! Fancy asking a budding Pulitzer Prize winner to choose between *The Blackberry Bush* or *My Dog Rex*. In the end I plumped for *The Blackberry Bush*, ingeniously weaving it into the plot as the hiding place for my young lovers as they cowered from the horse-riding, truncheon-wielding police. No doubt I'll get some right-wing fascist marking my paper and I'll be given a U grade, but I don't care. Like all authors of integrity, I refuse to compromise my principles in order to write a pile of sanitised pap.

Must go – *Dynasty*'s about to start.

Saturday, 13 June 1984

Dear Anne,

Sometimes I think I might die of loneliness, I really do. Karen is over at Jasper's helping him dye his hair back to blonde, Joe is at the allotment harvesting yet more disconcertingly deformed carrots and Helen – well, Helen might as well be from another planet for all we have in common. I'm a fifteen-year-old young woman, for God's sake, consumed by affairs of the heart and matters of the mines. Does she not realise that the prospect of spending an entire Saturday at a donkey sanctuary in Epping Forest is about as appealing as a date with Neil from *The Young Ones?* I have to say, the way she stormed out of the house when I refused to go with her was really quite childish. I think I will make the most of this time on my own to practise French-kissing my pillow.

Tuesday, 16 June 1984

Dear Anne,

My two O levels are officially over. Yippee! Still have all my other exams to come, but can't be bothered to revise. Have found an excellent quiz in *Blue Jeans* called 'Wilting Wallflower or Wild Rambler?'. Think I will do that instead.

Well, I don't believe it! I've been over my results twice but I definitely got mostly Cs. There must be some kind of typing error or something – according to *Blue Jeans* I'm a 'Wilting Wallflower'!

Mostly Cs.

Oh dear. When it comes to guys, as Limahl would say, you really are 'too shy-shy'. Stop hiding behind those National Health specs and braces and invest in a pair of stiletto pixie boots and a boob tube. The way you're going you'll be getting your bus pass before you get a snog!

Well, I've never heard anything so ridiculous in all my life. Me? A wilting wallflower? I don't think so. Anyway, I've had a snog now, thank you very much. They obviously haven't got a clue about these matters.

Oh, God! Maybe I *am* a wilting wallflower. After all, I'm practically sixteen and I've only ever had one French kiss. The way I'm going I'm sure to be a virgin when I reach the age of consent. Oh, the shame of it! *Blue Jeans* are probably right. I'll probably still be a virgin when I'm drawing my pension – destined to die a shrivelled-up hymen-intact hag. How tragic it will be to drift through life never aware of what it is to be proper woman, to be the maiden aunt to Karen and Jasper's brood of children. Is there really any point in going on?

Panic over! I have just redone the quiz and, upon reflection, I've discovered that for a lot of the questions

where I'd been putting C as my response I really should
have been putting A. For example, when they asked:

> When 'Against All Odds' comes on at the school disco are
> you most likely to be found:
> A. Smooching with the school hunk.
> B. Slow-dancing with his best mate.
> C. Skulking on your own in a dark corner.

I initially put C because at the last school disco I did end
up in a darkened corner, but that was only because I'd
spotted nerdy Norman Jenkins making a beeline for me, all
bum-fluff and boils in his beige cords. And, besides, every
time 'Against All Odds' comes on in my bedroom I
fantasise about smooching with Jed (who would definitely
be the school hunk, were he still at school). That's the
problem with these quizzes, really. Although I'm technically
still at school, in reality I have outgrown naff discos and
school hunks. How can I really expect a quiz aimed at
children to apply to me?

Friday, 3 July 1984

Dear Anne,
 I feel awful, neglecting you for over two weeks, but what
with exams and writing to Jed, my literary juices have been
feeling quite drained. I just had to write to you tonight,
though – you will not believe what has happened. Jasper
has chucked Karen! The carrot-topped cad! It all started to
go wrong a couple of weeks ago when Karen took some
peroxide over to his house to dye his hair back to its
original blonde. (Since collapsing with beret-induced heat-
stroke Jasper has gone right off Che Guevara.)
Unfortunately, however, he has not gone right on to Jasper
Carrott, otherwise he might not have minded when Karen

rinsed off the peroxide before it had had a chance to develop properly. He took one look at his Belisha-like barnet and hit the roof. Mrs M had to restrain him while Karen fled in floods of tears. When Debbie found out what had happened she offered to go round and rectify her daughter's hairdressing disaster and, much to Karen's relief, Jasper grudgingly agreed. However, the damage was done. The captain of Jasper's rugby team had called round in the interim and, before you could say juicy Outspan, the whole team knew of his follicular *faux pas*.

Karen felt awful, but no amount of tortured apologies on Care Bear notelets could make a difference. For a whole week Jasper refused to see her or take her calls until finally, last night, he summoned her to Chez Montague. Karen was ecstatic – she even nipped to the chemist to buy a packet of *Femfresh*. However, a romantic reunion was obviously not on the cards (if only she'd given herself a reading before catching the train to Moor Park, she could have saved herself the heartache and the fifty-pence fare.) Karen says she knew something was wrong the minute she arrived and Mrs M offered her a sherry – not even Mr M is allowed to touch the sherry! Then Jasper swanned into the lounge, his now white-blond hair poking out from beneath a skullcap.

'I've decided to embrace Judaism,' he informed her, while munching a matzo, 'so, due to our conflicting faiths, I'm afraid we will no longer be able to see one another. Besides, I leave for Israel in three days' time.' And with that he bade poor Karen 'Shalom,' and returned to his bedroom – no doubt to brush up on his Hebrew.

Apparently Mrs M was a tower of strength, telling Karen she would gladly volunteer to circumcise her heartless son – without anaesthetic – and giving her a bottle of Pomagne for the train ride home. By the time Karen arrived at my house she had her banana clip on sideways and a chronic case of hiccups.

'What am I going to do?' she wailed, thrashing around on my bed to 'Time After Time'. I muttered sympathetic nothings and forced a packet of malted milks down her throat.

'I could become a Jew too.' She sniffed, hopefully. 'I already support Spurs.'

I shook my head and sighed. 'I don't think so, Karen. It's not worth it. By the time you'd be ready to convert he would have moved on to some other craze. Let's face it, in the couple of months we've known him, Jasper has been a clubber, anarchist, pacifist, Communist, Dungeons-and-Dragons head and now a Jew. This time next week he'll probably have discovered the joys of Hare Krishna.' Well, there was no point giving her false hope and, besides, Karen could do so much better than Jasper. She left here in floods of tears and wasn't in school today. I am about to go round to her house to help her do a tarot-card reading and, no doubt, listen to huge amounts of Tears For Fears. Oh, well, what are friends for?

Saturday, 3 July 1984

Dear Anne,

I know this sounds horrible but I'm so glad Karen and Jasper have split up. My parents have bought this awful new game called Trivial Pursuit and they can't stop playing it. Basically it involves moving around a board answering questions in order to collect the pieces of a pie. It wouldn't be too bad if it weren't for the questions. They are just so obscure. I mean, who really cares which Mexican emperor died in 1527 from a stomach bug? Even the entertainment category was a big let-down – there wasn't a single question about *Dynasty*. If Karen and Jasper were still together I would have had to spend my entire Saturday night playing the damn thing. After one and a half torturous hours, with not a single piece of my pie to my name, I made my excuses and left. Even four hours of 'The Hurting' and analysing the motives for Jasper's flirtation with Judaism seemed preferable to that punishment. Never has the term 'bored' game seemed more apt! Somehow I just can't see it taking off.

Sunday, 4 July 1984

Dear Anne,

I finally plucked up courage to phone Jed, and fortunately this time I got through to him straight away. He seemed to be really pleased to hear from me. Apparently things are getting a little tense in Nottingham – Blidworth is one of the only pits in the area that is still on strike. 'Sometimes I wish we lived in Yorkshire.' He sighed.

I tried not to gulp in horror. It's bad enough him living in Nottingham, let alone another hundred miles further north.

'Why?'

'Well, at least the strike's solid there. We're right out on a limb in Blid'th. Never mind, as long as the other lads stay solid we should be all right. How did the exams go?'

'Oh, pretty crap.'

'You're kidding. Why?'

I gave a worldly sigh. 'I don't know. I found it hard to concentrate – what with everything else going on in this country at the moment my exams seem pretty irrelevant, really.'

'No, they're not. What about your career as a writer? Don't make the same mistake I did, Cat. You've got to grab every opportunity life throws at you.'

I was quite taken aback by his response – I really thought he would have appreciated my gesture of solidarity, not lectured me like one of my parents. Thankfully Jed changed the subject. 'So, when are you going to come up and see us, then? Now you're a lady of leisure.'

'Oh, I don't know. Do you still want me to? Won't I get in the way, what with the strike and everything?'

'No, not at all. In fact, you could help out. The wives have set up a soup kitchen in the village – they could probably do with an extra pair of hands.'

'Oh, right.'

Jed laughed. 'Don't worry, I'm only messing. After what you went through in Orgreave do you think I'd drag you up here just to work in a soup kitchen? I won't be able to take you anywhere flash, mind, not in my current financial predicament, but if you like the outdoors there's plenty of places we can go. I can take you on my tour of Sherwood Forest. I don't suppose you're a Robin Hood fan?'

I thought of Michael Praed, with those great puppy-dog eyes and revealing green tights, and smiled. 'Oh, yes, I think he's fantastic.'

'Sound. I'll take you on the Robin Hood tour of Blid'th, then.' Jed adopted the nasal tone of a tour guide: 'Highlights include the cottage where Maid Marian used to live and the bridge where Robin and Little John had their infamous scrap.'

Oh, Anne, it just gets better and better. As I lie here in bed, beads of sweat trickling down my face, I can't stop fantasising about Jed and me riding through Sherwood Forest on horseback, my arms wrapped tightly about his waist, my hair billowing out behind me. Finally we come to a halt and Jed, clad in dark green jerkin and tights, pulls me from the horse to cover me in kisses. As we sink on to the blanket of leaves beneath us and Jed pulls at my pale blue satin gown all I can hear is the haunting whisper, 'Robin – the hooded man,' echoing through the trees. It beats being chased around a coke plant any day.

Sunday, 28 July 1984

Dear Anne,

Oh dear, yet again I have neglected you, but with so much going on I'm afraid my poor diary has remained gathering dust under my bed for two whole weeks. I had to write to you tonight, though – I am far too nervous to sleep. Tomorrow I am going to Nottingham. Tomorrow I am going to stay with Jed! I still can't believe my parents have agreed to it. Of course, they didn't at first.

'No way!' Helen exclaimed, spraying muesli all over the kitchen table, when I first broached the subject.

'But I want to do something useful with my summer holiday,' I implored. 'Going to work in a miners' soup kitchen would be such a worthwhile cause. You know how important the miners' plight is to me – it's just like you and your African sisters.'

Helen chewed thoughtfully on a piece of dried banana. 'Oh, I don't know, Caitlin. It's an awfully long way to go, you're not even sixteen yet – who would be responsible for you?'

I bit hard on my lip to prevent myself shouting, 'I'd be responsible for myself, you stupid woman, stop treating me like one of your five-year-old pupils!'

'Bob would, of course. I'd be staying at his house with him and his wife.' I closed my eyes and prayed Helen would miraculously forget all about his sex-on-legs son.

'And Jed,' Helen added. God, she can be shrewd when she wants to be.

'Yes, and Jed and his sister Maxine.'

'Hmmmm, I'll have to speak to your father – and to Bob.'

I ran round the table and gave her a sort of hug. 'Of course, of course. Oh, please, Mum, please let me go, it would mean so much to me to be more politically active. It's all right for you, you were a student in the sixties, I need to have a cause to fight for. Surely you of all people can understand.'

'Mum?' Helen gazed at me quizzically over the pot of camomile tea.

'What?'

'You just called me Mum, not Helen.'

'Oh. Oh, yes.' I looked at her curiously – was this a good or bad thing?

Helen took my hand and squeezed it. 'I'll see what I can do,' she said, smiling warmly.

And by the end of the day it was all sorted. Helen had convinced Joe that they should encourage my new-found political fervour – after all, hadn't they been nurturing it since the day I was born? – then phoned Bob to check if it really was all right for me to stay for a few days and to offer to pay for my keep.

I went to bed that night the happiest woman alive.

Tonight, however, is quite a different story. I don't remember a time I felt so nervous – not even my cringeworthy flute solo for the Harrow Youth Orchestra comes close. It was bad enough going up to Orgreave but this time I'm not facing the prospect of a solitary day with Jed. This time I'm facing the prospect of nearly a whole week in Jed's house, with Jed's family and no Mrs M for moral support.

Chapter Seventeen

Monday, 29 July 1984

Dear Anne,

Well, I have to say this is quite a different experience from my last coach journey. National Express really know how to look after their customers. Not only does the ventilation funnel in the ceiling work but they also have a hostess called Donna, who walks up and down the aisle asking if everything's okay and if she can get you any beverages. Seeing Donna really makes me wish I was blonde – she looks just like Marilyn Monroe, or at least she would if Marilyn Monroe had had a penchant for gold plate. I've never seen so much jewellery on one person. I had decided on a distinctly low-key look for my journey north. Following my ra-ra rashness at Orgreave I was determined not to make the same mistake again and, after lengthy deliberation, plumped for my FRANKIE SAYS RELAX! T-shirt and my black drainpipes with the gold-zip feature. Just to be on the safe side, though, I've crammed the rest of my wardrobe into my sports bag – I'm determined to appear cool and sophisticated during my stay in Blidworth if it kills me. For the rest of the journey I'm going to study the cut-out-and-keep guide to overcoming shyness that *Photo Love* has so thoughtfully featured this week. Not that I'm shy or anything but I thought it might come in useful, should any awkward situations arise. For example, there is an excellent tip on the art of good conversation. Apparently you must always ask 'open-ended' questions, preferably requiring the other person's opinion on something. They even give a few examples like, 'What do you think about Martina Navratilova winning Wimbledon for the fifth time?' or 'What's your opinion of mismatching fluorescent socks?' The worst thing you can possibly do is ask a 'closed' question, which will just be met with a conversation-stopping yes or no.

'Have you been waiting long?'

'No.'

Upon arriving in Nottingham and clapping my eyes on Jed, my new-found conversational skills were temporarily abandoned on the floor of the coach along with *Photo Love*. I retrieved my bag from the pile on the roadside and attempted to start again.

'So, what do you think of National Express coaches, then?'

'I dunno – I've never been on one. Here, let me get that.' Jed took my bag and hoisted it over his shoulder. The sight of his toffee-brown biceps flexing beneath the white of his T-shirt made me catch my breath. So did the picture of Margaret Thatcher emblazoned across his chest. Jed noticed my bewildered stare. 'It's even worse than Jimmy Saville, isn't it?' he said, with a chuckle. 'Here, look, we've all got 'em.' Jed pointed to the lettering at the bottom, which declared, 'The Enemy Within'.

'Hmm, I think I prefer mine,' I said, puffing out my chest proudly.

'Yeah, me too,' Jed replied, with a wink. 'It's good to see you again, Cat.' And before I knew what was happening he'd kissed me lightly on top of my head. 'Come on, let's get the bus, me mam's dying to meet you. She's even got the posh tea-set out!'

Jed's mum, Lizzie, is really lovely. The minute I saw her

beaming face and bustling manner I knew we were going to get on. Besides, it's impossible to feel afraid of somebody who looks just like a little china doll, all shiny skin and twinkly eyes. And she smells so nice too, a mumsy mixture of soap and cinnamon. I couldn't believe it when she smothered me in a hug the minute I walked in the door.

'Come in!' she cried. 'Let me get a good look at you. Jed's told me so much about you.'

Jed turned crimson and groaned. 'Mam!'

'But you have, son. I hear you like reading,' she said, ushering me through to the living room. 'Our Jed's a real bookworm too. Gets it off me, he does. I do love me Catherine Cookson – can get through one of hers in a day. Not like his dad here, or his sister Maxine, proper square-eyes, the pair of them.'

'There's nowt wrong with a bit of telly,' Bob grunted, from an armchair in the corner, the remote control balancing on his stomach like a surfboard riding a wave. 'All right, Caitlin, love, make yourself at home.'

If I had to pick three words to describe Jed's living room it would be china shire horses. The place is full of them: standing majestically on the mantel, trotting proudly across the window-sill, even gazing through their water-coloured blinkers from behind gold frames on the wall. In keeping with this equine theme the stone-clad chimney-breast is covered with horse brasses, horseshoes and rosettes. It was quite a surprise, therefore, when my eyes came to rest on the photographic portrait of a young woman on top of the television set.

'That's our Maxine,' Lizzie explained, following my gaze.

'Our Maxine' was absolutely stunning. With her dark glossy hair, heavy-set eyebrows and expertly applied makeup she looked just like one of Debbie's flamenco-dancing figurines.

'What does she do?' I asked, quite shamelessly in awe in the face of such beauty.

Lizzie sniffed. 'She works as a waitress in a cocktail bar.'

Jed and I looked at each other and smiled.

'We haven't quite managed to turn her round and turn her into someone new yet.' Jed smirked.

'Oh, very funny, son,' Lizzie retorted, flicking Jed with the end of her tea-towel.

'Don't – don't you want me?' Jed replied, hiding behind a cushion to escape another tea-towel flick. 'Come on, Mam, get the tea on, Cat's starving.'

Everything is different up here – especially the meals. For a start they have tea, not supper in the evening. Dinner is apparently served at lunch-time! We dined on Findus crispy pancakes, chips and beans, with side-plates of white bread and butter triangles and endless cups of tea from a shire-horse teapot. It was delicious. Helen would probably have had a cholesterol-induced heart-attack at the very sight of it!

After tea Jed took me for a walk around the village. It looked very nice – rows of little cottage-type houses leading up to a lovely old church on top of the hill – but, to be perfectly honest, I was far too busy enjoying being with Jed to notice much else. As we ambled along the narrow streets, discussing the strike and different books and joking about Spam and, of course, Frankie Goes To Hollywood I didn't once need to resort to my guide to overcoming shyness. The conversation flowed like PG Tips all night. Even when we got back to the house we didn't stop talking until almost two in the morning. And then it was only because Jed has got to get up at five to go on the picket line.

As I lie here alone in Jed's bed I wonder if we are ever destined to spend a night together or if he will always be doomed to sleep on a sofa downstairs from me. I can hear somebody opening the front door. It must be the magnificent Maxine. I wonder if she is half as beautiful in real life. I do hope so. And I hope she likes me. Part of me wishes Jed had a younger sister, who played with Sindy and collected Care Bears. It wouldn't be nearly as daunting. I can hear her now, creaking about on the landing outside my room. What is she doing? God, I hope she doesn't come in. I want to be looking my best when I meet her. I wonder if she'll give me any beauty tips.

Tuesday, 30 July 1984

Dear Anne,

I slept so lightly last night I'm not even sure if I ever properly dozed off. At five o'clock I heard Jed and Bob getting ready to go to the picket line and from that moment on I was wide awake. I lay there listening to the trickle of the tap in the bathroom, the click of the kettle downstairs and finally the front door shutting behind them and their voices trailing off down the street. The dawn light was already filtering in through the red and white curtains, casting the room in a pale glow. It felt weird being in Jed's room, surrounded by his things. If Jed's living room is a shrine to shire horses then his bedroom is without doubt a shrine to Nottingham Forest Football Club. I studied the poster on the wall next to me – a row of mullet haircuts adrift on a sea of red nylon and ribbed white socks. I rolled over to survey the rest of the room. There wasn't much space for anything other than the bed, a small wardrobe and a black leather armchair, strewn with clothes. On the floor next to the wardrobe there was a ghetto-blaster speckled with flecks of white paint and on either side two piles of books teetered, an assortment of George Orwell,

rock anthologies and football annuals. On the floor right
next to the bed my copy of *Catcher in the Rye* lay open –
Jed was on page one hundred and twenty-five. With
nothing better to do I picked it up and began to reread it,
trying to imagine which parts would have made Jed laugh.
At 7.02 a.m. I heard Lizzie singing 'Agadoo', as she
crossed the landing and went downstairs. I was torn
between the prospect of joining her and having to practise
my new open-ended conversation techniques or the
boredom of lying in bed with no hope of returning to sleep.
My head was beginning to pound so I got up and rooted
through my bag. All of a sudden I hated my clothes.
Nothing seemed right, and the more things I tried on the
worse my head began to ache. Wrestling my way back out
of a pair of circulation-stopping pedal-pushers, I ended up
putting on the same T-shirt and trousers as yesterday. For
a bit of variety I piled my hair up into a pineapple and
after hurriedly applying some mascara I crept downstairs.

I don't know why I'd been so worried. As soon as I
peered around the kitchen door Lizzie greeted me with one
of her sunny smiles. 'Come on in, love, sit yourself down.
Tea's brewing.'

Two pots of tea later my headache had disappeared. I
also knew all about Lizzie's fondness for Ted Rogers, the
problems she was having with her thyroid gland and how
I'd been made an honorary member of the Blidworth
Women's Group. 'I'll take you down there later, love, so
you can meet all the girls. Bob said you wanted to give us
a hand.'

I remembered Helen's phone call to Bob and forced a
smile.

Lizzie patted me on the arm. 'I'm sure our Jed'll be
whisking you off somewhere later,' she said, with a knowing
grin.

At that point Bob and Jed popped in for some breakfast.

'Any sign of Madam?' Bob enquired, as he opened the post.

Lizzie sniffed. 'Don't be silly – she won't surface until dinner-time. She didn't get home till gone two.'

'How did you sleep?' Jed asked, sitting down in the chair next to mine.

'Fine thanks.' It was ridiculous – it had only been about seven hours since I'd last seen Jed yet, once again, I was tongue-tied.

'Bribing bastards!' We all jumped as Bob brought his fist crashing down on the breakfast table, causing the teacups to quiver on their saucers.

Lizzie put her arm across his shoulders. 'Is it another one?' she asked.

'Aye.' Bob scrunched the letter he'd been reading into a ball and stuffed it into the bin.

'We've been getting letters from the Coal Board offering us money to go back to work,' Jed explained, dipping a piece of toast into the yolk of his fried egg.

'Scab money. Come on, son, let's get back to the line.' Bob gulped the last of his tea and got to his feet. 'I'll see you later, love,' he said to Lizzie, and kissed her on the cheek.

'I'll be back at dinner-time to take you out,' Jed said, looking at me anxiously, 'Will you be all right with me mam till then?'

'Of course she will,' Lizzie replied. 'I'm taking her down to the Welfare to meet the rest of the girls.'

I smiled nervously at Jed and took a deep breath. 'I'll be fine.'

And actually I was. Fine. Despite all my initial nervousness, the women's group was a right laugh. They're just like the girls from Mike Baldwin's factory in *Coronation Street* – all smoker's coughs and crude jokes. I never knew

that your fanny could fart! Apparently Lizzie's best mate
Brenda can't even remove a tampon without letting one
rip! When they heard how far I'd come to help they all
seemed quite impressed and they didn't act as if I was
stuck-up at all. It probably helped that within ten minutes I
had mysteriously developed a Cockney accent to make Jim
Davidson proud. Everything went fabulously until we ran
out of sugar.

'Be a love and nip home and get the packet from the
pantry,' Lizzie said, handing me her door keys. 'I'd go
myself but I have to get the soup on – the first lot of lads
will be here in a minute.'

'No worries, mate,' I replied, taking the keys and
wondering what the hell a pantry was.

It was simple enough to find my way back to Jed's – he
lives at the top of a hill and the Miners' Welfare is at the
bottom. However, as I drew level with the house my heart
sank. A huge Harley Davidson was parked outside,
surrounded by heaps of records all higgledy-piggledy as if
someone had just flung them there. I studied the covers:
there seemed to be an overwhelming predominance of long
hair and leather.

'And you know where you can stick yer Meatloaf!'

I ducked as 'Bat Out Of Hell' came flying past me,
landing with a clatter against the motorbike.

'Come on, Max, it was an accident. It was dark, I'd had
fifteen pints of Burton's.'

I turned to see the back of a man clad from head to toe
in leather gesticulating wildly on the doorstep. He was so
huge I couldn't make out whom he was talking to but I
could certainly hear her.

'An accident?' she shrieked. 'You've been on at me for
years now to take it up the arse. That was no accident,
Derrick, that was rape.'

I stood rooted to the spot. *Rape?*

'Rape?' The man snorted. 'Oh, do me a favour, Max, the only rapist round here is you.'

'Get out of here,' the woman screamed, 'before I take the wood chopper to it!'

'All right, all right, I'm going.'

Before I had a chance to flee back down the street the man turned round and, in doing so, created a clear view of the doorway. They both stood there staring at me, Derrick, with his greasy ponytail and droopy moustache, and Maxine, with her scarlet négligé perfectly matching her flushed cheeks. 'And what are you staring at?' she snarled.

'I, er, I'm Caitlin. I've just come to get some sugar from the pantry. I can come back later if you want.' Oh, God, how I wanted to leap on that motorbike and race off like a bat out of hell. Unfortunately Derrick beat me to it.

'Well, come in, then,' Maxine barked, making a strange shaking gesture with her hand at Derrick's departing back.

I walked into the kitchen and gazed around helplessly for something that might be construed as a pantry.

'So, you're the famous Cat,' Maxine said, lighting a cigarette and leaning back against the kitchen counter. I couldn't help noticing that she had the most enormous nipples, which protruded like bullets from beneath her négligé. Although she looked a lot older than her photograph, she was still just as striking and very, very tall.

'Yes, er, whereabouts is the pantry? Is it outside?' I stammered, feeling about as cool and sophisticated as a used teabag.

Maxine peered down at me as if I were deranged. You'd never have thought that she was the one barely dressed.

'Is it outside?' she repeated, in a voice that sounded like the Queen's. 'No, love, it's inside, so's the toilet by the way. Gosh, we'll be as civilised as you southerners soon.'

She flung open a cupboard door and brought out a packet of sugar. 'Is this what you're looking for?'

I nodded.

'Right, then, you can run along now, can't you?'

Somehow I managed to get my head to nod before turning on my heel and bolting.

I didn't properly recover until about an hour later when Jed bounded into the soup kitchen and handed me an emerald green marble. 'I found it down the road and it reminded me of your eyes,' he said, smiling sheepishly, then turned to Lizzie. 'What have you got for us today, Mam? Steak and chips? Caviar and champers?'

Lizzie lifted the lid off the steaming pot of soup. 'Potato and leek, I'm afraid,' she said, with a giggle. 'Would Sir like it with bread or without?'

'Oh, with, please.'

'Brenda, fetch our Jed some bread.'

Brenda handed Jed two slices and winked. 'There you go, love. Now, you know where to come if you want some seconds, don't you?'

Jed looked at me and raised his eyebrows. 'Aye – what a big heart you've got, *Grandma!*'

Brenda shrieked with laughter. 'Ooh, you cheeky devil.' Then she turned to me and prodded me in the ribs. 'You'll have to be quick on your feet with this one, won't she, Lizzie? He's got an answer for everything.'

The rest of the lunch-time went by in a blur of bread-buttering. As the miners clattered in and out I basked in the glow of Brenda's remark. She seemed to take it for granted that Jed and I were an item. It was as if, bit by bit, my dream was becoming reality. Every now and then I would look up from my buttering behind the counter to see Jed laughing and joking with his mates and every time he would catch me looking at him and smile. It was as if our eyes were drawn together by some sort of magnetic force: like moths to a flame or northerners to a teapot. By the time the hall had cleared I was in a state of euphoria. Something was bound to happen between Jed and me today, I just knew it.

But what do I know? After all, I'm just a 'wilting wallflower' who can't tell a pantry from a cupboard and always asks close-ended questions. How can I ever hope to get a boyfriend? Oh, Anne, I feel so dejected as I lie here alone beneath a pair of Nottingham Forest curtains while the object of my desire sleeps soundly on a sofa downstairs, yet again. Don't get me wrong. We had a lovely afternoon – Jed took me into Nottingham to see the film *1984* and then we all had fish and chips for tea (thankfully Maxine was working again). We spent the rest of the evening playing gin rummy with Bob and Lizzie, which was a really good laugh, especially when Bob got caught with the ace of diamonds up his sleeve, but nothing happened. Jed was friendly enough, but there was no holding hands, no quick pecks, let alone lingering Frenchies and, to make matters worse, when Bob and Lizzie announced that they were going to 'hit the hay', I yawned and said, 'Me too.' I didn't know what else to do. If I'd just sat there Jed might have asked me to leave and let him get some sleep and that would have been too embarrassing for words. But by coming upstairs I may have blown my one chance at some pash. I am *so* crap! Jed's going off me and his sister obviously hates me – I may as well just leave tomorrow and stab myself with a candle for the rest of my life.

Chapter Eighteen

Wednesday, 31 July 1984

Dear Anne,

Well, thank God I didn't – leave today and turn to a phallus of a waxen nature, I mean. Otherwise I might never have got to experience the real thing. Or at least felt the real thing and given it a bit of a rub. Oh, my word, what a day it has been! Sometimes I think we need to be plunged into the depths of despair in order to appreciate the heights of true ecstasy, I really do.

After my desolation of last night, today started far more promisingly. I was awoken by a knock on the door at 7.08 a.m. Thinking it was Lizzie I called, 'Come in,' only to recoil in horror when Jed appeared, a freshly showered vision clad only in a pair of shorts and carrying a tray.

'Here you go, m'lady, breakfast in bed. Now will Madam be requiring a morning newspaper with her tea and toast?' Jed placed the breakfast tray on the floor beside the bed and awaited my response.

Far too concerned about the state of my hair to worry about the state of affairs, I shrank back into the bed stammering, 'No, no – it's okay – honestly.'

'Right, then, I'll leave you to it – oh, I thought you might like to wear this on the picket line.' Jed handed me his *Enemy Within* T-shirt.

'Thank you,' I yelped, from beneath the duvet.

I had a shower, cleaned my teeth and got dressed, which thankfully was a far less stressful procedure than yesterday. Jed's T-shirt went really well with my pedal-pushers and as I pulled it over my head and smelt his smell next to my skin I had to have a bit of a sit-down. Once the tingling had abated I went downstairs to find Jed alone in the kitchen.

'Your hair looks nice,' he said, staring at me over his copy of the *Daily Mirror*. 'You look like a mermaid with all those curls.'

'Thanks,' I muttered, grabbing some toast from the rack and vowing to end my days of scrunching and backcombing for ever.

After breakfast we went to join the picket line outside the colliery. Bob and Lizzie were already there, with about a hundred others. The atmosphere was pretty jovial, considering the ungodly hour, everybody milling about drinking tea from Styrofoam cups and making fun of a man called 'Lard-arse'.

At about ten o'clock Jed and I left the picket to go on the 'Official Jed Weyman Robin Hood Tour of Blidworth'. It began in the rather unsavoury sounding Blood and Guts Lane. This was where Robin Hood and Little John fought each other for the right of way and Robin ended up being rather unceremoniously flung into the adjacent stream. In an attempt at authenticity (or so he assured me afterwards), Jed proceeded to re-create this scene, casting himself as Little John. All I knew was that one minute we were standing peering through the brambles at a babbling brook when suddenly Jed had swept me into his arms and was running down the bank shouting, 'Nobody crosses Little John!' I had no alternative but to cling to his neck and press myself against him as tightly as possible. It was fantastic! Only when we got perilously close to the water did Jed come staggering to a standstill and we collapsed into a heap on the ground.

'Why did you go to bed so early last night, then?' he asked breathlessly, propping himself up on his elbow.

'I – uh – I thought you might be tired,' I stammered. The rays of sun filtering through the hedgerow above flickered on Jed's face like fairy-lights.

He laughed. 'I never get tired. Me mam says I must have swallowed a packet of Duracell when I was a nipper.' Jed coiled one of my curls around his finger. 'Anyway, how could a bloke get tired when he's with you?'

In that split second I think my entire being ground to a halt – my heart stopped pounding, my eyes stopped blinking, my body froze – and he kissed me. It was the most tender, gentle kiss I think I'll ever experience. Everything just seemed to slide into place. Our arms slipped around each other, our legs entwined and our tongues – well, it was as if they were Torvill and Dean gliding effortlessly around our mouths with all the grace and passion of 'Bolero'. It seemed to go on for ever: it was as if we lost the need to breathe or swallow, with our kiss becoming our sole source of sustenance.

'Bloody hell!' Jed exclaimed, when we finally came up for air. 'What happened there?'

Gazing up at his heart-shaped face and sun-flecked hair, I realised that we were both shivering. Shivering in the stifling heat.

'Can I kiss you again?' he whispered, lying down so that his face was level with mine.

I nodded and closed my eyes and once again I lost myself in a wave of bliss as Jed dusted me in kisses. Across my brow, on each of my eyelids, then tracing a path down my neck and back up to my earlobe. Although I didn't yell, '*Hun, hun, hun, hin, hin, hin!*' I couldn't help a little moan escaping before his lips found their way back to mine and once again we became entwined. I don't know how long we lay there like that, just exploring each other with our lips and tongues, it might have been half an hour, it might have been half a day. I lost all sense of time or bearings. Eventually we managed to tear ourselves apart.

'I suppose I ought to get on with the tour,' Jed murmured. 'I have to say that this sort of thing has never happened before. Weyman Tours pride themselves on their professionalism, you know.'

I giggled. 'So this isn't the spot where Robin Hood and Little John had a snog, then?'

'No, it is not,' Jed retorted. 'That was a bit further up the bank. I can show you where Maid Marian waited for Robin on their wedding day, though.'

Although Ashfield Cottage was built on the site of Marian's house, with its whitewashed walls and blackened beams it's easy enough to pretend it's the real thing. As I gazed up at a lattice window tucked beneath a gable I could just picture Maid Marian leaning out, waiting anxiously for her betrothed. I turned to Jed and smiled. 'You're so lucky, you know, living somewhere like this. Somewhere so rich in history.'

Jed let out a snort. 'Yeah, it must be terrible living in London with bugger-all to do and see. I tell you something, Cat, and you must never, never tell me dad I said this, but part of me hopes the pit does get closed down after the strike. Don't get me wrong, I don't want Thatcher to win or owt, but at least if the pit was shut I'd have the perfect excuse to get out of here. It's a such a big world out there – I don't want to be stuck in this bloody village for the rest of me life.'

'Where would you go?' I asked, attempting to gaze nonchalantly down the street while praying he didn't say Outer Mongolia.

Jed grinned, 'London, of course. Rumour has it the streets are paved with gold.'

I allowed my eyes to meet his and we both smiled.

'Come on, let's go to the Black Bull for a bit of snap.'

Thankfully 'snap' means food up here, not a riotous card game enjoyed by the under-fives. We spent the next hour feasting on cheese cobs and cider in the beer garden of a lovely old pub opposite Ashfield Cottage. Next stop on the 'Jed Weyman Tour' was Friar Tuck's Well, and then we headed off into Blidworth Woods. Jed led me along a trail called Robin Hood Way right into the heart of Thieves Wood. I don't care what he says about it being boring up here, the place names are fantastic – Blood and Guts Lane beats Bridge Street any day. It was lovely and cool in the woods with the tapestry of branches providing a natural sunscreen.

'Rumour has it this here tree was where Robin first kissed Marian,' Jed announced, in his tour-guide voice, as he led me up to a huge oak. He leaned back against the wall of bark and caught one of my hands in his. 'Weyman Tours offer an authentic reconstruction at no extra cost,' he said, pulling me closer.

'Oh, well, I do want my tour to be as authentic as possible,' I murmured – no 'wilting wallflower' me! It was only on the walk home that I found out Jed had picked that tree at random, but I decided to withhold my letter of complaint. The spine-tingling extras of Weyman Tours more than compensated for any deliberate distortion of historical fact.

It wasn't until we got home for tea that things took a dramatic turn for the worse. Maxine was seated at the kitchen table, all silky skin and satin boob-tube – it was her night off. 'So where have you pair been all day, then?' she asked, as soon as we walked through the door.

'I've taken her on the Robin Hood tour,' Jed replied.

'Ooh, how lovely.' Lizzie sighed, filling everyone's cups with tea. 'Did you see Ashfield Cottage?'

I nodded. Maxine's presence had rendered me speechless once again.

'It's bloody kids' stuff, if you ask me.' Maxine sniffed, ignoring her tea to continue painting her nails – the black varnish was as shiny and lustrous as her hair, which cascaded in loose ringlets about her face.

'No, it's not,' Lizzie retorted. 'I love the Robin Hood story – stealing from the rich to give to the poor.'

'That's right, love. He was like the Arthur Scargill of the middle ages.' Bob chuckled. 'Here, Caitlin, do you want some butter for your bread?'

I nodded and took the butter dish.

'So, Cat, how old are you again?' Everything that came out of Maxine's painted, pouting mouth seemed to be accompanied by a sneer.

'Fifteen – almost sixteen,' I muttered, buttering my bread furiously, not daring to look up.

Maxine let out a little snort of laughter. 'Right.'

'Sweet sixteen, eh?' said Bob, with a sigh. 'Oh, to be a teenager again.'

'What do you mean "again"?' Lizzie retorted. 'In all the years I've known you you've never acted a day over twelve!'

'It must be tough being an old fossil, eh, Max?' said Jed, and something about the steely tone of his voice made me look up in surprise. It was the first time I'd heard him angry.

'Shut up,' Maxine snapped.

'Well, I don't suppose you can remember much about your teenage years, can you? Although nothing much has really changed, has it? Still living at home, still working in a bar, still—'

'I said shut it!'

'Right, that's enough, you pair,' Lizzie interrupted.

We spent the rest of tea munching awkwardly at our pie and chips and listening to Lizzie and Bob natter on about a friend of theirs who'd just won a caravan on *Bullseye.*

It was a huge relief when the final dregs of tea had been drained from the pot, the dishes had been cleared away and Jed and I could set off for the Miners' Welfare club. Even the stares of Jed's mates as we walked into the smoke-filled bar were easier to take than Maxine's bitchy remarks. It also helped that 'Two Tribes' was pounding out of the jukebox, reminding me of Karen and our friendship, and I felt a bit stronger. At least somebody out there liked me.

'This is Cat,' Jed announced, to the group of young men seated in the corner nearest the door. I was greeted with a chorus of all-rights, how's-it-goings and good-evening – somebody even said miaow! But at least they were friendly; at least they were smiling beneath their moustaches. One hour and two halves of cider later I felt like one of the gang. At times it was difficult to understand their accent but, from what I could make out, Jed was the worst player on the colliery football team: he had once been sick all over the ref during an East Midlands Cup Final and for some reason they all called him Shakespeare.

'It's because I was once spotted reading a book,' Jed explained to me, during a break in the banter.

I don't think I've laughed so much in ages – until the door opened and in walked Maxine.

A cheer went up from Jed's mates.

'Here, Max, I've been keeping your seat warm.'

'Hey, Max, what have you done with Derrick?'

'She's told him to get on his bike.'

'Yeah, she's finally realised I'm the man for her.'

Maxine turned and fixed us all with her cool stare – I don't think I've ever seen anyone look so beautiful and so nasty all at the same time. She reminded me of the Queen in *Snow White*.

'You're not even man enough to lick the shit from my boots, Tom Whittaker. Now, get your arse up to that bar and get us a drink.' Tom, a burly hulk of a man with a huge scar snaking down his forearm, obediently leapt to his feet and scuttled off to the bar. To my absolute horror Maxine squeezed on to the seat next to me. 'Budge up a bit, Cat. You should have told me you were coming out for a drink – I'd have done something with your hair.' Staring at me disdainfully, Maxine lit up a cigarette. 'Don't you wear makeup down in London, then?'

Jed put his pint down on the table. 'Some lasses don't need to shovel on three inches of slap before they can leave the house, you know.'

Exhaling a thin talon of smoke from her perfectly glossed mouth, Maxine ignored Jed and continued to stare at me.

'Mind you, you probably aren't allowed to wear makeup yet, are you, love? Being a *schoolgirl* and all.'

If she had hollered it through a loud-hailer, I don't think Maxine could have said 'schoolgirl' any louder. I stared at my hands, clasped together on my lap, and prayed for something or somebody to save me.

'Come on – let's get out of here.' Jed got to his feet and pulled at my arm.

'But I've only just got here,' Maxine said.

'Oh, I'm sure you'll be all right. You're surrounded by booze and fellas, what more could you need? Besides, there's something I've got to show Cat.'

'Aye-aye?' said Tom Whittaker, returning to the table with Maxine's drink. 'I hope you've got a magnifying glass, love, you'll need it with Shakespeare here,' and he nudged me in the ribs and laughed.

'Hmm, well, don't do anything I wouldn't do,' Maxine said sulkily.

'Great – we'll be spoilt for choice, then, won't we?' Jed retorted, and led me out of the club.

'I'm sorry about Max,' he said, as we ambled up the hill. 'She can be a bit of a bitch at times, but once you get to know her she's all right.'

I tried to nod in agreement, but somehow I couldn't imagine 'getting to know' Maxine. She'd obviously written me off as an immature irritation from the moment she laid eyes on me.

Jed stuffed his hands in his jeans pockets and stared straight ahead. 'Me mam says she had her heart broken when she was younger and she's never properly recovered. Some lad did a runner with her best mate or summat and it left her all bitter and twisted. Poor Derrick's had to bear the brunt of it. Sometimes I don't know what he's doing still sticking around, the grief she puts him through.'

Suddenly I saw a glimmer of hope. Perhaps Maxine was human, after all. How awful to lose your first true love to your best friend. I tried to imagine how I would feel if Jed ran off with Karen. No wonder Maxine seemed so full of hate. I decided not to give up just yet – at least I wouldn't have to take her barbed remarks personally any more. 'How long have she and Derrick been together?'

'Oh, about ten years, on and off. They met at a Jethro Tull convention. He's asked her to marry him about seven times now. Poor lad.'

As we drew level with the church on top of the hill Jed came to a halt.

'There's something I want to show you,' he said, opening

the wrought-iron gate and ushering me into the
churchyard. 'It's the highlight of the Jed Weyman Tour.'

I followed Jed round to the far corner of the yard,
weaving my way through the worn old gravestones, leaning
like crooked teeth in the moonlight. I felt tingly with fear
and excitement.

'Here we are,' Jed declared proudly.

I peered round him to see a strange little tower
constructed from old stones, standing alone under the
branches of a yew tree. It was about four feet tall with a
large, hexagon-shaped base, tapering off to a pyramid
formation at the top. It was quite unlike anything I had
ever seen before.

'What is it?' I asked.

'It's a grave,' Jed replied, crouching down on the grass
beside it.

I searched in vain for some kind of inscription on the
mossy stone. 'Whose?'

'Will Scarlett's – he was Robin Hood's cousin.'

'Really?' I felt a shiver run up my spine as I imagined
the remains of one of Robin's merry men lying just a few
feet away, right beneath those stones. 'How did he die?'

'He was killed by one of the sheriff's men at Guy of
Gisborne's defeat. They made this gravestone out of some
of the remains from the old church.'

I sat down next to Jed and gazed at the stone. It felt so
weird to be at the graveside of somebody famous. Of
course, Helen and Joe had regularly dragged me off to
Highgate to see Karl Marx's final resting place, but this
seemed so much more intimate. Just Jed and I and Will
Scarlett huddled under the tree in the moonlight.

Jed put his arm around my shoulders. 'I wish you
weren't going tomorrow, Cat. It's so nice having somebody
up here that I can talk to like this. Don't get me wrong, I

love all the banter with the lads, but with you I can talk about anything. And you kiss a lot better than them too!'

That formed the perfect cue for us to take up where we had left off in the woods, only this time it wasn't quite so gentle and timid. This time the true depth of our passion was unleashed – we must have looked just like Pam and Bobby Ewing as we rolled about in the moonlight, tearing at each other's clothes and caressing each other's bodies. I can't believe I've finally felt a penis!

And now, as I lie here once more beneath Jed's Nottingham Forest curtains, my body still throbbing and my mouth still raw, I may officially be a virgin still but I am teetering on the edge of true womanhood. I may not have had my perfumed garden sown by Jed's lance, but at least it's been given a bit of a rake.

Have to go – somebody's knocking . . .

                                        Thursday, 1 August 1984

Dear Anne,

As I sit here on yet another coach being whisked away from Jed yet again, not even the delectable Donna and her offer of a selection of hot beverages and tasty snacks can wrench me from my gloom. As soon as we pulled out of Nottingham bus station and Jed's waving figure disappeared from view, a dull ache started inside me and with every mile that we speed down the motorway, every mile further away from Jed, it is developing into a crushing pain. It's so unfair. I feel as if I've spent most of my life feeling lonely and misunderstood and now when I finally find a soul-mate they have to live in Sherwood flipping Forest!

Feeling a little bit better now. Donna saw me crying and gave me a free carton of Um Bongo and a Lion Bar. She also gave me a piece of invaluable advice after I poured out my heart to her over Jed. Apparently when they were on a Butlin's holiday in Skegness, Donna's fiancé Wayne announced that he was going to stay on and become a Redcoat. Donna was heartbroken. But just a fortnight later he came crawling back proffering his profuse apologies and a box of Neapolitans. Wayne had missed Donna terribly and he couldn't come to terms with the fact that the Knobbly Knees contest was rigged. 'Love always finds a way,' Donna said, before patting me on the head and hurrying off to put out a small fire in the toilet. I have to say the service level on National Express coaches is second to none.

Love *does* always find a way and after what happened last night I am convinced that what Jed and I have is real.

When I heard the knock on the bedroom door last night I knew it was him and my heart began to flutter like the wings of a pit canary.

'Come in,' I whispered, and as the door creaked open Jed's silhouette appeared in the frame.

'I can't sleep,' he whispered.

I shoved my diary down the side of the bed and hoisted myself upright. 'Neither can I.'

'Is there room in there for another?'

I nodded and wriggled back as far as I could against the wall.

Jed gently eased the door shut behind him and tiptoed across the room. He was only wearing a pair of boxer shorts and as he climbed into the bed I could feel the warmth of his skin instantly seeping into mine.

'Come here,' he whispered, wrapping one of his sinewy arms around me. It was the weirdest sensation. Because as we lay like that, with practically every part of our bodies touching, there was no need for kissing or caressing, there was no need for words. For that couple of hours before Jed had to sneak back downstairs, as our lips rested upon each other's and Jed stroked my hair I felt we had become as close as two people could possibly get. And that is why I'm determined not to be sad any more. Jed has shown me what it feels like to experience true love and, from this moment on, I vow that my heart will be full of joy, not bitterness.

Chapter Nineteen

Late Saturday afternoon

I really don't know what made me piss in Sam's bottle of Aqua Libra – all I do know is that when I flung my diary at the wall I was so consumed with anger and resentment I had to seek some kind of revenge. Sam's half-drunk bottle of herbal elixir, sitting so smugly on the kitchen counter, seemed like the perfect victim.

Once I had screwed the lid back on, given the sides of the bottle a quick wipe and returned it to the fridge I reluctantly repaired to the bathroom to take a shower. Sam and the kids would be home shortly, I might as well make the most of what little peace and quiet I had left and, besides, I had a 'hot' dinner date to prepare for. I stripped off and looked at myself in the mirror. My body hadn't changed much since I was a teenager – I still had no cleavage to speak of and over the past few months my loss of appetite had also led to my loss of saddlebags and post-pregnancy paunch. I ran my fingers through my hair and wondered what Jed would have made of my feathered crop. Perhaps I ought to start growing it again.

I told myself not to be so ridiculous and raised my arms to do a quick pit-stop. They were hairier than George Michael's chin. Excellent. Now for the old bikini line. My pubic area was displaying an Afro to make Lenny Kravitz proud – I wondered absentmindedly if my pubes would form a thatch of natty dreads if I left them unattended for much longer. I was delighted to observe that some had broken free and were skanking their way up towards my belly button. This sight, coupled with my greyest, saggiest period pants, should surely put paid to any carnal desires Sam might unleash upon me later. I binned my Bic and stepped into the shower.

Slowly but surely as I let the warm soapy water wash over me I felt a sense of calm set in. As I ran my hands over my body, massaging the suds into my skin, I closed my eyes and imagined that my fingers belonged to Jed, all brown and scuffed and strong. For the first time in years I could almost picture him in my mind, his golden hair glistening wet, his toned arms pulling me towards him, his mouth closing on mine. My heart began pounding, my face began throbbing – I was getting hotter and hotter. Christ I was burning – I was being scalded alive. I wrenched at the shower door and burst out on to the bathroom floor, yelping in agony.

'Wipe my bum-bum!'

'What the —' On top of my third-degree burns some shampoo had managed to trickle into my eyes and I stumbled around blindly, feeling for a towel.

'Wipe my bum-bum!'

I rubbed my eyes furiously, then managed to prise them open a fraction. Just enough to see a pair of miniature buttocks, bent over in my direction, awaiting a wipe. For God's sake!

'Frankie, what have I told you about flushing the toilet when somebody's in the shower?'

Frankie turned to look at me imploringly. 'But I was scared of my poo – it kept growling at me.'

'I'll be the one growling at you in a minute. Where's the towel gone?'

Frankie handed me a square of toilet paper. 'Here you go, Mum, you can use this if you want.'

'Gee, thanks!'

I wiped my smarting eyes on the tissue and turned off the shower – there was no towel anywhere to be seen. Just as I was about to check the airing cupboard, the bathroom door burst open and in charged Megan, like a prepubescent pop princess possessed. Her eyes were staring wildly, her lips were pursed, even her curls seemed to be springing from her head in outrage.

'You little freak!' she screamed, launching herself upon her beloved only brother. 'Look at what you've done to Britney!'

Even I was shocked when I examined the plastic figure being brandished in Megan's fist. With its savagely cropped hairstyle it bore far more of a resemblance to Bryan Adams than Britney Spears.

'She wanted a feather cut,' Frankie whimpered, shuffling behind me, his shorts still around his ankles. 'Don't worry, Meg, it'll grow back.'

Megan glowered. 'No, it won't, you little retard – it's a doll and doll's hair doesn't grow back, ever!' Then, without a word of warning, Megan shoved me to one side and proceeded to batter Frankie about the head with her mutilated mannikin. I slipped on the pool of water that had formed at my feet, lost my footing and twisted the same ankle I had sprained the day before. For the second time that afternoon the bathroom became filled with red mist.

'Right, that's it! Give her to me!' I yelled, grabbing Britney from Megan's grasp. 'I am absolutely sick to death of this. You,' I said, waving Britney in Frankie's face, 'are more than old enough to be wiping your own bum and you,' I turned to Megan and raged, 'should learn to appreciate real music. There's only one place Britney Spears belongs and that's down here.' And before I knew what I was doing I had shoved Britney half-way down the toilet bowl and flushed the chain.

Of course, I instantly regretted it. Megan's screams immediately added a migraine headache and temporary deafness to my list of ailments. Frankie found it pretty amusing, though – until I turned to him and snarled that Scooby-Doo was next on my hit list.

'I hate you, I hate you,' Megan shrieked, retrieving Britney from the toilet. 'You are *so* not my mum any more. Just you wait. I'm going to email Britney and tell her what you've done and she'll come and adopt me and take me to live in her new mansion in Louisiana and then you'll be sorry.'

'*Oh, yeah*', I wanted to shout, '*just try me!*'

'Kids, kids, what's going on?' Sam called up the stairs in his oh-so-calm-toxin-free-I-love-t'ai-chi voice. 'Is everything all right, Caitlin?'

'No, it's not – just do something with them, will you?'

I rushed across the landing to my room and slammed the door. I couldn't let Sam see me crying. I wrapped myself in the duvet, lit up a cigarette and began to sob. What the hell was wrong with me? Why did I always end up hurting the people I loved? Starting with Jed and now my own children. I wasn't fit to be a mother – just as, all those years ago, I wasn't fit to be a girlfriend.

Chapter Twenty

Friday, 2 August 1984

Dear Anne,

The first thing I had to do today upon waking was get over to Karen's for some twenty-four-carat gossip. Actually, the first thing I had to do was face a debriefing from Helen over the Marmite on oatmeal toast. I had already prepared a wide selection of picket-line tales and soup-kitchen anecdotes but, to my surprise, she seemed more concerned with the sleeping arrangements.

'Bob and Jed have to get up every day at five o'clock to go on the picket. Bob says he's never seen Jed so eager to get to the pit.'

'So Jed slept on the sofa?'

'Yes. Honestly, Helen, you wouldn't believe the spirit of solidarity on that picket line – it was quite moving, it really was.'

'And Bob and his wife were there all the time?'

'Where? Oh. Yes, of course they were. Bob keeps getting sent letters from the Coal Board offering him money to go back to work. Scab money, he calls it.'

'And Jed's sister Maxine. What was she like? Was she working in the soup kitchen too?'

'God, is that the time? Look, I really must get round to Karen's.'

Once I had filled Karen in on all the juicy details – which took about three hours forty-five minutes – I knew I had to ask her the burning question that had been plaguing me ever since my graveside encounter on Wednesday night.

'Karen, can I ask you something?'

'What?' Karen whispered.

'Are you okay?' Karen looked rather ashen-faced and the way she was slumped across her bed, eyes glazed, she bore a rather unsettling resemblance to a zombie from one of her dad's video nasties.

'Yeah, I'm fine, just feeling a little tired, that's all.'

'Oh, right. Try eating another biscuit. Anyway, you know when you and Jasper, you know – did it?'

'Yes.' Karen sprang into an upright position, her eyes sparkling back to life.

'Well, what direction did his you-know-what point in?'

Karen grabbed a chocolate digestive from the plate. 'How should I know? I didn't have a compass on me at the time.'

I blushed furiously. God, now I was even becoming a wilting wallflower in front of my best mate.

'No, I don't mean what geographical direction, I mean,' I took a deep breath, 'did it poke straight out or did it sort of go upwards?'

There, I'd said it. I took a biscuit and slumped back against the wall.

Karen began to snigger. 'Oh, I see.'

'It's just that when I imagined a man getting an erection I always assumed that his you-know-what would point straight out, you know, like a Dalek. But Jed's seemed to go right up like a—'

'Tent pole?' Karen offered helpfully.

'Yes, exactly. Like a tent pole.'

We both collapsed in fits of giggles, which wasn't particularly cool or sophisticated of us but I think we were just enormously relieved.

Of course, it all makes perfect sense now. I mean, how else would it be able to go up inside you? Bit by bit I am evolving into a woman. I know it's only a matter of time now before I truly come of age.

Friday, 9 August 1984

Dear Anne,

What I want to know is, why is a blowjob called a blowjob when all you have to do is suck – and maybe give it a bit of a lick? Thank God Karen gave me a demonstration on that carrot. Imagine if I'd been getting intimate with Jed and started to blow on his willy – what would he have thought?

Tonight has been a really good laugh, the perfect antidote to my week of toil in the soil. I have spent the past five days helping Joe harvest his crop of mutated vegetables at the allotment. With their puny physique, his potatoes bear far more of a resemblance to Prince Edward than a King Edward and as for the carrots! Before you think I've taken leave of my senses I only agreed to do it for the money (£2.50 a day – the tight sod) but as I pick at the calluses forming on my hands and rub the aches and pains from my back I have to ask whether I need the money that badly. Surely not even the limited edition Trident Terror mix of 'Two Tribes' is worth resembling Alan Titchmarsh for? And those are just the physical scars. Imagine my embarrassment when I was about to leave for Karen's tonight and Joe gave me a carrier-bag full of misshapen vegetables. 'Take these over to yer woman's,' Joe said with a smile.

Has he no shame? 'Why? What for?'

'Why do you think? To eat, of course.'

I thought of Debbie on a Sunday morning, tottering

around her kitchen, singing along to Shakatak while opening tins of baby carrots and perfectly formed new potatoes. I don't think I've ever seen her with a vegetable peeler in her hand.

'I don't think they eat real vegetables,' I tried to explain.

'Well, all the better – this'll show them what they're missing.'

I pictured Debbie grimacing as she struggled to remove the peel from one of my father's deformed carrots, inadvertently slicing off her false nails in the process or shrieking with horror as a maggot crawled out of one of the rancid potatoes.

'Honestly – I really don't—'

'Oh, g'way, will yer?' said Joe, bustling me out of the door with my bag of worm-riddled wares. 'They'll love it.'

'God, how gross.' Karen shuddered, peering into the bag. 'Why is there so much mud?'

I shrugged my shoulders. 'It's not the mud you should be worried about, it's the wildlife. Don't worry, I'll dump them in the bins on my way home. Where is everyone?' For once Karen's house was eerily quiet.

'Oh, they've gone down to my aunt Shelley's for the night – she's having a sausage sizzle. So, you know what that means?'

I nodded excitedly – it meant raids on the mini-bar and the cigarette supply under Karen's parents' bed followed by boogying to Frankie Goes To Hollywood on the downstairs record-player.

Two Advocaat-and-Babycham cocktails later we were well pissed.

'God, I am so drunk,' I slurred, collapsing on to the couch. Then I remembered what I had always longed to do if left alone in Karen's house. 'I don't suppose we could try on some of your mum's clothes, could we?'

Karen staggered to her feet. 'Yeah, okay – baggsy I get the white leather pencil skirt and boob tube.'

As I teetered towards the mirror in Debbie's gold sandals and purple catsuit I suddenly thought of Maxine. Huh, if she could see me now she wouldn't be so cocky. I backcombed my hair until it was practically sticking out from my head at right angles. That would show her. And as for not being allowed to wear makeup, well, Debbie's huge beauty palette had soon put paid to that. Okay – so I hadn't quite got the hang of blending my colours yet and my eyes looked more like a panda's than Pan's People's, but at least I didn't look like a schoolgirl.

'My name's Maxine and I think I'm so cool just because I work in a cocktail bar and have nipples the size of bricks,' I sneered at my reflection.

Karen burst out laughing as she zipped up her patent thigh-length boots. 'Come on, let's go and get a top-up. When do you think you'll see Jed again?' she asked, as we stumbled back down to the mini-bar.

'Who knows?' I replied, sighing theatrically. Jed had asked the same question in the letter I'd received that morning. I had calculated that one more week's toil at the allotment would provide my coach fare, but I wasn't sure if my parents would let me go again. 'One thing I do know, though.'

'What's that?'

'I'm going to be fully prepared for the pash this time. In fact, I was hoping you might give me some tips.'

Karen nodded eagerly, 'Yeah, of course,' she replied, in her finest woman-of-the-world voice. 'What do you want to know? I can lend you my candle, if you want.'

'Er, no, you're okay. I was just wondering how hard you have to blow – you know, when you give a blow-job?'

Karen choked on her drink, showering her white leather

ensemble with yellow spots. 'How hard do you have to *blow?*'

'Yeah. Should it just be a gentle whisper or should you pretend it's a candle on your birthday cake and really go for it? I don't want to make a fool of myself.'

Karen was on the floor by this point, her patent-clad legs flailing about wildly.

'What is it? What did I say? Come on, Karen, what's so funny?'

'You don't blow, you wally, you suck,' Karen gasped.

'Yeah, yeah, very funny.'

'You do – you have to suck it, like a lollipop.'

'Yeah, right. So why isn't it called a *suckjob* then?' I retorted.

'I don't know,' Karen replied, hoisting herself upright and wiping the streaks of mascara from her face. 'Look, I'll show you, if you like. Where are those vegetables?'

I passed her the carrier-bag.

'Right, a carrot ought to do the trick.' But Karen hadn't figured on my dad's deformed carrots. 'Blimey, what's happened to them? Why are they all such weird shapes? Look at this one.' She held a carrot aloft – with its two spindly heads it looked more like a tuning fork. Finally she found one that was just about the right shape and size to be loosely construed as a penis. 'Okay,' she said, gingerly taking hold of the broad end of the carrot. 'You take hold of his you-know-what by the base and then you bring your lips around the top, like so.' Karen put her mouth round the pointy end of the carrot. Just the thought made me want to retch – as far as I'm concerned carrots are only fractionally better than Brussels sprouts. 'And then you move your mouth up and down as you suck – I won't do that bit because of all the mud, but do you see what I mean?'

I nodded, trying really hard not to look appalled.

'After a while you can go on to do deep throat.' Karen lit a cigarette and reclined on the couch. 'That's what Jasper liked me to do – although I have to say I found it a bit uncomfortable.'

'What's deep throat, then?' I hardly dared ask.

'Deep throat? Oh, it's when you go all the way down.'

I looked at the carrot in horror – it must have been at least six inches long.

I've decided not to bother with blowjobs after all. On balance, sex seems far less complicated – even in the stab-with-a-lance position.

Thursday, 15 August 1984

Dear Anne,

Excellent news! My great-aunt Breda has died. Now, I know you must think that was a very heartless thing to say but, believe me, if you had ever experienced her acid tongue and spinster spite you would understand my lack of remorse. Besides, her departure from this mortal coil means that Helen and Joe will be departing for Dublin tomorrow – leaving me home alone until next Tuesday. Oh, how will I cope without the smell of cabbage and the sound of banjo all weekend? It also means I'll be free to phone Jed without Helen coming into the hall to polish the letterbox every five minutes, like she did tonight. Yippee!

Friday, 16 August 1984

Dear Anne,

11 a.m.

They've gone. It feels so strange to be alone in this house. Strange yet quite wonderful. The first thing I did was take the ten pounds Helen had left on the kitchen table (in case of emergency) and go down to WavyLine and buy the following emergency supplies:

Ten B&H
No Polo mints
One bottle of lemonade
One bottle of Coke
One loaf of sliced white bread
One packet of Findus crispy pancakes
One sack of Alphabites
One box of banana-flavoured Angel Delight
Jackie magazine

As I sit here positively drowning in E numbers and filling my bedroom with smoke I feel deliciously debauched, I really do. A woman of the world, pining for her absent lover, recording her innermost thoughts in her journal and listening to Neil from *The Young Ones* wail about the hole in his shoe.

11.30 a.m.
Am starting to get a little bored. Why did Karen have to agree to help out in the salon this weekend? That Angel Delight has left a really strange taste in my mouth. Wish I'd bought some Polos now.

11.45 a.m.
Well, I must say *Jackie* was a bit of a let-down this week. The photo story was about a girl with glasses who couldn't get a date, yawn, yawn, and the problem page was about whether or not you can get pregnant standing up – again. I think I might start getting *Cosmopolitan.*

Oh, no – somebody's knocking on the door. I bet it's the milkman. Well, there's no way I'm paying him, however long he keeps knocking. Jesus, is he ever going to go away? What the hell is his problem – shouting through the letterbox like that? Oh, my God, oh, it can't be. Can it? It is. It's Jed.

Chapter Twenty-One

Dear Anne,

As Barbra Streisand would say, I am a woman in love – with the emphasis on *woman*. I now know what it means to come of age – to have had my hymen torn asunder. I wish I could report that the world seems an altogether different place, that things have taken on a golden hue, that everything seems familiar and yet different somehow. But, to be perfectly honest, apart from a dull ache in my nether regions things are pretty much the same as they've always been. Externally anyhow. But in my heart it feels as if a gaping chasm has been filled.

When I flung open the front door and found Jed standing there, grinning from ear to ear, with his motorbike helmet in one hand and a tin of Spam in the other, I thought I was going to combust with joy.

'I – I thought you were the milkman,' I stammered, rooted to the spot.

Jed laughed. 'Sorry, madam, I am the Spam man. How many tins would you like today?'

'Oh, just the one, please,' I replied, trying to regain my composure. 'Would you like to come in for a cup of tea – or do you have to get on with your deliveries?'

'Oh, a tea would be lovely and I wouldn't mind a Spam sandwich if you've got one going spare. It's a bit of a trek from the depot to your house, you know.'

Still trembling slightly I led Jed into the kitchen where I prepared a mountain of Spam sandwiches on snowy white, ready-sliced bread.

'I still can't believe you're really here.' I sighed, pouring us both a glass of Coke.

'You don't mind, do you?' Jed asked anxiously. 'It's just that when you told me yesterday that your parents were going away I thought I'd pay you a surprise visit. I was going to do it next month for your birthday but you'll be back at school then, and the way the strike's going, I may have to sell the bike pretty soon.'

'Are things that bad?'

'Aye, it's getting that way. Me mam's even talking about putting her gold-plated horse's head in hock! So, do I get a kiss for coming all this way to see you?'

I stood up and shuffled around the kitchen table towards him. 'I don't do this kind of thing with any of my other delivery men, you know,' I said, as I drew level with Jed.

'I should hope not,' Jed replied, getting to his feet. 'God, I've missed you, Cat, give us a hug.'

I can't begin to describe how good it felt to be back in his arms – like little Jimmy Krankie, I just couldn't stop grinning.

'Well, now that I'm the guest of honour I hope I'm going to get a guided tour of Pinner.'

I stopped grinning. How could Pinner possibly compete with Blidworth and its rich history of Robin Hood?

'You see that house over there? The one with the red door?'

Jed peered over my shoulder across the tree-lined avenue. 'Aye.'

'Well, that's where Bob Holness lives.'

And, as if on cue, the door swung open and out stepped His Royal Holness, all tangerine tan and glistening teeth.

'Ooh, can I have a pee, please, Bob?' Jed sneered, under his breath. I could tell he was distinctly unimpressed.

'How dare you ridicule our resident star of tea-time TV?' I shook my head in mock disgust at Jed's ignorance.

'Oh, I'm sorry. I'm sure in five hundred years' time Bob Holness will have gone down in national folklore alongside Robin Hood.'

'Very funny. Well, I did warn you. Pinner is the boredom capital of the world, but at least our local celebrities are still alive. The witch from *Rent-a-Ghost* lives just round the corner.'

Jed clutched the trunk of a tree for support. 'You're kidding! Hazel the McWitch lives here? Take me to her immediately – I'm her biggest fan!'

'Well, at least you're guaranteed a celebrity-sighting in Pinner,' I retorted. Secretly I was rather impressed by Bob Holness's appearance – it was the first time I'd seen him outside *Blockbusters*. He looks a lot smaller in real life.

'And how do you know Will Scarlett wasn't with us that night?' Jed whispered ominously. 'Watching over us like a guardian angel?'

I shivered. 'Come on, let's go to the park.'

When we had stationed ourselves by the pond in Pinner Memorial Park, surrounded by supplies of Coke and crisps, Jed began to confide in me.

'I am so sick of this bloody strike,' he said, throwing a handful of broken crisps to the ducks. 'It's different for me dad. He sees it as some kind of historical struggle – this bloody great battle between good and evil – but I just can't see the point. I'm not sure what we're fighting for.'

'How do you mean?'

'Well, why should I fight for the right to be a miner? To crawl around in the dirt, miles underground just to make some other bugger rich. Where's the glory in that? Where's the glory in dying at fifty of emphysema? I tell you, Cat, as soon as strike's over I'm out of there.'

'Oh.' I stared at the pond, where a flotilla of ducks was steaming its way over to us.

'Don't look so gloomy. It means I'll be coming down to your neck of the woods.'

I looked at Jed hopefully. 'What do you think you'll do? For work, I mean.'

'Oh, I don't know, but I'm bound to find summat – this is the eighties, everything's booming apart from the coal mines. As long as it's above ground I don't care. I could be a groundsman and look after these little fellas.' Jed nodded at the ducks waddling their way up the bank towards him and scattered the rest of his crisps on the grass. 'You never know – if things work out, in a couple of years' time we could have a place together. I could help you through college. I could even go to night school meself.'

As soon as the words left his mouth an image formed in my mind. Jed and I lying together on a bed in a tiny studio flat, Jed tanned and muscular from his outdoor job, me pale and interesting, scribbling away in my notebook. Helping each other with our college assignments before making love all night long. It all sounded so perfect, so preordained.

Without saying another word we got to our feet and headed home. With every step of the way my heart pounded louder at the thought of what was to come (and I mean that quite literally!). By the time we got to my bedroom I was sure Jed could hear the deafening thud. Hoping to drown it out, I put 'Careless Whisper' on the record-player and cranked up the volume. As Jed gently peeled off my vest top two voices began squabbling inside my head. *Don't let him do it,* one voice urged, *you have no breasts, you have no experience!* While another, quite shameless voice (it even had a slight American drawl) urged me to abandon all inhibitions and rip off his clothes too! On and on the voices raged within my head, on and on my heart pounded within my ribcage, and on and on George Michael echoed around my bedroom. Until suddenly we were both naked under the duvet.

'Hello,' Jed whispered, cupping my face in his hands.

'Hello,' I whispered back. My whole body was shivering and, for some reason, even my teeth were chattering.

'Are you okay?' Jed asked, stroking my hair away from my face.

I nodded cautiously and winced as the needle on the record-player jerked its way back to the rest. There was a plop of vinyl upon vinyl and then – humiliation to end all humiliation – Neil from *The Young Ones* began wailing about the hole in his shoe. Why hadn't I remembered my earlier play-list?

Jed stretched out a muscular arm and turned down the volume. 'Can I ask you something, Cat?'

'It's not mine, honestly. Well, it is, but it was a mistake. I thought it was funny at first but—'

'I'm not talking about the record, although it does confirm my suspicions about your music taste. No, I, er, just wondered. Are you? Have you? Is this your first time, you know, with a bloke?'

It's funny, really, because I had planned all along to lie, to regale Jed with tales of my sexual prowess, but when it came down to it, when I found myself lying there naked in his arms, I felt no need to prove anything to him. For the first time in my life I felt confident being myself.

'Yes, it is,' I replied, staring at the ridge of muscle rippling across his chest.

Jed took my hands in his. 'I see. Well, listen, I don't want you to do anything you don't feel ready for. I don't

want you feeling pressured into anything. I'm happy just to
lie here kissing you all afternoon. You just let me know
what *you* want to do.'

I felt strangely close to tears. The voices in my head had
fallen silent, and as we lay there kissing, I knew that the
time was right. And when it did eventually happen, when I
felt Jed ease himself inside me it felt like the most natural
thing in the world, which I suppose it is, really, isn't it?

Afternoon faded into evening and still we remained in
bed. I got up only to answer a phone call from Helen.

'Oh, everything's fine. Just doing a bit of reading before I
go round to Karen's.'

And from Karen.

'*Oh, my God!* Jed's here. Came down on his motorbike
for a surprise. And guess what, my perfumed garden has
been sown – well, not sown literally because he used a
johnny, but you know what I mean. Of course you can –
come round tomorrow night, about seven.'

We dined on a midnight feast of Findus crispy pancakes
and Angel Delight, and drifted off to sleep just as the pale
white light of dawn began to filter its way through the
curtains.

Our lips were the first to awake. Gently pressing against
each other until they formed a kiss. The rest of our bodies
followed sleepily, our limbs wrapping their way round each
other until once again I felt that slight burning sensation
and Jed was inside me.

'Good morning,' he whispered, pressing himself against
me.

I clung to him and smiled – I felt warm and tingly all
over. I don't think I'd ever felt so good on waking – not
even Christmas morning could compete.

After we made love Jed insisted on going downstairs to
make some tea. I took the opportunity to look in the

mirror. I couldn't believe the image staring back at me: my external appearance could not be further removed from the way I was feeling inside. With my matted mane and bloodshot eyes I looked more like an alley cat than a sex kitten! I tugged a brush through my hair and wiped the mascara from my cheeks before diving back into bed.

'So, what have you got in store for me today?' Jed asked, as he returned to the room with two steaming mugs of tea. 'The *Rent-a-Ghost* tour of Pinner or perhaps we could go and stalk Ronnie Barker?'

In the end we went to Watford market. Jed managed to haggle me a copy of 'London Calling' by the Clash for 99p. 'It's time you listened to some decent music.' And I spent the rest of Helen's emergency fund on a bottle of Merrydown cider.

By the time we got home it was gone seven and Karen was waiting on the doorstep. I glowed with pride when I noticed her jaw drop open in awe.

'Karen, this is Jed.'

'Hello,' she said, blushing furiously

'All right?' Jed said, with a grin. 'I've been hearing a lot about you. I understand you're a big fan of Shakin' Stevens.'

Karen stared at me blankly.

'Take no notice of him,' I said, unlocking the door. 'He fancies himself as a bit of a comedian.'

'Oh, right.' I don't think I'd ever seen Karen so dumbstruck. It was great to be the confident one for once.

'He's gorgeous,' she hissed, the minute Jed went upstairs to fetch an ashtray.

I shrugged nonchalantly as I poured out three glasses of cider.

'Cat tells me you're a bit of a Mystic Meg on the quiet.' Jed placed the ashtray on the kitchen table and sat down on the chair next to mine. My heart skipped a beat as I felt his hand rest upon my bare knee.

Once again Karen looked uncharacteristically embarrassed. 'Well, I do a bit of tarot reading,' she replied, taking a large gulp of cider.

'Sound. You couldn't give me a reading, could you? I wouldn't mind knowing what the future's got in store.' Jed threw me a sideways smile.

Karen fumbled around in her rucksack – I couldn't help noticing she still had *Jazzy J* written in Tippex across the strap. 'Okay,' she said, placing the deck of cards on the table in front of her. 'I haven't been doing this all that long, so you'll have to bear with me.'

'Sure.' Jed pulled his chair right up to the table and rubbed his hands together eagerly.

Karen picked up the cards and began to shuffle. 'Do you have a specific question in mind? Is there anything in particular you'd like to ask the cards?'

'Yeah. I want to know if I'm ever going to get away from the bloody pit,' Jed replied. 'Am I ever going to be anything other than a miner? I guess I really don't want to pick the ace of spades!' he added, with a chuckle.

'They're tarot cards not playing-cards, stupid,' I said, raising my eyebrows at Karen.

Karen giggled and passed the pack to Jed. 'Okay, give them a good shuffle and try to concentrate on the question you want answered while you're doing it.'

Jed took the cards and shuffled them with the speed and ease of Paul Daniels – I half expected him to begin throwing them in an arc formation from one hand to the other.

'Right,' he said, handing them back to Karen. 'Now what?'

'Now,' Karen responded in her finest Mystic Meg voice, 'I am going to lay the cards in the Celtic Cross Spread.'

Jed looked at me quizzically.

'Well, the first card represents you,' Karen announced, holding a card aloft. It bore a picture of a court-jester type figure so engrossed in sniffing a rose he seemed blissfully unaware he was about to fall off a cliff.

'It's the Fool, 'I shrieked, clapping my hands with delight.

'Oh, very funny.' Jed gave me a playful dig in the ribs. 'Well, that's a good start.'

'It is, actually,' Karen said reassuringly. 'The Fool denotes a fresh new beginning, involving joy and excitement. It's the same card Jasper got three weeks before he went to Israel,' she added bitterly.

'Oh, well, I don't want that much of a new beginning,' Jed responded, looking a little concerned. 'London will do me.'

'Okay, well, the next card denotes possibilities or problems.' The card Karen was holding displayed a rather haughty-looking Queen of Swords. 'Right, well, as this card is reversed I'm afraid it symbolises a bit of a problem. Is there somebody close to you who comes across as being cold and aloof? Somebody who can be harshly critical and extremely stubborn?'

Jed let out a bitter snort. 'Aye. Me loving sister.'

I couldn't help smiling smugly.

'Well, be on your guard with her as she may present a bit of an obstacle.'

Jed nodded.

Karen picked up another card from the spread. 'The Ace of Swords reversed,' she announced, before leafing through her instruction book. 'Sorry about this – I haven't got them all memorised yet. Right, well, this card represents your best course of action and it is telling you not to put any more pressure on a particular person or situation or you are in danger of pushing them over the edge.'

Jed stared at the card blankly.

'Now I'm going to look at your past influences,' Karen declared, as she picked up the fourth card. 'Pass us a fag, Cait.'

I lit her a cigarette and passed it over. I had to admit I was quite impressed with the professionalism of Karen's reading – she had obviously been making the most of all her spare time since Jasper left.

'Okay, you've got the Three of Wands reversed, which basically means you've been far too passive, waiting for life to happen to you rather than taking any action yourself.'

Jed nodded enthusiastically.

'Now I'm going to take a look at the current atmosphere in your life.' Karen picked up a card and flicked through her book. 'It says here that you are fed up with the general boredom of your life. You need to shake yourself out of this rut by taking a holiday, redecorating your surroundings or doing something completely new.'

'Bloody hell, she's pretty good at this, isn't she?' Jed remarked.

I beamed with pride at my fortune-telling friend. 'Spot on,' I replied. 'Your bedroom could certainly do with a makeover – you could get rid of those awful curtains for a start.'

'Oi, they're Nottingham Forest's finest,' Jed retorted, 'So, come on, then, do they tell you anything about the future? Can you see what's going to happen to me?'

Karen picked up a card with three swords on it. 'Well, this card denotes your short-term future. Oh.' Jed and I stared at Karen staring at the card. She suddenly looked a bit embarrassed. 'Well, this card seems to suggest that you're going to be involved in some kind of love triangle.'

'God, that's exactly what I got,' I exclaimed, feeling a little cold inside.

Jed looked bewildered. 'What do you mean, love triangle?'

'Well, I'd have thought that was pretty obvious,' I couldn't help snapping. Could Jed have somebody else on the side?

'Not necessarily,' Karen replied, studying her book. 'It says in here that the triangle could take many forms. It could be between you, your mother and your sister or you, your best friend and your girlfriend. However, all three people are going to get hurt through the choices that will have to be made.'

All three of us sat in silence for a moment.

'Well, I'll just have to keep me eye on you, then, won't I?' said Jed, giving my hand a squeeze. 'I saw the way you were looking at Tom Whittaker that night in the Welfare.'

I squeezed his hand back and began to laugh. What was I worrying about? It was only a stupid tarot card – they couldn't all be right.

Karen breathed a sigh of relief. 'Right, let's take a look at your home environment. You've drawn the High Priestess, which means . . . which means . . .' Karen furrowed her brow. 'Hold on a second.' She flicked through the book, 'Okay, it means that you need to trust your intuition and don't take things at face value – look for the answers to your questions within your own heart.'

Jed frowned slightly. 'Okay.'

'And finally, 'Karen said, with a flourish, 'your long-term future.'

Jed's face lit up expectantly, 'Yes?'

'Oh.'

'What? What is it?' I asked anxiously, something about the frown on Karen's face told me it wasn't prophesying a studio flat in London with a Pulitzer Prize-winning lover.

'I just need to double-check,' Karen muttered, flicking through her book once more. 'Hmm.'

'Come on, it can't be that bad. Can it?' Jed said, laughing nervously.

'Well, I'm afraid it says here that the Ten of Swords reversed means great pain or heartache will be inflicted upon you intentionally by a person or situation. Sorry.'

Well, this was turning into a great night! Part of me was wishing that Karen had stayed at home with her chocolate digestives and Tears For Fears and forecast her own doom. Judging by her hangdog expression I think Karen was sharing these feelings.

'Bloody hell, I wish I'd never asked now,' said Jed, reaching for the bottle of cider, 'Couldn't you have just told me that Fate saw me wearing yellow at a jumble sale or summat? That's what Mystic Meg would have said.'

Karen and I laughed weakly.

'Oh, come on, don't look so depressed – you're not the ones about to suffer great pain or heartache.' Jed clutched his chest theatrically, 'Please don't do it to me, Cat, don't run off with Tommy Whittaker, have some compassion.'

I laughed and gave him a hug, 'Oh, all right, then, if you insist.' The thought of me cheating on Jed with anybody else was too ludicrous even to contemplate – I was far too worried the reverse might happen.

Karen put her cards back into her bag and got to her feet. 'I really ought to be going,' she said sheepishly. 'My dad's got a new video nasty out – *Revenge of the Roller-boot Ripper*. It was lovely to meet you, Jed.'

Jed smiled as he stood up. 'Yes, you too, even if you did thoroughly depress me.'

'I'm so sorry.' Karen's face blushed crimson. 'Like I said, I'm new to the tarot so I'm sure it wasn't an accurate reading.'

'Hey, don't worry, I'm only messing. It was really interesting to see how it works, but I think I'll stick to playing-cards in future – I seem to have a bit more luck with them.'

'Yeah, he's the village Snap champion,' I piped up, before getting tickled almost to death.

After Karen left we went straight up to bed and it was wonderful to feel consumed by passion rather than nerves. It didn't hurt as much either. Afterwards we lay under the open curtains, sharing a cigarette and gazing up at the violet sky, without saying a word, for a long, long time. Finally Jed broke the silence to voice my own thoughts: 'I'm dreading leaving tomorrow.'

I snuggled up to his chest. 'Me too.'

Jed kissed the top of my head. 'Meeting you, it's like I've finally woken up. I've finally realised where I belong and what I should be doing. Or, rather, where I *don't* belong and what I *shouldn't* be doing. I just feel as if I've wasted too much time. I don't want to waste another second.'

My eyes filled with tears.

'Hey – what's up?' Jed wiped my face with the side of his thumb. 'Don't get upset.'

'I'm not, I'm just so, so happy. I didn't think it was possible to feel like this.'

Jed laughed. 'Me neither. Oh, sod it, we've waited this long, what's another couple of months apart? The strike'll be won once winter sets in and then we can start to make proper plans. But until then,' Jed rolled himself on top of me, 'I really think we should make the most of our time together.'

We stayed in bed for as long as possible on Sunday morning before Jed took me for lunch (or should I say dinner?) at Fletcher's Fish and Chip Bar.

'One day I'll take you out for a slap-up meal somewhere

dead posh,' Jed said, handing me the squeezy bottle of ketchup.

But as our eyes met across the blue and white plastic tablecloth I knew that, for as long as I lived, no dinner date would ever beat that first one with Jed. Never again would a chip taste so saltily succulent, never would the vinegar-soaked batter encasing a piece of cod taste so beautifully bitter-sweet.

Chapter Twenty-Two

Early Saturday evening

'Caitlin, I've booked a table for eight o'clock at the Peacock Hotel.'

As soon as I heard Sam's voice calling up the stairs I stuffed my diary and cigarettes inside the record-player and crammed about half a packet of Polos into my mouth.

'Can I come in?' Sam enquired, from the other side of the door.

'Hold on.' I scanned the room frantically for something to wear. I grabbed my Frankie T-shirt from the bedside cabinet, pulled it over my head and arranged the duvet across my lap. 'Okay.'

Sam edged his way cautiously around the door. 'I thought you might like a drink.'

'What is it?' I asked, eyeing the pale yellow beverage suspiciously.

'Aqua Libra. It's an excellent pick-me-up, crammed full of essential vitamins. Have you been smoking?' Sam sniffed the room like a suspicious beagle.

'No,' I replied sulkily, grinding the Polos between my teeth.

Sam placed my Aqua Urethra cocktail next to Jed's Davy lamp on the bedside cabinet. 'Well, I hope you're getting changed for dinner,' he said, with a nervous laugh.

'Why? What's wrong with what I've got on?' I demanded,

glancing down at my T-shirt. 'Eighties retro is all the rage at the moment, Sam.'

'Yes, but aren't you supposed to spend a fortune on modern interpretations rather than drag out the genuine article from— Where on earth have you been keeping it all these years? The garden shed?'

'Oh, for Christ's sake, Sam. You ought to take this T-shirt's advice and RELAX!' I leapt to my feet and pointed at the faded black lettering.

Sam's eyes seemed to be fixed on something a bit further down. I followed his gaze to my raga-muff, sprouting out from beneath the frayed edge of off-white cotton. 'Oh, for God's sake, is that all you can think about?'

Sam's face flushed. 'Well, *think about it*'s all I can do, these days, isn't it?'

I stared at him defiantly and, as usual, Sam's eyes were the first to break away.

'I'm sorry, Caitlin, I'll go and see to the kids while you finish getting ready,' and with that he turned and shuffled out of the door.

It didn't take me long to finish getting ready – only as long as it takes to locate one's nastiest pair of knickers, pull on a frayed denim mini-skirt, stuff a miniature Davy lamp in the pocket and run a comb through one's hair (the crop rather than the Afro). By the time I got downstairs Karen had arrived, all fluffy blonde mane and Britney videos.

'Ooh, thanks, Auntie Karen. Look, Dad, look what Auntie Karen's got me. You're *so* the best auntie in the world!' Megan shot me daggers as she flounced into the living room, clutching her new tape to her chest.

'I see you still have a fondness for video nasties, then,' I remarked, from the kitchen doorway.

Karen turned in surprise. 'What? Oh, right. Well, I thought

Megan and I might practise our dance routines a little later on. Nice outfit, by the way.'

Karen and Sam were both staring at my T-shirt. Karen stifling a grin, Sam a grimace.

'Auntie Karen, can I French-plait your hair?' Frankie ran over to Karen and gazed up at her imploringly.

'Yes, of course you can, sweetie, as soon as Mummy and Daddy have gone. I've got something for you too,' Karen pulled a purple-clad plastic doll from her bag. 'It's Daphne from Scooby-Doo.'

Frankie gazed at the doll in awe. 'Oh, wow! Look, Mum, look at her hair.'

I felt a stab of guilt. We were already one day into the bank-holiday weekend and I hadn't done anything for my kids except scream at them and flush their toys down the toilet. How dare Karen come over here and make me feel even worse about myself? How dare she be so effortlessly kind and affectionate? I looked at Karen, Sam and Frankie all standing there staring at me, and felt like some hapless tourist who had carelessly meandered into their happy family snapshot. If Sam had been married to Karen their bank-holiday weekend would have been a blissful bonanza of cinema trips, family tickets and meal deals.

But it wasn't my fault, really – how could it be? I was never meant to be here – I didn't deserve to be here. I was just a big impostor.

'I'm going to get my handbag,' I muttered, choking back the tears as I fled upstairs.

'Are you okay?' Karen asked, poking her head around the bathroom door.

I looked up from the wash-basin. 'Yeah, fine. Just a little tired, that's all. I didn't get much sleep last night.' I gave my eyes one more douse with cold water before pressing a towel over my face.

Karen perched herself down on the edge of the bath. 'Look, if it's about what happened last night, you know, with the ouija board I've got a confession to make.'

I lowered the towel and looked over at Karen. She was wringing her hands anxiously in her lap.

'I just wanted to get you back for the Cadbury Finger joke. I never meant to upset you. I should have thought. I'm sorry.'

So Karen had been moving the glass, after all. Perhaps if she had owned up immediately it would have made a difference, but not now. Not now that I had unleashed the memories. Now there was no going back.

'It was just all such a long time ago. I had no idea it would still upset you. You have to get over him, Cait. You can't stay trapped in what-ifs and if-onlys for the rest of your life.'

'No, you're right,' I replied. 'Maybe one day you have to find the answers to those questions. Maybe one day you have to find out – what if?'

'Oh, God, you're not going to do anything stupid, are you, Cait? I'd never forgive myself if my stupid prank led to you – well, broke up your marriage. Can't you see what a wonderful husband you've got in Sam? Can't you see how much he loves you?'

'Jed loved me,' I murmured, smearing moisturiser around my swollen eyes.

'Yes, but Jed—'

'Don't worry, Karen, there's no way any of this is your fault. It was bound to happen eventually. Is it really so bad of me to want to know what might have been?'

Karen shook her head sorrowfully. 'No, I suppose not. Just don't forget you've got two lovely kids and a husband who adores you, that's all.'

I looked at my adoring husband over the top of my gold-embossed menu and sighed. What on earth made him think

I'd want to come to a restaurant that didn't serve chips? They didn't even have them hiding under their French alias of *pommes frites!* I studied the menu once more for something vaguely appealing. The food on offer perfectly reflected the décor of the Peacock Hotel – a hollow victory of style over substance. I gazed up at the mock Tudor beams, undoubtedly lovingly carved from MDF, and glanced at the sea of sepia faces staring down at me from the wall – purchased, no doubt, from Old Artefacts Are Us or whoever supplied these olde-worlde pubs with their pseudo-antique props. I returned to the menu. There was absolutely nothing appetising about the appetisers, unless you enjoy un-wrapping a 'delicious' filo parcel of rotting cheese or get off on the thought of a pulverised duck's liver. And as for the main courses, well, the staple ingredient might be okay – personally I don't have anything against a piece of steak or chicken or even lamb, for that matter – but why, oh, why do they have to go and ruin it by dressing them in the most vile concoctions imaginable? Whoever thought that chicken wrapped in wilted spinach leaves made a mouthwatering combo had obviously not eaten for quite some time. What on earth was wrong with golden breadcrumbs?

And then, of course, there was the gut-churning prose. Whoever wrote the menu really ought to consider a career as a short-story writer for *Gal Pal* magazine. 'A butterfly of chicken breast, resting gently on a bed of mashed potato, infused with the cheeses of three different counties and drizzled in a delightful sun-dried tomato sauce.' Or, even better, 'Our staff will be delighted to introduce you to our desserts.' As our waiter headed over to our table, notebook at the ready, I pictured him leading a rather bashful-looking slice of choco-late cake by the hand: 'Mr Delaney and Ms Kennedy, it is a great honour for me to introduce you to our Belgian Truffle Gateau, hand-baked on the banks of the river Seine and lovingly dusted in powdered sugar.'

'Caitlin?'

'What? Oh, pleased to meet you.' I automatically extended my hand, feeling somewhat dazed.

The waiter looked at me, bewildered, before giving my hand a cursory shake. 'Pleased to meet you too, madam. Now, what will it be for the starter?'

I stared at the menu frantically. 'Oh, er, could you acquaint me with the soup of the day?' Surely I couldn't go too far wrong with a humble bowl of soup.

'Certainly, madam. Our soup of the day is carrot and broccoli, infused with the juice of a pomegranate.'

I nearly hurled all over the starched linen tablecloth at the thought. 'Oh, on second thoughts I think I'll have the duck liver pâté.'

'Excellent choice,' the waiter lied. 'And for your main course?'

'Could I have the medallion of lamb, nestling on a bed of wild saffron rice and suffused with a lime and coriander sauce?'

'Certainly. And can I get you something to drink?' The waiter automatically turned to my tediously teetotal husband. 'Would Sir like to see the wine list?'

'Oh, there's no point showing that to him, 'I piped up, 'unless, of course, you stock low-alcohol Lambrini in your wine cellar. I hear two thousand and one was a particularly good vintage.'

'I'll have whatever my wife would like,' Sam responded defiantly.

I grabbed the list and scanned it for the highest alcohol content. 'We'll have a bottle of Double Bay chardonnay, please.'

The waiter sniffed. 'Right you are, madam.'

My first glass of wine barely touched the sides: getting pissed was the only way to numb the excruciating embarrassment of being one half of the silent couple from hell. Sam and I used to laugh at such couples back in the good old days – we were so smug then, maybe a little too smug, as our eyes scanned the restaurant for our prey. Oh, how we'd laugh at the deafening silence emanating from their table, the vacant, sulky stares, the sullen demolition of the meal. It was only now I was beginning to see how much we had needed those couples to detract from our own shortcomings, to reassure ourselves that at least we weren't that bad, at least we had our kids and careers to talk about. But not any more. I couldn't think of a single thing I wanted to say to Sam. Fortunately, however, we were in the presence of an even greater evil: the obnoxious couple from hell were seated to our right and taking great pleasure in stealing our limelight.

'I wish to make a complaint!' the man bellowed across the restaurant, all beetroot face and bluster. He was brandishing a piece of meat on a fork causing great drops of French onion and Burgundy gravy to plop on to the pristine tablecloth below. He was about fifty and clad in the red braces and stripy shirt that only a merchant banker would wear. It was difficult to tell how old his wife was: the way she was slumped across the table pouring wine down her throat she looked like one of the living dead. Her skew-whiff hairpiece and smeared makeup weren't doing her any favours either.

'I'm sorry, sir. What seems to be the problem?' Our waiter was back, and if he'd possessed a forelock it would have been tugged right out by the roots.

'This steak is the problem. It's bloody disgusting. Get me the manager.'

'I'm sorry, sir, the manager has gone away for the weekend. Perhaps I could get you something else? Would Sir care to have another look at the menu?'

'You've got to be joking. I wouldn't eat another morsel in this place. Call the manager immediately.'

'I'm sorry, sir, the manager is in Shepton Mallet visiting

his niece. Now, what seems to be the problem with the steak?'

'What seems to be the problem?' The man waved it around wildly, splattering the waiter's shirt with brown flecks. 'It's more gristle than meat – that's the problem. I wouldn't give it to my dog!'

'No, she had the lamb!' I couldn't resist commenting with a guffaw.

'Caitlin,' Sam hissed, 'they might hear you.'

'So what? Stuck-up pricks. Honestly, Sam, I don't know why you brought me here. It's hardly my kind of place.' I refilled my glass with wine. Sam's remained virtually untouched.

'What's wrong with it?'

'It's so poncy and pretentious. Why couldn't we have gone to a Pizza Hut or something?'

To my surprise Sam hit the table with his hand – a little bit harder and I'm sure it would have made a noise. He looked at me with disgust. 'Well, I'm so sorry for trying to make an effort here. I'm so sorry for wanting to take my wife somewhere nice. Perhaps I should have just taken you to the local working-men's club – is that more *your kind of place?*' Sam picked up his glass and drained it in one. 'Yeah, I'm sure you'd love that, wouldn't you? A night of fruit machines and pork scratchings. God, I'm so sorry I didn't follow my dad into the building trade. Then you could have dragged our kids down to the pub every Friday night to get the housekeeping off me before I pissed it up the wall. Later on our kids could have lain awake listening to me beat the crap out of you and not be able to do a thing about it. Is that more *your kind of thing?* Well, I'm so sorry, Caitlin, for wanting something a bit better for my family.' Sam fumbled in his pocket for his wallet. His hands shook as he scattered a sheaf of notes on the table. 'Come on, we're going.'

'But—'

'But what? Do you know something, Caitlin? I'm getting a little sick of constantly being made to feel inferior. All I want to do is be a good husband and father. Why do you think I spend so much time and effort trying to improve myself? It's all for you, but I can't compete, can I?'

'Can't compete with what? I don't know what you're talking about.' My heart was pounding as I attempted to take his hand, but he snatched it away.

'I'm not stupid, Caitlin. Do you think I don't know what's going on? I saw that bloody lamp. I know what that T-shirt's about. You've been thinking about him again, haven't you?'

I looked down at the tablecloth and my teeth began to chatter.

'Well, I've had enough – I'm sick of trying.' And with that Sam turned and marched out of the restaurant.

As I fumbled for my handbag and stumbled to my feet I realised that the entire restaurant had fallen silent and all eyes were on me. Even the gristle-hating grumbler and his lush of a wife were looking at me in horror. I heard my chair clatter to the floor as I turned on my heel and fled.

Unsurprisingly the drive home was silent. I think we were both too close to tears to risk talking. As soon as we got home, Sam went upstairs to bed, leaving me to make my awkward excuses to a worried Karen and a fed-up couple of kids. 'But we haven't finished watching the Britney video,' Megan wailed.

'I'm only half-way through the plait,' Frankie joined in.

'Oh, God, what happened?' Karen whispered, following me into the kitchen, where I poured us both a stiff lemon squash and vodka.

'He knows,' I said glumly. 'Sam knows what I've been thinking about and he wants me to make a choice. I think he's had enough of me.' I was snivelling now like a baby.

Karen tore off a piece of kitchen roll and handed it to me. 'Oh, come on, there's no way Sam would ever finish it with you. He's angry, Cait – you both are – and you've got to be careful. There's a very good reason why anger is just one little letter away from danger, you know.'

I smiled weakly through my tears. 'And who told you that? Oprah, I suppose.'

'No. Actually it was Sally Jesse Raphael, but that's beside the point. You have to sort things out with Sam. You can't let your anger with the past keep ruining your chances of a happy future.'

'I know. I know.' But as I nodded to Karen and took another gulp of my drink all I really knew for sure was that any future I had lay firmly rooted in my past.

Chapter Twenty-Three

Monday, 9 September 1984

Dear Anne,

Yet again I have been neglecting you, but now that I have Jed to write to there seems little point in replicating my musings in my diary. Besides, I don't think my wrist could take the strain, especially now that school has started and I'll have heaps of homework on top of everything else. I hope you don't think I'm just a fair-weather friend – if anything I must be a bleak-weather friend – but don't we all tend to turn to our diaries in times of sorrow rather than joy? Our diary is the one companion who will listen to our outpourings of woe without uttering a patronising remark, stifling a yawn or stuffing a chocolate biscuit. I know I can count on you, Anne, to be there for me in times of stress, to lend an ear when I can't turn to Jed because I don't want him thinking I'm a miserable cow. Times like this evening, for example.

Oh, Anne, how I hate school! As I traipsed into my maths class with a heavy heart and even heavier rucksack I wanted to hang my head and wail. I don't think I've ever felt so out of place – apart from at the Methodist disco – and, like the disco, the cause of my misery was exactly the same. I felt like a woman surrounded by children, a woman trapped inside a child's uniform, trapped inside a child's body. I punched 55378008 into my calculator and turned it upside down. Must I remain BOOBLESS for the rest of my days? Will I never get a late surge of hormones to my chest area? I can't believe I'm going to be sixteen next week and my bra size is still a measly 32AA!

Saturday, 21 September 1984

Dear Anne,

In an attempt to prove to you that I am not just a bleak-weather friend I am writing to you in the best of birthday cheer. So, I have finally come of age. Well, of course I really came of age some weeks ago, but at least it is now official. I am finally allowed to buy cigarettes, elope and have sex – who wants the right to vote in this police state anyhow?

I got an extra-long letter from Jed this morning, together with a homemade card and a book. On the card he had printed 'Birthday Greetings from Blidworth' above a heart-shaped collage of leaves. Each leaf had been carefully chosen for its colour, emanating from a bright yellow centre into waves of orange, red and finally green. It was beautiful. Inside he had enclosed a piece of stone chipped from Will Scarlett's grave.

'Ooh, that's really spooky.' Karen shivered when I showed it to her.

'Why?' I asked, bewildered. I was overjoyed to have something tangible to remind me of Jed, apart from the little Davy lamp. One of these days I'm going to have to pluck up the courage to ask him for a photograph.

'Well, you shouldn't desecrate somebody's grave like that – they may come back to haunt you.'

'Oh, Karen, you've been watching too many of those creepy videos. Speaking of watching things, I don't suppose we could put *Robin of Sherwood* on, could we? It is my birthday.'

I love watching Michael Praed and pretending he's Jed. Imagining it's me being swept into his arms is the closest I can get to the real thing at the moment. I think I'm going to read the book Jed sent me. It's called *On The Road* and inside the cover Jed has written, 'To my very own Sal Paradise', whatever that means.

Sunday, 22 September 1984

Dear Anne,

Sal Paradise is a young writer who meets an outgoing character called Dean Moriarty and together they travel across America – 'on the road'. Maybe one day Jed and I will travel the world – I can just see it now, me on the back of his motorbike clinging to him tightly, like a modern-day Robin and Marian, with the wind in my hair and a thrill in my heart, visiting all the places and meeting all the characters who will go on to feature in my novels, and encouraging Jed to write a book of his own. Since meeting Jed I feel as if the whole world is opening up to me – like some war-time liberator he has marched into my prison of a life and flung open the door.

Saturday, 28 September 1984

Dear Anne,

Spent the afternoon at the cinema with Karen and her kid brothers watching *Ghostbusters*. On the way home we encountered something strange in our neighbourhood – a ghost from Karen's past called Jasper. Back from his satsuma-picking sabbatical, he was shopping for last-minute supplies for uni – I assume from the sausage roll he was stuffing that he has turned his back on Judaism. In fact, judging by his Paisley shirt, brown hair and the bunch of

twigs protruding from his back pocket, I think our Jasper is
now worshipping at the altar to misery that is Morrissey.
Karen's brothers and I nearly wet ourselves, especially
when he started talking in a bizarre Mancunian accent,
telling Karen he was 'right sorry, fings had never worked
out between 'em' and that she 'were a right crackin' lass'.

My amusement was short-lived, however. As soon as we
got back to Karen's we had to listen to 'Master And
Servant' continuously for three whole hours – and the
packet of chocolate Bourbons ran out after the first thirty
minutes! By the end of the night I truly felt like a
'Girlfriend In A Coma'!

Thursday, 11 October 1984

Dear Anne,
The NUM have been fined and had their funds taken
away. As soon as I heard the news I rang Jed – he seemed
pretty cheerful, though. He says that now the weather's
getting colder the coal will start to run out and then the
government will have to back down. Helen and Joe have
decided to run a miners' support stall on Pinner high street
every Saturday morning and they want me to help. Oh,
Anne, I am torn between my loyalty and devotion to Jed
and the abject embarrassment I will have to endure from
the sniggers of my passing schoolmates.

Friday, 12 October 1984

Dear Anne,
Can't believe the news. The entire government were
nearly wiped out by a bomb in Brighton last night. It feels
as if the whole world has gone mad this year, what with the
threat of nuclear war, police and miners fighting in the

fields and now a gaping great hole in the side of the Grand Hotel and three people dead. Perhaps the Spam man was right after all, perhaps this really is the '1984' that George Orwell prophesied. I can't believe Princess Diana has called her baby Harry – it sounds like the name you'd give a dustman! I wonder how many children Jed and I will have. If I had a boy I'd have to call him Frankie – if only to annoy Jed!

                              Saturday, 13 October 1984

Dear Anne,

Well, as predicted the miners' support stall was a rather testing experience, to say the least. It was all right for Helen. She stationed herself firmly behind the trestle table, well away from the stampeding hordes of Saturday shoppers, so that she could 'deal with any enquiries', but Joe and I had to stand in the middle of the street shaking our buckets and fending off enquiries about why we didn't just 'piss off back to Russia'! Even worse, we were the ones who had to do all the shouting! I'm afraid I could feel the onset of one of my sore throats so I was reduced to muttering, 'Dig deep for the miners,' while being shoved out of the way by some browbeaten young mother or walking-stick-wielding old fogey. It wasn't so bad after the first hour, somebody had actually given me fifteen pence in coppers so at least I had something to rattle, and Joe managed to shout well enough for both of us. But then came the sight I had been dreading: like Clint Eastwood swaggering down Main Street itching for a bar-room shoot-out, the Mattress appeared on the horizon, one hand on her trusty steed, Rambo, the other brandishing a loaded copy of the *Sun*.

'Well, if it isn't the little murdering-IRA-Paddy-weirdo-

miner,' she rasped, before gobbing a greeny into my
bucket. As I watched her totter off down Bridge Street all I
wanted to do was fling down my bucket and cry. I fumbled
in my pocket for a tissue and felt the Davy lamp.
Wrapping my fingers around the cool metal I thought of
Jed and at once felt strong again. As I watched the
Mattress's purple-flecked legs and two-tone hair disappear
around the corner I realised for the first time that I was the
lucky one, not her. She might be able to pick on me now,
but not for much longer. One day soon I'll be out of
Pinner, I'll be living my life to the full with Jed, and what
will she be doing? She'll be stuck in a flat on the estate
with that flea-ridden dog and a litter of snotty babies –
that's what.

As soon as we packed up the stall I went into
Woolworths and bought myself a bar of Dairy Milk and 'I
Just Called To Say I Love You', which has to be my theme
tune at the moment, the amount of times I'm calling Jed.
I'm dreading the phone bill arriving, I really am.

Saturday, 20 October 1984

Dear Anne,

I bet you never thought you'd hear me say this, but I
had the most amazing time on the miners' stall today. Oh,
it started off grimly enough. The weather has turned foul,
and as I shivered inside my fingerless gloves and velveteen
snood I have to admit I was tempted to creep beneath the
trestle table and curl myself into a ball. I gazed at the
welcoming light of the Paphos coffee shop, beaming like a
beacon across the rain-slicked street.

'Shall I go and get us a hot drink?' I offered.

'Great idea – I'll have a pint of London Pride with a
brandy chaser.' Joe chortled.

Helen shot him daggers from behind her 'enquiries' desk. 'Don't be so silly, Joe. I'll have a cup of decaff, please, Caitlin, and get your father the same.'

'Decaff my arse,' Joe bellowed. 'If I'm not allowed any alcohol then I'm bloody well having the most caffeinated coffee in the house!'

Raising my eyebrows in despair I made my way over to Paphos. Thankfully there was a long queue, Saturday morning being the peak time for the more senior inhabitants of Pinner to partake of a cup of tea and a cream slice. The place was a seething mass of blue rinses and beige stockings. As I stood in line, soaking up the heat from the industrial-sized tea urns and spluttering coffee percolators, I prayed that the old fossil in front of me would never finish counting out her coppers. Unfortunately she finally made it to one pound eighteen and it was my turn to be served.

Balancing the Styrofoam cups on top of one another I wove my way through the gridlocked traffic back to the stall. I was so busy concentrating on not spilling the drinks that I didn't notice anything untoward.

'Here you go,' I said, placing the cups on the table, 'Coffee is served.'

'Well, that's charming, that is! We come all this way to lend a hand and we don't even get a drink!'

For the first time on miners'-stall duty I managed to raise my voice to a shout (in fact it was more of a scream): 'Jed!' I spun round and there he was, brandishing a bucket and grinning from ear to ear. Completely forgetting my parents' presence I leapt into his arms, unable to stop the tears of joy spilling down my face. 'What are you doing here? When did you get here? How long—'

'Steady on.' Jed laughed, holding me tightly. 'One question at a time. I came down with me dad. We just got here. It's only a flying visit, I'm afraid.'

I turned to see Bob standing next to Joe, chuckling to himself.

'Well, well,' he said. 'I can see why our Jed were so eager to come down here with me – looks like he's got himself his own personal support group.'

Bob and Joe laughed loudly.

'You're not kidding,' said Joe. 'And from the size of our phone bill I'd say he's also got himself a personal helpline!'

My frozen cheeks rapidly began to thaw with embarrassment. 'Dad!'

'Right, Caitlin, do you want to help out behind the table and let the men do the collecting?' Helen's barked question sounded far more like an order.

'No, it's okay, I'll carry on here.' It may have sounded like an order, but it was still a question and a closed one at that.

I took my bucket and sheet of stickers and stood next to Jed proudly. Let the Mattress come along now, I thought. Let her feast her piggy little eyes upon Jed and his leather jacket and oil-stained jeans. Let her gaze at his freshly cropped hair and his still-tanned skin, and let her see the way those flinty eyes sparkle every time he treats me to a grin. But, of course, she never showed. Not that I was all that bothered – I was having far too much fun. Working on a miners' stall with Jed and Bob was a totally different experience from working with my parents. It was more like taking part in a comedy sketch, the amount of wisecracks that went on. Between the pair of them they managed to charm their way into the affections of most of the passers-by. Not one person asked them to go back to Russia – or even Nottingham. On the contrary, an unprecedented number of shoppers actually chuckled and offered messages of support as they walked past and an even more unprecedented number of people took the trouble to stop and put money into the buckets. The time flew by.

'Right, then, let's get this lot home and us to the pub,' Joe announced, once the sea of shoppers had turned and headed home for lunch. After nearly four hours on the stall my stomach was growling, my feet were aching and my fingertips were numb with cold, but I felt deliriously happy. Every time I looked at Jed I wanted to pinch myself (and kiss him!).

'Excellent idea,' said Bob, rubbing his hands and stamping his feet. 'Bloody hell, I'm colder than a Bejam's burger.'

'Is it all right if I take Cat for a bit of lunch, Dad?' Jed asked, as he helped fold away the table. 'I can meet you back at their house a bit later.'

Bob turned to Helen and Joe and winked. 'Oh, listen to him, wanting to take ladies out for lunch when we haven't got two ha'pennies to rub together.'

Jed's face flushed. 'Well, how are you going to be paying for your beer in the pub? I was only going to get a bag of chips or summat. And, anyway, it's out of my bike money.'

'Steady on, son, I was only messing.' Bob pulled a worn leather wallet from his jacket pocket and fished out a five-pound note. 'Here you go, get her a piece of cod as well.'

Jed smiled grudgingly. 'Are you sure?'

'Of course I'm sure. Jesus, son, get out and enjoy yourself for a bit. I'll see you back at the house at about five.'

Like grains of sand, every second of my afternoon with Jed seemed to slip through my fingers, and the harder I tried to cling on to them, to make time stand still, the faster it seemed to drain away.

'Why the long face?' Jed asked, playfully planting a dollop of ketchup on the end of my nose.

I wiped it away and summoned a feeble smile. 'I just wish we had a bit more time, that's all. We always seem to be racing against the clock. I can't imagine what it would be like to live in the same place, to be able to see you whenever I wanted.'

Jed reached into the brown-paper bag and fed me a chip. 'Come on, shall we go and sit under one of them?' He pointed to the cluster of pine trees standing majestically in the corner of the park.

I nodded and followed him along the winding footpath. A pine-scented mist hung over the park – it was as if somebody had been let loose with a giant can of Elnett.

Once we were seated beneath the ferny canopy Jed handed me my parcel of fish and chips and positioned himself in front of me. 'Now, listen,' he said, 'I want no more of that kind of talk. You need to read *The Dharma Bums* by Jack Kerouac. Have you finished *On The Road* yet?'

I nodded. 'Yeah, it was great.'

Jed smiled. 'I thought you'd like it. Well, I'll send you *The Dharma Bums* next. It's not as good as *On The Road*, but it gets you thinking. It's all about Zen Buddhism,' he explained

I stared at Jed blankly.

Jed laughed and bit into a chip. 'Our Max reckons I'm turning into Neil from *The Young Ones* – hippie-dippy shite, she calls it, but I tell you what, those Buddhists have got one thing right.'

I gazed at Jed expectantly, oblivious to the chips going cold on my lap.

'They say that we have to live life in the moment, that there's no point dwelling on the past or the future. Who cares that I've got to go back to that bloody picket line tonight? Who cares that I haven't seen you for weeks? We're together now, aren't we?'

I nodded at Jed and smiled.

'So, do you know what I'm going to do?' Suddenly Jed was on his hands and knees, prowling towards me with a huge grin on his face, like Tigger about to pounce.

Giggling, I put my chips on the ground and shook my head.

'I'm going to seize the moment, that's what!' And with that he sprang forward, pushed me back on to the ground and pressed himself against me. His lips were warm and salty, and as his tongue slid inside my mouth I felt a wave of contentment wash over me.

Jed was right. As we flailed about, losing ourselves in the moment, I also managed to lose all of my nagging doubts and frustrations – not to mention various articles of clothing. It was only when we came to leave and I found myself retrieving my tights from what looked suspiciously like the entrance to a rabbit warren that it dawned on me just how recklessly I had behaved. What on earth would Helen have said if I'd been arrested in Pinner Memorial Park for indecent exposure? It would have been the biggest news to hit Pinner since Barry Cryer belched at the annual horticultural society awards!

So as I sit here alone in my bedroom once again, thinking of Jed speeding his way back to Nottingham on the back of Bob's bike, I'm determined not to be morose. Like a true Zen Buddhist, I think I might try meditating instead.

Chapter Twenty-Four

Tuesday, 6 November 1984

Dear Anne,

I MUST I MUST IMPROVE MY BUST!

For the past three weeks I have been thrusting my way
through a series of bust-improvement exercises Karen
discovered in *Woman's Own*. Admittedly, from the droopy
bosoms displayed in the diagrams, they are designed for
women who already have breasts but, let's face it, any
alteration on nothing has got to be an improvement. Two
hundred chest expansions every morning certainly can't
make it any smaller!

Loads of miners have started going back to work. I know
I should feel sad but part of me can't help hoping that it
will all soon be over and I can see Jed again. Jed is feeling
confused too. He hates the strike-breakers, but at the same
time he's worried about his parents and what the lack of
money is doing to them. Their phone's been cut off and
they've even started to ration their teabags!

Saturday, 10 November 1984

Dear Anne,

Karen dragged me along to the cinema tonight to see
one of her gruesome horror movies. I don't know about
Nightmare on Elm Street, it was more like a nightmare on
Naff Street! Talk about a load of rubbish. Every time I

looked at the baddy with his ridiculous nine-inch nails I couldn't help thinking of Maxine and her shiny black talons. Jed is getting really pissed off with Maxine (hee hee!). In his last letter he called her a 'spoilt cow'. Although she is the only one bringing any money into the house at the moment she is still blowing most of it on makeup and clothes. Jed is furious because he gave his mum nearly every penny of his bike money. When Maxine waltzed through the door last Saturday with the new ZZ Top album, Jed wanted to smash it over her head. Shame he didn't – the wanton witch!

Saturday, 17 November 1984

Dear Anne,

We have started collecting clothes and toys for the miners' children on the stall. People are being really generous now. Every time somebody puts some money in my bucket I think of Bob and Lizzie and Jed and the number of teabags they could buy with each donation. I am missing Jed so badly it is starting to physically hurt. My heart is literally aching – of course, it could be all those damn chest exercises!

I MUST I MUST *INCREASE* MY BUST!

Please, God, let them have grown a cup size by the time I next see Jed. Of course, the way things are going there's a good chance my breasts will have grown four cup sizes and be dangling around my waist before we are reunited!

I am so bored at the moment – bored of writing letters, bored of going to school, bored of my bothersome breasts.

Wednesday, 28 November 1984

Dear Anne,

Fantastic news! Bob is arranging a Christmas disco at the Miners' Welfare to say thank you to the Harrow Support Group. It was Jed's idea – 'If I don't see you soon I'm going to go mad,' he wrote in his latest letter. Oh, Anne, it's so wonderful and reassuring to think that he is missing me as much as I am missing him. I have to admit there have been times recently when I have become terrified he may get sick of waiting and find somebody else in Blidworth – somebody nearer his age who speaks just like him. I think of Karen's tarot-card reading and the love triangle she prophesied for both of us and my heart becomes paralysed with fear. One night I even dreamt I saw Jed walking arm in arm with another girl and instead of a handbag she was carrying a teapot!

Thursday, 6 December 1984

Dear Anne,

J BN HPJOH UP SVO BXBZ!

No, I have not started speaking Martian – I have just devised a cryptic code for matters of a top-secret nature. I know my ferret of a mother would not be able to contain herself if she came across this journal and there are some things that I can't afford for her to read. My current cunning plan being one of them. I know I have to do it, I really have no alternative, but if Helen were to find out it would ruin everything.

Anyway, the miners' disco has all been arranged. A coachload of us will be going up to Blidworth on Saturday 22nd. It will be the first time I'll have been to a disco with Jed. I wonder how he dances. Oh, God, I hope he isn't one of those men who shuffle from side to side looking like he's on a day-release from Broadmoor! I have been practising my routines like crazy. Madonna's new song is brilliant. As I leap about my room in my lacy fingerless gloves and fishnet tights I think back fondly to the day when I was a virgin being kissed for the very first time. Oh, how I love being a woman of the world, a woman who makes love *à la carte* and lives in the moment. I've started putting socks down my bra – it makes me look more like Madonna.

Saturday, 15 December 1984

Dear Anne,

One week to go till the miners' disco. God, I am so excited. My plan is coming along swimmingly too. Yesterday Helen told me that she and Joe had decided not to go to Blidworth, after all. They have had a blazing row. Last Friday night Joe ended up staggering off to the allotment at closing time and falling asleep in the potting shed. When he stumbled through the kitchen door the following morning, a clump of peat behind his ear, Helen went ballistic. 'God, you spend so much time at that bloody allotment you're even beginning to think of it as home!' she seethed, stabbing her poached pear with a fork.

Joe smiled sheepishly and pulled a runner-bean cane from his pocket. 'Olive branch?' he offered feebly.

Helen hasn't spoken to him since.

'So as your dad and I won't be going I've asked my headmistress, Mrs Montague, to take you,' Helen informed me this morning, with a smug grin.

'Okay,' I replied, with an even smugger grin. If only Helen knew that entrusting me to the care of the drunken Mrs M was a bit like entrusting your favourite satin sheets to Freddy Kruger!

Saturday, 22 December 1984

Dear Anne,

God, I am so excited! Spoke to Jed last night and just
the sound of his voice gave me goosebumps. What is it
going to be like when we are reunited this evening? The
preparations for my plan are firmly in place, my nails have
been painted (black really has to be the worst colour when
you're suffering from passion-induced quivers!), my
crucifixes have been polished and my ankle boots have
been shined. My bag is packed and hidden behind the sack
of compost in the porch. As I take a last nostalgic look
around my bedroom I feel like a prisoner about to wriggle
my way down an escape tunnel. I give my trusty old
record-player a pat on the lid – farewell, my friend, you
have served me well, seen me through my shameful Shakin'
Stevens days right through to my current era of
sophistication, but now I must be off. I look at all the eyes
staring down at me from the wall through a mascara gauze,
Holly, Paul, Mark *et al* – so long my pin-up pals, it's time I
joined my very own real-life pin-up, I'm sure you'll
understand. I have spent so many years in this room
dreaming of my release that now the moment is upon me I
can't help feeling a little emotional. But I'm sure I'll be
back for a visit in a year or so, once the dust has settled.

Chapter Twenty-Five

Monday, 24 December 1984

Dear Anne,

Well, here I am, back in my blasted bedroom again, somewhat sooner than planned, and with the mood my parents are in, I'm not likely to be going anywhere else for several years. My sentence has been extended with all hopes of parole cruelly dashed! The one good thing about my confinement is that it gives me plenty of time to describe to you the events of the past two days. (I will probably have ample time to write my first seven novels as well!)

Shortly after I recorded my previous diary entry, Mrs M arrived to take me to the bus station, looking suitably headmistressy in her pearl twinset and tweed coat.

'Now, no drinking, Caitlin,' Helen hectored, as she eyed me up and down suspiciously. I had on my decoy black boiler-suit and no makeup. I looked like a cross between Gary Numan and Joan Baez.

'Good Lord,' Mrs M shrieked, from the doorstep. 'There'll be none of that kind of behaviour while she's in my care. Just relax, woman.'

Helen beamed with relief. 'Yes, of course, Marjorie. Well, have a nice time.'

'We will,' we sang in unison. As the door closed behind me I grabbed my bag from its hiding place and followed Mrs M to her car. As soon as we pulled out of the estate

Mrs M put on a Slade tape and a flashing Santa hat. 'It's Chriiiiiiiiiiiiiiistmas!' she shrieked.

'Yeah – get out the Murraymints,' I cried.

'Sod the Murraymints, get out the Christmas punch,' Mrs M replied, pulling a Thermos flask from the glove compartment. It was the kind of flask your grandparents would fill with chicken soup and take on a daytrip to Hove. Mrs M, however, had filled it with the entire contents of her drinks cabinet and from the taste of it, half a bottle of white spirit! I felt as if the entire lining of my mouth had been stripped away with my first swig.

Once we got to Harrow bus station I rushed to the toilets where I ripped off my boiler-suit and clambered into my Frankie T-shirt, Karen's black leather mini, a pair of fishnets, black leg warmers and my boots with the gold zips. I left my makeup for the coach, which thankfully I applied *before* I had any more of Mrs M's punch. Mrs M herself had undergone somewhat of a transformation – she had removed her tweed coat to reveal a saucy Santa outfit to match her hat.

'I won't tell if you don't,' she said, with a knowing wink. 'Now give me all the latest on your hunk of spunk – are you still courting or is he available?' She looked at me hopefully then took a swig from her flask.

For the rest of the journey I regaled her with tales of Jed. It was great to have such an enthusiastic (if a little inebriated) audience. Sometimes Karen can appear a little distracted during our heart-to-hearts, the way she yawns and sighs and flicks through her magazines. But not Mrs M. By the time the coach pulled into Blidworth she was positively oozing alcohol and emotion, like a tub of brandy butter that had been left out in the sun.

'Oooh, young love,' she murmured, between hiccups. 'I wish I could say I remember it well, but that bastard of a husband of mine has bled me dry.'

As the coach negotiated the narrow Blidworth streets down to the Miners' Welfare I felt a surge of panic and excitement. I grabbed Mrs M's Thermos flask and took a swig – I don't know about Christmas punch, it was more like a Christmas head-butt the way it left me reeling and seeing stars. I have to admit I was quite grateful, though – at least it helped to numb the initial embarrassment as we all trooped off the coach and into the club. It was a bit like that film *American Werewolf in London* or, rather, *Harrovian Do-gooder in Blidworth*, the way everyone put down their pints and stared at us. Thank God Bob was on hand with his welcoming grin and cheery banter. 'Come in, come in, make yourselves at home – there's grub at the back and plenty of ale behind bar.'

Trying not to look too desperate, I cast my eyes around for Jed. *Where was he?* Then I heard a whistle and someone call my name. 'Cat!'

I turned to see Jed leaning against the bar with his eyes closed, holding a sprig of mistletoe above his head.

But before I could say, 'Headmistress-on-heat', Mrs M had zoomed past me, lips puckered and hat blinking wildly to launch herself on Jed. Pinning him against the bar she managed to hold him in a clinch for at least thirty seconds.

'Bloody hell!' Jed gasped, as he wormed his way out from beneath her boulder-like bosom and staggered to freedom – his face was streaked crimson from a mixture of embarrassment and lipstick. 'What the hell's she been drinking? I thought I was going to pass out!'

'Well, I'll have some of it, if there's any going spare,' chuckled a man standing next to Jed. From the scar running down his colossal arm like a seam, I realised it was Tommy Whittaker.

'Oh, there's plenty going spare if you play your cards right, young man,' Mrs M bellowed, straightening her hat and adjusting her breasts. 'Now, what does a lady have to do to get a drink in this place?'

Tommy looked at Jed and me and winked. 'Don't you worry, love, I'll see to the drinks.'

As Tommy fished in his pocket for his wallet Jed and I exchanged coy glances.

'Well, that didn't exactly go to plan,' Jed said, looking at the mistletoe wistfully.

'Well, you know what they say – if at first you don't succeed. . .'

Jed flung his arms around me and planted a huge kiss on my lips. 'Merry Christmas, Cat.'

I buried my face in his jacket and inhaled the rich smell of leather. 'Merry Christmas.'

'Did you bring your things?'

'Yeah – no problem.'

Jed smiled and took my hand. 'Brilliant. This has gone from being one of the shittiest Christmases ever to one of the best. How long are you going to stay?'

I bit my lip and looked at the floor. 'I don't know, really – three or four days?' I hadn't told Jed of my secret plan to stay with him for ever: I had decided to wait until the moment was right for that revelation, and as a chain of people snaked past us doing the conga that moment was definitely not now.

'What do you think your parents will say when you don't come back tonight?' Jed shouted, above the music.

I shrugged my shoulders. 'Who cares? It's not as if they can drive up here and get me, is it? And, anyway, they're far too busy being pissed off with each other to be bothered about me.'

Jed led me over to a small table in the corner. 'Oh, don't tell me they're fighting in your house too?'

I nodded woefully – it would have sounded far too

heartless to admit that my parents' row had made my life
easier this past week.

Jed pulled out a couple of chairs and we sat down. 'I tell
you what, our house has been a war zone lately, what with
me dad fretting about scabs and our Max acting like Lady
Muck. Some days I just want to get on me bike and get
out of there. And then I remember that I haven't even got
a bike any more because of the bloody strike.' Jed looked at
me and sighed.

I picked up one of his scuffed brown hands and kissed it.
'Come on, what happened to all of that "living in the
moment" stuff?'

To my relief, Jed's face broke into its customary grin.
'Sorry,' he said sheepishly, then leapt to his feet. 'Come on,
they're playing our song – have you got any Spam we can
dance round?'

Laughing, I followed Jed to the small circular dance-floor
as '1984' boomed out from the speakers. Jed is such a
good dancer – it was fantastic watching his toned body
twist this way and that and thinking that it belonged to me.
He even managed to look sexy dancing to 'Nellie The
Elephant'!

The evening flew by in a smoky haze of sausage rolls,
speeches and singalongs. By the end of the night any
awkwardness had disappeared, with the burly miners and
their bourgeois supporters all united in a common cause –
to get as blind drunk as possible. Bob and Jed entertained
the crowd with a song about sixteen tons of number-nine
coal, and as everyone cheered them on I thought my heart
was going to burst with pride. How had I – the class
'weirdo' – ended up with somebody as popular and fun as
Jed? What had he seen in me that nobody else had? And to
think I had been heartbroken when Alex Moon and Jasper
Montague hadn't fancied me – Jed was worth a million of

them. As 'The Power Of Love' came on and Jed led me on to the dance-floor I felt like the belle of the ball – a modern-day Cinderella in glass ankle boots. But as the song faded out and the DJ bade everyone farewell, it was the equivalent of the clock striking midnight. I looked around in panic for my fairy godmother.

'Where's Mrs M?' I asked Jed. 'I've got to tell her I'm not going back.'

Jed shrugged his shoulders and squinted around the club. Somebody had turned on all the lights, replacing the fairytale glow with a harsh glare. 'Come on, we'll look outside,' he said, taking my hand.

I followed him out into the icy cold night, my heart pounding. What would I do if Mrs M caused a scene? If she dragged me kicking and screaming on to the coach? She was a headmistress, after all, a figure of authority and respect, a role model to three hundred children, and my mother's boss. We eventually found her snogging Tommy Whittaker behind the bins, her saucy Santa outfit hitched up around her waist to reveal the largest pair of floral satin pants I had ever seen.

'Ah, Caitlin!' she gasped, when we prised her away from Tommy's colossal physique. 'I was just coming to look for you. There's been a bit of a change of plan. I'm afraid I won't be coming back on the coach tonight, after all.'

I raised my eyebrows and looked at Jed. He, however, was busy grinning at Tommy like a Cheshire cat.

Mrs M attempted to straighten her dress and careered sideways into the bin. 'Good grief, it's a landslide – the whole pit's about to collapse!' She clung to Tommy's arm for support. 'You see, Caitlin, this young man has kindly offered to show me his collection of brass etchings.'

Jed stifled a snigger and Tommy scuffed the toe of his boot into the ground.

'It would be terribly rude of me to decline, but I feel awful leaving you in the lurch. Will you be okay going back on your own? I'll make sure one of the others gives you a lift home from the station.'

I took a deep breath. 'Well, that's just it, Mrs M, I'm not going back either. I want to spend Christmas with Jed – I don't know when I'll get to see him again.'

'Quite so,' Mrs M empathised. 'Well, this is wonderful news. I'll feel a lot better knowing you're in safe hands tonight.' She snorted loudly and gave Jed a knowing nudge. 'I'll go and tell the driver we won't be coming back to Harrow and then I'll call your mother and tell her we've missed the coach. We can discuss our return in more detail in the morning. Now, come along, young man, I'm just itching to get a look at those etchings!'

And with that Mrs M frogmarched a sheepish-looking Tommy to the coach.

Jed was laughing so hard I thought he was going to be sick. 'Wait till the lads hear about this,' he gasped. 'Our Tommy getting hold of Dame Edna – God, if only I'd had a camera.'

'Did you see her pants?' I spluttered.

'Did I see them? I think I've been blinded by them!' Jed grasped my arm and rubbed his eyes theatrically. 'Come on, then, time for phase two of our plan.'

Phase two was informing Jed's parents about their unexpected house guest. It was also where our plan began to fall apart. When Bob and Lizzie arrived home from the Welfare to find me sitting on their sofa next to Jed they were unimpressed, to say the least.

'What the 'eck's going on?' Bob demanded, his trademark grin nowhere to be seen. 'Why isn't she on the coach?'

I glanced anxiously at Lizzie, hoping for a reassuring

smile or the offer of a cup of tea, but she looked positively distraught, hovering behind Bob in the doorway.

'I've asked Cat to stay for Christmas,' Jed replied, placing his hand on my knee.

'Oh, have you now?' Bob turned his glare upon me. 'And do your parents know about this?'

I shook my head and gazed at my lap.

'I see. So when were you planning on letting them know? Or were you not going to bother and just let them go out of their mind with worry when you didn't get home tonight?'

'All right, Bob, go easy on her,' Lizzie said, slipping past him to perch on the arm of the sofa. 'Don't you think you should have asked them if it was okay beforehand?' she asked gently.

Bob made a snorting noise. 'Asked *them* – what about asking us? This is our house, son. Your mother and I have a right to know who we've got coming to stay in it.'

Jed sighed wearily. 'For God's sake, it's Christmas, Dad. What's so wrong with wanting to spend a little time with my girlfriend?'

Bob raised his eyes in despair. 'Yeah, it's Christmas, and we haven't got a pot to piss in and you want to play the host with the most. How can we be expected to look after a guest when we can't even look after ourselves?' With an exasperated sigh, he slumped down in his armchair.

Lizzie patted my shoulder. 'I'm sorry, love, it's nothing against you, it really isn't, it's just that things are so difficult at the moment. It's not really the best time for us to have anyone to stay.'

'Not for you, perhaps, but what about me?' Jed demanded, getting to his feet. 'What about what I want?'

'Well, well, what have we here?' I looked up in horror to

see Maxine towering in the doorway. Her raven hair was gleaming and her heavily shaded eyes glinted with curiosity.

Jed groaned. 'Keep your nose out, Max, this is nowt to do with you.'

'Oh, really? Well, seeing as I live here I'd say it has everything to do with me.' Maxine pulled off her stiletto-heeled boots and sashayed into the room. 'So,' she said, staring at me from in front of the fireplace, 'what the hell is *she* doing here?'

'She's staying here as my guest, that's what,' Jed replied defiantly.

'Oh, really? And did Mam and Dad know anything about this little arrangement?'

Lizzie shook her head. 'No, we didn't, but don't worry, Max, we're sorting it out.'

'There's nowt to sort out!' Jed shouted. 'I've invited Cat to stay for a couple of days, end of story.'

'And don't you think you should have asked Mam and Dad if it was okay for your little friend to come and visit?' Maxine enquired, nonchalantly holding up her perfectly glossed talons for inspection.

'I told you to keep your nose out of this,' Jed snarled, turning on Maxine. 'It's got sod all to do with you who I invite to stay here.'

'Oh, yes, it has when they're poncing off *my* parents.'

'You what?' For a split second I thought Jed was going to punch Maxine: his whole body seemed to tense like a vice. 'You've got no right to accuse anyone of being a ponce. Who the hell do you think you are, swanning in here in your tarty clothes calling all the shots? Cat's done a million times more to help us than you. You haven't been on a single picket line since strike began. What's up, Max, afraid you might ladder a stocking or worried you might run into one of your tricks?'

The room echoed with a resounding crack as Maxine slapped Jed's face. Jed staggered backwards, clutching his cheek.

'Are you going to let her get away with that?' he shouted at Bob. 'Or are you just going to sit there doing bugger-all while she takes us all for a bunch of mugs?'

Bob looked at Lizzie in despair before turning back to Jed. 'Now, come on, son, let's all just calm down – you shouldn't have talked to your sister like that.'

'I shouldn't have talked to her like that? What about the way she was talking about Cat? Jesus, what is wrong with you pair? Why do you always let her get away with murder?'

Lizzie got to her feet and put an arm round Jed, 'Come on, love, let's go and get a cup of tea and talk about what we're going to do.' She turned to me and smiled weakly. 'I'm so sorry, pet, we're all under so much pressure at the moment, especially with Christmas coming. I hope you understand.'

I nodded numbly before silently reciting my thirteen times tables – anything to distract myself from the reservoir of tears that had formed behind my eyes. Jed gave my shoulder a quick squeeze before he followed Bob and Lizzie grudgingly into the kitchen. Unfortunately Maxine failed to follow suit, choosing to sit next to me on the sofa instead.

'Satisfied now, are you?' she whispered.

'What do you mean?' *Six times thirteen is seventy-eight.*

Maxine shifted herself sideways so that she was staring straight at me. I could feel her dark grey eyes boring into the side of my head like a double-barrelled shotgun. 'Now you've upset my parents.'

'I didn't mean to,' I gulped. *Seven times thirteen is ninety-one*

'Bullshit,' Maxine hissed. 'You swan up here with your

lah-de-dah voice and your crappy books, thinking you're so
much better than everyone else, thinking we're some kind
of charity case. Well, we don't need your help. Jed doesn't
need your help. You're just a distraction to him while the
strike's on. You're a novelty, that's all. As soon as strike's
over you'll be history, love.'

Eight times thirteen is . . . But it was too late – the
floodgates had burst open and a gigantic sob was
unleashed. I stumbled to my feet, awash with misery and
shame. As I fumbled around blindly for my coat and bag,
all I knew was I had to get out of there – I couldn't stay in
that house for another second. I didn't care if I had to run
all the way back to Harrow.

I made it as far as the church before Jed caught up with
me.

'What did she say to you? I'll kill her, I swear, Cat, I'll
kill her if she said anything else.'

I shook my head and wiped my face with the back of my
hand, but the tears kept spilling from my eyes in streams.

Jed pulled me to him. 'I'm so sorry, Cat. I had no idea it
was going to be like that. They're bastards, the lot of them.
Come on, we'll go round to Tommy's – see if we can take
a look at his etchings.'

I laughed feebly, but Maxine's words had left me empty
inside. Was that how I'd managed to get Jed? By being a
novelty? A distraction from the hardship of the strike? I felt
vulnerable and scared.

Once again Mrs M proved my unlikely saviour.

'Good grief, girl, what on earth's the matter?' she asked,
from the shadowy recesses of the hall as Tommy Whittaker
let us into his flat.

'There's been a bit of bother over at ours,' Jed explained.
'I don't suppose we could crash on your floor for the night,
could we?'

'No problem,' Tommy replied gruffly, and led us through to a tiny living room. A black leather settee took up most of the far wall, beneath a huge framed photo of some footballers holding a trophy aloft. In the corner a portable television set was balanced precariously on what looked like an old bar stool. 'Take a seat,' Tommy said, gesturing to the settee with one hand while attempting to hold the tiniest of towels around his waist. I tore my eyes from the forest of dark hair creeping down his torso and perched on the edge.

'Are you all right, my dear?' Mrs M asked, pushing past Jed to sit beside me. She was clad in her flashing Santa hat and a huge black donkey jacket. As I glanced up I noticed her floral satin pants draped on top of the television and felt an awful urge to giggle.

'Yes,' I gasped. 'Jed's parents were a bit upset, that's all.'

Mrs M snorted. 'They weren't the only ones – your mother didn't take too kindly to the news either.'

I groaned. 'Oh, God, what did she say?'

'Well, she seemed a little perturbed that you were spending the night with Jed, but don't you worry, I put her straight.'

My heart sank even further. 'What do you mean?'

'Well, I reminded her of what happened to Romeo and Juliet when they were kept apart.'

Tommy let out a guffaw. 'Can I get you a beer, Romeo?' he asked, giving Jed a playful dig in the ribs.

'No, you're all right,' Jed replied. 'I wouldn't mind seeing *what's on TV*, though.' Jed looked pointedly at Mrs M's pants before smirking back at Tommy.

I was too concerned about Helen to appreciate the joke. I could just picture her standing in the hall in her ethnic woven nightshirt, slamming the phone down on Mrs M.

Mrs M put her arm round my shoulders and gave me a

squeeze. 'Don't you worry, my dear, I'll get you home safe and sound tomorrow, but until then –' she stood up and grabbed Tommy by his spare hand '– follow my example and have some fun!' And with that, the most unlikely pairing since Elton and Renate John traipsed off to the bedroom.

Jed looked at me and smiled weakly. 'So.'

I shrugged my shoulders.

Jed cleared his throat nervously then sat down beside me. 'Do you fancy watching a bit of telly? I've heard there's *pant*omime on ITV.'

'I'd rather watch the Pink *Pant*er on BBC One,' I replied, with a grin.

Jed's brow furrowed into a frown. 'Of course, there's always that film Mac*Knicker* on BBC Two.'

I groaned and pushed Jed back on to the settee. 'That was terrible.'

'All right, all right, no need to make a *thong* and dance out of it!'

'Stop it! Please!'

'Only if you give me a kiss.' Jed pulled me on to his lap and cupped my face in his hands. 'I'm so sorry, Cat, about earlier. I feel dead shitty about the whole thing.'

'Don't worry. Anyway, it hasn't gone totally wrong – we still get to spend a night together.'

Jed looked at me and smiled. 'Aye, we certainly do.'

After we had made love Jed went and fetched a blanket from the hall cupboard and we snuggled up together on a makeshift bed of leather settee cushions. As I buried my face in his taut, muscular chest I inhaled deeply, determined to savour every second I had with him, every second I had to wallow in his smell, to be soothed by his heartbeat and to drink up the warmth from his satiny skin.

'Cat.'

'Yes.'

'I love you.'

A fountain of fireworks cascaded before my eyes. Jed loved me. He loved me! I wasn't just a novelty or a distraction, after all. But before I had a chance to respond a shriek resonated throughout the flat.

'DIG DEEPER, BOY! DIG DEEPER!'

Jed sat bolt upright. 'What the fuck?'

'That's the way, that's the way.' Mrs M's voice rang out from the room next door. 'Dig deep for the miners, boy, dig deep. Oh, yes, that's more like it! Aaaaaaaaah!'

Jed and I clung together in fits of laughter as a frantic banging beat against the wall. Finally there was a strangled moan and it all fell silent.

'Oh, God, that was gross,' I said, with a shudder, snuggling up to Jed once more.

'Yeah, tell me about it. And it ruined my big moment,' Jed added wistfully.

I looked up at him and smiled. 'No, it didn't.' I wriggled my way up so that my lips were level with Jed's ear. 'I love you too,' I whispered.

Jed let out a huge sigh of relief, 'Thank God for that. I thought after tonight you might have decided to call it a day.'

I put my arm around his waist and clung on to him tightly. 'No way.'

My whole body melted as Jed began stroking my hair.

'Cat.'

'Yes?'

'Merry Christmas.'

The following morning Tommy and Jed dropped Mrs M and me off at the coach station in Nottingham. We must have looked a right motley pair, Mrs M in her Santa outfit and me in my disco attire, both of us still bearing the

bruises of the previous night's makeup. For the first time
ever I didn't feel completely devastated at having to leave
Jed. Now he's told me he loves me I feel a new sense of
security, a new-found confidence wrapping itself round me
like a quilt. Besides, my conversation with Mrs M on the
way home was far too interesting to allow me to wallow in
any self-pity.

'Can I offer you some advice, Caitlin?' Mrs M asked,
offering me a Murraymint as well.

I nodded and grabbed the mint gratefully – the inside of
my mouth tasted worse than school dinners.

'You've got somebody who really loves you there. Don't
let him slip through your fingers.'

I looked at Mrs M curiously. The tone of her voice was
different, softer and more serious than usual.

'You mustn't ever make the same mistake I did and
settle for second best.'

'What do you mean?'

'I live in a loveless marriage, Caitlin. It's been loveless for
years, but we made an agreement to stay together for
Jasper's sake.' Mrs M brought one of her starched
handkerchiefs out of her handbag and blew her nose
loudly. 'For sixteen years now I've had to turn a blind eye
to my husband's little liaisons with flibbertigibbet nurses at
the hospital. Oh, I know you probably think I'm just some
drunken old fool, some eccentric old buffoon who can't
keep her hands off the cooking sherry, but drink is all I've
had to numb the pain.'

I looked at Mrs M in shock. 'Oh, that's terrible. How
awful for you.'

'That's why you must promise me never to make the
same mistake. Never sell yourself short. You're a beautiful
girl, Caitlin, and Jed is a lovely boy. Don't let anything ruin
what you've got.'

I nodded solemnly. 'I won't.'

'Now, don't look so grim, girl, anyone would think I'd just told you Santa doesn't exist!' Mrs M's voice raised itself to its usual bellow.

'I'm sorry, it's just that I feel so bad for you – I had no idea.'

'Good grief, don't be sorry for me. My misery is over.'

'How do you mean?'

Mrs M took a bottle from her handbag and doused herself in Tweed. 'Well, Jasper's off at university now, which means that my penance has finally come to an end. What do you think last night was about?'

'Oh, I see. So are you and Tommy going to get it together, then?' I fought to keep any trace of incredulity from my voice.

'Good heavens, no. I was just checking everything was in working order. It's been quite some time since my triangle *d'amour* saw any action, you know.'

I remembered Mrs M's mating call of the previous night and grinned. 'And was it? In working order, I mean.'

'As well oiled as a tin of sardines,' Mrs M replied, with a contented smile.

So, Anne, as I contemplate a Christmas bereft of cheer, charm or even turkey (Helen is making a nut roast), I know I must count my blessings. For this year I have been given the greatest gift of all – the gift of true love. Now that I have met Jed I know I will never end up like poor old Mrs M, trapped in a lifetime's loveless existence.

Chapter Twenty-Six

Midnight – Saturday

Trembling, I put down my diary and turned to my essential bedside companion. It was almost midnight – the witching hour. As I lay there shivering in the stifling heat I felt as if I had entered some strange twilight zone world where nothing made sense any more. Was it really only a day since I'd found the Betterware Breakdown prostrate on my driveway? Was I really a mother of two who drove a Range Rover and wore Jimmy Choos, or was I still a teenager mooching about in my bedroom in my Frankie T-shirt? Was I happily married to the man of my dreams or was I still in love with Jed?

I felt the truth battering away at my mind like a tidal wave and a flurry of memories piled themselves up like sandbags against the assault. Sam and I walking down the aisle surrounded by a sea of smiling faces, Sam beaming widely as he turned to kiss his bride – his bride flinching as she walked out into a glare of sunshine and a fistful of confetti. But, let's face it, how many people can truly say that their wedding day is the happiest of their life? How can it be, when all you can think about is keeping your father from playing his banjo at the reception? The honeymoon is probably the best indicator of matrimonial bliss. I cast my mind back to the silky beaches and sumptuous cocktails. The gallons of sumptuous cocktails. Perhaps the writing is on the wall when you need to consume sixteen Harvey Wallbangers in order to consummate your marriage. But you paper over the writing and the cracks with a montage of excuses: *friendship is far more important than lust, we can grow to love one another, at least he'll never hurt me, it's better than being on my own.*

I sat upright with a start – I had *not* ended up like Mrs M, trapped in a loveless marriage. Sam was a fine man, he would never cheat on me, he would never let me down. From the moment he found me, swept up in that freshers' fair, a fractured emotional shell, he had set about sticking me back together again with an endless supply of love and compassion. And he had stood by me ever since – the perfect husband. In sickness and in health, Sam had always been there for me – reassuring me when my smear test came back abnormal, cheering me on as I completed my first (and last) half marathon. For richer and for poorer, Sam had always put me first, spending any bonuses on family holidays or a new family car, working flat out so that I could take a year off after the birth of each of our kids. For better and certainly for worse, Sam had always been my rock. What the hell was I thinking of, hurting him like this? I staggered to my feet and made my way across the landing to Sam's bedroom. To *our* bedroom. I tapped on the door nervously.

'Come in.' Sam's voice was soft and welcoming.

I edged open the door and crept in.

Sam was sitting up in bed reading a copy of *Here's Health*. 'Oh – I thought it was one of the kids,' he whispered, putting down his magazine. 'Is everything all right?' His eyes looked bloodshot, as if he had been twelve rounds with George Best. As if he had been crying.

'Oh, Sam,' was all I could manage, before the tears started to flow from my own eyes. I stood there, pigeon-toed in my Frankie T-shirt, like some frightened schoolgirl desperate to climb into her parents' bed and be reassured that everything was going to be all right.

'Come here.' Sam patted the smooth space on the bed beside him.

I peeled back the duvet and crawled in. 'I'm so, so sorry,' I sobbed. 'I don't know what's wrong with me at the moment.'

'It's all right.' Sam stroked my hair. 'Just let me help you. Let me love you.'

I closed my eyes and felt my shivers begin to dissipate as Sam held me to him. 'Let me love you, Caitlin,' he whispered, over and over again, like a mantra, soothing all of my fears away.

As his hands worked their way up inside my T-shirt I could almost hear the squeak of leather as I thought of Jed lying on top of me on Tommy Whittaker's sofa.

'Are you all right?' he whispered, as he peeled off the T-shirt.

'Yes.' I sighed, as I felt him take one of my nipples into his mouth and tease it gently with his tongue. My whole body began to quiver as Jed worked his way down my body, leaving no inch of skin unkissed.

'I've missed you so much, Cat,' Jed panted, his teeth brushing gently against my earlobe.

I moaned with relief as I finally felt him inside me.

'God, I want you so badly, Caitlin, it's been so long.'

I froze. He called me Caitlin. Jed never called me Caitlin. I opened my eyes and, like a scene from a sci-fi movie, Jed's heart-shaped face morphed itself to oval, his grey eyes turned to blue and black curls sprang from his head. Jed had turned into Sam.

I screamed and pushed him off me. 'What are you doing?'

Sam shot out of bed as if he had been burned. 'What do you mean? I thought you wanted me.'

I leapt out of the other side of the bed and pulled my T-shirt back on. I felt hysterical. 'You're not – you're not—'

'I'm not what, Caitlin?' Sam's eyes sparked with fury. 'I'm not good enough? Not working-class enough? Not *him?*'

I leant against our wardrobe, trying to get my bearings.

Sam marched around the bed to stand right in front of me. 'Well, no, I'm not him and I never will be, but I'm your husband, the father of your children.'

My heart was pounding furiously. I'd never seen Sam so angry. What was he going to do? I caught a glimpse of his clenched fists and, for a split second, I thought the unthinkable before Sam recoiled in horror. I watched as he stumbled back round the bed, pulling on his dressing-gown as he went. 'My God, Caitlin, what are you trying to do to me?' He collapsed on the bed, his whole body convulsing with awful silent sobs. 'I know how badly you were hurt,' he gasped, 'and ever since we met I've been trying to help you get over it, but you don't have the monopoly on pain, you know.'

I nodded helplessly.

Sam wiped his face with the back of his hand. 'For years now I've put up with coming second best because I didn't want to lose you, but I've never really had you at all, have I? You've always been in love with him. And how can I possibly compete with a ghost from your past?'

I could feel my legs begin to buckle under me. 'No, don't say that.'

'Don't say what? It's the truth. Don't you think it's time we both faced up to it.

I stared wildly at Sam for a few seconds, then fumbled blindly for the door. As I careered out on to the landing his parting words ricocheted around me like gunshots.

'Don't you think it's time you made the choice, Caitlin? Him or me?'

Chapter Twenty-Seven

Tuesday, 1 January 1985

Dear Anne,

HAPPY NEW YEAR! I hope you sense the determination with which I make that statement – I thought the capital letters and exclamation mark would help to demonstrate my resolution. And, speaking of which, apart from being happy in 1985 I have only one other New Year's resolution and that is to be with Jed. Unfortunately there would appear to be a conflict of interest in this house, with my parents resolving to sabotage my happiness by whatever means necessary. Take last night for example, New Year's Eve, a crucial turning point in the plot of our lives. Like the end of a chapter, the way you see an old year out can either leave you breathless with anticipation at what is to come or make you scream out loud with bored despair. Let's face it, a night of the Dulwich Dubliners at O'Flaherty's public house is hardly what you would call a page-turner!

'But Karen's parents are having a disco,' I implored. 'They've hired the lights and the glitter-ball and everything.'

'I don't care if they've hired Terry Wogan,' Joe replied, fishing a piece of potato from his beard. 'You're coming out with us.'

'But I hate Irish music.' I looked at Helen in despair, 'Please Hel – Mum, please, don't make me come.'

Helen was busy applying an extra coat of lip-salve in the reflection from the kettle. She looked up at me wearily. 'After what happened in Blidworth we just can't trust you to go out on your own. Now, go and get ready, please.'

'But I won't be on my own – Karen's parents will be there.'

Helen snorted. 'And that's supposed to reassure me, is it?'

I leapt to my feet. 'God, you're such a snob. What's wrong with Karen's parents? At least they know how to have a good time. At least Debbie doesn't think Max Factor is the name of a game-show host!'

'Caitlin, that's enough!' Joe shouted. 'Now go and get yourself ready.'

I came back downstairs wearing my navy boiler-suit and a fearsome scowl, determined to make them pay for ruining my night. But, no matter how hard I tried, my parents remained oblivious to my tortured expressions and fitful sighs. They were far too enraptured with the God-awful band. As soon as the Dulwich Dubliners shuffled on to the minuscule stage, all beer-bellies, beards and banjos, the crowd turned into a foot-stomping, pint-wielding mob. Even Helen was tapping her toes – it was excruciating. I ended up seeking sanctuary in the ladies' where a woman named Cathleen gibbered on at me for half an hour about her husband Seamus and his problems with 'the gout'. If she hadn't supplied me with a steady stream of free cigarettes I think I would have flushed myself down the toilet in despair!

As the clock struck midnight I locked myself into one of the deserted cubicles and thought of Jed. 'Happy New Year,' I whispered, coiling my fingers around the little Davy lamp in my pocket. As the cheers wafted through from the bar I closed my eyes and imagined I was in the

Miners' Welfare in Blidworth, in Jed's arms. What a start
to the New Year that would have been.

But just because one chapter finishes badly it doesn't
mean you should discard the entire book. So, as I embark
upon this new chapter in my life, it is with a sense of
overwhelming optimism – for I feel certain that 1985 is
where our lovers will finally be brought together to live
happily ever after.

Monday, 7 January 1985

Dear Anne,

I returned to school to a state of pre-mock hysteria. I
can't see what all the fuss is about really – the proper
exams aren't until June. So, in my determination not to
peak too soon, I smuggled the following letter from Jed into
my maths textbook and read it for the fiftieth time since it
arrived this morning.

> *Dear Cat,*
>
> *Thanks for the card. Happy New Year to you too. I was
> thinking about you when the clock struck twelve, wondering
> where you were and who you were with. It never crossed my
> mind you'd be on your own in a toilet – although I'm pretty
> glad you were. I'd been imagining you in the middle of some
> party with some posh bloke with loads of O levels slobbering
> all over you. Sometimes I get dead jealous, thinking of you
> all the way down there with other lads queuing up in the
> wings, but then I tell myself not to be soft. I know I can trust
> you, Cat, you're my best mate, for Christ's sake. Sometimes
> I don't know what I'd do if I didn't have you to talk to or
> write to. Nobody up here understands me the way you do,
> nobody up here finds the same things funny. The other day I
> went down to the Welfare to get a bite to eat and Brenda*

gave us a Spam sandwich. I wish you could have been there, Cat – I could have done with the laugh.

Have you been watching the news? Thousands have started going back to work now and morale's getting pretty low. Me mam and dad are barely talking – I try and stay out of their way as much as possible. I've been out walking a lot, round by our old haunts. Some nights I just go up and sit by Will Scarlett and remember that night I brought you there. Then I start freezing me arse off so I go round to Tommy's for a beer. I'm still giving him grief about Dame Edna! Another reason I can't stand it at home at the moment is our Max. I know big sisters are meant to be bossy but she takes the frigging biscuit. She's always on at me about summat – I still haven't forgave her for the way she spoke about you. Anyway, Cat, it looks like it won't be long now before strike's over – I just wish that we could have won it. It's all starting to look like such a waste. As soon as I'm back on my feet again (or back on me bike again) I'll be down there and then no one can stop us being together. My sister might want to live at home until she's drawing her pension, but not me. All I want to do is get out of here and start a new life with you.

Good luck in your exams and keep up the writing – one of these days I'm going to find that diary of yours and see what you really think of me!

All my love,

Jed x

I decided to include Jed's letter here because it fits in so well with the new, positive chapter in my life. Seeing our shared dreams written down in black and white makes me feel even more hopeful about what is to come. I can't believe he gets jealous about me too. I can't believe he thinks I've got a 'queue' of other blokes waiting in the wings! Karen's going to crack up when I tell her that bit!

Wednesday, 16 January 1985

Dear Anne,

It's been over a week now since I got a letter from Jed. I wish they hadn't had their phone cut off and I could phone him to check he's okay. Mind you, the way the strike's going he's probably too busy on picket lines to write. Had my first mock exam today – French, *c'est magnifique!* Don't get me wrong, I can't bear languages (apart from English, of course!) and I had been particularly dreading this exam, but the most fantastic thing happened half-way through. I was sitting at my desk, chewing a pencil and trying desperately to remember whether a chair was male or female (!) when I heard a bizarre noise at the back of the hall. A snuffling, giggling noise, a bit like a hysterical pig. Which was not completely wide of the mark. We all turned round to see the Mattress slumped over her desk, literally foaming at the mouth with laughter.

'What on earth is ze matter with you?' Madame Henri exclaimed, racing down the aisle brandishing a ruler. 'You are causing a disruption, you silly girl.'

To which the Mattress snorted even louder. 'Why don't you piss off back to France, Garlic-breath!'

There was a collective intake of breath followed by a ripple of nervous laughter as everyone watched to see what would happen next. I took the opportunity to glance down at Angela Braithwaite's paper and made a mental note that a chair is, in fact, female.

Madame Henri rapped her ruler down on the desk with a resounding crack. 'How dare you speak to me in zis way?

What have you been doing back zere? What is ze meaning of zis?' She grabbed a bottle from the Mattress's desk. The Mattress, it would appear, had been too busy inhaling Tippex thinner to waste any time conjugating verbs.

'What does it look like, Snail-lover?' the Mattress sneered, applying a coat of lipstick to her chin.

'Get to ze headmaster's office immediately!' Madame Henri shrieked. 'I will not tolerate zis insolence!'

The Mattress lurched to her feet, sending her chair clattering on to the wooden floor. 'Why don't you go to hell, the lot of you?' she yelled, her off-white blouse straining at the buttons to reveal glimpses of the black bra beneath. 'I don't need to be here, learning to speak like a Frog. I've got a job lined up for me down the bingo. I wanna be out there earning proper cash, not stuck in here with a bunch of kids.'

The Mattress then gave us all an extremely mature two-fingered salute before marching, somewhat unsteadily, out of the hall. Surely she's got to be expelled now? I still can't believe she got away with locking Mr Pertwee in the stationery cupboard last year!

Friday, 18 January 1985

Dear Anne,

Jed still hasn't written. It's been almost two weeks now, well, eleven days, but it feels like eleven months without a single, solitary word. I have written twice since his last letter. Maybe he's had to ration stamps or something. I know – I'll write him a quick note tonight and send him a stamped, addressed envelope. He's probably been too embarrassed to ask me.

Friday, 25 January 1985

Dear Anne,

Excuse my appalling handwriting but, as Swellen from *Dallas* might say, I'm feeling shlightly pished. At Karen's tonight I drank about half a bottle of Strongbow before starting on her dad's home brew. It was vile but I had to drown my sorrows somehow. Unfortunately, however, like rubber floats, my sorrows keep bobbing back up to the surface to torment me even further.

Jed still hasn't written, he didn't even use my SAE to drop me a note. Every morning when the post plops down on to the mat my heart skips a beat. *Please, please, please*, I pray silently as Helen rifles through the envelopes, smiling as she spots this month's *Anti-Vivisection News*. Sod those animals, I feel like screaming, your own daughter is having her heart ripped apart here, without an anaesthetic! But I bite my lip, bin my breakfast and tell myself that I'm bound to hear from him tomorrow. But I'm not am I? Something has gone wrong. The question is, what?

Reasons for Jed not writing:
1. He has had an accident on the picket line and is unable to write, or phone, or get anyone else to write or phone on his behalf.
2. All of his letters have gone missing in the post.
3. He has decided to finish it, but hasn't got the nerve to tell me.
4. The 'novelty' has worn off and he is no longer interested in a Pinner schoolgirl.
5. He has met somebody up there whom he can see whenever he likes.
6. He has had somebody else up there all the time and I was only ever a bit on the side.

Okay, so the last one might be a bit far-fetched but I have just spent the evening with Karen and her extensive collection of Tears For Fears. Jasper has left her so disillusioned with the male race that she is hardly the most positive of shoulders to cry on. I wish she hadn't reminded me of that bloody love triangle she prophesied. The thought of Jed dumping me is hard enough, but the thought of him with someone else is unbearable.

Chapter Twenty-Eight

Sunday, 27 January 1985

Dear Anne,

Have spent most of today writing and rewriting a letter to Jed. No matter what I say it always sounds wrong – too stroppy, too soppy, too desperate. My bedroom floor is littered with scrunched-up balls of paper and I still haven't done one bit of revision for tomorrow's history mock. I wonder if that's what Jed and I have become – history? Maybe I should just write him one single line:

HAVE I BEEN CHUCKED?

But the sad fact is, I don't think I could bear to hear the answer. I'd rather carry on like this, clinging to the ever-diminishing hope that there is some perfectly simple explanation for his silence. Perhaps he got a chance to write over the weekend and his letter will arrive tomorrow.

Monday, 28 January 1985

Dear Anne,

No letter. It's getting to the point where I can't think about anything else. I feel as if I'm sliding down a dark tunnel back to my old life of loneliness and boredom, only this time it's even worse – this time I know exactly what I am missing. Not even the news that the Mattress has been expelled to pursue her career as a bingo caller can wrench me from the mire.

Thursday, 31 January 1985

Dear Anne,

I can't stop crying. I feel like a desperate woman. I feel like Sue Ellen when she found out about JR and Kristen. I did something so embarrassing tonight. Helen and Joe were at the Miners' Support Group meeting and I was home alone. Home alone with the phone. Every time I walked past the damn thing I felt as if it were calling to me. It wasn't ringing or anything, it was just that I couldn't shake the thought that it was my only possible connection to Jed. The only way I could find out what has happened to him. I managed to ignore it for nearly an hour, but I kept thinking of reasons to go downstairs, reasons to walk past it in the hall and finally on the way to the kitchen for my fifth glass of Ribena it got too much to bear and I grabbed the receiver and dialled Jed's number.

In the split second before I got the out-of-order tone I thought my heart might explode it was beating so fast. *Please let it ring*, I implored silently, but the shrill, discordant beep that followed seemed to sum everything up perfectly. It was just what Jed and I had become – disconnected. However, once I had the telephone in my hand I became a woman possessed. I was determined to get through to Jed somehow. Before I knew what I was doing I had acquired the telephone number for the Blidworth Miners' Welfare from the operator and was dialling it with trembling fingers. As soon as I heard the ringing tone I knew I wouldn't be able to speak – how could I hound him in his local pub? That's the kind of thing Helen does to Joe, but they've been married twenty years. I couldn't put the phone down either, not even when a voice at the other end said hello. I put my hand over the mouthpiece and strained to make out the background

noise. A mixture of chatter and music drifted down the
line. Was Jed there? Was that *his* laughter I could hear
ringing out in the background just above the beat from the
jukebox? 'Hello, hello,' the voice at the other end barked,
and still I couldn't bring myself to replace the receiver and
sever my only link left with Jed. Then, with a sharp click,
the line was cut. I now know what they mean when they
say the silence was deafening. It seemed to slice through
my eardrum like a knife.

Saturday, 2 February 1985

Dear Anne,

Like the miners I have gone on strike. Only I have
ceased all work supporting their cause. Why should I go
and freeze my backside off collecting money for Jed's
teabags and Spam sandwiches when he can't even be
bothered to write and tell me it's over?

I HATE HIM! I HATE HIM! I HATE HIM!
Helen was surprisingly understanding when I told her I was
too depressed to help on the stall, but then isn't her sole
aim in life to revel in my misery?

I HATE EVERYONE!

Thursday, 7 February 1985

Dear Anne,

Well, one week to go until Valentine's Day. I have
decided to buy Jed a card. Not a really slushy one or
anything, just something cool and jokey. Maybe that's
where I went wrong before, maybe I was coming on too
strong and scared him off. Perhaps he thought I was a
silly lovestruck schoolgirl. If I can just choose the right
kind of card – the kind of card somebody like Madonna

would send – he might change his mind. Oh, Anne, sometimes I wish you could talk and tell me if I'm doing the right thing. The truth is, I just don't know what to do for the best.

Saturday, 10 February 1985

Dear Anne,

I am so angry. I can't believe I spent nearly an hour after school last night looking for exactly the right kind of card for Jed. Why the hell did I bother? I mean, it's not as if he's going to send me a card, is it? No. If he's buying a card for anyone this year it will be for his new girlfriend. The longer his silence has gone on the more obvious it becomes that he has met somebody else. Why else would it be so hard for him to write to me and let me know it's over? Last night I couldn't sleep I was so angry. How dare he do this to me? How dare he treat me like some silly child he can cast aside as soon as the novelty wears off? His witch of a sister was right – she probably knew what he was playing at all along. Well, one thing he didn't reckon on was that I'm not some stupid doormat. I'm not just going to fade off into the background as if I never existed. I gave him everything and the least I deserve is an explanation.

Today I went back to the Miners' Support stall and I shouted for all I was worth. My new-found fervour certainly paid off – I had twenty quid in my bucket within an hour! After two hours it had gone back down to four pounds seventy. I know that stealing from a charity should be a hanging offence and no doubt I will be condemned to an afterlife of hell-fire and eternal damnation, but I had to get my coach fare somehow. I don't know when I'm going to go and how I'll get away with it, but as soon as the opportunity arises I'm going back to Blidworth to get some answers!

Thursday, 14 February 1985

Dear Anne,

OH, MY GOD! I can't believe what I have just done. And what I am about to do! Today started predictably badly, being Valentine's Day and all. Of course there was no card from Jed and, even worse, I had to choke down my breakfast watching Joe beaming at his heart-shaped raffia card (no doubt hand-woven exclusively for Oxfam) before he presented Helen with a box of carob-coated gingers. I couldn't say a word to Karen on the way to school, especially after she showed me the card she got from Jasper. Who does he think he is signing it from the 'Lancashire Love Lord'?

I marched into maths to be greeted by a particularly Wanksome Wainwright.

'Now, now, Miss Kennedy,' he whined, 'don't be so aggressive with the furniture. Was it really necessary to slam the lid of your desk quite so hard?'

I glowered at him over the top of my algebra book. His greasy black hair and pasty skin would have looked far more at home at a peeping Toms convention. 'Sorry, sir,' I muttered, trying hard not to retch.

Wainwright sidled his way down the classroom to my desk. I could smell his repugnant breath at ten paces. 'And what's all this?' he sneered, pointing to the yellow sticker on my blazer lapel.

'It's a sticker, sir,' I retorted, and somebody behind me sniggered.

'I can see that,' he said, blasting his breath unbearably close to my face, 'but why are you wearing it?'

'Because I want to,' I replied.

'But *why* do you want to?' The backs of his pale hands crawled with bulging blue veins as he tapped his fingers on my desk

'Because I do,' I replied, with an exasperated sigh. What the hell was his problem?

'*Because you do*,' he mimicked. He was so close now I could see a yellow film clinging to his teeth like the skin on a bowl of custard. 'Why don't you tell us all what it says?'

A deathly hush fell over the classroom. All I could hear was the blood pumping through my head. Pound. Pound. Pound.

'Why?'

'What do you mean, why?'

'Why should I tell everybody what it says? They can read, can't they?' I fixed my stare on the seam of his insipid pink shirt. One of his buttons had come undone and I could see about an inch of pallid paunch, sprinkled with wiry black hairs.

'I'm perfectly aware that they can read, Miss Kennedy, but I'd like you to read it for them.' He suddenly raised his voice to a yell: 'NOW!'

I jumped in surprise. 'It says, "Dig deep for the miners,"' I mumbled.

'It says what?'

'"Dig deep for the miners".'

'I see. And are you a miner, Miss Kennedy?'

'No.'

'And is this a coalfield?' He gestured at the sea of stupid spotty faces all clinging to his every word.

'No.'

'Well, I think you should take it off, then, don't you?'

'No.'

'I beg your pardon?'

'I said *no!*' I shouted, getting to my feet.

'But you're not a miner and this is not a coalfield so I really don't think you have any business defacing your school uniform with such things.'

'You don't have to be a miner to wear one of these stickers,' I retorted. 'And you don't have to be a wanker to be a good teacher,' I added, under my breath.

'I beg your pardon?'

I looked at his beady little eyes staring at me, full of hatred and contempt, and something inside me snapped. I had better things to do with my time than be bullied by some shrivelled-up loser, like go to Blidworth and find Jed. I put my books into my bag and pushed back my chair.

'Where the hell do you think you're going?' Wainwright screeched, his voice as grating as fingernails on a blackboard.

'To find myself a coalfield,' I replied, without bothering to look back.

What happened next is all a bit of a blur. I can vaguely recall Wainwright's shrieks echoing after me as I raced down the corridor, but I just put my head down and kept running and running. I didn't stop until I'd got to Pinner station and ordered my ticket to Victoria and I didn't draw breath until I was seated on the tube and rattling my way towards London. Hurriedly removing my school tie and buttoning up my winter coat I reached into my bag for my lip-gloss and eyeliner. Once I had given myself a quick makeover I felt a lot less conspicuous. This, coupled with my anger at Wainwright – and Jed – seemed to fire me with a new-found confidence, propelling me through the crowded concourse at Victoria, up the steps, around the corner and all the way to the coach station.

Even now, as the coach flies past the sign for Nottingham, the usual flurry of butterflies in my stomach are being swatted away by angry thoughts. *How dare Wainwright patronise me like that in front of everyone? How dare he ridicule me for my political beliefs? How dare he treat me like a child? How dare Jed treat me like a child? How dare he use me and then cast me aside?*

However, the moment I was deposited by the number 511 bus outside the Black Bull pub in Blidworth my angry thoughts were instantly replaced with nagging doubts. I looked at the beer garden, deserted and bedraggled in the February drizzle, and remembered the day Jed had taken me there for lunch. The day of my 'Weyman Tour of Blidworth'. I thought of Jed laughing and tanned, munching his cheese cob and flicking pieces of onion across the table at me. Jed wasn't a cruel person. He wasn't a love-rat like JR Ewing, he was caring and thoughtful – just like Bobby. As I ambled up the hill I recalled his letters and their curious mixture of tenderness and bravado. I thought of the Jed beneath the cheeky exterior, the Jed who had wiped the mascara from my face when I cried and sent me numerous little gifts in the post. Why would he have bothered doing all of that if I was only ever some fleeting distraction?

By the time I reached the top of the hill I had virtually ground to a standstill, such was my state of confusion. Unable to bring myself to walk down Jed's road I turned right into the churchyard and made my way to the far corner and Will Scarlett's bizarre gravestone. A large drop of water unleashed itself from a branch overhead and trickled down my face like an ice-cold tear. I shivered and pulled up the collar of my coat. It was hard to believe that the last time I had been in the churchyard it had been hot enough to cavort about semi-naked. It had seemed so special then, so magical, but now in the unforgiving grey mist it seemed nothing but dreary and cold. I looked at the stone construction in front of me, and suddenly it dawned on me that perhaps Jed brought all his girlfriends here. Perhaps he gave them all a piece of stone as a memento. Perhaps the stone he'd sent me hadn't been chipped off the grave at all, but had just been lying on the ground somewhere. Had I been the unwitting victim of some awful cemetery swindle?

The church clock struck three, prompting a flurry of wings, both in the surrounding trees and my stomach. At nine o'clock this morning I had been arriving at school in Pinner and now, six hours later, here I was in Blidworth. Although I felt sick with nerves I knew I couldn't come all this way and leave without some kind of explanation. Jed would probably be on the picket line with Bob, and Maxine would be working, but hopefully Lizzie would be at home. I could just ask her to tell me the awful truth before returning to Pinner to drown myself in Smiths records and torture myself with Dungeons and Dragons.

Breathing in nervous little gasps I made my way out of the churchyard and down Jed's road. Like a circus drumroll my heart beat louder with every painted front door that I passed until, with an almost deafening crescendo, I reached his, painted bright red like a warning sign. Somehow I made it up the short path but my trembling hand didn't seem able to make contact with the doorbell. Just as I leant against the wall for support the door burst open and Jed flew out. He was moving so fast, pulling on his leather jacket as he went, that he didn't even see me at first. When he did he stood motionless for a second, staring at me in disbelief.

'What are you doing here?' he asked, in a cold, hard voice. 'Shouldn't you be at school?'

I looked at him in surprise. Although there was no denying it was Jed he seemed so different. Gone was the cheery grin and, instead of twinkling, his eyes seemed to be glinting with rage. His transformation left me feeling scared and bewildered.

'I, er, came to see you. I thought as it was Valentine's Day—'

Jed laughed bitterly, before turning to walk away. 'I really haven't got time for this now,' he called over his shoulder.

I watched him heading off down the road and my disbelief turned to anger. To ignore my letters was one thing, but to ignore me when I had come all this way was another. 'You selfish bastard!' I called after him, in a pitifully wobbly little voice.

Jed stopped dead in his tracks, then turned slowly to face me. I can't begin to describe the expression on his face: a horrible mixture of fury and contempt. 'What did you call me?' he asked, in a controlled voice.

I clenched my fists tightly inside my coat pockets. 'A selfish bastard,' I repeated, a little more steadily this time.

Jed looked at me long and hard then broke into a bitter laugh. 'Yeah, that's me all right – a good-for-nothing bastard. You're much better off without me, Cat, so why don't you do yourself a favour and sod off back to your cosy little life? You've had your fun, now get back to your studying and leave me alone.' And with that he turned on his heel and marched off down the road.

I felt dizzy with sorrow and confusion. Why was he so angry with me? What had I done? Then, out of the corner of my eye, I saw a figure appear in the doorway. Wiping away my tears I turned to see Maxine glowering at me from the doorstep.

'What the hell are you doing here?' she barked, pulling her black satin robe around her. In the split second that I allowed myself to look up at her face I noticed that she wasn't wearing any makeup. Her eyes seemed so much smaller and quite bloodshot.

I couldn't bring myself to talk, to tell her of my
humiliation. I was sure she had probably witnessed it all
from the window anyway.

'Did he tell you to get lost?' she sneered.

I looked at her bare feet obscuring the faded WELCOME
on the doormat and noticed that her toenails were also
painted black – with not a single smudge. I nodded meekly,
with not a shred of self-respect remaining.

Maxine snorted. 'What did I tell you? Now, why don't
you piss off back to London once and for all? Go on – piss
off!' she yelled, as if I were some flea-ridden cat that had
strayed up her path. To the sound of the door slamming I
picked up my bag and slunk off down the road.

It's now seven o'clock at night and, once again, I'm on a
coach speeding away from Jed. But this time I am not
consumed with feelings of love and bitter-sweet sorrow.
There's nothing sweet about the way I currently feel. For
as long as I live I will never forgive him for treating me like
this and I will never forgive myself for being so stupid. I
feel completely numb. I don't care what kind of
punishment my parents or Wainwright have got in store for
me – nothing will ever be able to hurt me again after this.

Chapter Twenty-Nine

Sunday morning

'Who's it going to be, Caitlin – him or me?'

Squinting, I could just make out Sam's silhouette, standing on top of a sack of porridge oats, brandishing a revolver-shaped carrot.

'Don't be so stupid,' I mumbled, rolling on to my side. 'And turn that bloody searchlight off!'

After a few seconds, when Sam failed to respond I opened my eyes a fraction and realised that there was no carrot-shaped revolver, there was no Sam and that the searchlight scorching the backs of my eyes was the sun, blazing through the open window like a blowtorch. I wriggled into a semi-upright position and tried to get my bearings. My eyes scanned the saucer of cigarette butts, shredded Polo wrappers on the window-sill and the diary on the floor, surrounded by clusters of sodden tissues, before finally coming to rest upon myself, curled up at the foot of the bed. I couldn't remember falling asleep. I couldn't remember anything much. My mind was a jumble of thoughts: who had I argued with last night – Sam or Jed? It was like I was hurtling along on a ghost train with haunting voices echoing all about me.

That's me all right – a good-for-nothing bastard . . . I'm your husband, the father of your children . . . Sod off back to your cosy little life . . . What are you trying to do to me? . . . Don't you think it's time you made the choice, Caitlin? Him or me? . . . Him or me?

Like the moment when the ghost train crashes through the doors into the brilliant daylight I was hit by a blinding flash of clarity. Finally I knew what I had to do.

As soon as I'd showered and got dressed – I decided against the Frankie T-shirt, putting it back into its box along with the lamp, stone, book and the single – I crept downstairs to make myself a drink. It was only just seven o'clock and the kids and Sam were still asleep. Or so I thought.

'Going somewhere, are you?'

I nearly dropped the carton of orange juice in fright. I peered round the door of the fridge and saw an ashen-faced Sam standing by the table, nervously twiddling his wedding ring. Nodding, I took a glass from the shelf and attempted to fill it with juice; my hands couldn't stop trembling.

Sam marched over to the fridge and flung open the door. 'You're going to Nottingham, aren't you?' he asked, and slammed a packet of bacon on to the counter.

I tried to swallow a mouthful of juice but my throat seized up and I spluttered it all over the floor. 'I have to,' I rasped.

Sam took some sausages from the fridge. 'I don't suppose we've got any black pudding in here, have we?'

I shook my head sorrowfully. 'I have to do it, Sam. It isn't fair on you for us to carry on like this.'

'Oh, please,' Sam snorted, 'don't try to make out you're doing this for me. When have you ever done anything for me? God, I could murder some hash browns.' He picked up the sausages and bacon and flung them back into the fridge, 'Sod it – I think I'll take the kids to McDonald's for breakfast.'

I crept up behind him and gingerly placed a hand on his shoulder. 'Sam, please.'

'Please what? Jesus, Caitlin, what do you expect me to say? He shrugged away my hand and marched to the kitchen door. 'Okay, fine,' he said, without turning round. 'Do what you have to do – it's not as if I haven't been expecting this.'

'What do you mean?' I lowered my gaze to my feet and nervously traced a crack in the floor with my toe. I heard Sam turn round but couldn't bring myself to look at him.

'Look, Caitlin, I've been prepared for this moment since the day you told me about him and what happened between you. It hasn't been easy, you know, living in dread for all these years. God knows, I've tried to make things okay, tried to make you forget all about it, but obviously it wasn't quite enough and, to be honest, I don't know what more I can do.' I heard Sam take his car keys from the shelf by the door. 'So go, do what you have to do. I just want you to know that I'll always be here for you, Cait, you'll always be the love of my life – I only wish that one day you could say the same about me.'

As I drove down the tree-lined avenues of Pinner, part of me wanted to do a seven-point turn and join Sam and the kids in their hash-brown fest at McDonald's, but as soon as I reached the motorway and put my *Hits of the Eighties* CD on the stereo I felt an eerily familiar feeling: the old magnetic force that had propelled me up to Orgreave all those years ago. As I cranked up the air-conditioning and leant back into my seat I thought of the fusty furnace of a coach and my Murraymint-munching companion. I rummaged about in the cardboard box on the passenger seat for the last of my Polos. What would have happened if I hadn't made that first journey up to Orgreave? Would Jed and I ever have got it together? I doubted it. It suddenly hit me how downright sneaky life can be. How a seemingly innocuous decision can go on to have repercussions for years after – if not for ever more. What if Helen hadn't believed my story about revising in the library? What if Mrs M had had me thrown off the coach? What if I'd had to stay in Pinner that day? How differently would my life have turned out? How much easier would it have been? But, then, I would never have got to know Jed. Controlling the steering-wheel with my elbows I removed my wedding ring and slung it into the glove compartment.

As I sped along the country lanes, suppressing a nervous giggle at the sign for Blidworth Bottoms, I experienced yet another identity crisis. A quick glance in the rear-view mirror seemed to confirm that I was indeed a thirty-something, with the beginnings of crows' feet clawing at the sides of my eyes, and a quick glance about my Range Rover certainly suggested that I was successful, if a little messy and disorganised. The fact that I was driving at all meant that I had to be grown up and yet I felt exactly as I had all those years ago when I first arrived in Blidworth. Like a frightened little schoolgirl. Had I ever truly grown up? Or had part of me remained frozen since that day in 1985?

As I drove through Blidworth everything seemed different from how I remembered it – faded and ragged around the seams – and for the first time I was struck by how unreliable memories can be. A huge bolt of fear surged through me. What on earth had I expected? Things change. People change. People move on. As I parked the car I felt sick with nerves. It was like some awful action replay of that miserable Valentine's Day all those years ago. I clutched the steering-wheel tightly and reassured myself that I was no longer a naïve schoolgirl. I was a successful writer, a mother, a wife, a woman. Okay – I was a woman, but that was something, at least. I couldn't be patronised or fobbed off any more. All I wanted was an explanation. Surely I was entitled to that. God knows, I'd paid my penance. I grabbed the cardboard box from the seat beside me and got out of the car.

It was like opening an oven door, the heat was so intense, and by the time I had walked the few yards to Jed's house beads of sweat had burst through my skin and begun to trickle down the side of my face. Somewhere in the distance a dog barked and I could hear the inane laughter of a Sunday-morning DJ drifting over the motionless air. I clenched my hand into a fist and rapped on the door. Sweat began pouring from my face as a cacophony of voices vied for attention inside my head. *Are you mad? Do a runner! They won't still live here. Do a runner! You're going to look like a complete nutcase! DO A RUNNER!*

Just as I was about to turn and do a runner I heard the rattle of a chain and the sound of several bolts being pushed back. I stood there transfixed as the door creaked ajar.

'Yes?' a woman's voice rasped from the other side.

'Oh – er – I don't know if you can help me, but I'm trying to track down the family who used to live here back in the eighties. The Weymans.' I stared expectantly at the door, noticing that it was still the same red paint – only now it was chipped and peeling.

'And who the hell are you?' the voice behind the door enquired.

'My name's Caitlin. Caitlin Kennedy.'

The door swung open to reveal a large, middle-aged woman clad in a tea-stained, towelling robe. A cigarette dangled precariously from her bottom lip and her peroxide-blonde hair sprouted from her head like clumps of gorse. She looked as if she'd just walked off the set of *The Jerry Springer show* – the week they were doing 'Help! My Mom Looks Like a Trailer-trash Trollop'.

'So. You finally made it, then?'

I looked up in surprise. 'Pardon?' Surely I didn't know this bloated blimp? The hard grey eyes stared back at me sullenly and the penny dropped. 'Maxine?'

'Well, I suppose you'd better come in, then, hadn't you?'

As I followed her into the kitchen my mind whirred into action. Of all the possible outcomes this was the only one I had not foreseen. It was also by far the worst.

'Cup of tea?' Maxine barked, grinding her cigarette into an overflowing ashtray and immediately lighting another.

'Yes – yes, please. That would be lovely.' Oh, God, I sounded just like the Queen.

Maxine slammed down the kettle and took an almost empty bottle of Scotch from the cupboard. 'You don't mind if I have something a little stronger, do you?'

'No worries.' God, now I sounded Australian. It was ludicrous, really. Even after all these years – which seemed to have treated me far more kindly than they had Maxine – I still felt like an awestruck kid. I looked at her pallid jowls hanging down from her face like lumps of dough. What had happened to those chiselled cheekbones? What had happened to that raven hair? How had she turned from glossy goddess into such a washed-out wreck?

'Well, go through, then.' Maxine gestured angrily at the living-room door, as if she had read my mind.

My face flushed. 'Yes, of course. Sorry.' Clutching my cardboard box, I shuffled off into the living room before stopping dead in my tracks. There he was. There was no mistaking the impish grin, the sparkling grey eyes. It was Jed. Everywhere I looked. Pictures of him lined the walls, the mantelpiece, the windowsill; even the drinks cabinet contained a passport-sized photo of Jed inside a tiny heart-shaped frame. There was not a shire horse in sight.

'Oh, my God!' I sank on to the sofa, tears streaming down my face. All of those years spent wishing I had a picture of him, trying desperately to reconstruct some kind of photo-fit in my mind. Even when he came to me in my dreams I could never get him to turn round, to show me his face. And now it was everywhere. It was as if I had seen him only yesterday, it was so familiar. The brown skin crinkling at the corners of his eyes, the slight dimple on his chin, the jaunty expression. A great blanket of grief descended on me and, as it sucked the air from my lungs, the pain was excruciating.

'There you go.' Maxine slopped a mug of tea on to the coffee-table in front of me.

'Thank you,' I spluttered, trying desperately to fight my way up for air.

'Don't mention it.' Maxine stubbed out her cigarette in an ashtray usefully mounted upon a brass stand and took a hefty swig from her glass.

'Where are your parents?' I asked hesitantly.

'Retired to Bridlington. Been there for years now. Couldn't face sticking around after the strike – and everything.'

I nodded.

'So, what do you want, then?' Maxine narrowed her cold grey eyes at me.

I looked down at the carpet. It was a tapestry of fag burns and assorted stains. 'I had to come.'

'What for? Morbid curiosity? Fancied a nose?'

'No, it's not like that. I think about him all the time. It was starting to drive me insane.'

'Took your bleeding time, didn't you?' Maxine placed her bloated hands upon her bloated hips. 'If you think about him all the time, how come you never came sooner? Let's face it, love, he was only ever a bit of rough to you, wasn't he? A bit of excitement. And now you've come back for one last thrill.'

I raised my eyes to meet her stare. 'I loved Jed.'

'Yeah, right. That's why it's taken you seventeen years to come and see him.' Maxine took a cigarette from her dressing-gown pocket and rolled it between her fingers. Like the paint on the front door, her scarlet nail varnish was peeling and chipped.

'How could I have come before? I was absolutely heart-broken – not to mention guilty.' I slumped back into the settee, beset with the old familiar feelings of shame.

'What do you mean, guilty?'

I took a deep breath. 'Well, it was all my fault, wasn't it? If I hadn't turned up here that day. If I hadn't been so horrible to him, called him those names, he wouldn't have got so worked up and he wouldn't have —' I tried to swallow back the onset of tears. 'How could I have come here and faced you all? I couldn't even face myself.'

Maxine sat down beside me on the settee, bringing with her a waft of stale cigarettes and booze. 'You mean you think it was your fault? For all these years you've been blaming yourself?'

I nodded, sobbing uncontrollably. 'Of course it was my fault. You should know – you were there. You must have heard what I said to him.' I turned to face Maxine. 'I just couldn't understand why he'd dumped me. I was young, Jed was my first love. I still believed in fairytales.'

Maxine gave a sarcastic snort.

'Look.' I began rooting frantically through my cardboard box for my diary, 'Read this if you don't believe me.' Practically tearing the pages out as I went, I turned to the entry for 15 February and passed the diary to Maxine.

Chapter Thirty

Jed is dead. I can't. I don't. How? Why? Everything feels totally surreal. I don't have to go to school. Helen has made me a cup of real tea with *two* sugars! When she appeared in my room at seven o'clock this morning I thought I was going to get another rollicking.

'All right, all right, I'm getting up,' I grunted, from the snug depths of my bed. We were supposed to be having a meeting with the headmaster at nine o'clock to discuss my 'unruly conduct' of yesterday. 'Who was that on the phone?' I peered, bleary-eyed, over the top of the duvet. Helen was standing in the doorway, her face soaking wet – I thought she'd just forgotten to dry it or something.

'It was Mrs Montague,' she whispered. 'There's some bad news.'

'Don't tell me – Jasper's converted to Islam and he's joined the PLO?' I retorted, with a snigger.

Helen perched on the edge of my bed and before I knew what was happening she was clasping my hands in hers.

'What's wrong with you?' I demanded, pulling my hands away in embarrassment. I think it was then that I realised her face was slick with tears not water. 'Mum? What's the matter?'

'It's Jed.'

My heart missed a beat.

'There was an accident on the picket line yesterday.'

'What do you mean, an accident? What kind of accident?'

'He was hit by a lorry.'

'What? How?'

Helen wiped her face with the back of her hand. 'I'm not sure exactly. Marjorie heard it on the news. There was some kind of scuffle and he fell into the road.'

'Oh, my God. Is he badly hurt? Is he in hospital? What's happened to him?'

'He's dead, Caitlin.'

For some strange reason I started to laugh. 'Don't be stupid. He can't be. I only saw him yesterday. He was fine.'

Helen grabbed hold of my arm. 'There was nothing they could do, Caitlin. He died before the ambulance arrived.'

I stared at Helen blankly. Her whole body was quivering like a jelly. 'What's the matter with you? Why are you crying? It can't have been him. It must be a mistake. I told you, he was fine when I saw him. Mrs M must have been confused. She's probably been at the sherry or something.'

Helen shook her head. 'It was definitely him, Caitlin. Your father's just gone down the road to get the newspapers. I'm so sorry.' Helen tried to put her arms round me but I pushed her away.

'What do you mean you're sorry? You hated me seeing him. You did everything you could to keep us apart.' I leapt out of my bed, shoving Helen aside. 'Is that what all this is about? Is it just some sick way of getting back at me for going up to Blidworth yesterday?'

Helen stared at me, horrified. 'No, of course it isn't. Caitlin, please, sit back down.'

But I couldn't stop pacing up and down my bedroom. 'You're sick – sick!' I screamed. Jed couldn't be dead. He was too young. Too full of life. She had to be tricking me.

Helen stood up and tried to put her arms around me. 'Caitlin, please. I'm not lying to you. I promise. Jed died yesterday afternoon. It must have been after you saw him.'

I sank down on the bed. 'But he was so—' I searched for the right word. 'Alive. It doesn't make sense.'

Helen sat down beside me and put her arm round me. 'I know,' she whispered. 'I can't quite believe it myself. Your father will be back in a minute with the papers – maybe they'll tell us a bit more. Would you like a drink?'

'Could I have a cup of tea?' I looked at her hopefully. 'Sure.'

'And could I have two sugars?'

As soon as Helen nodded I knew she had to be telling the truth – she would never willingly prepare me a drink containing caffeine *and* sugar unless something truly cataclysmic had happened. Jed had to be dead.

But as I sit here sipping my tea all I can think of is Jed at his kitchen table, refilling his mug from Lizzie's shire-horse teapot. How can it be true? I just can't believe that Jed will never be able to drink a cup of tea again. That he will never feel that warm, sugary trickle down the back of his throat. Or that he will never be able to eat another Spam sandwich. Mrs M must have got it wrong.

God, is Joe ever going to get back with the papers?

Oh, my God – I feel as if my whole world is falling apart. How can this be happening? How can it have happened? But it's here before me in black and white, in a national newspaper, for Christ's sake. So it has to be true, doesn't it?

MINER KILLED IN PICKET LINE SCUFFLE
A young miner was killed yesterday, in what appears to have been a tragic accident. Jed Weyman, 18, was crushed to death

by a lorry leaving the Blidworth colliery in Nottinghamshire. Weyman, who had worked at the pit since leaving school at sixteen, had been a regular on the picket line in Blidworth since the strike began. Blidworth has been one of the few Nottinghamshire pits to have remained on strike, but tensions were running high with the recent return to work by a handful of men. Eye witnesses report that Weyman arrived on the picket line late yesterday afternoon in 'an extremely agitated state' and began pushing his way to the front of the protest. Losing his footing, he fell through the crowd-control barrier and on to the road just as a lorry was leaving the plant. Despite the desperate attempts of his friends and several family members, including his own father, Weyman died before the emergency services arrived on the scene. An inquest into his death is expected to be held early next month.

How can Jed have been killed? He was so young and fit. So full of vitality. How can all that energy have been crushed out of him in just a split second? It doesn't make sense. Nothing makes sense. Young people don't die out of the blue like that. I remember when Granddad Kennedy died, the spasm of shock I experienced when Joe replaced the receiver and whispered, 'Me da's had a heart-attack running down the road after the pools man – keeled over and died before he could give him his coupon.' But as I clung to the sideboard for support, my feelings of horror were already being eased away by reassuring details. Granddad Kennedy was eighty-three years old; his skin had worn paper-thin and his eyes had begun to cloud over; it was only a matter of time before his heart wore out too. But Jed's skin is too smooth and brown to die, his eyes are too sparkly. I can't bear the thought of those giant wheels thundering over him, crushing all the life out of his body. It feels as if they're steamrollering their way across my heart.

I can't breathe, I can't see. Help me somebody, please.

Joe appeared in my doorway, looking ashen-faced beneath his beard. Apparently I had been screaming.

'Are ye okay?' he asked, glancing around the room anxiously.

It dawned on me that it was probably the first time he had ever set foot in my bedroom and I started to laugh hysterically. 'Yes, I'm fine. I just feel so confused.'

Joe hovered nervously. 'I know, Cait, I know. Do you want me to get you anything? One of those God-awful magazines you've always got your nose in?'

I thought of *Jackie* and *Blue Jeans* and their endless supply of love stories and problem pages. I somehow doubted that they'd have a quick fix for my current dilemma. Perhaps I ought to write in: 'Dear Jackie, what do you do if your ex-boyfriend goes and dies on you? Oh, and by the way, is it true that you can't get pregnant if you have sex standing up?' I shook my head and attempted a smile. 'No, it's okay, Dad. I just need to be on my own for a bit.'

Joe nodded, somewhat gratefully. 'Well, just give us a shout if you do. Your mother will be back soon – and she's arranged to have next week off.'

'What for?'

'Well, to be with you, of course.'

So, I was to be allowed a whole week off school. Normally I had to be suffering from a temperature of over 108 degrees before they'd let me have a day off. Oh, the times I would have given anything for Joe to let me have a week off and shower me with magazines, but now it was happening I felt absolutely terrified. I curled myself into a ball on my bed.

'Okay, then,' Joe said gruffly. 'I'll be downstairs if you need me.'

The rest of today has passed in a haze. I seem to be

frozen, both mentally and physically, only leaving my bed to go to the toilet, and I wouldn't even have to do that if Helen didn't keep bringing me so many cups of tea. All I want to do is lie here staring at my bedroom ceiling, fixating on the Artex bobbles. If I stare hard enough I can just make out the outline of a plump-breasted pigeon right above my head. It reminds me of a test we did in science once, where we were given a selection of images and asked what we could see in them. When it was my turn I saw a peacock (the Mattress saw a penis with three balls). Apparently the image you identify can tell a lot about your current mental state. I wonder what the underlying symbolism of a plump-breasted pigeon can be?

Somewhere in the distance I can hear our front door opening and Karen's voice. She is talking to Helen, but I can't make out what they're saying. Their low-pitched mumbling is quite soothing, really, a bit like a babbling brook. I've never known Karen talk to Helen for so long. I wonder what they're saying.

Karen finally made it upstairs.

'Oh, Cait, are you okay?' she cried, launching herself on me.

'Yes, I'm fine,' I responded, wriggling out of her embrace. Although her eyes were expertly made up as usual, I could tell they were puffy and bloodshot.

'Have you been crying?' I demanded.

Karen nodded silently, chewing on her bottom lip.

'What for?'

Karen looked at me in surprise. 'Well, for Jed, of course. And you. Oh, Cait, I'm so sorry.' And with that she began to sob uncontrollably.

'But why?' I asked, incredulous.

'Why what?' Karen spluttered between sobs.

'Why are *you* crying?' Why was everybody crying, apart from me?

'Because I'm upset. Because it's so tragic. What's the matter, Caitlin?' Karen stared at me in bewilderment.

'Nothing's the matter,' I retorted. 'Not with me anyway. It's everyone else who seems to be going mad.' I clambered out of bed and put 'London Calling' on the record-player. All of a sudden I had the overwhelming desire to shout and scream and if I couldn't do it then I'd let Joe Strummer do it for me.

'God, Cait, turn it down a bit, your mum will have a fit,' Karen urged, covering her ears with her hands.

'No, she won't.' I replied breezily. 'I told you, everyone's going mad around here today. Helen's been making me cups of tea all day, with real teabags and sugar and everything. They're even letting me have all of next week off. She'll probably be shouting at me to turn it up in a minute.' I sat down and studied the record cover. It seemed so long ago that Jed had bought it for me. I thought of him bartering away with the stall-holder in Watford market, pleading with him that he only had a pound left to save his girlfriend's music taste. His 'girlfriend'. I used to be his girlfriend. Jed used to be alive. I thought of those scuffed brown hands passing me the record and I traced the sleeve with my fingertips. Retracing Jed's. I thought of those strong hands cupping my face, entwining my fingers, caressing my skin, and a shard of raw pain sliced its way through my numb exterior. I couldn't bear the thought of those hands withering away to skin and bones before finally turning to dust.

I can't remember much about what happened next, but from the dull ache in the back of my throat I must have been screaming for quite some time. I remember flailing about, lashing out at the arms that kept being flung round

me and wondering why they couldn't just leave me alone.
I'm all right when I'm left alone.

Saturday, 16 February 1985

Dear Anne,

I don't know what's happened, but I don't seem able to
swallow. I've told Helen to stop making me so much tea –
it's taking me about three hours to sip my way through half
a mug. Every time I try to force something down it's as if
my whole throat seizes up and I start to retch. Once again
I feel chained to my bed. It's the only place I feel relatively
safe. As long as I just lie here and stare at the pigeon on
the ceiling – it's starting to look more like a pumpkin by
the minute – I feel okay. I'm caught up in an endless cycle
of grief and numbness and there's nothing I can do apart
from lie here waiting for the next wave of pain to unleash
itself.

I got Joe to buy all the newspapers again this morning
and I have made a little collection of clippings about Jed.
Today Tommy Whittaker was interviewed in the *Daily
Mirror*. He said he had never seen Jed as 'irate' as he was
on Thursday afternoon. And somebody else described his
behaviour as extremely out of character. The journalist
went on to talk about how tensions among the miners are
running high generally, with the growing return to work,
but it doesn't make sense to me. Jed was never that
bothered about the strike – if anything, he wanted it to be
over as quickly as possible so that he could get on with his
life. And now—

Oh, my God. It must have been me. It must have been
what I said to him that made him so angry. Of course –
why didn't I realise it before? He must have been on his
way back to the picket line when I arrived at his house and

called him a bastard and that was what put him in such a rage. The way he stared at me with his eyes full of contempt, the way he shouted at me to 'sod off' before marching down the street. I was the one who had got him 'in an extremely agitated state'. I was responsible for his death.

When Helen heard my wails she was up in my room in a flash, but nothing she could do eased my feelings of pain or guilt. Not even a bowl of butterscotch Angel Delight.

'I thought it might be easier to swallow,' she said, stroking my matted hair away from my tear-sodden face.

I shook my head and continued to sob.

'Caitlin, what is it? Talk to me, please,' Helen begged.

But what could I say? How could I tell my mother that I was responsible for Jed's death? That I was little better than a murderess. That I might as well have shoved him under the wheels of that lorry myself.

'If you're worried about missing the funeral, don't be. Joe's spoken to Bob and Jed's being buried on Tuesday. I'll come up with you. I can go and book the coach tickets now if you like.'

'He's spoken to Bob?' I felt sick with fear. Maxine must have told them all about my unexpected visit and how nasty I had been to Jed.

Helen nodded. 'Yes. He was obviously distraught, but he said you were more than welcome to come.'

'I can't,' I gasped.

Helen looked at me, puzzled, 'But why not? I've told you I'll come with you. I think it's important that you say goodbye.'

'No!' I shouted. 'I can't go to the funeral and that's final.' I could just picture Jed's family glaring at me across his open grave, with his evil witch of a sister hissing, 'It's all her fault,' to the tuts of the crowd and the sobs of his new girlfriend.

'But, Caitlin, I know how much Jed meant to you. This is the only chance you'll get to say goodbye. At least have a think about it over the weekend.'

'No,' I repeated. 'Jed might have been important to me but I wasn't important to him. He'd dumped me, Helen. That's why I went up there on Thursday – to find out why.'

Helen's mouth fell open in surprise, 'Oh – I see.'

'Yes, so I had already decided that I was never going up to Blidworth again – not even for Jed's funeral. Now, if you don't mind, I think I'll have a bit of a nap.'

Helen backed out of the door, taking her bowl of Angel Delight and an untouched mug of tea with her.

Oh, Anne, what am I going to do? How can I possibly carry on, knowing that I am responsible for another person's death? Jed was so full of life and I took that away from him. How will I ever forgive myself?

Sunday, 17 February 1985

Dear Anne,

I HATE HIM. I HATE HIM. I HATE HIM.

Why did he have to dump me? Why couldn't he have had the decency to tell me? All he had to do was write me a note, telling me it was over and why. Then I would never have gone up there to see him. I would never have called him a bastard (at least not to his face). And he wouldn't have got so angry. And he would still be alive.

Monday, 18 February 1985

Dear Anne,

A couple of weeks ago I was trying to think of what kind of Valentine card to send Jed and now Helen is asking me to sign a 'With Sympathy' card for his family. How can I possibly sign it? 'With deepest sympathy at being responsible for your son's death, all my love, Caitlin.'

Tuesday, 19 February 1985

Dear Anne,

Jed was buried today and it's all I can think about – his body being lowered into that hole. Jed hated being underground – did I ever mention that? It always made me laugh, the thought of a miner who hated the dark and hated being underground. And now he's going to be trapped down there for ever—

I wonder if he's being buried near to Will Scarlett's grave. I hope so. All day long I have clutched the piece of stone Jed sent me as if it's some kind of satellite link to the cemetery. My only connection to his burial. Why does the weather have to be so nice? I've had to shut my curtains to block out the sunlight. Jed would have loved a day like today. But I don't deserve to witness anything so beautiful – not now it's something I've taken away from Jed. Every day of my life from now on deserves to be dull and miserable, for every day is a day I have stolen from Jed.

Chapter Thirty-One

While Maxine read my diary I glanced nervously about the room. All around me Jed's eyes stared down accusingly – I felt like a prisoner on Death Row with the gilt carriage clock on the mantelpiece marking the seconds until my doom. Every time I heard Maxine turn a page I caught my breath. Perhaps she had never fully comprehended my part in Jed's death; perhaps she hadn't heard anything at all that day. Although I was practically paralysed by fear, deep down I longed to be absolved of my sins, once and for all.

On and on the seconds ticked away with still no response from my executioner. Surely she couldn't be that slow a reader. Maybe she was too horrified by what she had read to speak, but somehow I couldn't imagine Maxine ever being rendered speechless, especially with half a bottle of Scotch inside her. Perhaps that was it – perhaps she had fallen into a drunken stupor right beside me. Summoning all of my courage I glanced sideways. Maxine was staring straight ahead of her, the diary sliding off her lap on to the sofa.

'Are – are you okay?' I ventured, getting ready to run for the door.

Maxine stood up, causing me to cower back in my seat. 'Yeah. I'll be back in a minute,' she said, almost trance-like, before shuffling from the room.

Oh, my God. Where had she gone? What had she gone to get? I pictured her emerging brandishing a sawn-off shotgun and shrieking, '*This one's for my brother, bitch!*' before pumping me full of lead. By the time she returned, with a new bottle of Scotch, poking out of her dressing-gown pocket and a cardboard box tucked under her arm, I had become a quivering wreck.

'Drink,' she barked, handing me a smeared glass from the drinks cabinet.

I nodded, trying to ignore the smudges of lipstick around the rim as Maxine half filled the glass with Scotch.

'Fag?'

I nodded again, taking the cigarette with trembling fingers. So this was to be the condemned woman's last meal – a tumbler of whisky and a Superkings Extra. It seemed perfect, somehow. I took a swig of whisky and tried not to wince as it scorched the back of my throat.

'So, now you know,' I said, bending forward slightly for Maxine to light my cigarette. To my surprise her hands seemed to be trembling too, causing the flame to waver about alarmingly. She was probably suffering from DTs.

Maxine leant back into the sofa and let out a sigh. 'Oh, I know, all right,' she said, through plumes of smoke, 'but I don't think you do.'

I looked up from my drink. 'What do you mean?'

Maxine shook her head. 'I can't believe it. All these years you've been blaming yourself. Poor cow.'

'Well, of course I have – and don't tell me you haven't been blaming me too. You were there. You must have heard what I said to him. You must have blamed me for what happened.'

Maxine continued to shake her head sorrowfully. I could see the start of her raven roots pushing their way out of her scalp, contrasting starkly with the bleached ends. 'You haven't got a clue, have you?' she muttered. 'It wasn't your fault. None of it was your fault. Jed didn't dump you, there wasn't anybody else. He didn't die because of you. He died because of me.'

I turned to stare at Maxine, a rush of unfamiliar emotions coursing through my body. 'What do you mean?'

'It was me. The "evil witch", as you call me in your diary.'

My face flared. 'I didn't mean it – I was young, melodramatic, I—'

'No, you were right,' Maxine interrupted. 'I was a witch, I was a bitter, fucked-up cow and I was to blame for everything.'

'But I don't understand. How can you have been? How can *you* have made Jed finish with me like that, with not a word of explanation?'

'I hid your letters.'

'What?'

'I hid your letters from him. Every morning while he was on the picket line with me mam and dad I'd wait downstairs for the post and I'd take yours out and hide them in me wardrobe.'

'But why?'

'Because I couldn't bear how close you'd got.' Maxine sloshed some more whisky into her glass. 'It made me sick how close you were. The way he talked about you all the bleeding time, the way he used to look at you, the way he defended you that Christmas, and then the pathetic way he moped about the place when he thought you'd dumped him.'

'He thought I'd dumped him?'

'Yeah. God, you'd have thought Forest had lost the Cup Final the way he carried on.'

'But why didn't he write to me, then? Why didn't he try to find out why I hadn't written?'

'He did – once – but I overheard him asking me mam to post it for him, so as soon as he'd left the house I offered to do it for her.'

I looked at Maxine warily. 'Don't tell me. You accidentally posted it in a bin instead?'

Maxine shook her head. 'No, I hid it with yours. I've still got it, actually.' She bent down to rifle through her cardboard box.

Puffing slightly from the exertion she hoisted herself upright
and handed me a piece of paper. It was crumpled and worn at
the edges and there was no envelope. 'I'm afraid I read it,'
Maxine muttered, 'I read them all.'

I felt a surge of anger flooding my chest. How dare she have
read my letters? How dare she have kept them from Jed? But
as I carefully unfolded the tissue-soft paper and saw the faded
handwriting my anger was replaced with an attack of goosebumps. Seventeen years after his death I was to receive
another letter from Jed and the prospect elicited that familiar
nervous thrill.

> *Dear Cat,*
>
> *Well, what can I say? It's been over two weeks now since
> I got a letter from 'that London' and it's dawning on me
> that perhaps you're trying to tell me summat. The thing is,
> Cat, since the day I met you I've felt like we're living on
> borrowed time. It's a bit like when a football match goes into
> extra time and you're dreading the ref blowing for penalties.
> There was always summat at the back of my mind telling
> me not to get too involved. We're from such different
> backgrounds – you and me – and it always worried me that
> one day you'd grow bored of me. That one day you'd want
> to go off to university and get your degree in writing or
> whatever and I'd be left behind. The thing is, Cat, I'm not
> like the other lads round here. I've got dreams, I've got
> plans, just like you. And that's why I'd do anything to keep
> you. So I guess it's penalty shoot-out time and this is my
> last chance. Whatever happens between us, I'll still be
> moving away, once this bloody strike is over. I need a new
> start and I want you to be a part of it. So let me know what
> you think. Don't be afraid of hurting my feelings – I'd rather
> know if you've met someone else, or even if you don't love
> me any more. There's nothing worse than not knowing at all*

– it's doing my head in! I promise you, Cat, that if you don't want me any more I'll never bother you again.

All my love,

Jed

A tear trickled down my face and landed on Jed's name causing the ink to darken like new. 'How could you?' I gasped. 'How could you have kept this from me for all these years?'

Maxine chipped a piece of varnish from her thumbnail. 'I didn't think you cared. When you didn't show up at the funeral, I thought that maybe I'd been right about you, after all. I thought that maybe he was only a passing fling.'

I took a cigarette from the packet lying on the sofa between us. 'But I still don't understand. If Jed still loved me why didn't he try writing again? Or why didn't he call?'

'He was too proud. And I think he'd started to believe all the stuff I'd been telling him.'

'What stuff?'

'Oh, that you'd just been using him, that you must have met some posh lad down in London, that you were probably having a right laugh about him behind his back. That kind of thing.'

I looked at Maxine, slumped over in her shabby dressing-gown. What had made her such a poisonous bitch? Why had she been so determined to keep Jed and me apart? Something still didn't make sense. But a heady mixture of Scotch, nicotine and the oppressive summer air had descended on my brain like a fog and, try as I might, I couldn't put my finger on what it was that didn't quite ring true.

'I suppose you think I'm a right bitch,' Maxine observed intuitively, lighting herself another cigarette.

There was something about the way she said it, something about the nonchalant way in which she tilted her head back to exhale a flotilla of smoke rings that triggered off a demon-like fury in me. I leapt off the sofa and marched over to the fireplace. I wanted to kick her, punch her, scratch out those hard little eyes and rip out that vile hair from the roots – and if she didn't look exactly like Mike Tyson's negative I would have done just that. Jerry Springer would have needed more than Steeeeve to hold me back, I can tell you.

'Have you got any idea what I went through?' I shouted. 'Have you any idea how badly I was hurt? All these years I've thought that Jed didn't care about me – all these years I've been blaming myself and wondering what I did wrong and all along it was you. You were the one who forced us apart. Right from day one you went out of your way to get at me, with your snide remarks and your shit-stirring. But I don't understand why. What did I ever do to you? I was desperate for you to like me – did you know that? I actually looked up to you. Why couldn't you have just left us alone?'

'Because I was jealous.'

'But why?'

'Because I'd never seen him get so close to anyone before and I couldn't stand it.

'But why couldn't you just be happy for him? Look, I know you were hurt once. Jed told me all about it and I'm sorry. It must have been awful to lose your first love to your best mate like that, but that wasn't Jed's fault. It wasn't our fault.'

Maxine stared at me blankly.

Finally I began to gain some clarity. 'Oh, I get it. You lost your first love so you had to ruin Jed's too. You were that bitter and twisted you had to—'

'Jed *was* my first love.'

'What?' I grabbed on to the mantelpiece for support: this was beginning to get a little too *Jerry Springer* for comfort.

'Jed was my first love and I ended up losing him – twice.'

'What are you trying to say?' My stomach began to contract and a burning sensation rose to the back of my throat.

Maxine gulped down the remains of her drink. 'Why do you think I was so jealous? For eighteen years I'd had to love him from afar and then you come along and whisk him off his feet with your fancy books and your posh voice, and I couldn't bear it. Especially when I found out he was going to move down to London to be with you. I couldn't face the thought of losing him.' Maxine gave a bitter little laugh. 'Funny, really, because in the end I lost him completely.'

My brain felt even fuzzier than before. What exactly was Maxine trying to tell me? I looked at her and, to my surprise, I saw the unmistakable glisten of tears on her face.

She wiped them away defiantly with the sleeve of her dressing-gown and continued, 'It wasn't fair. All I ever wanted was for him to love me, but as the years went by he seemed to hate me more and more. I could tell by the way he looked at me. I wanted him to be proud of me, respect me, but he only ever saw me like all the others did. To him I was just a mouthy slut, an embarrassment.'

I released my grip on the mantelpiece and took a step towards her. 'That's not true. He used to defend you. You were his sister.'

'But that's just it, Cat.' Maxine peered up at me through tear-filled eyes. 'I wasn't his sister. I was his mam.'

Chapter Thirty-Two

'There – I bet you didn't see that one coming, did you?' Her dark grey eyes, Jed's eyes, bore into me and I backed up against the wall. Maxine's revelation was so preposterous I didn't even attempt to conceal my shock.

'Oh, my God. How come? I mean how did— Did he know?'

Maxine shook her head. 'No, my parents wouldn't let me tell him. We made a deal when I found out I was pregnant that if they were going to bring him up as their own he wasn't to be told the truth until he was an adult.'

I collapsed on to the sofa and took a deep breath.

Reading my mind, Maxine passed me my drink. 'I was only thirteen at the time, we'd gone on a caravan holiday to Scarborough and I got a bit carried away with this Scottish lad I met down the arcades. Tex, he called himself. I never even knew his proper name, but he was so handsome, so cool with his tattoos and slicked-back hair, I'd have done anything to make him like me as much as I liked him. Pathetic, really, 'cos of course he was just like all the rest of 'em, only out for one thing, and once he got it I never saw him for dust. It was my first time as well – I didn't think you could get pregnant first time.' Maxine gave a bitter laugh, 'Then three months later I find out I'm up the duff. I was shit scared – I'd have agreed to anything me mam and dad said. I didn't want a baby, for Christ's sake, I was still only a kid myself.

'But, then, as Jed grew up, as I grew up, things started to change. I used to hate me mam sometimes – the way he'd

always run to her for a cuddle when he fell over and want her
to tuck him in at night. To him I was always just a bossy big
sister. I remember one Christmas when I was eighteen and Jed
was coming up to five and about to start school, I begged them
to let me tell him the truth. I felt old enough to be a mam by
then. But they said, no, that it would only screw him up, and I
didn't want to mess him up right before he started school and
all. So I kept me gob shut, but inside I felt so fucking angry. I
felt like they had no right keeping my baby from me, but I
loved him so much I had no choice but to put him first. You
got kids?'

I felt so confused that it took me a couple of seconds to
respond. Finally I managed a nod.

'Well, you'll understand, then. As a mam there are times
when you'd put yourself through living hell for the sake of
your children.'

I recalled entire days spent watching Britney and Scooby-
Doo videos and nodded enthusiastically.

Maxine continued, 'So I tried to get on with me life. I met a
decent fella – well, when I say decent I mean he didn't sniff
glue and he didn't shag around or owt. Derrick, his name was,
but of course I could never give him what he wanted. I could
never have left Jed. So I stayed at home and made everyone's
life hell instead.' Maxine topped up her drink from the bottle
on the floor. 'I had me own little bit of power, see. I might have
agreed to go along with me mam and dad's plan but I didn't
have to make life easy for them. It's pathetic, really, the way I
used to call all the shots round this place. I thought it would
make me feel a bit better, but in the end all it did was turn them
all against me, even Jed – especially Jed.'

I shook my head. 'I can't believe he never found out.'

Maxine lit a fresh cigarette from the glowing butt of her old
one. 'Well, that's just it, he did find out – and it bloody well
killed him.'

'What do you mean?'

'Well, I'd wanted to tell him on his eighteenth birthday. They'd said to wait until he was an adult and I'd kept my side of the bargain, but there was always some bloody excuse. "Why don't you wait until the strike's over?" me mam said. "Things are stressful enough already." So I waited and waited, but the fucking strike just went on and on, and then you came on the scene and I'd never seen him so happy. And I couldn't bear it because I wanted to be the one to make him smile. I wanted to be the one he confided in. I used to hate the way he'd always have his nose stuck in one of those books you sent or one of your letters. And then, when I found out he was planning on leaving to go to London, I knew I had to do something.'

'So you started hiding my letters?'

'That's right.'

'And turning him against me.'

Maxine nodded. 'I just wanted him to myself for a bit. Can't you understand? I'd had to give him up to me mam for eighteen years and then, just as I was about to get a chance to finally be his mother, you come along and snatch him from under my nose.'

'But it wasn't like that. I wasn't trying to steal him away. I had no idea.'

'I know. I know. But I wasn't thinking straight, was I? All I could think of was that I had one chance to tell him the truth and try and start over with him before it would be too late and he'd be off getting wed, with kids of his own. I was desperate.'

I sighed. 'And then I went and ruined it all by turning up here on Valentine's Day and losing my temper with him.'

Maxine slammed her cigarette packet down on the arm of the sofa. 'No! You don't understand. What happened on Valentine's Day had nothing to do with you. Why would he have got in such a rage over you? He loved you, for Christ's sake, he would have done anything to get you back. But when you arrived I'd just told him the truth. I'd just told him I was his mam. I thought he'd be happy. I'd been dreaming of that moment for years and in my dreams he always gave me one of those grins of his and told me he was proud to be my son. Oh, I knew he'd be shocked, all right, but I thought he'd be glad to find out where he really came from. I didn't think for one minute he'd go mental the way he did.'

'Why? What did he do?'

'Well, he was sitting right where you are now when I told him, and at first he was just silent. And I was crying and laughing and couldn't stop yapping about how I just wanted to be a proper mam to him and I wanted him to get to know the real me. I honestly thought that he'd start crying too, but when I tried to put me arms round him he just lost it. He pushed me across the room and jumped up. "I've got a proper mam!" he screamed at me. "You're just a lying, stirring bitch." So then, of course, I gets going too and starts telling him a few home truths, like the only liars around here were me mam and dad and how they never let me tell him the truth and if he wanted to shout at anyone he should go and shout at them.' Maxine paused to take a swig from her drink. 'So that's what he did – or at least tried to.'

I sat staring blankly at the mantelpiece, with the carriage clock counting down the seconds, until the final piece of the jigsaw fell into place. 'You mean, when I arrived he was actually on his way to—'

Maxine nodded. 'Have it out with me dad? Yes. By the time he got to the picket line he was doing his nut. You must have read the reports in the papers. Of course you did. How could you have thought he'd got so angry over you?'

'But I called him a bastard.'

Maxine snorted. 'Yeah, well, he was that, all right, wasn't he?'

I turned to glare at her, but I saw that she was really crying now, great torrents of tears streaming down her face.

'That's why I couldn't believe it when I read your diary,' she sobbed. 'For all these years you've been blaming yourself and it was me who killed him. His own mother. It wasn't you who stole his life away from him, it was me.'

We sat there for a while, Maxine weeping uncontrollably while all I could do was stare up at one of the pictures of Jed. He must have been about thirteen, clad in his football kit and brandishing an eggcup-sized trophy as if it were the World Cup. His entire face was crinkled into a grin. God, how I'd loved that grin, the way the hint of mischief danced about his face like sunbeams. So I hadn't killed him, after all. Somewhere in the darkened recesses of my mind it was as if a cell door was creaking open. Bit by bit my body began to relax.

'Could I use your toilet?' I asked timidly.

Maxine wiped her nose on the back of her sleeve. 'Yeah, sure. It's an inside one and everything,' she added, with a sly smile.

I grinned back at her and, rather unsteadily, got to my feet. Feeling extremely spaced out, I hauled myself up the stairs by the banisters. As I reached the landing I couldn't resist peeking through the door just to my left – Jed's old bedroom. I caught my breath. Yet another faded snapshot from my past.

The red and white curtains had been sun-bleached to pink, and the football poster, with its row of mullet haircuts and skin-tight nylon, looked absurdly outdated, but apart from that it was exactly as I remembered it. The pile of books still teetered in a pile on the floor, their pages yellowing and brittle. I bit my lip as I caught a glimpse of *The Catcher in the Rye* half-way down. But even harder to bear was the sight of Jed's leather jacket draped across the back of his armchair as if he had only just flung it there before popping downstairs for a cup of tea.

Maxine didn't just have a cardboard box dedicated to Jed, she had an entire house. It was as if she had sealed herself away inside his tomb, like the devoted servant of an Egyptian pharaoh, doomed to rot away in his memory.

'This is where I come when I want to feel close to him. I sit in here for hours sometimes, just looking and remembering.'

I jumped in surprise to see Maxine propped against the doorway, her face puffy and tear-streaked with a black cobweb of mascara. She edged inside and took Jed's jacket from the back of the chair. 'Do you remember this?' she asked.

I nodded.

'It was like his second skin, wasn't it?' Maxine held the leather jacket to her cheek. 'Even on a day as hot as today he'd have the bleeding thing on. Silly sod.'

I thought back to all the times I'd buried my face in that jacket and inhaled the rich leathery smell – Jed's smell. Maxine was right, it had been like his second skin. My eyes began to fill with tears.

'So, do you want to go and see him, then?' Maxine put the jacket back on the chair and sniffed loudly.

'Yes, please.' For all these years I had absolutely dreaded the prospect of visiting Jed's grave, but now I couldn't think of anywhere I'd rather be.

'I'll just get meself dressed and then we'll get going.'

As soon as Maxine left the room I picked up Jed's jacket and held it to me, but his smell had long gone, drowned in the aroma of stale smoke and cheap perfume. It no longer smelt of Jed, it smelt of Maxine. I pictured her sitting in his room night after night, holding the jacket to her, clinging to what little she had left of Jed. What little she had left of her son.

When Maxine reappeared she was clad in a pair of lilac velour jogging bottoms and an outsized T-shirt emblazoned with a gold Kylie motif. I smiled wryly to myself as I followed her downstairs. Perhaps I should have worn my

Frankie T-shirt after all – Maxine would probably have appreciated it.

'I go up to see him twice a day normally,' Maxine said, lighting yet another cigarette as she shut and locked the front door behind us.

I shook my head as she offered the packet to me. 'No, thanks.' It was hard enough to breathe in the humidity outside without the hindrance of a lungful of smoke. 'What, every single day?' I asked, tucking my cardboard box under my arm.

'Yeah. I just can't bear thinking of him all on his own up there. Besides, it's not exactly far for me to go, is it?'

As we turned the corner, St Mary's church loomed down on us and I felt my heart skip a beat. 'No, no, it's not,' I murmured. But, even so, I couldn't help but feel sad at the thought of Maxine puffing and panting her way up to the graveyard day in day out, year in year out, and I felt certain that Jed would not have wanted it. Jed had been such a live-in-the-moment type of person he would have hated the thought of Maxine wasting her life like this.

As we made our way through the wrought-iron gate and along the stony path towards the church I felt more nervous than I've ever felt in my life before. Not even the time when my waters broke in the middle of Safeways came close to this. And yet now I was finally here I saw how preordained this moment was. I had simply been delaying the inevitable, burying my memories in the loft, hiding behind some wisecracking façade while all the time Jed patiently awaited me. The sound of our feet crunching on the gravel echoed through the lifeless air as we rounded the church. And there it was – exactly as I had remembered it – unchanged for hundreds of years, the yew tree proudly surveying the scene from its corner, its canopy of branches offering a tantalising respite from the unforgiving sun.

'He's just over here,' Maxine said, leading me past the yew

tree to a cluster of graves. My initial reaction was one of shock. I had been expecting Jed's headstone to be one of those polished granite affairs rather than the old-style grey slab before me. But when I read the inscription I was reminded again of how long ago he had died.

Jed Weyman

Born 27 March 1966

~

Died 14 February 1985

Beloved son of Elizabeth and Bob

'They didn't even let me have him in death,' Maxine whispered, as she bent to pick a stray weed from the rainbow spectrum of flowers covering Jed's grave like a patchwork quilt. 'How many kids have you got, then?' she asked, squinting up at me.

'Two – Megan and Frankie.'

'One of each, eh?' Maxine hauled herself back upright. 'You're lucky.'

'Yeah, it's nice to have the variety.'

'No, I mean you're lucky being a mam. Don't you ever take them kids for granted, you never know what's round the next corner.'

I thought of Megan's diva-like antics and Frankie-Daphne with his follicular fixation. How long had it been since I'd thought of my kids without some sense of fear or resentment? How long had it been since I'd thought of them and felt 'lucky'? I began to experience an overwhelming sense of shame.

'You still with your old man?' Maxine asked, looking pointedly at my wedding finger. My bare wedding finger.

'Yeah, I think so. I'm not exactly sure.' Had I ever truly been 'with' Sam? Undoubtedly I had been with him physically for the past fifteen years, but emotionally? And then it dawned on me. Maxine and I were exactly the same, with our cardboard boxes stuffed full of memories, our regrets and remorse keeping us anchored in the past, suspended in some awful state of purgatory. Oh, I might look a little more together on the outside, but how long would it be before my body gave up the charade and bloated itself like a balloon? I might not be marinating myself in Scotch just yet, but when was the last time I had made it through a day without the soothing elixir of a vodka and tonic? When had I last made an effort with my appearance? I might not have bleached the life out of my hair, but I had chosen to have it cropped off. Yes, we were exactly the same, Maxine and I, and Jed would have been heartbroken to see what had become of us.

'I suppose you must be feeling a bit better now?' Maxine asked, carefully scraping a clump of moss from Jed's gravestone.

I stared at her blankly.

'I mean, now you know the truth about what happened. You don't need to blame yourself any more, do you?' She fumbled about under a cluster of violets and brought out a miniature bottle of Jack Daniel's. 'I like to keep a supply up here in case I fancy a nip,' she explained.

'Oh. Right.' A graveside mini-bar – now that Jed would have approved of.

'Do you want one? I think there's still a couple of gins behind them bluebells.'

I shook my head and smiled. 'Oh, no, it's all right. You don't have any pork scratchings under there, do you? I'm starving.'

Maxine looked at me and smiled warmly. ''Fraid not – this is strictly a liquid bar.'

I shrugged my shoulders. 'Oh, well, it was worth a try.'

'Don't make the same mistake I did, Cat.' Maxine's face clouded over. 'Don't let life pass you by.' I saw that her eyes had filled with tears and all of a sudden I wanted to hug her.

'I won't,' I promised.

'You go back to those kids of yours and make the most of every single second you've got with them.'

I nodded, my own eyes now filling up.

'Come 'ere, love.'

And before I knew what was happening Maxine had pulled me to her and was patting me, somewhat awkwardly, on the head.

'I'll say one thing about our Jed, 'she muttered into my hair. 'He had far better taste than his mam. You're a good lass.'

'Thank you,' I whispered, before disentangling myself from Maxine's grasp. 'I suppose I really ought to get going – I've got quite a long drive back.'

'Are you sure? You don't want to stop for a bit of snap, do you? The chippy opens in half an hour.'

I shook my head. All at once I had become consumed by the bizarre urge to be with Megan and Frankie. The thought of them being so far away from me was creating a dull ache in the pit of my stomach. It was like the feeling mothers talk about when they leave their newborn babies with a sitter for the first time – only, in my case, it was arriving about eight years too late.

'Okay, then.' Maxine grabbed my hand. 'Listen, Cat, would you mind if we kept in touch? Nothing much, just the odd letter or summat. It's just that I don't really have a lot to do with me parents any more and you're the only other person I know who loved Jed.' She stared at me imploringly, her heavily lined eyes sunk like a panda's against her pallid cheeks.

'Of course I will,' I said, giving her hand a squeeze.

'I mean, I wouldn't blame you if you hated my guts, after what I've told you today, but I hope you understand that I never meant any of this to happen.'

'Of course I don't hate you.'

'You don't?'

'No – it was all just a tragic mess. Can't you see? Nobody was really to blame for any of this. Not me, not you, not your parents. It just happened, and it's up to us to try to find a way to move on with our lives. It's what Jed would have wanted.' Jesus Christ, was it really me waxing such words of wisdom or had I unwittingly been possessed by the spirit of Oprah Winfrey? Karen would have been proud. But as soon as the words left my mouth I felt a weight rising from my shoulders, for I knew what I was saying was true, and for the first time in years my life seemed so beautifully straight-forward.

'Thank you. Thank you so much,' Maxine whispered, and this time we hugged properly.

'You take care now,' I said, wiping my eyes, 'and I promise I'll write soon.'

Maxine grinned. 'Don't you go sending me none of those books of yours, mind. I'm afraid I'm not a bookworm like our Jed.'

'Oh, don't worry, I won't.' I thought of my extensive back catalogue of 'Tales with a Twist' and smiled wryly. 'I may have a few short stories you'd enjoy, though.'

As I left Maxine rummaging among the bluebells for the final bottle of gin I made a slight diversion from the footpath and headed towards the yew tree. There was one more thing I had to do before I left. Ducking beneath the sweeping branches I felt a shiver run up my spine. There, in the shadows, stood Will Scarlett's gravestone, with its bizarre hexagon base and pyramid top. As I knelt down on the grass next to it I could practically feel Jed's arm snaking around my shoulders.

'God, I've missed you,' I whispered, placing my cardboard box on the ground beside me. 'For all these years I've tortured myself with what-ifs and if-onlys because I thought that's what you would have wanted, but it's the last thing you would have wanted, isn't it?' A breeze began dancing through the leaves above me and I tilted my head back and closed my eyes. 'Oh, Jed,' I whispered, 'I've been so stupid, clinging to the past, drowning in guilt, letting my life just pass me by. But it didn't seem right to move on – not without you.'

Tears spilled out of the corners of my closed eyes. I tried to imagine what Jed would have said if he could have been there and I thought of the advice he gave me all those years ago in Pinner Memorial Park. *We have to live life in the moment, Cat, there's no point dwelling on the past.*

And suddenly it all made perfect sense. Our past can imprison us or it can set us free, but ultimately the choice is ours. I didn't *have* to spend the past seventeen years floundering in a sea of guilt and remorse, I had chosen to do so. Rather than turning my back on life, squandering opportunities and going through the motions out of some kind of warped loyalty to Jed, I should have used his death as an incentive to live my life to the full. That's what he would have wanted me to do.

I thought of Karen and the way she had used her past to fire her up the career path and out of Pinner, leaving the frustrations and restrictions of her childhood behind. And the way she had used her experience with Jasper to ensure that no other man would ever give her the runaround. I felt a pang of guilt as I thought of Sam. What finer example could there be of a person using the pain from his past to keep him striving towards his dream of domestic bliss, no matter how many obstacles I had thrown in his way? How easy would it have been for Sam to follow his father's example and crawl into the bottom of a bottle, continuing the cycle of pain and self-pity that had blighted his childhood? But, no, Sam had possessed the courage and fortitude to escape his demons. Quiet, mild-mannered Sam was the strongest of us all.

I wiped the tears from my eyes and crawled slowly towards

Will Scarlett's grave. I ran my hands over the hexagon base. It felt refreshingly cool, protected from the sun by the shade of the tree and a patchy carpet of moss. I edged my way round the stone, working my way up the slabs, tracing every bump, every crack with my fingertips until finally I found what I was looking for. About half-way up, one of the slabs of stone jutted out awkwardly. Not enough to cause any imbalance, but just enough for somebody to have been able to chisel off the top corner. I delved into my box and brought out the stone that Jed had sent me. It was slightly darker and moss-free, but when I slotted it into the gap it fitted perfectly. I sat back and smiled. I guess the feeling I was experiencing was what Karen would term closure, but as I picked up my box and got to my feet it felt more as if something was opening rather than closing. Instead of wasting years wondering *what might have been* I realised it made far more sense to focus on *what might be*.

As I walked towards the church gate, away from Maxine, away from Jed and away from Will Scarlett, my life suddenly offered up a wealth of opportunities. I could finally get to know my husband, I could allow myself to love my children. God, I could even attempt to write that Pulitzer Prize-winning novel! Shafts of sunlight filtered through the lattice framework of the gate, creating a golden mosaic on the ground. I took my mobile from my bag and scrolled through the phone book until I reached S for Sam. S for Saviour. S for Soul-mate? As my mind brimmed over with myriad possibilities I swung the gate shut without casting a backward glance.